The Penny Prophecy

Emma Sharon Rich

AmErica House
Baltimore

First printing

ISBN: 1-58851-225-8
PUBLISHED BY AMERICA HOUSE BOOK PUBLISHERS
www.publishamerica.com
Baltimore

Printed in the United States of America

for Jack

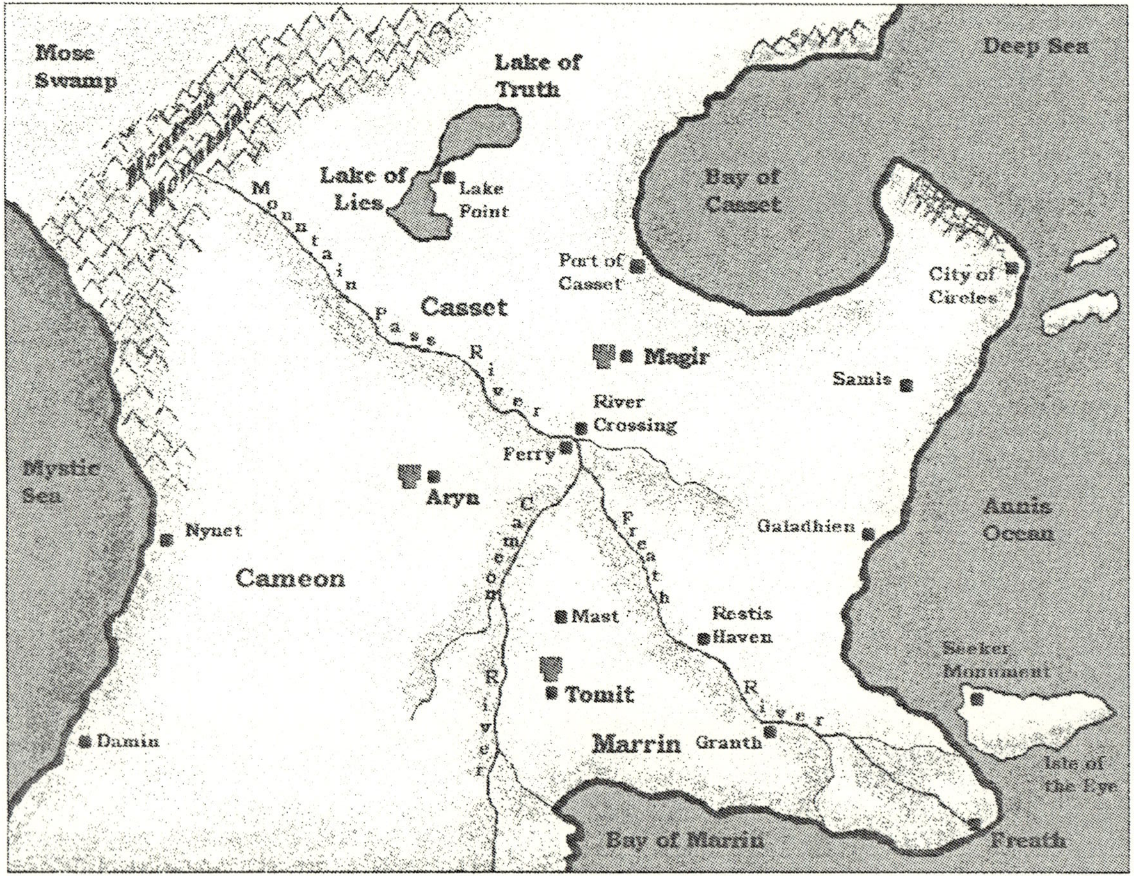
Mose Swamp
Lake of Truth
Lake of Lies
Lake Point
Mountain Pass River
Bay of Casset
Port of Casset
Casset
City of Circles
Magir
Samis
River Crossing
Ferry
Mystic Sea
Aryn
Cameon River
Freath River
Galadhien
Annis Ocean
Nynet
Cameon
Mast
Restis Haven
Seeker Monument
Tomit
River
Damin
Marrin
Granth
Isle of the Eye
Bay of Marrin
Freath

Prologue

The streets of Restis Haven bustled with midday activity. Street vendors filled the market square, their flimsy wooden stalls buckling under the weight of fruit, breads, brightly colored silks and other wares. Their urgent cries and calls rang through the rapidly darkening air as they strove to out-shout each other, trying to unload their goods before the storm that had been looming overhead all day broke. Men and women shopped or gathered in groups to exchange the news brought in by the merchant wagons. Beggars with yellowed eyes and swollen limbs – the stigma of the dreaded and fatal disease plaguing the realm – lay in dingy bricked doorways, pleading for bread or a few coppers. The smell of soured milk, yesterday's fish, and unwashed humans hung heavily in the air, nearly gagging Jaerak as he made his way through the crowded streets toward the bookshop.

Dressed in plain clothes – neutral colored trousers and shirt, a black cloak with the hood drawn up around his face, and leather boots – Jaerak Thorin wove warily through the throng of people. His face twisted with disgust when strangers brushed against him as they hurried past, and he tried without success to close his ears to the raucous noise of the city street. A solitary and reclusive man, the constant bustle and seemingly aimless activity of the city repelled him, but he had pushed aside his baser feelings to supply a more pressing need. He had hoped a city as largely populated as Restis Haven would allow him to live in anonymity and for a time it had been so. But even now there were people who would gladly shove a knife through his ribs if they spotted him, and that was an experience he was not eager to endure again. He was becoming too well known in certain circles and he realized he would soon have to move on. That was a difficulty with being an assassin, he mused to himself, and not for the first time. The money was good, more than good, but he could never stay too long in one place and Jaerak knew he had worn out his welcome in this town. The city had recently become flooded with mercenaries, assassins, and thieves – they came like hounds to meat at the first scent of unrest or war, and he often had to defend himself against rivals who were all too eager to eliminate their competition. It definitely did not pay to become too conspicuous in his line of work, and Jaerak was first and foremost a cautious man. He had been in enough fight-for-his-life situations to appreciate his expertise at saving his skin, and he had learned well to trust his instincts.

Business was brisk despite the impending storm, though people hurried to conclude their transactions, wanting to be safe in their homes before the downpour began. But as Jaerak approached the bookshop, large drops of water began to fall from the sky, spattering thickly against the cobbled street and booming thunder that for hours had sounded far distant now cracked with alarming immediacy. Swearing to himself, he hurried to duck under the awning of the bookshop just as the sky opened its floodgates and huge quantities of icy water instantly soaked everything in sight. Men and women scattered, scrambling for shelter like rats scurrying for the concealment of the shadows. Jaerak shuddered at the sight. The city when it was wet was even fouler than when it was dry. The rain never completely washed away the soot that covered nearly every surface, and mud and refuse clogged the streets for days.

Once inside the shop, Jaerak threw back the hood of his cloak and shook the rain from his eyes. He took deep breaths of the pleasant, musty fragrance of mold and dust that tickled his nose. He loved the scent of books and felt more at home in a bookshop than in any lodgings he might enjoy. A mangy white cat sauntered past, giving Jaerak a look that left no room for doubt upon whose territory he currently trespassed. The cat stopped and struck a pose, graciously allowing himself to be admired before he disappeared among the meager stacks in search of a nice, fat rat. Of which, Jaerak thought angrily, spotting a book whose binding looked suspiciously chewed, there were most likely many.

Jaerak caught a glimpse of himself reflected in the plate glass window, now streaming with a cascade of rainwater, and grimaced. At first glance, anyone would think him handsome, almost inhumanly beautiful, as if his features had been carved from softstone by a master sculptor. But upon closer inspection, they would see that the hard line of his cheek and jaw bespoke a ruthless and ungentle nature, and his eyes were cold and dull as flat steel. One touch from those eyes could send a chill racing down even the stiffest spine. But there was intelligence as well as cruelty in his face, and anyone with a grain of salt in their soul knew that Jaerak Thorin was not a man to be trifled with. He was a dangerous man, a man without conscience.

As always, there were few books on the shelves and even fewer that were worth reading. The Onnic, the Church's powerful and deadly army, had drastically reduced the variety of reading material by simply burning all the books the Triumvirate considered unsuitable. This left a rather dry selection consisting mostly of agricultural and religious books, subjects that had never even remotely interested Jaerak. But every once in a great while the Onnic missed something interesting, especially this far from Magir, the capitol of Casset and seat of the Onnic Order. Jaerak was constantly hunting for something new, something that might one day give him the means to pave the way for his ever-growing ambition, to satisfy his ever-growing hunger for power. He considered himself a scholar, though he had never attended any college nor been apprenticed in any trade. Between contracts, he read books and studied many subjects in the seclusion of his lodgings, though there was one subject in which he would not claim interest. He may not care one way or another about the Church in general, but he had no illusions as to what the Onnic would do to him if they caught him studying magic.

After a thorough search of the little shop to make sure he was the only patron there, Jaerak called for the shopkeeper, who had slipped out of sight as soon as he had entered. A bald, portly little man hesitantly emerged from the shelves, a worn, obviously beloved volume clutched to his chest as if it were a talisman that brought him comfort. His eyes were wide with fear and he gulped audibly as Jaerak turned his icy gaze on him. "Yes, my Lord?" he squeaked. Furiously blushing, he cleared his throat and tried again. "May I have the honor of helping you, my Lord?"

Jaerak looked at him with ill-concealed disgust. It never ceased to amaze him how readily most people allowed themselves to be controlled. *Find a man's weakness and he is yours*, he thought as he watched the man's face blanch with fear. "How many books have you found for me this time, Thomlyn?" he asked aloud. Sometimes the little man was able to find books of interest overlooked by the Onnic, but lately he'd had little to offer. Jaerak thought that maybe it was time to look for a new supplier – this one wasn't worth half a copper anymore.

Thomlyn started nervously and averted his eyes. The warm, almost gentle timbre of Jaerak's voice did not deceive him. "Well, Lord," he stammered, "nothing of the sort you are looking for has come through in a long time." He threw up his hands in a gesture of despair. "I am sorry, my Lord, but I have found nothing. The Church has been too thorough, and there have been two book fires in the city since last you came." Sweat beaded on his forehead as he tried to make himself small enough to squeeze into the corner, not an easy feat for a man of his girth. "Besides, I think they're getting suspicious of me," he continued, trembling visibly at the thought. "Last night I think they sent a night-search to the shop. I found the door ajar when I came in this morning, and some things had been moved in my desk."

Jaerak lifted his arm and casually but brutally backhanded Thomlyn across the face. Whimpering, the shopkeeper fell to his knees, nursing his cheek. Blood beaded on his lower lip and overflowed, leaving a crimson streak on his chin. Jaerak reached out again to pull him roughly to his feet, but before he could grasp the terrified man, a glimmer of strange yellowish light caught the corner of his eye. Abandoning the shopkeeper for the moment, who immediately and prudently ducked behind the wooden counter, he went to examine it.

The light was coming from a dusty shelf near the back of the shop, radiating from a small, slim book he had never seen before, laying crossways between two others. Upon closer inspection, he could discern the faint spell-web woven delicately around the volume that was the cause of that alien, unearthly light. He recognized it as an uncomplicated protective spell of Air, which caused the casual eye to pass over the book as if it were not even there. Why he could see it he did not know, but it was surprising enough to find a spelled book in this land that had spawned the Onnic army. Glancing indifferently at the cowering shopkeeper, Jaerak lifted his hand and traced his finger along the line of the spell-web, unraveling the simple pattern and freeing the book from the spell. Thomlyn's poor eyes nearly burst from his head as he witnessed this magic, but Jaerak ignored him as he took the book from the shelf.

It was very old, and the black leather that bound it was cracked and peeling dry. There was no title, nor author's name, but in one corner of the cover was a tiny faded symbol – an eye with a teardrop-shaped iris etched in green and gold. Jaerak's own eyes widened as he studied it. The eye was the Seeker symbol, and he had seen it only once before. It had been branded into the forehead of an unfortunate woman accused of being a magic user before she had been burned to death in the courtyard of the Church.

So this must be a Seeker book. Jaerak had never seen one before. To his knowledge, all such books had been burned by King Retik during the Onnic War over five hundred years ago. Surely, no Seeker would be reckless enough to write one since then, especially one that had obviously been to a printer's office. This book certainly looked old enough to have escaped that siege, though how it had come to be here was a mystery he knew would eat at him until it was solved. Restis Haven had been a popular Seeker city before the war. Perhaps this book was a relic from that long-ago era of magic and mystery. Questioning Thomlyn about the book was useless; the man was as sharp as softstone. Carefully, Jaerak opened the front cover, trying not to damage the delicate leather, and received another shock, this one all but knocking the breath out of him. There, right inside the front cover, was his enchanted mark.

All magic users have their own personal enchanted mark, which can be used like a signature. And, like a signature, no enchanted mark is exactly like any other. The Seekers had used them long ago to mark their belongings or spells, and he had discovered his own mark through working his magic in secret. He had never used it – the Onnic were uncanny about finding them. Yet, here was his own dodecahedron within a seven-pointed star staring up at him from the cover of a Seeker book he had never seen before. No mage could use the enchanted mark of another mage, so he must have put it there himself. Yet, he knew that he had not. His mind reeled as he tried to find an explanation, but none immediately presented itself. At least one mystery was solved. A sorcerer's enchanted mark never escaped the eyes of its master, so the warding spell had been ineffective on him.

Next to his mark, he saw two names – Gwynne Davanir and Silvya Brenn – and the name of a city penned on the page. Somehow, it did not surprise him as much as it should have that they were written in his own hand – the bold, spiked letters were unmistakably his. The implications were... well, he was sure there were bound to be implications, but he could not think of any at the moment. His brain had gone numb with shock. The names were unfamiliar to him, and the way they were written suggested they both belonged to one woman – not surprising, he thought, that a Seeker would change her name. How kind of his unknown benefactor to supply him with both.

Jaerak's mind raced with catlike speed, already hatching plans and devising schemes. He had the uncomfortable suspicion that he had just stepped into someone else's design, that he was being used like a puzzle piece. By itself, a piece of a puzzle has little meaning or coherence, but put together with others a pattern begins to emerge. He experienced a surge of hot anger at the thought of playing the part of a pawn in someone else's game, with no knowledge or understanding of the rules. But the unknown person or people involved would receive a nasty shock if they thought he would quietly play along. The rules were about to change.

Finding this book had been no accident. He was convinced that someone had left it for him, though the logistics of how and why continued to escape him. He would, of course, have to read the book to get an idea of the game being played, and then he would track this unknown woman down and question her. Perhaps she could give him a clearer picture of what he had just stumbled into.

Slowly he closed the book and turned to the shopkeeper, who was still trying to make himself invisible underneath the counter. Thomlyn was instantly on his feet, shaking and holding out his hands in what was supposed to be a reassuring gesture. "My Lord, I saw nothing," he said emphatically, though unable to keep the tremors from his voice. "You have nothing to fear from me, no my Lord, you needn't worry that I'll have a loose tongue. I never saw you do noth..." His voice faltered as Jaerak approached him, and the poor shopkeeper saw his own death in those cold, expressionless eyes. With only a cursory glance outside to make sure no one was passing by, Jaerak grasped Thomlyn by the chest and head and effortlessly snapped his neck, muffling the man's bleat of fear and pain against his cloak. He tossed the inert form to the floor, where it collapsed next to the well-loved book that had fallen from its lifeless fingers.

Jaerak turned to find himself facing the unblinking stare of the little white cat, and for a moment the two stared at each other, motionless. The cat was first to break the gaze and stood, deliberately turning its back as if Jaerak were no longer worthy of its notice. Stepping over the shopkeeper's crumpled body, Jaerak hid the book snugly under his cloak and stepped out into the now-deserted street, dodging through the rain as he made his way toward his lodgings.

"...There are forces greater than can be known by man, but none that are greater than is known by woman."

– From the Prophecy of the Eye of Truth

Chapter One

Wherever there is war, it seems naturally to follow that pain, suffering and despair touch the population with apparent taunting randomness until memories of past happiness and peace seem an elusive, mocking dream. Gwynne was no stranger to these shadowy phantoms of human suffering, but salt and stuff it, she thought, enough was enough.

Gwynne Davanir stood at the window of her tiny, ramshackle house, watching the waves of the sea crash up against the red rock cliffs that separated the City of Circles from the Annis Ocean. She was a slightly plump woman of middle years with a deeply lined face and graying hair, but her eyes were still clear, snapping with the sharp intelligence of a quick wit and unclouded mind. The lines and hair, she knew, made her look older than she truly was, but after enduring a life of persecution and fear she was apt to look upon them as trophies of her survival in a harsh and prejudicial world rather than a stigma of age and ugliness.

War... The word pounded inside Gwynne's head like the surf and she realized she was gripping the sill of the window so tightly her knuckles were white. She had been so sure that the talks between Marrin and Casset would result in the beginnings of peace. Instead, after only three days of negotiations, Queen Rhyssl el'Faria and her entourage had stormed out of Morgan's castle with the righteous air of having endured the deadliest of insults. The Queen had begun to escalate her army the instant she had returned to Marrin, and with her went the last hope of an alliance between the hostile monarchs. Already the blood of many soldiers, as well as of many innocent bystanders, had steeped the earth of the two kingdoms. For generations the wars had raged – the realms of Marrin and Cameon against the tyranny and terror of Casset and its army of the Onnic, the Church's deadly soldiers.

Gwynne sighed and unclenched her stiffened fingers. After this latest development, she had no hope that King Morgan el'Solcyne would back down or consider any compromise. He would not rest until he had scourged the land of his most hated nemeses. *Of which I am one*, Gwynne thought wryly – the much feared and nearly extinct Seekers of the Eye of Truth – the magic users.

Not that he has much reason to fear me any longer. The thought rose unbidden to her mind, and she quickly pushed it back down. Gwynne had known for some time that her powers were fading away, becoming stagnant and diminished through disuse. No amount of worrying over the matter could change that now, and such thoughts should remain locked away in that rarely visited vault in her mind that had long housed other thoughts and memories too painful to bear. With her own eyes she had seen Seekers – some friends, some strangers – tortured and mutilated by the Onnic, and she had no desire to join their martyred ranks. So she had established herself as an ordinary citizen and had lived many years as such, and if she could not lay claim to true happiness, she could at least acknowledge some small degree of contentment. But now, when circumstances forced her to reconsider her decision, her powers seemed to escape her as if she were trying to grasp a handful of smoke.

It was no use. The tightly locked vault had opened and her demons rapidly emerged, eager for freedom after such long captivity. In her youth, Gwynne had been proud to be a Seeker of the Eye of Truth. She had joined the few remaining magic users in the secret Search for the woman who, it was promised, would someday come and reset the balance of power across the lands – the Eye of Truth, the woman foretold in the Prophecies from the time of the Great Cataclysm. It was written that she would harness and unleash the Five Elements of Magic upon those whose hearts were black and tainted, and magic would once again flourish in the lands.

Once, long ago, longer than the memories of man or woman, Seekers had been revered and honored. They had built huge, shining cities and had walked among the population as healers and soothsayers, builders and teachers. Those cities now lay in crushed ruins and had long since been overgrown and forgotten. The gentle Seekers had been hunted down and destroyed like a pack of mad animals, though treated with less compassion than if they truly had been rabid beasts. Few were left, and those who possessed the talent for magic were forced to hide it out of necessity and self-preservation. But that did not stop King Morgan from continuing his reign of terror, sending his Onnic legions out on terrible witch-hunts that ultimately ended in death for the guilty and innocent alike. So, alone and hunted, the scattered remains of the once-powerful and respected Seekers continued their quest in secret and solitude, never giving up hope that the Eye of Truth would soon come and save them all from the hell that their lives had become.

Gwynne herself had always known she was somehow different from other people. When she was a small child, her parents had taught her that magic was wicked, the work of the Evil One. She had known, therefore, with childlike innocence that her special little games could not possibly be magic. There was nothing evil in her harmless and delightful pastimes, and she had continued to indulge in her secret world that each day brought new and wonderful discoveries. She had found that she could feel things in the earth, could talk to plants and help them grow, could understand the stories told by the stones that had lain upon the shore for countless centuries. Each tree in the wood had a name, each blade of grass a tale of seasons past. The flowers told her stories that were carried on the wind, and she could feel the vibrant energy of the sand under her feet as she walked barefoot along the chalk-white beaches. She had delighted in these things of beauty and power and selfishly kept them to herself, wanting no other to enter her little world of secrets. She would go off for hours and hide herself in the caves that riddled the high cliffs by the sea, and if her parents worried that she was a shy, introverted child, she had found her friends in the very nature of the earth and needed no others.

One day when she was twelve years old she had come home from her favorite walk to find her parents dead, their house burnt. She shuddered to remember her wordless horror as kind and tearful neighbors told her of the crimson-cloaked men who had come to question her mother and father. Receiving no suitable answers, they had torched the house with her parents trapped inside, unable to save themselves while the townspeople stood by and helplessly watched. They were only too well aware what would happen if they tried to intervene. It was at that moment Gwynne had realized that her innocent little games were evil – were *magic* – and she had torn herself from the kindly hands of the neighbor who held her and had run as if all the demons of hell pursued behind. She knew, as if the truth had been written in blood and fire across the heavens, that her parents had been murdered because of her, and when she ran she fled more from herself than from the fear of sharing their fate.

She had run until she could go no further. She had collapsed in a grove of trees, her bare feet bloody and swollen and her head reeling. She had had no food or shelter and the coming night was cold. She did not remember how long she had lain there, shivering miserably beneath the trees. She had tried to keep warm by covering herself with the dead leaves cast from the trees with the coming of winter, but the cold had seeped into her bones until she was numb. Finally, she had been found, huddled and half-frozen, by an old, old woman who had heard the child's weak cries while gathering jumpernuts in the forest. She had taken Gwynne back to her small hutch and over the next few weeks had nursed her back to health.

The old woman, known to Gwynne throughout her life only as Aunt May, had listened as she had sobbed out her story, and had brushed the tears away from her face with gentle fingers. She had tightly held her thrashing body when Gwynne awoke in stark terror from the nightmares of the two charred and blackened bodies, their bony arms reaching out to her in mute appeal and condemnation. Slowly but inexorably, Aunt May drew Gwynne out of the whirlpool of guilt and remorse into which she had flung herself, until one day the nightmares stopped and she found that she could smile, and sleep, once again.

It was only then that Aunt May told Gwynne the truth about herself. Aunt May was a Seeker of the Eye of Truth, a magic user. Gwynne had been astounded. It was impossible that the kindly old woman was an evil being, impossible to hate her or be afraid of her! Aunt May told Gwynne of the Prophecies of the Eye of Truth, the legends born of the Great Cataclysm that foretold the woman who would come and lead the world back to truth and balance with her gentle and terrible hand. She spoke of the Five Elements of Magic and gave Gwynne books to read; old books that looked as if they were hundreds of years old. Despite her fear, Gwynne had been unwillingly interested and had listened avidly to everything Aunt May taught her.

Eventually the old woman had encouraged Gwynne to delve again inside herself to find her own magic. At first, she had rebelled, afraid that terrible retribution would once again follow, but the pull of magic was too strong, too sweet to resist for long. So, at first with caution and trepidation as if probing a wound not long healed, she again allowed her magic to surface. Aunt May taught Gwynne everything she knew of magic and the Prophecies that would one day be her gospel. She devised long, exhausting lessons for her, always gentle and kind, yet intolerant of sloth or incompetence. Gwynne had flourished under Aunt May's tutelage, and had continued to grow in strength and confidence until her efforts outdid even Aunt May's own.

When Aunt May eventually died, Gwynne, a young woman then, had struck out on her own to start her Search, taking with her only one slim volume from the old woman's extensive library as a remembrance. But her Search had led only to dead ends and disappointments, and finally the threat of the Onnic army became too strong for her. She had seen too much death, had witnessed too many abominations for one lifetime, and the blood she had seen shed seemed to leave a stain on her soul that grew darker and spread farther each year. Besides... she had become too tired in body and spirit to run any longer. She had returned to the City of Circles, the place of her birth, under a new name to live in peace and anonymity. Even if someone had remembered old Fisherman Avin Davanir and his wife Erinne, they had long ago ceased to wonder what had become of their long lost daughter. She had hoped to end her days quietly studying her books, but it seemed even that small luxury would now be denied her.

She could not exactly pinpoint the moment when the uneasiness she had first sensed some weeks ago had changed into something darker, something infinitely more malevolent. It had gradually moved from a vaguely troubled feeling, subtle as a brush of butterfly wings across her consciousness, to outright terror dominating the forefront of her awareness. She only knew that for some time something, somewhere, was very wrong, and it was getting worse. Gradually there had emerged a subtle difference when she extended her senses to include the earth, the rocks, and the trees – a faint taint as if the earth had gone slightly sour. At first Gwynne had thought it due to the blood that had soaked the earth over the years, but after a time she knew it was something different, something bigger than war and stronger than blood. It was as if some foul substance had defiled the soil itself, though Gwynne knew it had not. It was merely communicating a message to her, a warning of danger and fear and worse things to come. And now that she had received the warning, it seemed she was powerless to combat it, and her mind railed with frustration and fear.

Gwynne recalled a passage from the Prophesies, still as fresh in her mind as the day she had first heard Aunt May speak it. *"When Earth, Fire, Water and Air become one to cry out with mute voices of unspeakable danger and fear, when Time itself seems to stop upon an era of madness, it is then, my Children, that you must search for me, for my time has come."* Well, she could not ignore that the earth was indeed telling her of danger, and for all she knew the other elements could be doing the same. She had never been able to connect to the other elements as she had the earth, and she no longer knew anyone who could tell her if the same sickness was present in the water or air or fire. An era of madness... Well, now that peace between Rhyssl and Morgan seemed doomed to nonexistence, a never-ending war that had already raged over five hundred years struck her as madness indeed. And who was she, Gwynne thought ruefully, to ignore the commands set down more than five hundred years ago by those who had first recorded the Prophecies from the very Prophets themselves?

But what could she do? Her powers had ebbed, and even if they had not she dared not use them. Not all Seekers captured by the Onnic were executed. Some were enslaved and used like hounds, forced by soldiers to seek out magic and betray its user. Gwynne shivered when she thought of those gaunt, blank-eyed creatures – the Esprys. No longer human, but neither were they animals, they hovered through a joyless, mercifully short existence under the pitiless power of their deadly enemies. She could only hope they retained no memories of the life they had once had or the people they had once been. She did not know what the Onnic did to reduce a human being to that imbecilic state, but she knew she would rather die than become one of them.

The vault of her mind cracked open a little wider, exposing the darkest depths of memory within. She thought then of a man, a man with beautiful dark eyes and a sweet, secret smile that spoke to her of the heady scent of wildflowers and stolen moments in the woods. A man who had been forced to betray everyone he had held dear, to forsake all he had lived and fought for. Her heart ached afresh when she remembered how he had looked at her those many years ago through eyes that were no longer beautiful, eyes that could no longer see her. He had spoken through lips that could no longer smile, which no longer remembered, and had betrayed her to the Onnic. Gwynne shook her head, slamming shut the door on memories too painful to bear and shied away from the image of the blank, vacuous face that bore no resemblance to the man she had loved.

Perhaps it was time to begin her Search again. She could think of nothing else of any use she could do, and she could Search without using magic if she must. Well, maybe she could. Only magic users can sense a like ability in others, and Gwynne suspected that she need not physically *use* magic to Search for the Eye. Her conviction that resuming her Search might be fruitful as it had not been those many years ago stemmed not merely from one relevant passage in the Prophecies. It was fueled by countless coincidences, too many to be ignored and too accurate to be dismissed. It was a whisper here, an event there, an uncanny occurrence that just so happened to resemble a telling sign from the Prophecies. If she was correct, and the Epoch of the Eye was truly upon them, recognizing the Eye of Truth for what she was would be the least of her problems.

The Prophecies, vague though they were, did give some clues to use as guidelines for the Search. According to the long-dead Prophets, the Eye of Truth would be born a commoner and carry in her veins no drop of noble blood. She would be incapable of uttering a falsehood or of harboring a deception. She would be human, but would have the blood of one of the Old Lines running through her veins. *That could not be too hard to spot,* Gwynne thought. The physical characteristics of the Hordon or Sabian bloodlines were easy to identify. If she ever ran across a seven-foot tall woman with violet eyes and ice-white hair she would bet a pint of salt she had just found her quarry, and haul her off to the Lake Point posthaste to face the test at the Mirror of the Eye. But the most obvious indication would be her magic. The Prophets had foretold she would be the most powerful mage history had ever known. The pull felt from such power would be as hard to resist as a piece of iron could resist a lodestone.

Gwynne chuckled at her audacity. How could she think that after so many thousands of Searches, hers would result in triumph where all others had failed? The Prophets had said little of who would find the Eye, except to say the successful Seeker would possess the talent for magic. They also claimed that the one fated to find her would be inextricably bound to her, their destinies merging forever into one. The ghost of a shadow passed over Gwynne's face, and she bit her lip pensively. She had envisioned herself living always alone, sentenced by fate to a lifetime of solitude. It was dangerous to get close to people, to let them into her heart only to suffer for the cavernously empty place they left when they died. She had felt the sharp, bitter pang of loneliness for many years, and because it was self-inflicted she had never complained. Now she admitted to herself that perhaps it was not only the Search that beckoned her, but the prospect of sharing the remainder of her life with someone. The person who found the Eye of Truth would never have to be lonely again.

Gwynne started violently as a loud rap sounded at her door, and she cursed her negligence for not perceiving the visitor earlier. There had once been a time when no one could sneak up on her like that, even as lost in thought as she had been. She composed her thoughts and smoothed her dress as she made her way to the door. Before she opened it, she pressed her hand against the wood as she always did, just to make sure no Onnic stood on the other side. At least there was one talent that had not deserted her. Satisfied, she opened the door just as the man she now faced raised his hand to knock again. For an instant, they stared at each other in speechless surprise.

The young man's surprise no doubt stemmed from her unexpectedly abrupt appearance, but Gwynne was in no condition to make such a coherent judgment. Before her stood a man about thirty years of age, lithe and supple of body with straight fair hair swept back from his brow, the ends just touching his shoulders. He had piercing, intelligent eyes of an indeterminate shade between blue and gray, and the waning light that cast its shadows upon his features accented his fine, high cheekbones. And such features...! Gwynne's normally excellent imagination failed her as she tried to find a word to express his perfect beauty. Sex appeal came to mind as she experienced a faint but regional flutter, a sensation she had not felt for many years, nor had she ever expected to feel it again.

The man recovered first. His smile was so blinding that Gwynne missed the first part of his explanation. She blinked, and forced herself to listen.

"...know it is rude to intrude upon you like this," the man was saying, obviously mistaking her dumbfounded expression for disapproval at his boldness, "but it was imperative I speak to you." He began to look uncomfortable, as her silence remained unbroken. "You are Gwynne Davanir, aren't you?"

"I... yes, I am," she stumbled. *By the Eye, woman, get a hold of yourself!* "I'm sorry, what did you say your name was?"

"Jaerak Thorin, my Lady," he said, accompanying the introduction with an elegant bow. "I have traveled from Magir to speak with you. If it is not convenient, I can return another time."

His manners were faultless, but something about him caused Gwynne to eye him with distrust. She could not put her finger on it, but there was something not entirely right about this impossibly beautiful young man. It certainly was not his face, which expressed only innocent ingenuousness, but she thought she should be cautious nonetheless.

"Of course you may speak to me," she said, smiling. "You must forgive my manners, but I so rarely have visitors. I sometimes forget how to receive them. Please come in." She ushered Jaerak into the foyer and offered to take his cloak.

"No, thank you, I cannot stay long," he explained.

"Very well. If you will follow me?" Gwynne led him into the front room that served as both library and living area. The furnishings were simple and austere, consisting of several comfortable chairs well past their prime and a long table untidily piled with papers. A smaller table was littered with used mugs and dishes that she had not gotten around to washing. Shelves and shelves of dusty books lined the walls, giving the otherwise shabby room a comfortable, homey atmosphere. Gwynne's most prized possession, a beautiful paper-thin blue and peach china vase, lorded over the room on its pillar-like table near the window. "I am sorry about the mess, but as I said before I don't often entertain. Please, sit down." She gestured to one of the chairs – the one that was not losing its stuffing – and took the other herself. All her senses were now alert, and she had not missed the gleam in the young man's eye when he had seen the shelves piled with books. "Now, what may I do for you?"

Jaerak took a deep breath and let it out heavily. "It is hard to know where to begin, my Lady. Perhaps I should start with some information about myself. I live in Magir, as I told you..."

"You told me you have come from Magir," Gwynne interrupted, smiling. "You did not say that you lived there."

Jaerak's eyes narrowed in amusement. "I can see you don't miss much. Somehow, I am not surprised. I will try to be more precise. I do live in Magir, and I have been a student there for several years. I study many things, at least, as many things as the Onnic will let me." Gwynne nodded her head to show that she, too, understood the restrictions enforced by Onnic censorship. "Well... I understand that this is a delicate subject, but..."

Suddenly, Gwynne felt her heart constrict, as if a great hand had grasped and squeezed it. She realized all too late why the man had so disturbed her. It was not his looks that had bothered her, but that he had addressed her by her true name, a name she had not used in more than thirty years. It amazed her that after so long a time she would still automatically answer to it, and if she had not been so distracted by his startling beauty she would have caught herself sooner. She cursed herself three ways for a fool as her mind raced desperately for a way to remedy her error.

Seemingly unaware of her shock, Jaerak continued. He took another deep breath and blurted, "I understand that you are a Seeker, and I wish to learn from you."

Gwynne felt the color drain from her face, and her hands became icy where they lay in her lap. She found herself on her feet and standing as far from the man as the room allowed with no recollection of having moved. She silently and incoherently cursed herself again, for she knew she was a picture of guilt and there was no way now to deny the charge. A cold lump of fear knotted in her guts as she stared in horror at the man before her. So long... she had evaded the Onnic for so long, and now it was all over. *How had he found her? How had he discovered her birth name?* She had been so careful, so cautious, and she could not think what she could have done to give herself away. She was buffeted by an unexpected wave of despair at the thought of having to abandon a Search she had only just begun to consider resuming.

"Please!" Jaerak exclaimed, rising from his seat. His beautiful face was a picture of gentle concern. "Do not be so alarmed. I mean you no harm at all, truly I do not." Gwynne did not move, and Jaerak raised his hands in apparent helplessness. "How can I convince you except to tell you that I, too, have a talent for magic? You see, I have a small ability for Fire."

Jaerak opened his hand, palm up, and stared at it, his dark eyebrows coming together in a frown of concentration. Gwynne felt a tiny tremor reverberate through her bones and she gasped aloud. Seemingly out of nowhere, a small ball of fire suddenly materialized above Jaerak's fingers, flickering and dancing on the drafts that swept through the room. Gwynne gazed at it in astonishment. It had been a long time since she had witnessed magic in practice. She focused intently and was barely able to recognize the ingenious, rose colored gossamer spell-web that twined through the fire and Jaerak's fingers, protecting his skin from the heat, cementing the flames to his hand, infusing them with magic. It took a great deal of effort for her to see any spell-lines other than those from the earth, but she could not bring herself to look away. It was so beautiful, and Gwynne, enthralled, found herself smiling like a fool. When Jaerak closed his hand into a fist, abruptly extinguishing the light, she experienced a pang of regret as keen as pain.

"I need to learn more before I can begin my Search," he said, and Gwynne's delighted smile vanished like the flames he had just killed. "I came here because you are the only other magic user I've ever heard of." He looked at her with a glimmer of amusement. "Perhaps I should have chosen my words more carefully, but it's not exactly a subject one can bring up casually, is it? Please, sit down again and talk to me."

"How... how did you find out about me?" Gwynne asked, unable to keep her voice steady. "Where did you learn my name?" She sank back into her chair as if her legs could no longer support her, and indeed, she was trembling so violently that her teeth chattered. She tightly clutched the arms of her chair to keep her hands from shaking and tried to take slow, even breaths. That tiny vibration, as gentle as a lover's touch, had completely unnerved her. It had, indeed, been a long time since she had sensed magic. Jaerak, once she was seated, resumed his own chair and reached into his cloak. Her heart seemed to stop its beating altogether as Jaerak drew a book from its voluminous folds. She, of course, instantly recognized it.

"Where did you get that?" she whispered. Her voice was hoarse and she barely recognized it as her own. She unconsciously reached out and grabbed Jaerak's arm, her fingers digging painfully into his flesh. "Tell me. Tell me, where did you get that book?"

Jaerak looked surprised at the intensity of her question. "I found it in a bookshop in Magir," he said, looking uncertainly at the white-knuckled hand that still clasped his forearm. "It has your name in it. That's how I found you. I assumed you were a Seeker, because of the symbol on the front." He held the small, slender volume out to her. With trembling hands, Gwynne took it, her fingers caressing the fractured leather lovingly.

It was the book she had taken from Aunt May's collection after the old woman's death so many years ago. It was one of Gwynne's most treasured possessions, not only for the love she felt for her long-dead mentor, but because it was her only tangible link to those who had first begun the order to which she had dedicated her life. It had mysteriously disappeared from her library some time ago, and as much as Gwynne had grieved for the loss, her fear of discovery outweighed softer emotions. She had lived in fear long after it had vanished, hoping the book had not fallen into the hands of the Onnic. How extraordinary, she thought, that it should return to her by way of this strange man from Magir.

She carefully opened the book and sure enough, there was her true name penned on the page beside her alias, as well as the name of the City of Circles. She noted, however, that her own hand had not written them. She was not such a fool that she would mark her name in such a dangerous manner, and she wondered who had done it and why. Apparently, she assured herself, trying to keep panic at bay, it was not to incriminate her, or else the Onnic would have come and done their unspeakable things to her long ago. There was nothing else on the page, and as she carefully flipped through the book she could see no other notations or marks that should not be there. Whoever had written her name had left no clues behind.

Jaerak Thorin had remained respectfully silent while Gwynne had examined the book, but now he spoke again and his quiet words chilled her. "It is true, then. The book is yours."

"Yes, it is mine," Gwynne answered. There was no point in denying it; her reaction to it had made that fact clearer than any words she could have spoken. Now she looked at Jaerak through more suspicious eyes. "But it was not I who wrote my name into it. How did you learn the meaning of the Seeker symbol? It is hardly common knowledge these days."

Jaerak looked uncomfortable. "I... I once saw a woman accused of using magic and... her trial was public. They..." His voice trailed off and the look on his face spoke of remembered pain and helplessness.

"I see," Gwynne said quickly. She, too, had witnessed Seeker trials, and she knew what was inflicted upon the accused.

Though her breathing had calmed and her tremors subsided, an urgent uneasiness continued to wash over her. She suspected that this man knew more than he was telling her, and thought he had deliberately confronted her this way to observe her reactions. His eyes, distant and unreadable, betrayed none of the emotion that was painted upon the rest of his face. Carefully keeping her own expression neutral so as not to betray her purpose, she sent out the gentlest mind probe, so light that the recipient would never realize what was being done. She was instantly blocked by the most powerful mind-shield she had ever encountered.

Surprised, Gwynne probed a little harder and was again repelled. Mindshields in mages were not uncommon, and even some non-mages sometimes had natural ones of which they are unaware, but never had she come across one that was so tight, so complete. Suddenly she realized this was why she had not known he was coming until he was at her door, and why she had instinctively mistrusted him before he had even spoken her name. If he truly was a student of magic and wished to follow the ways of a Seeker, he would have opened his mind to verify his intentions. Even if he was unsure of her, which would only be natural, she should have been able to sense something, some stray thought, some unchecked emotion. But there was nothing, not even a hint of what was going on behind those beautiful eyes of his. It was as if she had tried to probe a block of stone.

"I don't know who put your name in the book," Jaerak was saying as Gwynne brought her attention back to him. "I found it like this in the shop. I figured you must have owned the book, and you would know what it meant. So I decided to journey here to ask you about it."

Well, Gwynne thought, *the best way to find out why he is here is to let him tell me*. "Have you read it?" she asked aloud.

"Yes, but it didn't seem to be a real book. I mean, it just looked like a list of some sort."

"Yes, it is a list," Gwynne explained. "An inventory."

"An inventory? Of what?"

"Well, you have heard, of course, of the Onnic War?" Jaerak nodded an affirmative. "All right. Then you know that the Seekers were being massacred by the thousands, the tens of thousands. At that time, Seekers used what were called Pyaerea, or magic items, to aid them in their Search. Pyaerea were items that were created or enchanted by mages so their magic became inherent in the objects themselves. Used properly, they could augment one's powers, and even non-mages could use some of the more powerful Pyaerea. During the Onnic War, over five hundred years ago, many of these Pyaerea were confiscated by the Onnic and destroyed. So one Seeker, Melanrys an'Tereal, created the Dark Abyss. Have you heard of it?"

"No, what is it?" Jaerak asked, avidly interested.

"No one really knows. It is a place, so to speak, that cannot be entered without a certain key, a magic key." Gwynne tried to remember how Aunt May had described the Dark Abyss to her. "Some Seekers have described it in their writings as a pocket of space, or a gateway to another world. It is a place that does not seem to exist in time or space, and only magic users can enter it. The Pyaerea would be safe where no Onnic could find them. Creating the Dark Abyss took all Melanrys an'Tereal's strength, and in the end it killed her.

"Anyway, the Seekers put their remaining Pyaerea into the Dark Abyss and sealed it to protect them from the Onnic. But now no one knows where the gateway to the Abyss is, and knowledge of the key with which to open it has long been forgotten. This book," Gwynne waved it at him, "is the list of all the Pyaerea that still lie in the Dark Abyss, and their functions, properties and descriptions."

Jaerak looked thoughtful. "They could be a true asset to mages now, couldn't they?"

Gwynne looked at him sharply. "Not really. Much knowledge was lost during the Onnic War, including the knowledge of how to use many of the Pyaerea. The writings of the Seekers have been burnt and destroyed, and after the passage of so much time, no one remembers the stories passed down from the Seekers of the Onnic War. I'm sure that in time we could learn again, but the Onnic would not give us that much time." *Why is he so interested in this?* "Over the centuries magic has dwindled in our lands. By culling out and killing the magic users, the Onnic have made it very difficult for us to pass the talents down to our children. Most of us don't even live long enough to bear children, and the rest of us are understandably wary of forging permanent, intimate relationships." A shadow flitted across her face so fleeting that Jaerak was unsure whether he had actually seen it. Gwynne continued.

"The Onnic have destroyed our cities, our books, our knowledge and our history. Those born with magic today have no one to teach them, and more often than not their magic goes unrealized their entire lives. If the Eye of Truth is not found soon, there will be no one left to find her and then we shall be lost. Magic will die, and we will have lost a precious part of our lives and our heritage.

"The Pyaerea are useless without the knowledge and the wisdom to use them." Gwynne waved the book at him. "This book tells us what they are, what they look like, and what they can do, but the author did not think to tell us their secrets. If someone dropped the Anais Rod in my lap right now, I could tell them it was made by Cor of Restis Haven, and that he imbued it with the ability to call lightning at will. However, I would not be able to do it myself. For me, it would be a useless piece of crystal."

"But would the Eye of Truth know how to use them?" Jaerak asked.

Surprised, Gwynne thought about it. She had never considered that possibility. "Perhaps she would, but I don't know for sure. It's said that her magic will be so strong that I doubt she will feel the need for the Pyaerea."

"But don't you see? If she has the knowledge of the Pyaerea, she could teach the rest of us how to use them. Then, we would certainly be a formidable army for her to lead. The Onnic wouldn't stand a chance against us!" Jaerak's eyes, for the first time, held a spark of emotion. Gwynne was not sure she really wanted to know what that emotion was.

However, she continued to speak gently. "But these things are not what it means to be a Seeker of the Eye of Truth. We are not to be an army, with the Eye of Truth as our leader. Our aim is to put an end to war, not begin a new one. The Onnic war was devastating to us, by all accounts. One of the reasons we died in such incredible numbers was because most mages refused to use their magic to take another person's life. Magic users have always been scholars, teachers, and healers. The thought of using their magic as a weapon against another person, even to defend their own lives, must have been abhorrent to them. So many did not defend themselves, and they died. Their blood steeped the earth and stained the stones, and still they died, until they began to learn to hide what they were.

"Today we Seekers struggle, not only for our survival but with our ignorance. Those of us who were lucky enough to have a teacher rarely find someone we can pass that knowledge on to, and it therefore dies with us. None of us dares write that knowledge down anymore. The Onnic are unbelievably skillful at finding such books." She unconsciously stroked the leather of the book she still held. "A Seeker's ultimate goal is to end the suffering of the oppressed by Searching for the One who will come in our time of need. The Prophecies tell us that there will be the strongest need when we are at our weakest. In the last twenty-five years, I have met only two other mages. One of them is dead now and the other..." Gwynne felt a spasm of pain as she thought of the beautiful, blank face of the woman who had been her friend. "Well, the other one would have been better off if she, too, had died. The point is, we do not seek power, nor do we use our strength for our own ends. What little strength we have left we use for one purpose only – to fulfill the Prophecies."

"I see," Jaerak said, smiling mildly. "I never had anyone to teach me these things. Somehow I'd always pictured the Eye of Truth as a general, with all of us her soldiers, exacting retribution upon the Onnic for their years of oppression and torture."

"I don't think it will be exactly like that," Gwynne said dryly. "I think she will teach us all to live amongst one another again, the way it was centuries before. Before magic was considered evil, before people without our talents learned to fear us."

Jaerak nodded his head, his fair hair throwing golden lights. "I never knew how we had lived before. The history books I've read never told those stories. As for this book," he took it once again from her reluctant hands, "I just thought perhaps there might be something here that could aid us in the Search. I remember a reference to some stones with magical properties. Do you know of them?"

"Yes." Gwynne looked at Jaerak thoughtfully. "There were five altogether, each infused with an Element of Magic."

"I thought there were only four elements," Jaerak said, looking puzzled. "Air, earth, water, fire."

"The knowledge of manipulating the fifth element has been lost for centuries," Gwynne told him. "But long ago, Seekers considered time an element. They could manipulate it and use it as they could the others."

Jaerak's eyebrows shot up to his hairline. "What do you mean? How does one manipulate time?"

Gwynne shrugged. "I don't know. I never found a book that described it."

"And no one knows how to do this anymore?"

"No."

"Even if they had the Stones?"

"I don't know. It doesn't matter, anyhow. No one knows where they all are now."

"But if the book refers to them, wouldn't they be in the Dark Abyss?"

"I only know for certain of one that was placed there. All five were supposed to have been put into the Abyss, but according to the stories, only one actually made it – the Alchemist Stone. All the Stones had names – I cannot remember them all now – and they were made to be used together. They could be used separately, but their real strength lay in their unity. The Alchemist Stone was only one of the five. The rest were probably lost or destroyed before they could be saved."

"The Alchemist Stone. Let me see..." Jaerak carefully opened the book and gently turned the brittle pages. "Ah, here it is. There were five stones – the Alchemist Stone, the Philosopher Stone, the Aurora Stone, the Ephemeris Stone and the Zephyrus Stone. So, the Alchemist Stone was the only one that made it into the Dark Abyss? What were its properties?" Jaerak was now leaning forward as if to catch her words more quickly. *Aha! Now we are coming to the true matter of this interview!* Gwynne tentatively tried again to probe Jaerak's mind, but his shield had no cracks or chinks. Gwynne felt the uneasiness begin to creep back. If this man did indeed have magic, it must be very strong to sustain such a mind-shield for so long. His eyes glinted greedily, and he was biting his lower lip hard enough to leave bloodless marks where his teeth had sunk into the skin. Gwynne was not sure why he was questioning her. If he had indeed read the book as he said he had, he would have known what the properties of the five Stones were.

"I... I'm not sure I remember," Gwynne lied. Whatever else he wanted from her, she was certain that he had not come to learn the ways of the Seekers. But she could not guess at his ulterior motive, nor why he was so intent on questioning her knowledge of the Pyaerea Stones.

The lie was a mistake. Jaerak's eyes narrowed, and suddenly Gwynne wondered how she ever could have thought him handsome.

"You do not trust me," he murmured. "Not surprising, under the circumstances." Abruptly, Gwynne found herself unable to move.

He rose to his feet and Gwynne tried to struggle, helpless in the prison of Air he had constructed around her. Fear fogged her vision, but she could not even blink. She felt as if she were encased in stone.

"I did not expect to fool you for so long," he said, his voice a scathing rebuke as blinding panic clawed in her throat. "Oh, did I forget to mention I have a slight talent for Air, as well as for Fire? I'm sorry, but it is bad form to reveal all one's secrets. Now, you are holding back information that I need and really, it will be much quicker and easier this way than to pry it out of you with idle conversation."

Gwynne felt a sharp mental probe like a needle stab into her brain and unbelievable pain wracked through her head. Unable to move, or even to scream, she sat agonizingly helpless as Jaerak methodically raped her mind, sorting through memories and information, storing what was useful and discarding what was not. Gwynne had never in her life experienced such agony, such violation. A bewildering deluge of memories swam before her unblinking eyes as Jaerak brought them to the surface of her senses. His mind was too strong for her to resist, and she was too weak to throw up her own shield against him. Yet, even as he ruthlessly and repeatedly pierced her mind, she sensed something familiar about his touch, something oily and rancid and foul.

Finally, after several lifetimes, Jaerak withdrew and released her from the spell. She collapsed to the floor, sobbing and moaning, too spent to retaliate and too wounded to get up. She blinked repeatedly, her eyelids feeling like sand over her moisture-starved eyes. Jaerak laughed contemptuously as he picked up the treasured book and waved it at her.

"Remember, my Lady," and his voice made the title a mockery, "I have evidence enough to see you arrested and executed by the Onnic. I suggest you forget you have ever seen me, though something tells me we shall meet again someday. Believe me, I look forward to the pleasure." He turned to leave and Gwynne, gathering her last ounce of strength, called upon her powers of the Earth to help her. Jaerak's face turned from triumphant to terrified as the floor beneath his feet began to tremble. Objects in the room began to rattle where they sat, and the lovely vase fell from its pillar-like table and shattered, sending small, sharp pieces of blue and peach porcelain flying through the air. One piece cut deeply into Jaerak's left cheek as the ground gave one final heave that threw him off balance. Gwynne heard the snap of bone breaking as he crashed through the door and fell heavily onto the front step.

The earth once again became quiet as Gwynne, nearly unconscious with strain, lost the last of her strength and the emerald lines of the spell-web she had been trying to weave disintegrated between her fingers. The last things she saw before the blackness engulfed her was Jaerak dragging himself away from the house with his good leg, a tongue of orange and blue flame leaping from his fingertips, and a small curl of smoke no thicker than a fishing line floating up into the air before a soft breath of wind came to blow it away.

"...And so she will come, the Eye of Truth, and with her she will bring balance, and therefore peace."
– From the Prophecy of the Eye of Truth

Chapter Two

Aliane el'Gregarian, daughter of King Torrit el'Gregarian – King of Cameon and ruler of the Western Region – was bored.

She had accompanied her father on his trip to Magir because she had wished to see more of the world than merely Aryn, the city in which she had been born and had never left until two weeks ago. The journey itself had been fun, for her father was a wonderful companion and the lands they had traveled had been interesting. But now she was stuck in this huge, dreary castle with the very tiresome company of Princess Julane, daughter of King Morgan el'Solcyne, monarch of Casset and ruler of the Eastern Region. Their fathers were in a conference together and Aliane wondered wearily how much longer they would be.

She knew what they were conferring about, though her father had tried to keep it from her. He was going to ask King Morgan leave for one of his sons to court her in the hopes they would grow to like each other and eventually marry. Aliane knew that such an alliance between the two kingdoms would be a great stepping-stone in the pursuit of peace between the two monarchs, but in truth she knew she could never bring herself to love either son. Not even for her father.

She had met the Princes Larion and Paulis once before when she was a child, and they had both displayed a cruel streak that had frightened her. She remembered them as bullies and their particular brand of fun had sickened her. She had a vague, disturbing memory of a poor squirrel or some other small woodland animal that had come to its painful and messy end at the hands of the young princes.

Aliane was, by nature, a very kindhearted and compassionate young woman, and the rough manners of the two princes compared poorly with her gentle sweetness. At the same time her fiercely independent spirit resisted all efforts to dominate her – a trait, she thought, the princes would undoubtedly fail to appreciate. She had told her father that she did not wish to marry either man, but he had only laughed and suggested that perhaps they had changed as much in the intervening seventeen years as she had herself. And because she loved her father dearly, she had closed her mouth and said no more about it.

Being a king's daughter, even if only by adoption, had not spoiled Aliane. Torrit el'Gregarian adored his lovely young daughter, and would not for the world knowingly do anything to make her unhappy. He truly believed she could grow to like at least one of the princes. Aliane had been the daughter of his sister, but when her parents and Torrit's beloved Queen had been killed when she was only three years old, he had taken her into his home and had raised her as his own. He and his late wife had had no children themselves, and for twenty-three years she had stayed by his side. In all that time this was the first instance he had ever overridden an appeal she had made to him.

Aliane sighed and glanced up at Julane, who was expertly embroidering an elaborate pattern, in rather garish colors, onto a pillow cover. She thought Julane was very beautiful with her golden hair and deep blue eyes. But her beauty was somewhat marred by her tight-lipped mouth and the way she looked at everything through eyes constantly narrowed with suspicion. Julane had made it obvious from the beginning that she did not like or approve of Aliane, but in such a way that Aliane could not take official offense. She wished her father would hurry up and conclude his business so they could be on their way home. This may be the grandest castle in all the regions, she thought to herself, but she had seen no trace of happiness in it. She was eager to return to her own cheerful, if shabby, home.

She glanced at the rich carpets and gleaming wooden furniture, the heavy damask draperies and elaborately carved moldings, the priceless paintings and the lamps strung with jewels. Pretty, she had to admit, but ostentatious. She wondered how anyone could be comfortable with such luxury when people were dying of hunger and sickness in the plague camps outside every town in the realm. Morgan might be richer than her father, but he obviously used his money selfishly. Maybe if she married one of the princes she could actually do some good with such wealth... but no, she thought. If she wouldn't marry for power or political unity, she certainly couldn't marry for money, or even the opportunity to help people in need. She gratefully remembered that both princes were both out with Morgan's royal army, and were not expected to return any time soon. If Morgan agreed to her father's proposal, she would be spared the ordeal of meeting with them, at least for a little while.

Aliane looked down at the piece of raggedly stitched cloth in her hands and resisted the temptation to stick her tongue out at it. She despised embroidering. She would much rather be reading, or practicing with the new recruits down in the courtyard. She could hear them through the window; the clash of metal against metal and the rough voice of the Swordmaster rose through the misty autumn air and wafted through the polished stone and glass of the palace walls. Her father had always allowed her to practice with his recruits, but she did not think King Morgan would have quite the same ideas about a woman practicing with his soldiers-in-training. Especially, she thought smiling to herself, one that could no doubt beat the tar out of his boys judging from the uncomplimentary epithets coming from the Swordmaster. The recruits must be a new batch of boys from the outlying villages that kept King Morgan constantly supplied with the men he needed for his deadly armies.

But she had not wanted to embarrass her father, so when Julane had acidly suggested she put aside her book and turn to the more ladylike occupation of embroidering, she had complied without complaint. Now she was fervently wishing that she had complained after all. Her fingers, unused to a needle, were roughened and sore, and she surreptitiously tried to hide a bright spot of red on her cloth where a pricked finger had bled onto the pattern. She was already tired of Julane's silent, contemptuous sneers; she did not want to give the snooty princess any more reasons to snub her. Perhaps later Charis, the Swordmaster and captain of her father's guard, could find a secluded area for a spot of sword practice with her. She felt the need to work off the tension of prolonged immobility. *Who would have thought that needlework would be harder on the muscles and nerves than swordplay?* Aliane tried to ease the tightness across her shoulders without seeming obvious and hunched again over her work.

"So."

Startled out of her reverie by Julane's flat, slightly nasal voice, she again stuck her needle into her finger instead of her cloth. Julane had so seldom spoken to Aliane that her words seemed to explode into the air with unnecessary force.

"I wonder which of my brothers will be forced to marry you?" Julane continued, as if she considered marriage to Aliane only a slightly better fate than being burned at the stake. Aliane kept her expression smooth as she lifted her face to look at the beautiful, haughty princess.

"I'm certain I don't know. Perhaps King Morgan will find me undeserving of either."

Julane sniffed. Had the Princess been less refined, Aliane would have been tempted to call it a snort. "I wouldn't depend on it. Of course, you don't have much choice in the matter. It must be just an *awful* feeling, knowing your life can be bought and sold or traded away, though you won't be sold cheaply, will you? The price of your life is peace between our kingdoms. Such a peace has not been known for more than a hundred years."

An expression appeared on Aliane's face, a look that usually caused her friends, at least the ones who knew her well, to duck and run for cover. "I cannot be bought, and I will not be sold," she said evenly. "My father will not force me to marry anyone against my will."

Julane smiled. She had small, even teeth and her face suddenly seemed predatory. "We'll see. He may not have as much choice in the matter as he thinks he does, and my father has a way of... persuading... people to do what he wants. After all, King Torrit is not even your real father, is he?"

Aliane smiled back at her. By this time, even Charis would have been uneasy had she smiled at him that way. Julane did not even twitch an eyelash. "He is just as much my real father as if I had been born to him. And even had my parents lived, I would still be kin to him. My mother was his sister."

Julane raised her elegant eyebrows, her expression bland. "I was not trying to imply anything."

"I'm sure you weren't," Aliane murmured, pretending to study the uneven stitches on her cloth.

Julane looked at Aliane speculatively, her needle never pausing in its smooth, steady rhythm. "Somehow I don't think you would be quite right for Paulis. He prefers young boys." She went on, ignoring Aliane's astonished face. "Larion on the other hand does like his women, though I think he prefers them a little younger than you. You are pretty enough to satisfy him, though. I hope you are tougher than you look. I've heard that Larion can get... rough."

It was obvious to Aliane that Julane was baiting her, and enjoying it, but she was apprehensive nonetheless. She suspected that although Julane was saying such things to scare or annoy her, she spoke nothing less than the truth. Aliane decided she preferred the princess's stony silence to her conversation after all.

"Why is it you have never married?" Aliane asked, trying to smooth the waters. As soon as she spoke the words she wished them back unsaid, cursing her unfortunate tendency to say the first fool thing that entered her head. Julane shot her a look so cold that Aliane actually shivered. If she had ever wondered what pure, unadulterated hatred looked like, she need wonder no more. She had apparently inadvertently struck a nerve. Julane was several years older than she, and it must rankle that she had not yet wed. Neither

Torrit nor Rhyssl had sons, so she had been spared an arranged marriage for political purposes. However, surely there must be some noble house or royal family with a son who would be attracted to Julane's undeniable, though obvious, beauty. *She probably hasn't found a man who could put up with her*, Aliane thought to herself, just as Julane said in icy tones, "I have not yet met the man who comes up to my standards."

"Of course," Aliane said, hiding a smile. She could think of nothing else to say – at least, nothing polite that would befit a princess.

Silence again descended upon the room, and Aliane went back to her needlework with a quiet, relieved sigh. However, soon the silence began to grate on her nerves, and she again felt her muscles tightening in response to the tension.

Just as Aliane was about to toss convention and good breeding to the wind and run gibbering from the room, the door of the parlor opened and an elaborately costumed servant bowed himself inside to deliver a message from her father. King Torrit was ready to receive an audience with her in the main library if it was convenient for the Princess. Aliane thought it was more than convenient for the Princess and gathered up her belongings with alacrity. After a hasty but civil farewell to Julane, to which she received no reply, she sped from the stuffy parlor into the huge corridor.

The hall echoed with the voices of various servants and ministers of state and such, and Aliane looked around in confusion. She had no idea who all these people were; Morgan's castle was much more densely populated than her father's. A young woman carrying a pile of linens too large for her to see over bumped into her, knocking Aliane off balance and sending her needlepoint skittering across the glossy marble floor. The maid shot her a breathless apology, but did not check her hurried steps and soon she was out of sight. King Morgan must have put her in a lounge near the servants' stairs, she thought resentfully. Yet another subtle insult to herself and her father. Morgan and his daughter certainly were two scales plucked from the same serpent.

Though she was tempted to leave it where it was, Aliane retrieved her needlework from the floor, fearing someone might tread on it and hurt him or herself. She straightened, the small wooden hoop safely in her hands, to find that the footman who had delivered her father's message had disappeared. He was probably still leading the way to the library, assuming she followed behind him. Everyone else looked too busy to warrant interruption for directions to the main library, so she decided to find it for herself.

Aliane had not realized how large Morgan's castle was until she got lost in it. After several wrong turnings, she eventually found herself in a deserted corridor with gracefully curved wooden arches and rich tapestries hanging from high oak frames. Portraits lined the corridor walls, and elaborately bejeweled chandeliers spilled their golden lights onto heavy, expensive velvet rugs. Apparently, the best that Morgan had to offer was reserved for his private quarters. Aliane wandered through the hall admiring the tapestries and pictures, though comparing them unfavorably to the somewhat shabbier but more comfortable furnishings in her father's castle in Cameon. What was the point of having beautiful things when they were jealously stashed away where no one could enjoy them? When she acquired something beautiful she wore it or displayed it where all could admire it, not just an elite, privileged few. Though she could understand why Morgan would want to hide away some of these portraits, she thought with amusement, studying one especially horse-faced ancestor peering myopically at her from canvas and paint.

This passionate love of beauty was a trait inherited from her dead mother, as was her curly dark hair and trim, supple figure. Her indomitable spirit of will, which her father called "spunk" to her vast annoyance, was apparently not, for Torrit fondly spoke of his sister as meek and gentle with not a fiery spark in her soul. Aliane constantly perplexed him with her independent manner and propensity toward mischief. He could often be seen shaking his head with indulgent affection after hearing another of her exploits. But the world contained many interesting and wonderful things, and Aliane longed to go out and explore them all. She was no longer content to hear the stories of distant lands and wondrous sights told by her nurse and maids. She wanted to see them for herself. It rankled to know that nearly everyone in Aryn had seen more of the world than she, and merely reading about far-off lands and distant places no longer satisfied her.

It had taken a great deal of persuasion before her father had capitulated and decided she might accompany him on this trip to Magir, but in the end he hadn't had the heart to deny her. So many times he had told her, "My pretty, you are a Princess, and you must act as such. Your mother never stepped beyond the boundaries of Aryn, and your aunt the Queen never went further from the castle than her gardens, and she was perfectly content. There was only the one time..." He would abruptly stop, and on his face would appear the mask of grief that always came when he thought of the one voyage his young Queen had taken with Aliane's parents that had ended in tragedy at the bottom of a deep gully. Their horribly twisted and broken bodies had been found among the wreckage, along with the mad horse that had plunged over the edge, taking the carriage in which they rode with him. Aliane was not sure if her father had ever forgiven himself for not noticing the signs of madness in the stallion he had presented to his wife as a birthday gift, but for a long time he had blamed himself for the deaths of his loved ones. Out of love and compassion, Aliane tried to keep that tortured look from his face as much as possible.

Was it any wonder, she thought, that he was so loath to allow her beyond the palace walls? Aliane was used to her father's overprotective attitude, but in recent years it had started to chafe at her nerves. She had begun to resent that she was virtually imprisoned – in a gilded cage, she had to admit – because her parents and aunt had died over twenty years ago. Why, she was more likely to fall down the stone stairs of the palace than to meet misfortune in the world beyond! But her father remained unconvinced, and so she had remained locked away in her father's illusion of safety. That he had finally allowed her to accompany him on this trip gave Aliane some hope for her future. However, she knew she would never truly have the freedom to explore the world as she wished, especially if she had to marry one of the princes.

Seeing that no one was around, Aliane made a rude face at the tapestry she was examining. She had no memories of her mother, but thought that despite her grace and beauty she must have been very dull. She could not imagine living contentedly as she had – brought up to a life of royalty, an arranged marriage and solitude, constantly surrounded by servants and ladies-in-waiting. She preferred to think for herself, and her idea of proper behavior rather differed from the general understanding. Aliane wanted to *live* life, not have it lived for her. Sometimes she thought she would rather not be a princess at all, and would gladly relinquish the privileges that accompanied her rank if she could only have the freedom for which she yearned.

Aliane brought her mind back from her daydreams as she heard voices sounding somewhere nearby, muffled and indistinct as though coming through a closed door. Thinking one of them might be her father's, she followed the sounds until she stood outside a set of huge wooden double doors. They were closed tightly, and she was about to knock upon one of them when she heard the voices again, now clear and raised in anger.

"I'm telling you, something must be done! There have been reports..."

"Reports! There will always be reports, Masyl. And I am telling you I have not the manpower to follow every insignificant lead now that Rhyssl is escalating her army. If you want to pursue this, do it on your own time."

Aliane backed uncertainly away. Neither voice belonged to her father, but she recognized one of the antagonists as King Morgan. She had met him the day of their arrival, and his deep, bass voice was unmistakable. She had not intended to eavesdrop, but curiosity won over and she found herself with her ear pressed shamelessly against the door.

"Sire, have you forgotten what this war is about?" the man called Masyl asked, his voice chilly. "It is our duty, our sworn oath to look into these reports."

Aliane heard some shuffling, as if someone had pulled out a chair and sat down. "My dear Masyl, don't you think I know that? But, as *you* know, Rhyssl has harbored sorcerers in Marrin for years, and we need to flush them out first. That will weaken her position while at the same time achieving a higher goal. When we make an example of those heretic witches, perhaps the others will come forward willingly, hoping we will show them some mercy for their surrender. Rhyssl's army is becoming stronger every day, and I need all my men for the strike in Freath if we are to prevail. She has gained strong support in Freath, where we are most vulnerable. I cannot allow that city to fall to her."

"Yes, Sire. I understand that," Masyl replied. Aliane heard the scraping of a match being struck, and there was a pause while Masyl – whoever he was – apparently lit a cigar or pipe. "But some placating must be done if the Onnic are to be denied the pursuit of these reports. After all, this is what they were trained to do, and most of them do not have the patience to wait for a full-scale assault on Marrin." Pipe smoke, Aliane decided as the dusky scent reached her nostrils through the crack in the door.

"Poor Masyl," the King said, laughing. "And you are the one they always complain to. Very well, I will placate your troops, but I suggest you begin including loyalty and patience in the training of your Initiates."

"Sire," Masyl's voice was stiffly affronted, "my soldiers are the best that can be found in all the lands, and they all know my punishment for disloyalty." Aliane shivered at his tone, fervently glad it was not directed at her. She heard Morgan laugh again.

"Fine," he said, dismissing the subject. "Now, I have news from this morning's meeting with Torrit." Aliane pressed her ear closer to the crack, much interested. "He came to ask my permission for one of my sons to woo his precious daughter."

"Wonderful! And I trust you expressed your delight at such a plan?"

"Naturally." King Morgan's voice was oily and smug, and Aliane experienced a flush of anger at his disrespect. "It's perfect. His daughter, who I am assured is beautiful and charming, will marry Larion and that will give me the hold I need on Torrit. If he is allied to me, he cannot send much support to Rhyssl without the fear of angering or offending me. Since he has only the one daughter, there is no chance he can make a similar arrangement with one of Rhyssl's kin. Without the full support of his army, Rhyssl will weaken even more, which will more than likely cause some trouble between their lands. If I can get them fighting each other, it will undermine both their positions against me, and I can then lead a dual assault and conquer them both. Rhyssl's army will be stretched too thin to do much damage against me, and that trusting fool Torrit would never expect an overthrow of his throne from his own in-law."

"What was that?" The man Masyl's voice was sharp, interrupting the King's musings. Aliane pressed her hand to her mouth, forestalling another gasp. The first one had given her away. She frantically looked around for a place to hide and saw none. She could hear the men in the room push back their chairs to come investigate, and she felt panic rise in her throat. If she were found here... Suddenly, her eye alit on one of the huge tapestries, and praying that things were done here the way they were at home, she quickly slipped behind it.

Fortunately for her, tapestries in this castle were hung from high wooden frames over alcoves in the wall as they were in Aryn. This prevented discoloration of the walls and the mold that often grew on the backs of hangings that remained too long in damp corridors. She pressed herself into the shallow indentation, balancing herself on the narrow ledge that stood some inches from the floor. She hoped that no inconvenient parts of her anatomy interrupted the smooth, flowing line of the cloth, and she steadied the tapestry just as she heard the door open. The pounding of her heart was so loud that for a moment Aliane was afraid the two men would hear it. She held her breath and waited. She could not hear what was said, but evidently the sound she had made was chalked up to nerves or a rat, and the men went inside again. She stayed where she was for some moments, dust tickling her nose, until she heard the *snick* of the door closing behind them, and quietly came out from behind the tapestry. She hurried down the hall as fast as she could, for she was on the verge of a giant sneeze and did not want to be within hearing distance of that room when it came.

As she rounded the first corner, the sneeze could no longer wait. She muffled the extremely unladylike explosion with her handkerchief, thanking the Eye her father had made her carry it. She looked at herself with dismay. Apparently, no one had dusted behind those tapestries for years. Her dress was smeared with smuts of dirt and grit, and the dust balls that had prompted her sneeze clung to her hands and hair. She tried to tidy herself as she hurried down the corridor, her footsteps echoing in the vast, empty space. As she tried to smooth her hair and brush her dress, her thoughts returned to the conversation she had overheard.

That Morgan! Aliane again felt herself burning with anger. Thinking he could overthrow her father and use her as bait to start a war! Julane must have known something of his plan; Aliane recalled several of her comments in the lounge and considered them again with new understanding. Well, King Morgan had quite a surprise coming to him. She wouldn't marry his precious son if he put a knife to her throat! She stopped in her tracks, struck by a sudden thought. She could never tell her father what she had heard. Torrit would declare war against Morgan, and as much as she loved him she knew her father's army could never survive against Morgan's, even with Marrin and Rhyssl's formidable army behind him. And from what she had just heard, Rhyssl was going to need all her troops to defend against Morgan's armies in Freath. If she sent much support to King Torrit, she would be vulnerable in Freath, which was a very important and wealthy town with large ports and important trade routes. If Morgan gained control in Freath, all the regions would be more dependent on him, which was an unthinkable option. Aliane would have to come up with some excuse to refuse Larion. *Maybe I'll be lucky*, she thought wryly. *Maybe Julane is right and Larion is as nasty and supercilious as he was as a boy.*

She had to calm down. Hers was one of those unfortunate faces that revealed every emotion and thought that blossomed behind it. If she continued in this frame of mind, her father would know something was wrong and he would not desist his anxious questioning until he knew what was troubling her. She went in search of a powder room to comb her hair and splash some cool water on her flushed face.

Deciding finally that she was as clean as she could get without a bath and a change of clothes, she set out once again to find her father. She found her way back to the main hall, and asked a passing servant where she could find the main library. She was directed down a huge passageway to a set of massive oak doors chased with silver trappings. Taking a deep breath, she pushed them open.

The library was enormous. Shelves were built into every wall and reached from the floor to the high, vaulted ceiling. Every shelf was filled with books, all the same color and height, and Aliane found herself wondering if there was anything actually written in them or if they were there merely for display. A huge fireplace took up nearly one entire end of the room, and chairs and divans were tastefully arranged to suggest a cozy place to read. Seated on one overstuffed chaise lounge was her father.

All her anxiety evaporated as the King rose to meet her. Torrit had always seemed to her the epitome of strength and kindness. He was a huge bear of a man, and his stomach hung comfortably over his belt. Every visible inch of him was covered with thick, dark hair, as if to compensate for the ever-thinning hair atop his head. His brown eyes twinkled merrily and his smile lit up the room. Aliane felt a rush of affection for him, and she threw herself into his fond embrace, much to the King's surprise.

"Aliane! We were just about to send the search parties after you!" he cried, giving her a bone-cracking hug. "The footman was quite dismayed when he realized he had lost you." For a minute Aliane could not reply. She couldn't even breathe. Torrit released her and looked at her lovingly. "What happened?"

Aliane told him about the minor incident in the corridor that had caused the confusion. Torrit laughed, and Aliane felt herself smiling back, unable to resist her father's good cheer. "Well, you're here, that's all that matters. How was your visit with the Princess?"

Aliane made a wry face. "Fine, Father, if you like the cold, sneering type. She's beautiful, but her expression could curdle milk in a cow. How... how did your conference with King Morgan go?"

"Fine, fine," Torrit answered. "But let's not talk about that just now. Plenty of time for that later." He was absently brushing dust from his clothes while he talked, and he all of a sudden seemed to realize what he was doing. He studied his daughter more closely, noticing for the first time the smudges on her face and dress and the dust clinging stubbornly to her hair. Aliane felt blood rising to her cheeks and wondered what she would tell him if he asked her what she had been up to. To her relief Torrit just sighed, shook his head and said, "I don't even want to know. Just try to keep out of mischief while we are here, all right? I don't want any trouble with Morgan now that we have agreed on this next, vitally important step toward peace."

"Yes, Father," Aliane murmured. She did not say that she had already known of King Morgan's decision to allow his son to court her. She did not tell him of the fears growing in her breast and the dread of what lay before her. Always before she had been able to confide in her father, but now she felt small and alone, weighed down with the responsibility of her newfound knowledge. Suddenly her father seemed almost unbearably dear to her, and she silently and fiercely promised herself that she would spare him as much pain and trouble as she could. He had endured enough pain to last several lifetimes, and she would be salted and stuffed before she would allow herself to be the cause of any more. She squeezed his arm affectionately and asked, "Father, will it cause trouble for you when... er... if I refuse to marry one of his sons?"

"I don't think so," Torrit answered, smiling down at her. "I mentioned to him that you are a trifle... strong-willed, shall we say?" Aliane rolled her eyes and smiled back at him. At least he hadn't called her 'spunky'. "But he seemed pleased with the idea, and as soon as his oldest son Larion returns from the field he will come to Aryn to visit you. And," he added with mock severity, "I do hope you will give the young man a chance instead of refusing him outright. It is high time that you were settled down anyway."

Aliane sighed, but said nothing. They had had this discussion before, though it had never been resolved to the satisfaction of either. She hated the idea that because she had passed the threshold into womanhood she was expected to spend the rest of her youth at the beck and call of a husband. But the king wanted to see her safely settled down with a man who, in his wishful thinking, could manage to transform her into the proper lady he wished her to be. In all fairness to him, Aliane knew that King Torrit's exasperation with his daughter was merely a show, and he would have been sadly disappointed if she ever truly changed. He enjoyed her spirit greatly and often spoke of her with great pride and pleasure. But she did wish he would not push her so to marry. She was only twenty-six and already she was considered past the brink of spinsterhood. Of course, she had her share of girlish, romantic fantasies, but she would prefer to marry for love, not for politics. No doubt Julane would have jeered at such an idea.

Before Aliane could say anything to change the subject, which was understandably making her extremely uncomfortable, a page entered the library. He stiffly and pompously announced that it was nearly time for the midday meal, and King Morgan had requested their presence for a drink in the Grand Salon. Aliane hurried to her rooms to change, wishing, not for the first time, that she had been born a lowly peasant rather than a princess. She laughed bitterly to herself as she thought of all the girls in the world who secretly wished they had been born princesses. They had *no* idea what they were truly wishing for – a life of privilege, true, but also a life of restrictions and closed doors, inhibited freedom and thwarted desires. Perhaps someday, when this alarming new situation had been resolved and things had gone back to normal, she would be able to search for that elusive freedom.

She did not know how she would be able to sit across the table from King Morgan and speak to him pleasantly after what she had just heard, but she was determined to beat him at his own game. She *would* be pleasant, and when the time came, she would give him no leverage over her father. She could play games, too, and it was to her advantage that Morgan was unaware that the rules had just changed. So, with a lighter heart and cleaner face, she went out to meet her father and the page that was to escort them to Morgan's lounge.

"Magic is an abomination infesting the lands. It is wicked, abnormal and unnatural in the extreme."

– From the Onnic Book of Learning.

Chapter Three

"I believe I said that I did not wish to be disturbed." Masyl Vonnin glared at the young Initiate who stood nervously outside his office door. The boy swallowed and stood rigidly straight as he answered.

"Your Excellency, there is a man outside who says..." his voice dwindled and he flushed bright red.

Masyl looked sharply at the tongue-tied Initiate. "Well, boy? Either speak or stop wasting my time. If you have so much time to waste, I can speak to Master Boyan about it."

The Initiate flushed deeper, until his face matched the color of his robe. Struggling to remain at attention, he said, "Your Honor. The man outside says that you will wish to speak with him."

Masyl stared at the boy unbelievingly. "Who is it?"

"Your Excellency, he did not give me his name, and refused to answer when I questioned him. But he did say it was important."

Masyl sighed. Somehow, it was almost always important. He had absolutely no privacy for his studies and meditations any more. He did, however, have contacts with people who preferred to keep their names to themselves, though none had ever approached him here in the Cathedral before. Whoever it was would feel the sharp edge of his tongue; he had a reputation to protect, and being seen with the likes of any of them would likely finish him in the Onnic order. He had worked too hard and too long to allow that to happen.

"Send him in," he said shortly and the Initiate disappeared with more speed than grace. Masyl wondered who the visitor would be. Perhaps it was that man from Granth – he had been a valuable asset in the past. Pushing his papers aside, he sat back and waited for the Initiate to bring in his unexpected guest.

As always, being in the Cathedral soothed him. The smoothly polished green marble floors and exquisite statuary were pleasing to the eye, and his office, a large suite of sumptuous rooms situated near the back of the huge, ancient stone building, afforded an incredible view of Magir. The Cathedral was perched upon a high hill near the northern edge of the city, placing it higher than even the royal castle that had been built several hundred years later. The Cathedral was the heartbeat and lifeblood of Magir, and it was visible from every corner of the city, a constant reminder of the faith and regulations demanded by Triumvirate law. *Soon,* Masyl thought, soon that law would encompass the entire reaches of the three kingdoms, something he had always hoped he would see before his death.

He was unusually tired, and after his audience with King Morgan he had a great deal to think about and many preparations to make. He wished to rest. He hoped that whatever business this man had for him would be concluded quickly, for there were many things to plan before he could sleep that night. He felt a surge of resentment toward the King for putting so many responsibilities on his shoulders, but in truth he could not entrust them to anyone else.

People had often wondered how Masyl had managed to bring so many Seekers to trial, for he had tried and executed more witches than any other fifty Onnic priests together. Some had speculated he used magic himself to find them, though never in his presence. Any person who even hinted at such a thing would not live to see another sunrise. He had his methods – devious, he admitted, but it got the job done and he was serving the greater good by eradicating those heathen degenerates. It made his skin crawl to be near those animals – the Esprys – but he had to admit they worked, provided the conditioning was thorough and complete. It was unfortunate that they did not survive longer after the conditioning. The number of Esprys was running low, and every year there were fewer and fewer witches with which to replenish the supply.

A hard, athletic man in his youth, Masyl was now soft around the middle, gray on top, and in recent years had taken to sitting in his office rather than joining the Onnic armies on the hunt. It gave him satisfaction to know that despite his inactivity he was still feared as much as he ever had been in the past. People came from all over the lands to give him information, or to ask for his services. He employed many people, some within the Church, some without. With some, he had conducted business without the knowledge of the Church at all. He was sure that the Triumvirate, though he himself was a member, would never have sanctioned some of the seedier characters with whom he had dealt. He expected that this man would be one of his 'secular' employees.

But the man who entered the room was someone Masyl had never seen before. He was young, good-looking except for a ragged wound on his face that had not yet completely healed, and had an air of superior intelligence about him. As he approached the desk, Masyl noticed he walked with a perceptible limp. Masyl was a firm believer in first impressions, and his of this young man was one of instant distrust. This stranger looked completely and inappropriately at ease in the presence of so great and renowned a Priest. Masyl noticed that his eyes missed nothing; they darted around the room missing not a single detail and finally came to rest on his host.

Masyl felt anger welling up inside him as this impudent pup studied him; the way his eyes wandered over his features was insolence in itself. He forced the man to stand longer than courtesy allowed, knowing it would be uncomfortable for his lamed leg, while he subjected the man to the same scrutiny. He realized that this was a man of confidence and strategy. A man to be watched. Perhaps a man to be used.

Finally, he indicated a chair and the stranger seated himself. Masyl leaned forward to ask the man's name, but before he could speak the stranger himself spoke, his voice rich with all the arrogant assurance his manner implied. "I have information concerning a magic user," was his astounding opening statement. "She calls herself a Seeker of the Eye of Truth. The information I have could lead you to her and, if I am right, to much, much more. Are you interested in making a deal?"

Masyl was momentarily struck dumb, once again suffused with fury. A deal? He did not make deals with people, they came – they crawled! – to him to beg for his services. This man obviously had no idea who he was dealing with. "I do not make deals," he informed the man coldly. "But if you have information concerning a witch, I suggest you give it to me. And I should mention that withholding evidence about such a person is tantamount to being guilty yourself." *That should take the salt out of his attitude,* Masyl thought, smiling to himself.

But the man merely smiled back at him, as if he had expected such a reaction. Masyl made a conscious effort to control his temper and settled back into his chair. The man continued as if he had not even spoken.

"I have information you want about a woman who calls herself a Seeker of the Eye of Truth," he repeated. "You have something I want – the strength of an army and the power to use it. I am suggesting a fair exchange – the information I have could possibly make you the most powerful man in the land."

"I am already a very powerful man," Masyl said acidly, "and I have worked most of my life to become so. I am also very busy. What could you possibly offer to interest me in making a deal with you?"

"How about the chance to capture the Eye of Truth herself?"

Masyl again found himself speechless, but this time with astonishment. The idea was ludicrous. The Eye of Truth was mere fiction, a story made up by filthy witches to lend some purpose to their evil lives. He opened his mouth to protest, but the stranger gave him no chance to speak. "Hear me through. I have every reason to believe that the stories, the so-called Prophecies, are true. As you must know, Lord Priest, there are few things in this world that are truly impossible. This Seeker could lead you to the Eye of Truth, and if you destroy the woman of the Prophecies, you destroy the very heart of magic.

"The Seeker woman has given me information, and I can give you that and more. I can make you the most important man that ever lived. I offer you the chance to be the man that obliterated magic completely by killing its source – the woman of the Prophecies who is supposedly going to save the world with what you despise most – magic. If you let it happen, if you let her fulfill her destiny, then everything for which you and the Onnic have been working for over a thousand years will have been for nothing."

Masyl was astounded to find he was actually listening to the man. He was crazy, insane, out of his mind! Yet... the picture he had drawn had its appealing aspects. Masyl was vain enough to enjoy the thought of the fame and respect such a coup would bring him. But he was never a man to bargain easily, and this man had already insulted him. "Do I have only you to believe?" he asked with a hint of sarcasm in his voice. "Is your word alone enough to convince me of this ridiculous story?"

The man smiled crookedly. "Your Honor, my word will have to be enough or I will take my proposition elsewhere. I think that if you agree to my terms, you will find the evidence bears out my claim."

"*Your* terms?" The audacity of the man both amused and infuriated him. "We can talk about terms after you convince me your evidence is fact. Tell me how you know that the Eye of Truth is real and is... is..." Masyl nearly choked on the words, "...on her way."

"Not just on her way, but already here and waiting to be found," he replied, a wicked gleam lighting his oddly colorless eyes. "I can tell you only what the Seeker told me. She has information neither you nor I would have access to, and she has been using that knowledge to make plans. As much as you despise it, you must acknowledge the existence of magic and those who wield it know things the rest of us do and cannot. You have made an admirable attempt to rid the world of magic, but even you cannot be so naïve as to believe you have succeeded. You may have reduced their numbers, but you have not yet killed their spirit. The Search goes on, and one of these days they are going to find what they are looking for.

"If this Seeker is correct, and you are not, then what will come to pass will put your services permanently off demand. You will have to take it on trust. There is nothing else."

Masyl was shaken to the core of his being, and for a few moments he could not speak. He felt himself in the grips of a near-berserker rage and it took all his strength and determination to control it. Yet, despite his anger, he heard the truth behind the man's words. The number of witches found every year had been decreasing for some time, though he knew their filthy underground society still existed. Strange, he thought as the red film of rage faded from his eyes. He had never really contemplated what would happen if the magic users actually found what they were seeking. He had been present for many Interrogation sessions, where Catechists "persuaded" witches and blasphemers to talk. He had been a Catechist once himself, many years ago. The prisoners had babbled incessantly about their prophecies and the woman who featured so prominently in them, but it had never occurred to Masyl that the prophecies might be true.

Yet this man believed them to be true, that much was obvious. The Seeker he had spoken to must have told him more than he was admitting. But if the prophecies were true, and not just the pack of lies he had always believed them to be, then it might behoove him to listen to what the man was saying. However, it would not be prudent to appear to agree with him too quickly. Masyl prided himself on his ability to control situations and lead negotiations in the direction he wished. He had not achieved his current status by being careless.

"In my experience trust is earned, not blindly given," Masyl said. "I will need more than just your word."

The man brought a book out from under his cloak and handed it to Masyl. It was very old and his sharp eyes did not miss the little green and gold teardrop eye on the cover. Looking through it, he realized with a shock that it was a list of Seeker magic items created and used before the Onnic War. Well, today certainly was full of surprises. He had thought that no such record still existed. He looked at the stranger quizzically. "I could have you arrested and most likely executed just for having this in your possession. However, since you handed it over to me, I am willing to listen to your arguments." It was tempting, though, and the thought of the cocky young man being dragged away in chains to the Catechists made him smile.

"I took it from the Seeker woman. I offer you no arguments, I give you only facts. She will lead you to the Eye of Truth. You need only follow her."

Masyl looked at him thoughtfully. "Why do you believe?" he finally asked. "How did she convince you?"

The man's expression did not change. "Evidence," he said shortly. He obviously did not like having to explain himself. "It seems that many details from these Prophecies have already come true, just as had been foretold. For example, have you noticed that every year the winds from the north come earlier and earlier? This is supposedly one of the signs that the Eye of Truth is ready to be found. Also, the Prophecies mention a vast army sweeping the lands, and you must admit that, by your tireless efforts, the Onnic would apply. And do you remember the volcano that erupted in the Monteno Mountains several years ago? Well, that too is a sign from the Prophecies. The dropping sickness and the plague are others. There are just too many such occurrences to be coincidence, and we cannot afford to view them as such. It would just be too dangerous."

Privately, Masyl had his doubts about that. Anyone can claim to "prophecy" major, cataclysmic events and some of them, by the very nature of man and earth, are bound to come true. That it took this long for them to occur just reinforced his views that such coincidences do happen. He would need information a lot more specific than that before he could truly believe in these "prophecies."

"She will be powerful," the man continued, carelessly examining his fingernails. "She will use her magic to overthrow you and the Church. You are a good soldier, Vonnin. I am sure you have researched and studied the properties of magic. After all, you must learn about something before you can find its weaknesses to destroy it, correct?"

Masyl nodded impatiently, hardly even noticing the implied insult of the use of his surname that put the two men on equal footing.

"Then you know that magic basically consists of five elements, Air, Earth, Fire, Water and Time. Each magic user has a talent in one element, and perhaps an affinity for another, but it is rare to exhibit strength in more than one Element. All the Elements save one are of equal power, for each one cannot exist without the others. Fire must have air to survive, and it feeds on products of the earth as it burns. The earth cannot produce foliage without water, and it needs fire and air to preserve the delicate balance of nature. However, the most potent of these Elements is Time. It is the only one that can stand on its own, and it is the most important frame of reference for all the other Elements.

"I'm sure you have heard or read the stories of long-dead magic users with incredible power in their Element. There are stories of people who could quiet earthquakes, slow floods, calm destructive winds, or snuff out a fire consuming a city. Or, on the other side of the coin, they could cause all of these things to happen with equal ease. Now, imagine a person who has that kind of strength in *all the elements combined!* It doesn't matter how many men you have in your army, you would not be able to combat that kind of power. If the prophecies are true, and I have already told you I have every reason to believe they are, this power will be used against you, and it will destroy you. If this happens, we are lost.

"I have a plan that just might prevent such an occurrence. Perhaps you did not know that there is a test this woman, this Eye of Truth, must take to prove herself. She must look in a pool of water, the Lake of Chaos, otherwise called the Mirror of the Eye, at the Lake Point and it will tell whether or not she is the real Eye of Truth. This is the *only* way to identify the true woman of the prophecies. All you need to do is station your men at the Lake Point upon my command and wait for her and the Seeker to arrive. I am certain that this Seeker woman will bring a girl to look in the pool. If nothing happens, you will have two more magic users in your custody. If something does happen... well, you can imagine the victory that the Church would achieve through your efforts. You cannot lose."

Masyl drummed his fingers against his desk. "How do you know so much about magic?" he asked suddenly. In truth, he had not known half the information he had just been given, and his ignorance made him uncomfortable.

"The Seeker woman told me."

"Of course." A convenient explanation. "And what of your end of the deal? What would you wish in exchange for this information and everlasting fame?"

"I would have access to as many troops as I need, for I would join the hunt. You could have me instated as a Captain of the army if you chose. I will follow the woman while your men stand ready for my call. I would also want a legion to travel with me, and one to be sent south into Marrin to await my orders. That might be tricky with the restlessness between Rhyssl and Morgan, but I should be able to get them across the border. But most importantly, we *must* not kill the Seeker, not right away. We must allow her to continue her Search. If she does indeed find the Eye of Truth, I ask only one thing – that I have a chance to speak with the Eye in private before you take her away. Then she is yours to do with as you please."

Masyl stared, his insides twisting in sudden disgust. "You wish to speak with her? Doing so would instantly label you a traitor to the Church!"

The man scowled, his lips twisting into an ugly shape. "I am no traitor, and I have no intentions of going against the dictates of the Church. My reasons for needing to speak to the woman are my own, and they need not concern you. Or anyone else."

"You ask much, my friend. King Morgan has other plans for his soldiers; it would take quite a lot to convince him to allow several legions to go off on a wild boar hunt. However, if I agree to these terms, I must insist upon total loyalty on your part. If you renege on the vows I will require you to take before entering my army, I will have you before the Triumvirate so fast you will have no time to blink before the axe falls. If I find you have in any way been dishonest with me, the consequences will be the same. Is that clear?"

The man smiled. "You have my word, in writing if you request it. At the same time, I will expect you to hold up your end of the bargain. No one else need know about our agreement, but I expect to be granted my requests. If not, there are, as I said before, others I can go to."

"Of course." Masyl thought furiously. He still had grave reservations about entering into a contract with this man, but it was really too tempting to pass up. He looked as if he could command a regiment with ease, there was no cause for concern there. He had obviously had military training, the way he carried himself showed that beyond a doubt. Why should he not accept? He stood to lose nothing if he was lying, and stood to gain a great deal if he was not. And at the very least, he felt a profound satisfaction at the thought of prosecuting this arrogant salt-licker for collusion with a witch. "I shall write to King Morgan immediately to advise him that I have taken on a new Captain. You will speak your vows in his presence of course. But I warn you – the King likes to be betrayed even less than I. You will be watched."

"Fair enough. So will you." Masyl frowned at the enigmatic remark, but did not comment. "You will not regret your decision. Together, we will change the world, and when we are through the Church will have more power than it ever has in its history. We will make history ourselves, and people will be singing about you for many years. Your name will be coupled with Madagar of Damin and Sel of Aryn in those old songs of glory and fame."

"Yes, well, perhaps you can begin this great history by telling me the name of the Seeker we are supposed to follow."

The man grinned. "Look at the inside cover of the book you hold. I will see you in the castle for my oath three days from now. After that, I will wait here in Magir with my legion."

Masyl was confused. "Wait here? Why? Shouldn't you try to find her as soon as possible?"

The man grinned. "No need," he said. "I have every reason to believe that she will find me. We will then flush her out and follow her. Until then, good day and may health be yours." And with that, he strode from the room, closing the door behind him.

For a moment Masyl sat in silence, staring at the door that had not quite caught after the man's exit. He felt a little breathless and his heart hammered uncomfortably in his chest. He pulled out the panel that concealed the secret compartment in his desk and poured himself a liberal dose of the ouzaki he had stored there. He wondered uneasily whether he had just made a grave mistake.

He shuddered as the ouzaki burned a path down to his stomach and spread its comforting warmth through his body. Replacing the bottle and panel, he began to relax. He would not tell the Triumvirate of the agreement he had just made.

If the man was lying it would make him look a fool, and he could not allow that to happen. But if he were correct, the Council would undoubtedly understand his need for secrecy. They would berate him for failing to inform them of his intentions, while blithely ignoring the fact that if he had, they would have either impeached him or shamed him by accusing him of treason. Merely suggesting that the prophecies of the magic users were truth would be enough to begin proceedings against him. He would have to be careful.

Masyl replayed the interview over in his mind, and the more he thought about it the more he liked it. He had been unaware of the test that must be taken to establish the identity of the Eye of Truth. Somehow, that had never come up in the Interrogations. But he had also said that the Seeker woman would come here, to Magir. *Why would a witch come to the capitol of the Onnic army?* It didn't make sense. *Why would she seek him out?* If she prized the salt in her blood she would run long and far in the opposite direction.

He shifted in his seat, his uneasiness draping him like an ill-fitting garment. If Masyl got nothing else from the bargain, at least he could use the information he had learned today. The stranger seemed a mine of such information. Masyl did not like the thought that someone else knew more than he about such important matters. He would have to pump the man thoroughly, and if he decided he knew too much he could simply dispose of him after he became no longer useful.

Masyl chuckled to himself. He and his visitor seemed to have much in common. Perhaps it would work out after all. It would be interesting to see what would develop in the weeks to come.

He called for an Initiate to bring him a piece of good parchment. He would write to Morgan immediately. He would have no problem persuading the King to allow him the appointment of a new captain. He would simply say that it would be good to have a new authority figure, one that would be able to deal with some of those reports that the men were so eager to pursue.

A young boy, different from the first, brought the supplies he needed, and it was not until he was reaching for a pen with which to write that Masyl realized he had never learned the man's name.

"...The Eye of Truth shall know that which she had never learned and remember that which she had never lived."
– From the Prophesies of the Eye of Truth

Chapter Four

The day was dawning gray and bleak as Gwynne approached the outskirts of Magir. Clouds shadowed the sky with oppressive closeness and the taste of snow crept in silently with the morning. Gwynne shivered as a chill breeze penetrated her heavy woolen cloak. The streets were nearly empty and brown, brittle leaves whispered against the cobblestones as the wind tossed them to and fro as was its will. The sharp, crisp tang of late autumn was in the air and as Gwynne shifted uncomfortably in her saddle, she wondered whether she would live to see this winter through.

She pulled her travel cloak more tightly around her shoulders as she examined her surroundings. She was on a well-traveled road and the houses that flanked it were well tended and snug against the coming of winter. She saw few people about and assumed most families would be in their fields on such a day, preparing for the harvest and stocking their larders. The cold weather had descended so quickly that it must have taken many farmers unawares. She saw crops lying in ruin in the fields, bitten by the frost that lay like crystalline sugar on every surface, the delicate matrix of patterns crisscrossing itself as if designed by some fairy hand. Ahead she could see the ancient iron gates and guard towers that heralded one of the many checkpoints that were the only way to enter the city proper. Gwynne felt a twinge of anxiety and checked her pocket for the hundredth time to make sure the forged papers she carried were safe. She had been on the road nine slow, agonizing days and Magir was the first large city she had seen since she left home. Entering it would be the first of what she was sure would be many tests.

It was good to see civilization again. It had taken her weeks to prepare for the journey; the majority of her belongings had been burnt along with her house. She had been lucky to escape with her life, though she would be forever disfigured by the puckered burn scars on her face and body. *You'll pay for that, Jaerak Thorin*, she thought bitterly as her horse, Milyn, plodded complacently down the road. *Oh, yes. Someday you will pay.*

When Gwynne had eventually regained consciousness after her disastrous magical battle with Jaerak, she had found herself on the grass outside the inferno that had once been her house. She had been badly burned, but was miraculously still alive. How had she gotten outside? She had puzzled over the question for days, and the only reasonable explanation was so ludicrous she could not even contemplate it. It was impossible that Jaerak Thorin could have saved her life, impossible he had dragged her unconscious body from the noxious smoke and roaring flames that had devoured her house and everything in it. *Wasn't it? He had started the salted fire himself! But who else could have done it?* She certainly hadn't crawled out on her own.

It was with grim satisfaction that she remembered the distinct, if unpleasant, sound of breaking bone that meant Jaerak had been hurt as well. It served him right for coming along out of nowhere, shattering her peaceful life and destroying a lifetime of work and memories. *Well, that makes two houses I have seen burned to the ground for the sake of magic.* But she was no longer a girl of twelve and she knew there would be no Aunt May at the end of her path this time to comfort her when she wept. This time she could face her future with a bold face, though it harbored a frightened and unsure heart.

The incident had had one positive outcome, though – it had forced her to take action. Jaerak now had all the information she possessed; indeed, her head still ached from that horrifying invasion – and only the Eye knew what he planned to accomplish with it. Jaerak had her book, her name, her knowledge, and by far the strongest magic she had ever encountered. But what troubled her most was that fleeting moment of recognition when his mind had first touched hers. That feeling of ugliness and contamination had been so familiar, too similar to what she had already experienced in the earth to be a coincidence. Somehow, he had to be linked to it, and when Jaerak had sifted through her mind he would have realized she had caught the resemblance. He was no doubt already tracking her.

But why did he leave me alive? This was a question that had haunted her countless times since that day. Starting the fire had probably been done in a fit of temper fueled by her unexpected defiance, or perhaps it had been an involuntary defensive reaction to her use of magic. Whatever it was, she was certain he had not meant her to perish in the flames, so truly it must have been he who had rescued her from the blazing house. Gwynne remembered his cryptic statement about meeting again one day – she was sure it had been no idle threat. So presumably she was more use to him alive than dead. It was this thought that had sent her into a frenzy of preparation for leaving the City of Circles – fake papers under a different name, some gold, some clothes, some food. Fortunately, the fire had not reached her stables so she had not been forced to "acquire" another horse as she had the supplies. At least there was no need to disguise herself. The half-healed scabs on her face obliterated her features as no cosmetics or costume could. So, without even waiting for her burns to heal completely, she had left her home, hoping to be far away from the City when Jaerak decided he was in need of her "services" again.

As was her habit when she was tense her hands were clenched tight, and she found herself gripping the reins with unnecessary force. She noted ruefully that the leather had again broken through the tender scabs on her hand, and she wound the bandage tighter as blood seeped through the already crusted cloth. She would have to remain in Magir longer than she thought safe to allow her wounds time to heal. She would not find the Eye of Truth if she fell sick or dead on the trail. *And find her I will*, Gwynne thought determinedly. It was time, she would bet a pint of salt on that, and it was unlikely that the few remaining Seekers would be actively searching these days. She had never met *anyone* in her lifetime that could equal Jaerak's strength in magic, and it was possible that only the Eye of Truth could contain him. Gwynne knew that she – alone, aging, wounded and weak in magic – certainly could not.

So find her she must, and find her she would.

It would have been helpful, though, if the Prophecies had given a few more specific details about the bloody woman. *What would she would look like, when would she be born and where could she be found? It would have saved us a lot of trouble*, Gwynne thought irritably, *if the Prophets had just come right out and said what they meant. They saw everything else about her, couldn't they have told us her name?*

Gwynne's heart beat uncomfortably fast as she got in line at the checkpoint. This would be the first trial of her new identity, and if it failed she would be dragged before the Triumvirate for Interrogation. If that happened, her Search would be finished before it even began. She had been Interrogated once before, and she knew she would never survive another meeting with a Catechist. Sometimes, when she allowed herself to think of it at all, she wondered how she had survived it the first time.

There were few travelers this early in the day, so she found herself at the entrance booth in record time. A guard, looking bored, approached her and raised his hand as a signal for her to stop. He gave her burns only a cursory look and made no comment.

"Papers?" he said, extending his hand for them. Meekly, Gwynne gave them over. She felt sweat trickle down the back of her neck despite the chill of the morning. The guard glanced at them with an air of weary routine.

"Name?"

"Irena Savintalo," Gwynne said, trying to match his tone, as if she had answered to the name a thousand times.

"I see that you are a member of the Council of Cantos," the guard said, his voice quickening with interest. "May I see your mark for verification?"

"I am sorry, sir," Gwynne said meekly, "but as you can see, I have been in a recent accident." She pulled her cloak back and pushed up her sleeve, revealing one burn-covered arm. "My mark was burned away in the fire and they cannot replace it until the skin heals. But I have here a letter of reference verifying that Baron Cantos of the seventh line is, indeed, my sixteenth cousin eight times removed." Gwynne handed the guard another parchment.

"I see," the guard said, examining her arm with pity. "Yes, yes of course." He read the paper carefully. "Well, I think this will do, since it's stamped." He handed the papers back to Gwynne, who breathed a silent sigh of relief. "You may pay your donation and go through."

"Donation?" Gwynne was surprised. "For what?"

"The money goes to fund the armies against Marrin," the guard told her. "Right now, King Morgan needs all the help he can get. Ten silver, please."

How ironic, Gwynne thought as she dug the money out of her belt pouch. *I am helping to support an army that would like nothing more than to skin me alive and string me up by my gizzard.* But she handed the money over and asked, "Do you know an inn where I could get a hot meal and stable my horse? I'm staying in Magir for a few days, and I wish a comfortable room." She added another two silver pieces to the ten in the guard's hand for the information.

"Well now, the Fox and Falcon cooks a mighty good chicken, and the beds are fair comfortable," the guard said happily, pocketing the coins. Gwynne wondered how much of the "donations" ultimately ended up in the army's coffers. Not as much as was collected, she would guess. "Just ask for Telma Bartelt, the innkeeper's wife," the guard continued. "She's good friends with my wife. She'll take good care of you, if you can stand her flapping tongue."

"My thanks, sir, and a good day to you." Gwynne bowed her head to him and moved Milyn forward, making room for the next person in line. After she had gone a short distance, she found that she was trembling all over. She had passed the first test. It was unlikely anyone would question her claim to the Cantos line; it was the largest family in all the regions and the lineage was said to be volumes long. It had not been difficult to sneak into the archives and copy the family insignia for her papers.

Gwynne found the Fox and Falcon without difficulty – it was the largest, most popular inn in Magir. At least it so appeared judging from the noise that spilled from the half-closed doors. She dismounted in front of the stable, groaning as her sore muscles stretched and pulled. She tossed the reins to a stable boy and asked him why the inn was so full this early in the morning. He took one look at her and ducked his head, unable to meet her eyes as he answered.

"It's a Feast day, Lady," he said, leading Milyn into a well-spaced stall. "Some of 'em been at it fer some time now."

Gwynne was getting used to people's inability to look directly at her without pity or disgust, so she made an effort to sound friendly. "A Feast day? With the harvest not yet in?" She was surprised. She had figured all the farmers would be breaking their backs trying to gather what little of their crops could be salvaged from the frost.

"Harvest has already been, Lady. Crops were good this year." The lad turned his back and began removing bridle and tack. "Need anything from yer bags afore I store 'em?"

Gwynne retrieved a pack that contained extra clothes and her necessary articles and left the boy to his chores. Strange, she thought as she made her way to the inn. She had heard that the farmers had suffered a dry season this year, and that the early frost had killed off the already poor crops. Reports must have been exaggerated. Shouldering her pack, she pulled open the door and entered the Fox and Falcon.

As she stepped inside, the din hit her ears full blast with such force it almost knocked her back into the street. The commons room was filled nearly to bursting with people – men, women and children crowded together, making enough noise to raise the roof clear from the rafters. Despite the early hour, many people held mugs full of wine or ale, and roasted chickens and haunches of meat were piled on the tables. There was a raised platform at the far end of the hall and upon it musicians and singers played and sang with cheerful energy. None of them, it seemed to Gwynne's bewildered ears, were playing the same tune as the others. Jugglers and tricksters mingled with the crowd, delighting their audiences with the skills and sleight of hand of their trade and passing hats for contributions. Everyone appeared to be in a high and merry mood, and Gwynne wondered if she would be able to sleep if the revelry went on late into the night.

She tried to fight her way to the innkeeper's counter to ask for Telma Bartelt and reserve a room for the night, but everywhere she turned people painfully jostled her and she could not get through the crowd. One man, obviously on his third or fourth mug of ale, lurched into her and she cried out in pain as he rubbed against her half-healed burns. Instantly there were several dozen people around her, solicitously asking if she was all right. She blinked back her tears, nodded her thanks, and the crowd made room for her to proceed. One kindly young woman, plump and matronly, pushed Gwynne into a chair and cleared a table for her.

"Now, don't you worry about a thing dearie," she said comfortably. "You just tell me your name and I'll tell Koris to get a room ready for you. You'll want some breakfast, of course, and some of those burns look like they could use some oil. You just rest, you look fair salted. I'll take care of everything." Bemusedly, Gwynne told the woman her new name, and the angel in the guise of an innkeeper, who could only be Telma herself, bustled purposefully away, shooing curious people out of her path. In less time than Gwynne thought humanly possible, she returned bearing a thick plate full of ham, potatoes and eggs, and conversation full of information.

"Now, dearie, you just eat all of this up," she said, putting the plate in front of her. "My name is Telma, and Koris, the innkeeper, is my husband. He is getting a room all ready for you. Fortunately, most of these are a local lot," Telma waved a dismissive hand to the crowd, "so there are still plenty of rooms to let. Now, now, don't talk! Eat! You can ask questions when you're finished."

Gwynne closed her mouth on the thanks she was about to give and ate some ham instead. After the first bite, she looked at Telma in amazement, and appreciatively chewed another. The meat was as tender and flavorful as any she had ever tasted, and the hot tannin-bark drink, called tannis, was ambrosia. Cheerfully unaware of Gwynne's pleased surprise, Telma went on without a pause. "Of course, this is a Feast day, so it's extra special. With the harvest so good and in so early the Council thought a day of rest would do everyone a world of good, and so it has, my dear, so it has. Some of these people never set foot outside their homes, 'cept for a wedding or burying."

Gwynne swallowed and finally managed to get a word in edgewise. "But I thought the harvest was ruined by the frost," she said. "And as I came into the city I saw fields with crops still lying unharvested, dead and brown. How can this be?"

Telma frowned for a moment, thinking. "It's true that some was lost, but everyone saved enough to make up for it, I guess. Funny, I hadn't thought about it. But there's a gracious plenty this year, and everyone needed an excuse to celebrate what with the cold coming so early."

Realizing she would get no more information on the subject, Gwynne ate with good appetite. The food was more than excellent and she was hungry.

It was lovely to eat something she hadn't had to catch, kill or cook herself. She listened to Telma's pleasant chatter as she finished her breakfast, hoping to hear something interesting or informative. Unfortunately, all she got were in-depth analyses of the social habits of the greater part of Magir's population, many of whom Telma seemed to know personally. Gwynne was not surprised. Telma was the biggest, nicest, friendliest busybody she had ever met. *A good person to have as a friend,* Gwynne mused, *but not someone you would want knowing all your innermost secrets.* She had more questions she would have liked to ask, but she could not get another word in through Telma's wealth of gossip. When she had finished her meal, however, she interrupted a discourse on Farmer Hougan's latest limb ailments to ask where she could find some bookshops in town.

"Well now," Telma said thoughtfully. "I'm not what you would call much of a reader. No time for such things you know. Have an inn to run." Gwynne kindly did not point out that the inn seemed to be running fine while its mistress sat and gossiped with her. "But I think there's a bookshop a couple streets north of here. Old Harrin runs it, I think. Poor man, he lost his wife to the plague last year, but she would insist on helping them poor folk out in the camps. Never have I met a kinder, more generous soul than Mistress Harrin... What, are you off already?"

"I must," Gwynne said, standing. "But I will be back, I promise. Thank you, that was a delicious meal."

"Salt my soul, dearie, it weren't nothing. You come back for supper, and I'll give you something that will really stick to your bones, you hear? And don't go wearing yourself out wandering all over the city. Just look at you, the poor thing, practically burned to a crisp! I'll have some oil put in your rooms for you, it will ease the itching at night."

"Again, thank you," Gwynne said hurriedly, and escaped before Telma could cause any more fuss over her. Accustomed as she was to living alone, the kind woman's attentions embarrassed her. She made her way through the crowd, which parted for her in good humor, and stepped out into the street.

The cool, quiet air was a blessing after the stuffy noisiness of the inn. She stood for a moment, drinking it in like wine until a passing man shot her a strange look. She had become used to strange looks from passersby, but she wanted to attract as little attention as possible, so she pulled the hood of her cloak about her face and quickly moved on.

The layout of the large city was staid and unimaginative. Streets crossed each other at right angles with shops and offices situated in the commercial center and the outlying residential areas flanking the outskirts. Yet, the city did possess a certain charm. Brightly painted wooden signs hanging from their supports swayed in the chill breeze, and shop windows were filled with treasures from the far corners of the kingdoms and beyond. The streets were cleaner than some Gwynne had seen, and the cobblestones were old and had faded to dusky, pleasing colors. The more recent architecture was unremarkable, but there still stood some beautiful buildings of brick and stone that had been built by King Retik himself over five hundred years ago. And then to the south, high on a hill, the ancient palace of Casset lorded over the city, faced by the even more ancient Cathedral to the north. These tall, grand buildings ostensibly harbored the guardians of order and protectors of the people. *Right,* Gwynne thought bitterly as she looked at their graceful lines and towering turrets. *Protectors of non-magical people, anyway.*

The general air of the city, however, was one of consequence and prosperity. She noticed many people, intent as they were on their business, smiling or offering a kind word to passersby, and she smiled herself at the expansive aura of goodwill. Apparently, it was not only the proximity of alcohol at the Fox and Falcon that accounted for the cheerful mood she had observed earlier. It was a shame not everyone could live in such pleasant gentility. She came back down to earth with a sudden thud, remembering again her own problems. She had little time for dreaming.

Once Jaerak realized she had left the City of Circles he would undoubtedly come after her. But why? And why did he think she could lead him to the Stones he sought, for she was sure the Stones were at the heart of what he was after. He would not have sounded so interested in them if he had wanted information about something else. And how had her beloved book ended up in a shop? Who had taken it from her in the first place? Not Jaerak, of that she was certain. He had sought her out because the book had fallen into his hands, not because he had taken it from her. Lost in her thoughts, Gwynne found she had walked right past Harrin's bookshop and had to turn around and double back.

Old man Harrin informed her he had never seen the book she described to him, nor a man of Jaerak Thorin's description. It was obvious he knew nothing of the Seekers of the Eye of Truth. When she described to him the symbol on the front cover, he did not even bat an eyelash, and Gwynne was sure that if he had seen Jaerak he would have remembered him. He did, however, give her a long-winded description of the glorious history of his city and showed her several books from which he had no doubt purloined his flowery descriptions. In a town where much of the population had little time to read let alone spend hard-earned money on books, Harrin would be salted and stuffed before he let an obviously intelligent and literate patron just walk away empty-handed. Gwynne bought two books from him and he directed her to another place where she could make her inquiries.

At the other establishments the story was the same. They had never heard of the book, had never seen the man. After spending hours in various shops and finding no one who recognized her description of Jaerak, she was finally forced to conclude he had lied. He had not found her book in Magir unless it came from a private collector, but she clearly remembered him saying he had found it in a bookshop. Magir, though a large city, had relatively few bookshops, and she had visited them all. If Jaerak had truly lived there, had been a scholar there, she should have come across *someone* who knew him. A scholar... that gave her an idea. Perhaps she ought to visit the university.

But none of her inquiries bore fruit, and she finally had to face the truth. Gwynne was not entirely surprised, Jaerak must have known she would check his story. Therefore he must know, or at least suspect, where she was. Gwynne shivered at the thought. He had meant for her to come here, had told her a deliberate lie to divert her. Why? What could he possibly want from her that he had not already taken?

Gwynne felt the familiar flutter of panic in her belly. He was probably already in the city searching the inns for her. She had to get away before he found her. Of course, all he needed to do was talk to Telma; no doubt she would be more than happy to tell him about the poor old lady with the burns who had stayed at her inn. When it came time for her to leave, she would have to tell that kind lady she was heading in one direction and then immediately go the opposite way.

As she wound her way back to the Fox and Falcon, Gwynne wondered where she should go next. She had ridden south to Magir just to check Jaerak's story, and now that she knew it was false she had not a clue what to do next. Maybe she should continue south – news always traveled faster by water, and news was what she sought. She could follow the river and make her way to Marrin. She needed to find clues to the coming of the Eye of Truth, and it didn't help that she had no idea what to look for. Perhaps instead she should travel north towards the Lake Point, since the Lake of Chaos would be her final destination anyway. But the waters of the Mirror of the Eye would serve no purpose if she arrived there with no one to put to the test. Whatever she did, she had to get out of Magir quickly. *Jaerak is not the only danger,* she thought, catching a glimpse of a red uniform in the crowd. Onnic soldiers were everywhere here and her skin prickled at such close proximity.

As she turned again onto the main street, she saw, or rather heard, that the pandemonium at the Fox and Falcon had not ceased. If anything, it had significantly grown in volume. So, as soon as she reached the inn Gwynne made her way to her room to escape the noise, as well as Telma's tender mercies. Her room was small but comfortable, decorated with pretty curtains and bedclothes faded from the sun that streamed in through the wide window that overlooked the small garden at the back of the inn. Her things had been laid on a comfortable chair and the bed was turned back invitingly. The promised oil sat on a bed stand beside a sweet candle and a pitcher of water. Gwynne smiled as she poured some water into a porcelain basin and washed herself as best she could. Telma might be difficult to talk to, but she was kind. Finally, Gwynne was able to lie down, and she fell asleep almost before her head hit the pillow.

"A mage standing alone is like a single star shining in the heavens – but a mage standing in the company of others suddenly becomes part of a universe."

– Ancient Seeker saying

Chapter Five

When Gwynne awoke, she felt rested and refreshed. The soft pastel colors she could see through her window told her that the sun was setting and the rumble in her stomach told her it was time for supper. As she combed and re-braided her hair, she could hear that the commotion down in the commons room had by no means diminished – if anything the ruckus was louder and merrier. Gwynne sighed. Perhaps she could have supper in her room, she thought, but dismissed the idea at once. She needed to listen – or eavesdrop – on conversations downstairs that would probably be all the more interesting for the amount of liquor that no doubt loosened many a tongue.

Telma had been watching for her, and as soon as Gwynne appeared in the commons she was firmly grasped and deposited at a table. The noise was unbelievable. Tables had been moved aside to make room for dancing, and the number of musicians on the platform had increased. To Gwynne's relief, they were all playing the same tune this time, and men and women whirled around in a complicated dance that was unfamiliar to her. Telma had to shout to be heard over the din.

"Sorry, dearie, but I don't have time to sit and chat with you just now," she shrieked in Gwynne's ear. "Got to keep the customers happy, you know. But I'll bring your supper along soon, don't you fear!" Just then, someone called for her, and shaking her head in pretended irritation, she presumably went to see to the happiness of another guest. Gwynne raised her hands in thanks to the Eye, for sitting and screaming pleasantries at someone was not something she particularly enjoyed.

Gwynne sat back in her chair and surveyed the crowd. It was an extremely diverse bunch, including men and women, old and young, and Gwynne even saw some dwarfs. That was unusual. Dwarfs were extremely introverted and tended to remain in seclusion amongst themselves, and they rarely emerged from their mountain habitats to live among the people in cities. Everyone was in very high spirits, in every sense of the word, and Gwynne found herself smiling at the people around her. The gay mood was very infectious.

Without changing her expression, Gwynne sharpened her ears to catch snippets of the conversations taking place around her. It was a trick she had learned from Aunt May, to filter out background noise and only listen to the things one wanted to hear. It was a useful ability in certain situations.

Even so, she did not learn anything she didn't already know. For the most part people spoke of the early harvest and the prosperity of their farms or shops. Tales were told of uncommonly healthy livestock and news from the nearby fishing villages was of full nets and record catches. People appeared to be spending an inordinate amount of money at the shops and business was better than it had been in years. The sheep had given extra fine wool this year, and the threads and cloth it produced were a superior quality. She heard people say that the traveling merchants had done even better. Some of them had done so well they did not have to brave the snows this winter, but could stay with their families until the spring thaw. No one tried to offer explanations for these things, but thanked providence and the Wise One for a good, prosperous year. *Interesting*, Gwynne thought. And very unusual. In a time of political tension and imminent war, these people showed no signs of even being aware of any situations outside their own intimate communities.

A pretty young serving maid brought her supper, a delicious venison stew, rich with meat and vegetables and redolent with herbs, and Gwynne watched and listened while she ate. Telma did not reappear, she must have been busy tending to her flock just as a mother hen watches carefully over her brood of chicks. That was one woman who would never let a hawk or falcon into her nest, Gwynne thought, smiling. She finished her stew with embarrassing speed and mopped out her bowl with some excellent bread. Wandering around the city all day had sharpened her appetite, and she had not felt so hungry for days. She ordered a cup of wine from the serving girl who came to take her empty bowl, and sat back to enjoy the music and dancing.

A young man performing on the platform eventually caught her attention. He was unusually tall and stood out in the crowd of other musicians. He was playing a wooden flute, but was blowing into the end of the instrument instead of the side. Gwynne had never seen such an instrument before. A mouthpiece made from a reed had been attached to one end, and a series of holes were carved on top of the pipe. She idly wondered what it sounded like – she could not distinguish the tone of one instrument from all the others in the merry melody they played. But it was the man more than the music that held her attention.

He looked very young, not much more than twenty, with a long mop of curly dark hair that looked as if it had been trimmed with a blunt belt knife none too recently. He was pleasantly slim with well-built, broad shoulders, but Gwynne would notice these details later. For the time being her attention was focused only on the man's nose. It was a nose of lordly proportions, long and pointed with an eagle-like slope that seemed to put the rest of his face into shadow. It was quite the largest nose Gwynne had ever seen. It completely dominated the man's face, taking attention away from his other features, which were worth looking at as well, she later discovered. She watched as the song came to an end and the young man smiled at the applauding audience. That smile instantly transformed his face from a rather forbidding countenance to a warm and cheerful expression. Gwynne found herself smiling in response and applauded just as loudly as the rest.

The crowd began begging for another song, but apparently the man felt the need to wet his throat and stepped down from the platform. Giving in with good grace, the people parted to let him through, and as he made his way to the liquor counter he caught Gwynne's eye. She smiled and gestured for him to join her. With a quick grin of relief, he pushed through the throng to where she was sitting.

"My thanks," he said in a pleasant baritone. "I would never have found another table."

"My pleasure," Gwynne answered as the man seated himself and called for a server. "I enjoyed your performance and I wanted to ask you about your pipe. I have never seen one like it."

"You like it?" The man seemed pleased. "I made it myself. It was my trade before I decided the wandering life was more to my taste than carving instruments. My name is Thalan Dushar, and I am at your service."

"I am called Irena." At close range, the nose was even more impressive. Gwynne tried not to stare at it. "Could I hear your pipe? I couldn't make out the tone with all those other musicians playing at the same time."

"Playing very badly, you mean. I think all the musicians here are tone deaf." Thalan gave her a rueful grin. "But I certainly would be happy to play for you, my Lady." Thalan arranged his long, nimble fingers along the holes and brought the strange mouthpiece to his lips. The sound that emerged when he blew was a delight, low and mellow and silky. He played a few notes, and they floated through the air like a rich curtain of velvet that draped them with warmth and beauty. Gwynne was enthralled.

"May I try it?" she asked when Thalan had finished. He handed the flute to her and she tried to put her fingers in the same position his had been. But when she blew into it, the pipe emitted an undisciplined squawk that was nothing like the beautiful music Thalan had played. He laughed at her chagrined expression and took the pipe back.

"It takes a bit of practice, my Lady," he said as a server put his ale in front of him. "My thanks, sir," he said and gave the boy two silver pieces. He drank deeply and with obvious enjoyment, and Gwynne was fascinated by the way his nose reached nearly halfway down the tankard. Thalan put the mug down with a thump and sighed with contentment.

"Ah, that will put the salt back in a man's soul," he said with relish, wiping foam from his lips. "Now, my lady Irena, what brings you to the Fox and Falcon this fine night?"

Gwynne was ready with her story. "I am traveling to Freath to visit family," she told him. "I got a message that there has been some sickness, and I wish to be there."

"Plague? I'm so sorry." Thalan looked at Gwynne speculatively. "It would appear you have seen some trouble recently yourself."

"Yes," Gwynne admitted, glancing involuntarily at the scabs and bandages on her hands. They looked better, she thought. *Telma's oil must be working*. "That's another reason I travel south. My home burned, with all of my belongings in it, and I will stay with my brother's daughter's family until I am able to find new lodgings."

"Hard luck, that." Then the brilliant, flashing grin appeared again. "Probably the only hard luck you'll find in these parts. I have been here three days and I have never seen such fortune in one city before."

"I have noticed," Gwynne said. "It is very unusual. I had heard that the crops were poor this year, but it would appear I was mistaken."

Thalan nodded, looking puzzled. "I had heard the same, and the frost did come early this year. But the farmers seem to be prospering."

"Perhaps the information was misleading," Gwynne said reasonably. "You know how things can become exaggerated, especially if it is news of someone else's misfortune. Where do you come from?"

"Aryn originally, but I was apprenticed to a musician in River Crossing for five years. That was where I learned to make instruments."

Gwynne was intrigued. She liked Thalan immensely, and she could tell he was speaking the truth, for his face was the type that showed every passing emotion. At the moment, it revealed nothing but charming candor. But she wondered why a man of obviously good breeding and fortune would choose to live the life of a wandering minstrel. Carefully and delicately, she probed his mind, not wanting to appear rude by asking him straight out. No mind shield deterred her, so she proceeded with caution. What she discovered made her gasp aloud and withdraw immediately.

Thalan, oblivious to the whole thing, looked concerned. "My Lady, are you well? Are you in pain?"

"N... no," she said quickly. "I mean yes." Thalan looked confused. "I mean no, I am not in pain and yes, I am well. I'm fine, thank you for asking. But... I think we should speak again. In fact, I think you should meet me here, tonight, after everyone has gone home or gone to sleep."

Thalan looked puzzled. "Why? There *is* something wrong, isn't there? Something's happened. What is it? Did I say something to upset you? You can tell me."

"No, it's nothing like that. Nothing is wrong," Gwynne said firmly. "But I need to speak with you in private. Please, this is very important. Come back later tonight and come to my room, but make sure no one sees you. Will you do that?"

"All right, if it's that important, I will come." He still sounded confused.

"It *is* important. I will explain it all tonight," Gwynne assured him. "There is no need to worry. You must trust me." A loud noise caught her attention. "I think they are asking you to play again. Perhaps you should go."

Thalan looked up. "Yes, I should. This is how I make my living, after all." He looked at Gwynne, still not understanding her urgency. "I will come tonight. In fact," and the engaging smile came flashing back, "you couldn't keep me away now. You have sparked my curiosity, my Lady, and I never let mysteries go unsolved. Until tonight, then."

"Make sure no one sees you come," she hissed urgently as he stood up. "My room is the third one down the hall to the left." Thalan nodded and laughingly allowed himself to be led back to the platform for another round of music. Gwynne paid for her meal and wine and made her way slowly back up the stairs to her room. Once the door was safely locked, she threw herself down on the soft bed and thought about the interview that was to come. It promised to be very interesting, she thought. *Very interesting indeed.* When she had probed Thalan's mind, she had been completely unprepared for what she found, and her heart quickened with excitement as she remembered that unexpected jolt of recognition.

Thalan Dushar was a magic user, a Seeker of the Eye of Truth.

* * *

The knock did not come until two hours past midnight, but Gwynne was awake and waiting for it. She made sure that the man standing outside her door was the one she had invited before she opened it to admit him. Grinning mischievously, Thalan sneaked into the room and collapsed onto a rickety chair that groaned under his weight. Gwynne winced, but the chair held. *Telma must keep everything in good repair,* she thought fleetingly. The soft, flickering candlelight cast eerie shadows over Thalan's face, which might have looked malevolent save for an impish expression and that absurd nose. He was not exactly handsome, Gwynne decided, but he had a certain charm that one could be fooled into thinking he was.

"I had to avoid two chambermaids and the innkeeper's wife to get in here," he said, his eyes twinkling. "I wonder if she ever sleeps. By the... I mean, salt and stuff me, but that woman is nosy! I had to wait until she went into the kitchens before I could come up. I thought it would cause some talk if I were seen slipping into your room at this hour, and in the commons you seemed eager to keep this confidential. You did bring me here for a magical, romantic encounter, didn't you?" The young man grinned fiendishly at her, and Gwynne found her own lips curving up in return. The man's smile was irresistible.

"Well, not exactly romantic, but yes, magical," she assured him, keeping her expression bland and non-threatening. The grin froze on Thalan's face and he became very still. His expression would have given him away if she had not already known the truth. "Please believe that I mean you no harm," Gwynne continued gently. "In fact, I am very glad we happened to meet. I haven't had the chance to talk to one of my own people in many years, and there are so few of us left."

"So few what?" Thalan asked, trying to sound unconcerned and failing miserably.

Gwynne sighed. By the Eye, this was not going to be easy. After all, she had experienced a similar shock very recently and she knew how difficult this was going to be for him. "Come now," she said gently, "let us not play games. You are a Seeker of the Eye of Truth."

Shock showed plainly on Thalan's face, replaced almost instantly by fear. "I... I don't know..."

Gwynne reached out and touched him gently, and he visibly flinched away from her hand. "You have nothing to fear from me, Thalan. I, too, am a Seeker. I know what you are because I... pardon my rudeness... I probed your mind and saw your talents. You know, you really should learn to guard your thoughts whenever you are out in public. You never know when an Esprys might be around."

Thalan stared at her speechlessly for a moment. Then his face broke into a wide grin and he began to laugh. He covered his face and laughed and laughed until Gwynne began to look at him with some concern. Perhaps the strain... He raised his head, and she saw there were tears on his face and hands, small drops glinting in the candlelight as he pointed at her and laughed. Finally, gasping for breath, he got himself under control.

"By blood and bones, woman, you had me scared!" he roared. Gwynne quickly cautioned him to be quieter, and he went on in a milder tone. "For a moment there I thought that I was finished."

"Had I been anything but what I am, you would have been," Gwynne told him seriously. "You must have unbelievable luck to have come as far as you have without being caught. No," she said, smiling to take the sting out of her words, "you are not finished. In fact, I think that you have only just begun."

Thalan tried to make himself more comfortable in the chair, which was hard wood and all sharp angles and edges. "True. I only started my Search a short time ago. How did you know?"

"You are very young, and you have obviously not had much training," Gwynne explained, and then blushed at her tactlessness. She hurried on before he could comment. "And how could you have, with no one to teach you? There are so few of us left. If you had been taught, I would never have been able to see into your mind as I did."

Thalan made a wry face. "That, too, I fear is true. As you said, who was there to train me? I had to figure things out on my own, and so far the only thing I truly know is that I know nothing at all."

"Then you are already wiser than most people. How did you find out about the Prophecies?" Gwynne asked. "You were about to say 'By the Eye' before, weren't you? A very dangerous phrase to know. And you did not question me when I said you were a Seeker. So you know about the Eye of Truth, and you know about Seekers. The Onnic have taken considerable pains to ensure no one has easy access to such information these days."

"Well, that is quite a story. Would you like to hear it?" Gwynne nodded and Thalan gestured for her to take a seat on the bed. "All right. I was born to a wealthy merchant in the city of Aryn twenty-five years ago." He glanced at Gwynne with a sparkle in his eye. "Great beginning, don't you think?" Gwynne rolled her eyes and motioned for him to continue. "Well, my father and mother had a prospering trade contract with Marrin and were doing very well by it. They owned a great deal of land and they even had a small salt deposit on one of their plots. They became extremely rich from the trade of this salt. From the time I can remember, my father was priming me for the business so I could eventually take over for him when he stepped down. But I was never interested in business – I was always interested in music. My father, of course, did not consider music a suitable trade, but I was their only child so I was indulged. For a time, anyway.

"I studied with a master of music, a Monteno Mountain dwarf. It was in his house I found the books that described the Prophecies of the Eye of Truth, and he allowed me to read them after my lessons. My master had kept the books hidden for years. Not because he approved of magic, though I don't think he cared much one way or the other, but because he could not bear to see anything beautiful destroyed for any reason. The books had been in his family for generations and he knew the Onnic would confiscate and destroy them, perhaps imprison him if they were discovered."

"When did you realize you had magic yourself?" Gwynne asked.

"I didn't, really. My parents discovered it when I was very young. My talent lies with Water and I guess they finally realized why our land remained lush and green while our neighbors suffered from droughts. When I wished hard enough for rain, it rained. I didn't even realize what I was doing."

Gwynne was intrigued. "So what happened?"

"Well, it was my magic that finally persuaded my father that I was more suited for music than business. He was afraid – not for me but for his business – and he thought if I were busy with my music he could forget I was his son. Then I could not ruin his business with my flawed character." Thalan's lowered his eyes, leaving Gwynne to guess at the pain that hid behind them. "He finally took on an apprentice and proceeded to live as if I didn't exist. So one day I just packed up my things and left. I don't know if he ever even noticed."

"How awful," Gwynne muttered sympathetically. "Where did you go?"

"Oh, I stayed with Master Onyada for a time, learning to carve instruments and reading his books. I became interested in the Prophecies – they were the only things I had ever seen that gave my talent for magic any meaning. Once I had learned all I could from him, I decided to begin my own Search. I didn't know much of anything about anything then. I thought I had packed enough food and money for a year, but after four weeks of travel in foul weather I ended up in River Crossing with a lame horse, no food, no money, and no place to stay. I became apprenticed to an instrument maker there and when I had made a little money, I left. Since then I have been playing my pipe for my supper and a bed, and it has stood me fine. I never really searched or anything, I just kept moving from place to place. And so I ended up here."

"As did I," Gwynne said. "Though for very different reasons. Well, this could be fortunate for us both." She paused, trying to marshal her thoughts. It did not take much time to come to a decision. This young man could very well be the answer to her prayers.

"I have a proposition for you," she told him.

"Oh, really?" Thalan asked with a grin, raising one eyebrow in a wicked leer.

Gwynne laughed. "No, not that kind of proposition! I thought we had already established that there would be no romantic liaisons here."

"Right, sorry. So what do you propose?"

"I was wondering... would you like to travel together? I could give you some instruction on the use of magic, and you can be my traveling companion." She did not tell him that she wanted to teach him because her own magic was too weak to get them out of even a minor pickle, let alone a major catastrophe. The young man had possibilities; his magic was unschooled but quite strong.

"Are you serious?" Thalan seemed astounded at the idea. "I would forever be in your debt."

"Don't speak too soon," Gwynne warned him. "You haven't heard my story yet. Traveling with me could be a serious hazard to your health." Quickly, she told him about Jaerak Thorin, about her book that had somehow ended up in his possession, and his visit to the City of Circles. Thalan grew very serious as he listened to the tale.

"But that's unthinkable!" he exclaimed when she had finished. He looked at the scabs on her face and arms in horror. "*He* did this to you? How could anyone use magic for such evil?"

"It has been known to happen," Gwynne told him. "There are tales of sorcerers exploiting their powers and the powers of others for personal gain. Fortunately, it did not happen very often."

"Then you don't think you can fight him with magic?"

"Absolutely not," Gwynne said, watching him closely. "He is much too strong and far too driven. What I need now is information. What drives him, and why? What is he after, and what are his plans?"

"Yes, well, that confuses me," Thalan said thoughtfully. "If no one knows how to enter the Dark Abyss, what good will your book do him?"

"Well, he can use it now to incriminate me to the Onnic for one thing," Gwynne answered, remembering Jaerak's mocking words to her before he burned her house down in a fit of temper. "But he hasn't yet, and I don't know why. I know nothing about him, or what he wants, or even where he's from. He told me he was from Magir, but now I know he lied to me. I have been all over this city today, and no one has ever heard of him."

Thalan looked skeptical. "It's an awfully large city," he said.

"True," Gwynne admitted, "but he also told me he studied at the university here and no one there has ever heard of him either."

"Ah. Well. That does seem odd."

"He must have told me he was from here for a reason, what was it?" she wondered, her voice betraying her anxiety. "What does he hope to gain by luring me here with that story? We need to find out, because his magic is dangerously strong and he has a nasty taint of evil about him. I recognized it. I've felt it before in the Earth."

"Evil." Thalan's voice was so strange that Gwynne glanced at him in concern. His face looked like a mask in the candlelight. "What kind of evil?"

"Well..." *How best to explain it?* "It's like a well that started out clean, with clear water that tasted sweet, but became contaminated over a long period of time. No one would notice the contamination because it happened so slowly and no one would make a connection between the well water and the fact that people were getting sick."

Thalan smiled, a little sadly, she thought. "The water in the well is contaminated, my lady," he said. "I, too, have felt it. It still startles me how foul it feels, yet it has no taste of decay. I have wondered why."

Gwynne stared at him in astonishment. "Then it is true."

Thalan looked puzzled. "What is true?"

"The Prophecies. The Elements are coming together as a warning to magic users. The Prophecies say that when this happens, the Eye of Truth will be found shortly afterward."

"Really?" Thalan seemed intrigued by the idea. "So what do we do now?"

Gwynne eyed him quizzically. "We?" she asked, smiling.

Thalan's smile flashed across his face. He had lots of very white teeth, Gwynne noticed. "Yes, we! Do you think I could resist such a story? So, what do we do now?"

Gwynne grinned. "I love practical questions I can actually answer. We Search. Jaerak Thorin will not keep me from that. We will Search together, and we will go where the wind takes us. Who knows? We may actually find the Eye of Truth, and then our troubles will be over."

"Or perhaps," Thalan muttered so quietly that Gwynne had to strain to hear, "they will only have just begun."

"...The Eye of Truth cannot be known, but must be found. Only then will she see her own true power."

– From the Prophecy of the Eye of Truth

Chapter Six

"Come on, you puny weakling, work those scrawny little strings you call muscles!" The harsh voice of the Swordmaster cut through the crisp evening air like the blade of the sharpest sword.

Aliane, whose muscles were not particularly scrawny, though at the moment extremely sore from her vigorous workout, drove the point of her practice sword into the ground. She wiped away the sweat that was streaming down her face and stinging her eyes, and glared good-humoredly at the furious Swordmaster. "You wouldn't talk to me that way if my father were here," she accused breathlessly, pointing one grubby finger at him.

The Swordmaster grinned malevolently at her, one side of his face split by a deep, ugly scar. "Well, sweetheart, you want to play with the big boys, you have to get used to being treated like one, and your father would agree. And don't shove your sword into the ground, it dulls the tip of the blade. Now stand to!" He raised his sword and fell into a fighter's stance.

Aliane sighed and heaved her sword up. After nearly an hour of practice the weapon seemed to weigh almost as much as she did. Automatically, she got into position, and just in time, too. The Swordmaster came at her with a snarl and whirling blade, and Aliane fluidly blocked his thrust. They circled warily, testing for weaknesses and looking for openings. Back and forth they sparred until even the Swordmaster was dripping with sweat, and Aliane felt as if her arms were made of lead.

Finally, Charis dropped his sword and waved Aliane away. "Enough for today, you weary me with your ineptitude. Go back to your silk sheets and ladies-in-waiting where you belong."

Aliane made a face. "Charis, you know very well I can't stand ladies-in-waiting. Why do you think I put up with your ugly face instead of letting those mother hens stifle me to death?"

Charis winked at her. "Aye, and you're not bad for a spoiled little snip of a princess, at that."

"Thanks. See you tomorrow." She put her sword up on the rack and headed back to Morgan's palace, every muscle aching and strained. She grinned as she massaged her sore shoulder. If Julane could only see her now... Though upon further consideration it was probably better that she couldn't. The haughty princess would most likely faint dead away at the sight of Aliane in breeches, her face filthy, her body drenched in sweat and her hair straggling from its plait.

Aliane had managed to find time each day for practice with Charis, and the exercise made life in Morgan's castle at least tolerable. Charis had found a field near the men's barracks where they could practice in private, and they had taken to meeting in the early dusk before dinner when she would not be missed. She and her father had been in Magir five weeks now, and she was beginning to wonder if she was ever going home. The king of Casset and her father were still negotiating – over what, she did not know and no one had seen fit to inform her. As a result, she had been forced to spend more time than she liked in the company of the dull, beautiful Princess Julane. So far, her clandestine meetings with the Swordmaster had not been discovered, though she wondered if Morgan would be so keen to marry her off to his son if he knew she could probably equal the prince in a fight. *Hmmmmm*, she thought speculatively. Perhaps she should let herself be caught after all.

As she made her way across the stone courtyard, skirting scrawny dogs and flapping chickens, she spied a group of women near the main palace entryway. Their brightly colored silks looked incongruous against the mud-packed earthen ground and the gray stone walls. As soon as those ladies saw her, they would cluck disapprovingly – hence the mother hen image – and hustle her into her chambers before anyone could see her disgraceful state of disarray. Actually, a hot bath was just what she wanted, but not with those silly women bustling around her. They made her uncomfortable with their fussing. Sneaking a glance to make sure no one was looking, Aliane ducked around to the servants' entrance and went in that way. The first time she had sneaked in through the kitchens she had startled a scullery maid so badly that the poor woman had shrieked, dropped her cooking pot and run. But now the kitchen staff was used to seeing her and only bowed their heads to her as she passed. Aliane made it to her suite without being seen by anyone else and collapsed onto the luxuriously soft feather bed with a gusty sigh.

Charis always worked her as hard as he did his men – harder, it sometimes seemed. She chuckled to herself as she remembered the first time she had confronted him. She had been a child of thirteen and had barely had the strength to lift the practice sword she had taken from the armory. He had laughed at her when she had told him she wanted to learn to fight, and had dismissed her with a wave of his hand saying that little girls, especially little princesses, did not belong on the practice field. Thinking to prove herself as capable as anyone, she had swung the sword with all her might at his retreating back and the flat of the blade had connected with a resounding crack. In later years, Charis had joked that that was the only time in his career anyone had taken him unawares, for he had been pitched forward and landed with his face in the mud. After that he had decided he might as well teach her to use the weapon since she would obviously try to do it anyway, and for thirteen years – fully half her life – he had trained her. Once he had taken her on as his pupil, Charis had been determined to make her the best fighter she could be, and he had grinned sadistically while he watched her struggle through the grueling exercises he set for her. King Torrit had raised his eyes, shook his head and said nothing, as he usually did when his daughter confounded him.

A knock on the door disrupted Aliane's fond reminiscences, and she bade the knocker welcome. The door opened and a middle-aged and extremely corpulent woman entered. Shining silver hair caught up in a less than elegant chignon framed a face deeply tanned and finely lined. Hands on her wide hips, the woman glared accusingly at Aliane.

"So! Again you fight with that horrible man, again you disregard my suggestions! And just look at you. You are all sweaty and filthy and your hair... never mind. Into the bath with you." Lips tightly pressed with disapproval, she moved to help Aliane off with her clothes.

"Oh, Hernie, you say that almost every day," Aliane protested, laughing as she shrugged out of her leathers. "You may as well just get used to the fact that I am not a proper princess at all, and just love me for who I am." She unlaced her practice gloves and tossed them on the table, flexing fingers that were sore from gripping the handle of the practice sword too tightly.

"Aye, not a proper princess at that," Hernie muttered, glancing at the dirty gloves with ill-concealed disgust, "but not for want of my teachings or advice. Come now, into the tub... great gracious!"

Hernie's exclamation of surprise burst from her lips as she succeeded in removing Aliane's shirt and saw the purpling bruises spreading across her shoulders and back. *Salt and stuff it,* Aliane thought. *That's torn it.* Hernie could keep up a running commentary on the wicked shortcomings and carelessness of Charis for hours on end. Anyone who dared damage Aliane's royal skin deserved no less than a severe whipping himself, in Hernie's opinion. So she was quite surprised when the matron consoled herself with a muttered, "Criminal, that man, just criminal," and deftly removed the rest of her clothes.

Aliane sank gratefully into the steaming tub and relaxed, feeling her overworked muscles gradually begin to loosen. She watched curiously as Hernie bustled around the room, tidying up Aliane's cheerful clutter and brushing away imaginary specks of dust. Hernie had insisted upon accompanying Aliane and King Torrit on their journey – indeed, it had never occurred to the old woman to stay behind. Hernie had been so utterly scandalized when Aliane had informed her that her presence was not necessary that she had not brought up the subject again. On the day of their departure Hernie had been calmly and coolly waiting by the carriage that was to take them to Magir, and Aliane and King Torrit had said not a word when she firmly took her place next to her charge. They both knew better than to argue with her when she had made up her mind.

Hernie was the only servant who treated Aliane as a beloved though somewhat exasperating daughter rather than a princess. She had been with Aliane since she was a small child, and she had grown very fond of the irascible old woman. Now Aliane watched complacently as Hernie grumbled to herself while twitching the bed linen into place, but it was not until she had lain out one of Aliane's best ball gowns that she sat up and really began to take notice.

"Hernie, what's going on?" she asked, a dreadful foreboding coming over her.

"You be careful, I don't want to have to clean up a lot of spilled water. Sure and you haven't forgotten that Prince Larion is arriving tonight? And you out playing warrior in the yard until all hours! Hurry up or you will be late. Your father and that... *king*... have gone to a lot of trouble for you tonight." Her voice dripped with venom and despite the sinking in her stomach, Aliane suppressed a smile. Hernie, for reasons unknown, had taken a violent dislike to King Morgan and had been pleased with Aliane's wholehearted agreement with her opinion of the despicable monarch. Aliane idly wondered what Morgan had done to incur the portly housekeeper's righteous displeasure. Then the import of Hernie's words forced themselves into her consciousness and she slipped in the tub, getting a ducking for her carelessness. She surfaced, sputtering with swallowed rose water and indignation.

"Tonight?" Aliane was aghast. She launched herself to her feet, splashing more scented water on the floor. Ignoring Hernie's yelp of protest, she steadied herself against the side of the tub. "Already? What day is it? Salt and *stuff* it, I thought I had more time." She stepped out of the tub and into the robe Hernie had waiting for her, ignoring the disapproving look Hernie shot her for her language. King Morgan and her father had been planning a welcoming reception for the prince for days and she would, of course, be expected to attend. Aliane groaned silently. She had not been looking forward to this, and now that the time was upon her, she had to think fast. She had been trying to put this day out of her mind, and it seemed as if she had truly succeeded. It certainly had sneaked up on her quickly. Or perhaps Larion, being privy to Morgan's plans, had hurried home more quickly than he had originally intended.

Over the past weeks, Aliane had managed not to dwell on the conversation she had overheard in Morgan's castle that day. But now the memory of the two men's confident, treacherous voices caused a fresh stab of resentment to flash through her body. She could never marry Larion. To do so would give King Morgan far too much power over her father. Even without that foreknowledge, she could never marry into the Onnic order. That had surprised her father as well, she thought. King Torrit had not known the prince had been instated as an officer into the Onnic army, and she knew he was displeased that he had not been told. She had to think of a way to refuse Larion without giving offense, because she certainly couldn't tell anyone the real reason for refusing his inevitable proposal. She was almost sure that Larion knew what his father planned, and the extra power he himself stood to gain would make him a persistent suitor.

On the other hand, she was afraid of what would happen when she inevitably refused the prince. Her father may be confident it would cause no difficulties between he and Morgan, but Aliane was not as sure or as trusting as King Torrit. She would not put it past King Morgan to use her refusal as an excuse to declare war on him. He obviously wanted her father's lands, and aimed to divide his loyalty from Queen Rhyssl. Aliane did not doubt he would use every underhanded trick in his arsenal to obtain his desires. With growing dismay, Aliane realized she was in a terrible position and no matter what choice she made her father would still be hurt by it. For the first time in her life she felt completely alone. Always before she had been able to bring her problems to her father. This time she felt terribly isolated and lost without his wise counsel. She had no idea what to do.

Aliane felt a profound and unexpected urge to abandon her duties altogether and ride off into the night, searching for adventure and freedom from royal obligations. Those duties had been weighing heavily on her in recent weeks. Perhaps she could even begin her own secret Search, a thing she had dreamed about for many years. She had always kept her magic talents hidden from everyone, even her father. They seemed so small, so harmless to create such a furor that would certainly arise if anyone knew of them. And they gave her such joy. Whenever the wind blew, she could hear the secret whispers of the air surrounding her and the clouds above. The breezes laughed with her as they played with her hair and stole her hats, and she felt and respected the power behind the gale forces that sometimes come with the heavy storms. She knew very little about the Prophecies, but she had heard enough to fuel her desire to participate in the ancient Search with her fellow magic users. She had learned of the Eye of Truth long ago when she was just a little girl. She had slipped a silver coin into an old beggar woman's hand, and the woman had said, "May the Eye smile down on you, child." Aliane had asked who's eye she was talking about, and the beggar woman had told her a delightful fairy tale about magic, a prophecy and a savior. In later years, Aliane had tried to find out more about the stories, but had learned little. She knew just enough to feel a twinge of excitement at the thought of joining the Search for their as of yet unnamed benefactor.

With difficulty, Aliane shook away her dreams and dismissed such frivolous ideas. She could not abandon her father after he had taken such trouble to arrange this courtship. She would just have to concoct a plan to get rid of Larion that would allow him no cause for offense. Aliane's face dimpled as she unconsciously smiled. Perhaps she could make herself really annoying around the prince, forcing *him* to refuse to marry *her*. Morgan certainly could not blame her father if his own son decided to look elsewhere for a wife. Then perhaps later she could follow her heart and choose her own path. Her father could not keep her safely cooped up in one palace or another forever. *No*, said a treacherous little voice in her head. *He'll only keep you until he finds you a husband who will take up where he left off.*

Coherent thought became increasingly difficult as Hernie began to get her ready for the ball. Aliane endured with stoic silence as her hair was washed and dressed, grimacing as Hernie pulled a comb through the long tangled strands. But when she was finished Aliane's hair fell in raven-dark, shining splendor to her waist. It was an annoying encumbrance when she was at fighter's practice, but she could never bring herself to cut it. She knew it was beautiful, and she enjoyed the delightfully feminine feeling she got when she knew she looked her best, despite the allegations of certain people that she was a hopeless tomboy. After all, sword practice was not the only pleasure in a young woman's life. Hernie held out the gown for her to step into, and Aliane said with surprise, "But Hernie, aren't you going to put my hair up tonight?"

"I thought it would be better not to," Hernie said dryly. "This dress has quite a low back, and your hair will cover your bruises."

"Of course," Aliane murmured wryly, getting into the gown. "We wouldn't want the prince to think that I participated in anything so unprincesslike as physical exercise, would we?" Hernie shot her a warning look, and she subsided. She did not want the maid to suspect her intentions. As much as she loved the old woman, she knew what a hopeless gossip she was. Hernie fastened the dozens of tiny hooks and eyes that ran down the back of the gown and went to get her shoes while Aliane contemplated her reflection in the full-length mirror.

The gown was very beautiful, a shimmering dark green that brought out the emerald of her eyes. It fit her slender body closely and full, flowing sleeves gracefully draped arms that were perhaps a little too heavily muscled from hours of sword-play. Her cheeks were rosy, her hair shone in the candlelight, and she looked bewitchingly pretty. Her mouth twisted as she regarded herself. Tonight she would rather be wearing a shapeless garment that hid her curves, and look as drab and dreary as the lowest scullery-maid. Larion had no doubt been instructed by his father to woo her as ardently as possible, and looking as she did now would only encourage him. Abruptly, she turned away from her reflection, suddenly feeling as if she were in some way betraying her father and herself at the same time.

"Well, Hernie?" she asked as the woman came back into the chamber holding a pair of shoes, dyed a deep green to match the dress. "How do I look?"

Hernie raked her with critical scrutiny and sniffed. "You'll do all right, I suppose. Here, put these on. But I guess if you are out to catch a prince, you would want to expose your bosom in that manner."

"Oh Hernie," Aliane laughed, "you are terrible. It isn't that bad, and may I remind you that you chose this dress for me yourself."

"Humph," was the only reply. Hernie was the only person Aliane had ever known who actually said 'humph'. Hernie fastened a choker of emeralds around Aliane's neck and put a matching emerald and diamond comb in her hair. "Well, you should do your father proud anyhow. Just remember to keep your feet together when you sit, and don't laugh too loudly, and for fortune's sake, don't contradict everything the prince says to you..."

"But what if he says something that I disagree with?" Aliane asked mischievously, adjusting the cascade of curls over her shoulder.

"Well, you needn't be strident about it, anyway," Hernie conceded. "Just try to act in a way that becomes a princess, because that is what you are, young lady, like it or not!"

"But there are so many 'don'ts' about being a princess," Aliane complained, tugging at the neckline of the dress. It really was rather low, now that she thought about it. Hernie slapped her hands away and she left off her fussing. "No one would think it strange if a barmaid or a peasant girl had opinions and aired them in public."

"And what do you know about being a barmaid? Believe me, child, the life of a working woman is not to be envied, not even for the freedom of speaking your mind whenever you wish. Now you just remember everything I told you, and behave yourself. You go down now, your father will be waiting for you."

"Just one more thing," Aliane said, reaching for her jewelry box. She opened it and withdrew a delicate golden ring set with a single stone and slipped it on the third finger of her right hand. The stone was unlike any other she had ever seen. It was about the size of a man's thumbnail and shimmered with a rainbow of colors. Citrine, diamond, emerald, sapphire, and ruby all streaked together in a spectrum of light and color, as if a fairy hand had touched and smeared the hues of a rainbow like paints on an artist's palette. Hernie looked at the ring and sniffed.

"It doesn't go with the dress. The emerald one would be better."

Aliane firmly closed the jewelry box. "This was my mother's, and I want to wear it tonight." Under her breath, too softly to be heard, she added, "Plus, I'm going to need all the luck I can get." The ring had been a gift from Ronen el'Faria – Aliane's real father – to her mother on their wedding day, and it was one of the only treasures she had that had been her parents'. Hernie looked at her sharply and told her not to mutter, it wasn't ladylike, but said no more about the ring. Stifling her irritation, Aliane, after one last look in the glass, left the room and headed toward the Grand Ballroom, where the reception was to be held.

As Aliane descended the stairs, she took a deep breath to calm her nerves. She truly did not want to disappoint her father, so she vowed silently that she would be on her best behavior that night, at least when he had his eye upon her. There would be time enough later to convince Prince Larion that he thoroughly disliked her. She reminded herself that she would not be forced to marry the prince no matter what happened. Once this uncomfortable courtship was concluded and done with, one way or another, she could breathe easily and not worry about being a tool in her father's ruination. At least she fervently hoped so. Her nerves were beginning to fray under the strain.

She was watching her feet as she walked, careful of the narrow heels of her shoes, and she did not look up until she stood before the open doorway that led to the large ballroom. So it was not until she was practically inside that the full effect of the display hit her. Her mouth dropped open, and her only thought as she surveyed the room was, *By the Eye, he isn't fooling around, is he?*

Crystal chandeliers strung with every conceivable color jewel hung from the high ceiling, flinging their rainbow lights to every corner of the room. Against the length of one wall were long tables covered with heavy damask cloths upon which every available delicacy was laid out. An elite group of musicians quietly prepared and tuned their instruments, and a large area of the floor had been cleared for dancing. There were elaborately carved chairs at the head of the room, covered with rich red velvet and obviously meant for the royal family. She hoped that she would not be expected to sit up there. It was an arrangement designed to show the royal persons to their best advantage, and she did not relish the thought of being on display for everyone's scrutiny. Every surface in that huge room shone, sparkled, or richly glowed and the effect, to Aliane's dazzled eyes, was appalling. It looked as if they expected the Eye of Truth herself instead of a bachelor prince.

King Torrit stood by the tables, engaged in directing the kitchen servants where to place the huge, elaborate ice sculpture of – Aliane blinked – surely not... *Prince Larion himself?* But it was, and a rather good likeness, too, she had to admit. There was no gainsaying that the prince was handsome. She closed her eyes and sighed. Her father was trying so hard. It was truly a shame she would have to crush his innocent hopes. Finally, the placement of the ghastly sculpture apparently pleased him and he turned and saw her standing in the doorway.

"Aliane!" he boomed, coming over to engulf her in the folds of his rich blue velvet tunic. "My poppet, you look so pretty. How do you like the room?"

"It... it is amazing, Father," Aliane said truthfully.

"I noticed you were looking at the ice sculpture. I had it specially made for tonight," the king claimed with pride. "But you outshine any of my decorations, my dear." He beamed at her and a smile tugged at Aliane's lips. It was almost impossible to remain in a bad mood around her father. He surveyed his daughter with pride, and he glanced at her finger as the lamplight caught the stone in her ring, sending glimmering reflections of color across its surface. His eyes clouded for a brief moment, and then the warm smile showed itself again. "Your mother's ring," he said softly, taking her hand to examine it more closely. "I haven't seen this in a long time." He smiled sadly down at her, and Aliane felt a wash of pity flow through her body. He had lost so very much.

"Do you mind?" she asked, clasping his huge hand in her own small one.

"Mind?" Torrit looked at her in surprise. "Of course I don't mind. I gave it to you so you could wear it, so you could have something your mother treasured. I think it's very appropriate that you wear it tonight. I just wish she could be here to see you today. She would be so proud of you, my dear. As am I."

Aliane smiled affectionately. "Thank you, Father. I wish she could be here, too, as well as..." She hesitated, not knowing if what she wanted to say would be too painful.

To her relief, King Torrit smiled and squeezed her hand. "Yes, and my dear wife, too, I know. Tracia also would have been proud of you. I know you don't remember her, but she loved you very much."

Aliane smiled back at him, though she felt the prick of tears gathering behind her eyes. "I wish I did remember."

Torrit cleared his throat. "Yes. Well. We must make this night a memorable one. You look so very beautiful, my dear."

"Thank you. When is the prince due to arrive?"

"At any moment, my pet." The king's face cleared, and a look of anticipation sparkled in his eyes. "We should get to the receiving line. Morgan is already there and the guests are starting to arrive. We shouldn't keep them waiting in the salon too long."

Dutifully, Aliane took her place in the welcoming line, her father taking his place beside King Morgan at the head. She saw Princess Julane standing with her father, resplendent in silver brocade and lace, diamonds dripping from her hair and ears. She was smiling in anticipation, and Aliane was astounded at how pretty she was when the sullen, suspicious look was absent from her features.

The footmen began to announce the guests, and Aliane surreptitiously shifted from foot to foot with impatience. She disliked the ritualistic and ceremonial aspect of palace life – it took up so much time and was so salted boring! But she knew her duty, and as the guests began to file in, she stilled her fidgeting and smiled graciously. She was surprised by the extent of the guest list – some people had had to travel quite a distance to attend. There were even representatives from the noble houses of Cameon present, some of whom she knew, some she didn't. She smiled at all of them, touched fingertips with the women and allowed her hand to be kissed by the men as courtesy demanded. Apparently, her father was not the only one eager to see her married off. The list was interminable, and as name after name was called out, Aliane's thoughts wandered from the here and now to the sweeter call of daydreams as she automatically went through the motions of welcoming the guests.

Suddenly she was jolted back to reality when one young man – she had not heard the name called out for him – grasped her by the shoulders and planted a light, lingering kiss upon her cheek. Outraged by his impertinence, her hand flashed out and slapped him smartly across the face before she could form a coherent thought. Instantly a shocked silence flooded the room, followed closely by the small murmurs and gasps her action had provoked.

The young man standing transfixed before her stared at her in utter disbelief, his cheek reddened by her blow and, Aliane suspected, rage. His fingers still held her shoulders, and now they tightened painfully as if only his iron will prevented him from shaking her until her teeth rattled. One hand was over a particularly tender bruise, but she scarcely felt the pain. Aliane stared right back at him, her heart pounding, trying to control her temper. Through her fury she could see that the man was probably somewhat past thirty and handsome, though not in any way she found particularly attractive. She noted that his features were too hard and the line of his jaw too stiff for her tastes. Too late, she also saw the royal insignia that was pinned on his collar, and color flooded her pale face as she finally realized her mistake.

"Oh dear," she said, looking at the man in consternation. "You... You are Prince Larion, aren't you?"

"Yes." Larion pulled himself up so that he was towering over her. "And I must say I was expecting somewhat of a different welcome into my father's house, Princess."

"I must apologize," she said, mortified, as her father left his place in line to approach them, his face as shocked as her own. She vaguely remembered a fanfare and flourish of music, but had not connected them with the arrival of the prince. "I am afraid I was dreaming, and I didn't hear your name called. I thought you were taking unacceptable liberties."

"I hope there is no offense?" King Torrit said, sounding very hopeful indeed. "My daughter sometimes loses track of what she should be doing," he shot her a reproving glance, "but I am sure she did not mean to insult you so."

"No, of course I didn't," Aliane said, truly aghast by what she had done. Though truth be told, it was not a bad start to her crusade to persuade Prince Larion to dislike her. Still, she felt a flood of remorse as she looked at King Torrit. Her father was trying so hard, and she just humiliated him beyond belief. She glimpsed Julane behind Torrit, craning her neck in an undignified manner to get a better view of the scene. The smirk on the haughty princess's face stung Aliane's pride awake, and again facing the prince she drew herself up to her fullest height. Which, she had to admit, wasn't much.

"I hope you will accept my humblest apologies, Prince Larion." She made a deep curtsy, mostly so she would not have to meet his eyes. She was afraid her thoughts would be mirrored in hers.

Larion looked down his nose at her bowed head as if she were a servant who had just dropped a bowl of scalding hot soup in his lap. "I suppose I can make an allowance, this once," he said, his voice dripping with sarcasm. "I just hope I won't have to defend myself if I ask the Princess for a dance later."

"Of course not," Aliane replied, repressing her irritation at his tone. "You took me by surprise, that's all."

"Well!" Torrit said cheerfully. "Now that that is all cleared up, allow me to get you a glass of wine, your Highness, to toast your safe arrival."

"Are there no servants to do the serving, Sire?" Larion asked contemptuously. "In my mind, a king should never soil his hands doing a menial's work, and I believe my father's palace is amply staffed."

Well, that clinches it, Aliane thought as her father signaled one of the "menials" to get the wine. Prince Larion was still a condescending, supercilious, spoiled jackass. He watched loftily as a servant brought him his wine, and he sniffed it suspiciously before he deigned to take a sip. When he turned to face Aliane again, she saw there was a reddened patch in the shape of a handprint on his cheek, and she experienced a sudden, unexpected urge to giggle. She tried to get her face under control – she had caused enough embarrassment already. By the look on Prince Larion's face, she was not entirely successful. Not only was he a jackass, she thought as she took his arm to be led to the head of the ballroom, but he also had absolutely no sense of humor, which in her opinion was the greater evil.

The room began to buzz with excitement as the guests clotted together in their little social cliques. Aliane had to stifle another gasp of laughter as she realized that this incident would be gossiped about and spread around for a long time to come. These people loved gossip, and in their narrow little minds and dull, predictable lives this event would keep them happily occupied for months. Aliane felt a stab of pity towards them as she maneuvered around the room and felt their greedily curious eyes constantly upon her. They had been brought up this way, and it wasn't necessarily their fault they couldn't see past their own aristocratic noses. She had probably done them a favor by adding a little scandal and excitement to their lives.

Suddenly a thought struck her and she stopped, looking wildly around the room. Had Morgan seen what she had done? The King had been at the head of the line with her father, so he must have seen what happened. But she had not seen him with Julane just after the incident. Where had he been? She spotted the king across the room speaking to a man she had never seen before. She couldn't see very well through the crowd of people, but the stranger looked to be middle-aged and gray-haired, and he was wearing plain clothing rather than the rich finery that distinguished the other guests. She wondered who he could be. He must be someone important to divert the king's attention away from his party. Just then, both men glanced in her direction. She quickly looked away, pretending she had not seen them and slipped from sight back into the crowd. *Well, if he had not seen the slap,* she thought ruefully, *he would learn about it soon enough.*

The rest of the ball went off without incident, and if it had not been for Larion, Aliane might have enjoyed it. She loved to dance, but she did not like the way he pulled her close to him, or how he grasped her hand so tightly that she felt pins and needles afterward. His conversation lacked any spark of interest for her, and it took her almost no time at all to become heartily bored with his company. He seemed only concerned about himself and spent most of the night recounting his valorous deeds in battle, some of which sickened her to the point of nausea. When supper was announced, Larion took her arm with a possessive air that made her extremely uncomfortable and escorted her into the dining hall. She nearly groaned aloud when she saw the seating arrangements – she was to sit between Larion and an ancient duke or baron or something, who was so deaf that the only way to talk to him was to scream in his ear. Her father had been placed at the very opposite end of the table, so it looked as if decent conversation was not on the menu for her that night.

The kitchen staff had outdone themselves with the food. King Morgan had obviously ordered every conceivable kind of delicacy to welcome his son home. Among the more prosaic roast beef, swan and chicken were a brace of quail, an entire roasted boar and a roasted peacock with the feathers stuck back on, giving it a horribly lifelike appearance. Aliane did not eat any of the peacock, but she ate voraciously of the other dishes. Exercise always made her hungry, and she had not eaten since that morning. When she noticed Prince Larion watching her with ill-concealed contempt and disapproval, she felt another bubble of laughter rise in her throat, and she nearly gurgled inelegantly into her soup.

The night went on with seemingly endless chatter and dancing and music and noise. Aliane danced with many of the young nobles, and she did her duty to the more elderly ones as well, including the deaf baron who constantly told her to quit mumbling and speak up, for salt's sake. She found the nonstop conversation exhausting, and all too often when she turned her head she found Prince Larion looking at her, his face inscrutable and his expression giving away none of his thoughts. She found this very disturbing, especially since she suspected that she didn't really want to know what was going on behind those stony eyes of his. By the end of the night her nerves were stretched to an almost unbearable degree, and as soon as it was polite to do so she excused herself from the festivities and slipped away from the ballroom.

She breathed a gusty sigh of relief when she was safely back in her room with Hernie undressing her and getting her ready for bed. The only bright spot of the evening, in her opinion, was her initial introduction to Larion. How glad she was that just once, even unknowingly, she was able to smack that superior, egotistical, self-centered man right where it hurt him most – his pride. She would have to explain to her father that it just wouldn't be possible to marry that awful man. She suspected he would understand. She had the notion that Torrit had not thought highly of the prince either, and surely Larion's first impression of her had not been a favorable one. The prince did not seem to like much about her at all, and Aliane had gotten the impression throughout the evening that he was as set against the match as she. If she had only not seen that cold, calculating look on his face so often during the night...

The next morning when Aliane joined her father in the huge, elaborately decorated breakfast room for the morning meal, she was surprised to learn that the prince had left some hours before. Torrit told her a messenger had come in the night and that Larion had been called away to join his legion on an important mission.

"He received orders from that new captain Morgan instated," Torrit told her, looking doubtfully at the concoction of swan's eggs, cheese, roasted ham and spun sugar on his plate. He took a tentative bite and smiled, chewing more vigorously. "Mm. I'll have to see if Cook can reproduce this one."

"What new captain?" Aliane asked, waving away a servant who kept trying to put boiled hummingbird eggs in honey sauce on her plate. Not that she was really interested. She was too busy feeling relieved that she wouldn't have to sit across from Larion at the breakfast table that morning – it would have been enough to sour her appetite. Not that the hummingbird eggs weren't doing a good job of that by themselves, she thought sourly, noticing that despite her attempts to fend him off the servant had somehow managed to get a big spoonful of the glop on her plate.

"I heard Morgan tell Larion he has brought on a new man to lead the search for magic users," Torrit explained. "What was his name...? Ah, well, it will come to me. Apparently, he's rather ruthless. Anyway, rumor has it some old woman was trying to escape from the north, and Larion is to help track her down. I guess she's been seen here in the city, and Prince Larion was ordered to meet with this new captain of Morgan's. But I'm afraid the poor thing doesn't have much of a chance with the Onnic after her."

"I didn't know that you sympathized with the magic users," Aliane said, feeling a rush of pride for her father.

"Well," Torrit said, a little shamefaced. "I just don't think anyone deserves the treatment they receive. They are human beings, after all."

Yes, Aliane thought sadly. We are human beings, but are accorded none of the rights the rest of humanity take for granted every day. She felt a profound sympathy for that unknown Seeker being hunted down like a criminal, guilty only of possessing a gift that struck fear into the hearts of those who did not understand it. She, of all people, understood what it was like to live in fear of discovery, not allowed to choose your life or tell anyone what you were. She thought her father would probably understand about her talent for magic and would not despise her for it. But she knew his protection would be meaningless if the Onnic ever got wind of it.

Aliane spent the rest of the day in her quarters, thinking. When Hernie came to her door asking to hear about the ball, Aliane dismissed her, saying she wished to be left alone. Hernie, who had of course heard about what happened from the other servants, assumed she was too embarrassed to talk about it. *The dear child is just upset,* she thought as she made her way to the kitchens for a snack, *and no wonder!* Such a poor first impression to make on the prince. And he so handsome, she had heard from the kitchen servants. But the child would get over it in time. Only the young were capable of such depth of feeling when they humiliated themselves in front of those they are trying to impress.

But Aliane was not embarrassed or humiliated. Indeed, for the moment she had forgotten the incident had ever happened. She was more concerned with truth, with justice than with petty embarrassments. She thought long and hard, and after what seemed like an eternity of soul-searching, she came to a decision. Silently creeping down the servants' stairs, she slipped outside into the courtyard without being seen. She made her way to the guest barracks where her father's guards and soldiers were being housed and knocked on the door. Charis looked at her in surprise when he pulled it open, and followed her in bewilderment as she beckoned him to join her in a secluded, remote grove of trees where they could talk in private. When she quietly told him what she wanted, he was moved to protest.

"But your Highness, I don't think..." he began. Aliane raised her hand, and he fell silent.

"Can you get the information for me or not?" she asked.

Charis looked thoughtfully at her for a moment, and then his lopsided grin emerged, though not as heartily as it usually did. "If you don't get it from me, you'll find another way, eh? All right, I'll have it for you tomorrow. We can have an early practice." He hesitated, uncharacteristically uncertain as if he wanted to ask a question but wasn't sure he really wanted to know the answer. "But what...?"

"I can't say, Charis," Aliane said. She laid her hand on his arm in a rare display of affection. "Don't worry, I won't do anything stupid. I just want to know."

"All right, all right." Charis' voice was rough with surprise. Aliane suppressed a smile. The hoary old Swordmaster really was fond of her, she knew, but he was not prone to displays of emotion.

"Thank you Charis. I'll see you tomorrow. Early, just after first light." Charis nodded and returned to the barracks, closing the door after him. Aliane made her way back to her room with none the wiser, and with a lighter heart allowed Hernie to put her to bed.

"You must be quiet and modest, never speak unless spoken to, never laugh above a whisper and never show excess of emotion."

– From the Book of Etiquette on Royal Behavior, by the Lady Pomfrey de Frothingham.

Chapter Seven

The sun was shining gloriously over the land as Aliane made her way up the hillside where she and Charis had been holding their daily practice sessions. She hoped Charis had some good news for her, since she suspected the rest of the day would be a trial for her nerves and her patience. She would have to endure yet another excruciating breakfast with Princess Julane – her father was again closeted with King Morgan in meetings for the day. She suspected her behavior at the ball the other night would be thoroughly discussed, and she hoped her father would not have to bear recriminations for her actions. After all, it was not his fault. He had done his best.

She had awakened early, even before Hernie had come to bring her morning tea. She thought over her plan again and again, and the more she thought about it, the more determined she became. It was time, she thought, to put into practice all those high and lofty thoughts about freedom and justice. If Charis had been able to procure the information she wanted, she might have the opportunity to help someone else even if she couldn't yet help herself. She had responsibilities to her father and her station – she accepted that. But that was no reason to sit back in a comfortable castle with her hands folded meekly in her lap while an innocent woman was pursued like a virgin through a whorehouse. Not when she could do something to prevent it.

Charis was already waiting for her at the top of the hill when she arrived. He glanced at her as she approached and she instantly knew he had the information she sought. She could also tell he was having serious reservations about giving it to her. He shifted uncomfortably from foot to foot and after that initial glance would not meet her eyes. He knew, then, that the information he possessed could be dangerous to her and was unwilling to aid her if it meant putting her in harm's way. Well, she would just have to persuade him to cough it up. She needed that information and she wasn't going to let even an expert swordsman stand in her way.

She stopped in front of him, hands on her hips, her eyes and body projecting her determination, proving her resolve. "Well, Charis?" she asked, gazing at him directly.

He said nothing, and still would not look at her. He was definitely going to need some persuasion. She changed tactics. "Charis, listen to me. I've known you almost my entire life. You have helped me and worked with me when no one else would. You've taught me, not just about fighting, but about honor. You've never seen me just as a princess, or a girl, or a woman, or a fighter. You know that I am all those things, and much more. Can you honestly look at me and say you would have me stand by and do nothing? Should the woman I've become, the woman you have helped shape through the years, sit back and let this injustice happen?"

Charis shifted again uncomfortably. "This is different," he said finally, his face set in stubborn lines. "This is not the same as rescuing a kitten, or defending a kitchen drudge against an unfair accusation. This woman... well... there's nothing good that can come of mixing with the likes of her."

"Good? Good for whom?" Aliane's voice rose with outrage. "Good for me? Or good for her? She's a person, salt and stuff it, and I'm going to help her with or without your assistance! I would much prefer to have someone I trust at my back. I don't know what you believe or how you feel about... well... certain things, but I do know you have spent your life defending what you believed was right, putting your life on the line for those who needed you. Would you deny me the same right? I'm not stupid, Charis. And, thanks to you I can take care of myself."

Charis finally raised his eyes to hers, and she was surprised at the emotion she saw in their hazel depths. He had never shown her a great deal of sentiment, but obviously he now struggled with a painful conflict. "I'm thinking there's no one who can take better care of herself than you," he said slowly, and with a certain amount of pride. "I've seen to that, yes, but if you get in the middle of this there's nothing that can protect you. Not me, not your father, not your skills or brains or beauty or status, not anything. If you get caught, it won't matter a lick of salt what I believe! My first duty is to your safety, and the safety of your father."

"Charis, they're going to kill her!" Aliane cried, her self-control slipping. "Just for being what she is! For being *who* she is. I can't just let that happen!"

"I know." Charis was silent for a moment, and Aliane could see the inner battle he fought behind his eyes. He had always made it clear that his first loyalty was to his king, but she had not realized he felt such a strong loyalty towards her as well. She was absurdly touched by the knowledge, and she looked at Charis through eyes brimming with tears. That did it. In all his years of service Charis had never seen his princess shed a single tear, not even as a child when she had been hurt or frustrated or angry with him, and he was not about to be the cause of the first. He sighed, and Aliane knew he would tell her the truth.

"All right. I heard that Larion is meeting that new captain at The Dancing Waters Inn in the north city. That's all I can tell you."

"Today?" Aliane prompted. Charis sighed again and closed his eyes.

"Yes, today. This afternoon." He reached out and gripped her arm. "Aliane, promise me you'll be careful? I know what they can do. I've seen what they can do."

"I will. I promise." She stood on tiptoe and gave him a kiss on the cheek, absurdly touched by his use of her first name. "Thank you Charis. I'll make sure she knows you helped me find her. And I'll be all right, I promise. I'll be careful, and I'll be back before you know it. But this is something I have to do. You understand, don't you?"

Charis grasped her by the shoulders and looked down at her. "Yes, child, I understand. But for the salt of St. Petrius, don't ever tell your father what I've done this day. He would never forgive me for putting you in harm's way." He looked as if it would be a struggle to forgive himself, and Aliane felt a rush of affection for him.

"I promise," she said. "Now, how about a little sword practice before I head to the north city?"

Later that morning, Aliane told her father she was going for a ride and not to expect her back for dinner. Thinking she meant only to trot along the palace trails, he waved to her, saying only, "Make sure you take someone with you, pet." Aliane did not answer, she merely smiled and hugged him. She went to her room and changed into her freshly laundered practice clothes – breeches, shirt, leather boots, jerkin and bracers. She grabbed a sword and a crossbow from Morgan's armory and went out to saddle her father's horse, Frigget. She slung the sword across her back but strapped the crossbow to her saddle. Better to have two buckets when your house is on fire than one, she thought as she grabbed a handful of bolts. She wasn't as good with a crossbow as with a sword, but she felt better knowing she had some extra protection. Aliane felt her heart lighten as she rode through the gates of the courtyard, making her way into north Magir toward information about the only other source of magic she knew existed.

* * *

She found The Dancing Waters without difficulty, though it was a small, quiet inn set away from the noisy street. As she approached, she saw how the tavern had come by its name. The inn was one of several buildings that made up a large square, in the middle of which was a beautiful white marble fountain shaped like a slender young woman dancing down a garden path. Sprays of water from her fingertips flashed through the air and the marble flowers under her feet sent tiny jets of water flying all around the lovely figure. The sunlight reflected off the droplets causing bright, gem-rich colors to flicker here and there, as if they, too, danced with joy on the autumn breeze. Aliane was charmed. It was so beautiful.

She entered the inn and headed for the dining hall. She hoped Larion planned to rendezvous with his new captain there rather than taking a private room for their meeting. It would be awkward indeed if they used a different room. She did not want to be caught snooping outside their door like an eavesdropper. Almost being caught by his father in the same position had been quite bad enough, she thought. Being caught by Larion himself would be infinitely worse.

There were quite a few travelers breaking their journeys in the dining hall, weary from their travels and sitting with drooping, tired heads over their meals. Aliane looked at them with interest as she sat down and wondered who they were and where they were going, where they had been and what they had seen. One man looked to be a merchant, and she thought he could be traveling throughout the land to buy materials and sell his wares. Another man wearing a long black robe with an air of dignified authority might be a magistrate. Two women of middle years sat at a table together – one plump and pretty, the other lean and plain. Aliane speculated as she watched them. Perhaps one was a companion to the other. Or maybe the pretty woman was running away from her husband, or the homely one on her way to a clandestine meeting with her secret lover. Aliane chuckled at the thought. More likely they were on their way to visit a friend or family member in a neighboring town. Aliane turned to look at the other patrons and caught a glimpse of a man who was also scanning the room as if searching for someone. He was sitting away from the others, alone in a corner where the shadows concealed him and he would escape the notice of a casual observer. But once Aliane had seen him, she could not take her eyes off him.

He was the handsomest man she had ever seen. He looked to be only a few years older than she, and what she could see of his body was lithe and strong. His straight, molten gold hair fell to his shoulders and threw back the flickering firelight that touched him even in the shadows. She could not see his face clearly, but what she could see made her breath catch in her throat. He was dressed in plain but expensive-looking clothes, and he, too, appeared to be waiting for someone. Aliane could just imagine the person he was waiting for... he must have a string of lovers as long as the Mountain Pass River.

Just then, as if he had somehow sensed her thoughts, the young man looked in her direction and caught her eye. He smiled at her and Aliane felt her heart give a startled thump. For some inexplicable reason, she shivered as if she had just been touched by something cold.

Aliane quickly lowered her eyes. She struggled to control her breathing. Through her confusion, she couldn't tell if she was excited by the beautiful man's attention or if she wanted to escape it. She glanced up again and saw he was still looking at her, a small smile playing on those chiseled lips. She felt her blood quicken and her heart pounded in her breast. But before she could look again away, the man's attention was diverted to the doorway of the dining lounge, and it was clear from his expression that the person he had been waiting for had arrived. Aliane turned to follow the direction of his gaze, and when she saw the man who had just entered the room, she felt the blood drain from her face.

The man was Prince Larion.

Aliane quickly turned around and looked down at the surface of the table. The beautiful man in the corner must be the new captain that Morgan had instated. The witch hunter. She felt absurdly disappointed. *Of all the people in the city....* She almost felt betrayed, which was silly, she told herself firmly. Just because someone was beautiful on the outside did not mean they were as angelic as their appearance advertised. *Still,* she silently wondered, *why him? Why did it have to be him?*

As the prince approached, she drew the hood of her cloak more closely around her face, fervently hoping Larion wouldn't recognize her. After all, the last time he had seen her she had been wearing her finery, looking as primped and pampered as a princess should. Surely he wouldn't see the pretty princess he had danced with in the picture of the drab peasant girl she fondly believed she posed now. She didn't move as Larion brushed by her table on his way to sit with the handsome man in the corner. Larion had not even looked at her, and Aliane felt a rush of overpowering relief. Larion sat down at the beautiful man's table and soon the two of them were deep in conversation. She took a deep breath, willing herself to stillness, and sharpened her ears to catch the words that floated through the air to become lost in the gabble of voices that hovered between her and the two men. She concentrated, and little by little she was able to filter out those other sounds until she could hear only their voices. They were, she hoped as she listened avidly, as unaware of her presence as they were of her interest.

* * *

Prince Larion eyed the young woman speculatively as he made his way to the table. He wondered what the Princess of Cameon was doing in The Dancing Waters with no chaperone and no entourage. Obviously, Torrit was not with her – he had not seen the royal carriage in the yard, nor had he seen his horses in the stables. She appeared to be quite alone. Very strange. Larion smiled. The innocent, foolish girl, thinking she could deceive him. She had obviously not wished to be recognized, but it would take more than plain clothing and undressed hair to hide the princess Aliane's startling beauty. Her presence was a mystery that would have to wait, however, and he turned to the man sitting across the table from him.

"Captain," he said, bowing stiffly. He did not like the look of the fellow.

"Sire," Jaerak replied, half standing to bow in return. He somehow managed to make the perfectly polite gesture appear rude and insulting. He gestured for Larion to sit, and the prince obliged with poor grace.

"So why did you want to meet here?" Larion asked, signaling a passing server for a drink. "Don't you think meeting at the palace would have been more appropriate?"

Jaerak smiled, the faint white scar on his cheek drawing fine lines from the corner of his mouth. "I had my reasons for wanting to be private."

"Are you saying my father's palace is insecure?"

"Yes." Jaerak waved his questions away. "But that is not important. We have other things to discuss."

Larion swallowed his outrage as the server placed his drink before him, and he waited until the boy had departed before he spoke again.

"I suggest you take care what you say," he said, lifting his glass. "It would be a shame if someone misunderstood your statements and accused you of treason." He took a swallow of his drink and made a face. "Faugh. What is this liquor they serve here? It's vile. Anyway, I received orders from my father to meet you here, so here I am. I've been informed that you are now a commander in the Onnic army. Strange that we have never met before."

"Yes, I am now a Captain." Jaerak replied, ignoring Larion's last, pointed statement. "I've been brought in for a very special task. It is something that will require your... discretion."

Larion narrowed his eyes. "My discretion can always be counted upon."

"Very good. Then I have new orders for you."

"Orders from my father?" Larion asked with surprise. Any orders from King Morgan usually came to him directly.

"No. I shall be relaying your orders to you regarding this matter personally. You need not ask from whom they come."

Larion stirred impatiently, frowning at this deviation from normal protocol. "Very well. The orders?"

Jaerak drew a piece of parchment from his travel cloak and slid it across the table to Larion. "In this letter you will find the name and description of a woman. When next I contact you, you are to proceed to the Lake Point and wait for her there."

Larion stared at the other man in disbelief. He broke open the seal of the parchment and read the contents of the letter. As promised, it contained one name – Gwynne Davanir. He read aloud, "...a woman of middle years, graying brown hair, stout, with burn marks on her face and body." He looked up in confusion.

"I'm not sure I understand," he began.

Jaerak frowned. "It is very simple. Upon my orders, you and a legion of your men are to go to the Lake Point and wait for this woman." Jaerak tapped the parchment where it rested on the table. "When she arrives, she will very likely have someone with her. A woman. You and your men shall detain them, but will make sure, with your lives, that no harm comes to them. I and my men will not be far behind, and when we arrive, we shall take them into our custody."

"Wait just a moment," Larion said furiously, pushing the parchment away from him in a gesture of rejection. "Are you telling me that you want me to take a legion of men into the far north in winter and... and *wait* for this person? And then just hand her over to you?"

"And whoever she might have with her," Jaerak reminded him harshly.

Larion picked up the parchment read it again. Then, he contemptuously tossed the paper down onto the table. "You do not need me for this... this nursemaid's task! I can station four good men there, I'm sure they would be able to handle one old woman, even if she does have someone with her."

Jaerak's eyes glittered dangerously, and Larion suddenly felt the hair on his arms stand on end.

"No," Jaerak said slowly, as if speaking to a man who lacked wit. "This is no nursemaid's task. I need seasoned men there, and you are one of the best. This woman and her companion must... *must* not be allowed to escape. Do not underestimate them, Prince. They are very, very dangerous."

"They must truly be witches, then," Larion said, his interest quickening.

He had thought his father had fed him a load of pigswaddle when he had started talking about Seekers and magic users. If he were to apprehend a witch, it would prove to his father that his trust and responsibility were not misplaced. Magic users were getting harder and harder to find, and it would raise his credibility considerably if he could claim to have captured one – or better yet, two! King Morgan might even be persuaded to raise his rank in the army and he could then perhaps pay off some of those troublesome debts he owed. He lowered his voice and whispered, "Are they to be tried? And how do you know they will go to the Lake Point?"

Jaerak got to his feet. "You shall not ask any questions. When I send word, you will do as you are ordered. You will stay in Magir until I contact you. When I do, you shall take your legion to the Lake of Chaos and wait for the woman... or women... to arrive. You are to hold them in your custody until I arrive. Then you shall be given new orders. You are not to discuss your orders with anyone. Is that understood?"

Larion bridled at the Captain's tone, but he held his temper in check. Now was not the time to confront this dangerous man, and he was dangerous, of that he was sure. That time would come later, and when it did it would give him great pleasure to hurt him very much indeed. There was something bigger going on here, and Larion was determined to discover what it was. He would use his patience and discretion while necessary, for he was far from a stupid man. He took another swig of his drink and his mouth twisted at the taste.

"Yes, Captain," he said, his voice level, giving away nothing. "I understand completely. I will assemble my men immediately and await your further orders."

"Very good." Jaerak sat down again and leaned back in his chair, evidently satisfied. "You shall make your father proud."

Larion's lips twitched. "That," he said, spitting out the words with angry precision, "would be a feat indeed."

Jaerak smiled without humor. "Perhaps you can take a message for me back to the palace. To the Cathedral, actually." He took another rolled up piece of parchment from his carrysack. "This must go to the hands of Masyl Vonnin, and no other. Can you oblige me?"

Larion burned with silent anger. First a nursemaid, and now a delivery boy! It cost him dearly to hold his temper in check, but he managed it. He took the parchment.

"I'll see that he gets it." Larion rose. "Now, I have some business to attend to on a more personal note. If you will excuse me?" It gave him great satisfaction to take his leave of this odious man before he had been dismissed. Jaerak only barked out a short laugh.

"Indeed," he said, smiling. "Ah, the lovely maid you were watching so closely earlier. I saw her myself, and must admit I was intrigued. That sort of beauty is rare, and must be coveted when it is found. If you hurry, you might catch her. She left several minutes ago."

Larion bowed at the waist, as short an inclination as courtesy allowed, and strode towards the doorway. As he approached it, Jaerak's voice, calling his name, halted him. He turned to see the man watching him through narrowed, icy eyes.

"Remember, Prince Larion," he said, his tone making a subtle mockery of the title, "if anything happens to those women before I get to the Lake Point, I will personally take it out of your hide. Trust me when I say you would not find my displeasure pleasant."

Larion again bent his head a mere fraction and whirled to stalk out of the room. Jaerak's mocking laughter followed him, and he heard one last parting shot as he headed for the front door. "Enjoy the maid, my prince. She's the last you'll see for some time."

The man missed nothing! He had not seen Aliane leave, but Jaerak obviously had. He left the inn and emerged into the crowded street. Looking around, he could not see the princess anywhere. Well, he thought, tucking the message parchment into the pocket of his jacket, he would see her again at the castle before he left on this ridiculous mission and demand to know what she had been doing there. If he were expected to marry the wench, she would have to understand that she could no longer behave in a manner unbecoming his station.

He turned to walk towards the stables and collided with an urchin who was charging down the street with absolutely no regard for the safety of others. Larion managed to regain his balance, and the sharp blow he aimed at the boy missed as the child ducked in a practiced maneuver and sprinted away. His vile humor increased. If children could not behave themselves, they should be collared and chained like dogs until they learned a little respect. He fastidiously brushed off his coat and entered the stables. He would have a few words to say to his father about this assignment. He was too valuable a soldier to waste up in the north waiting for a couple of women! But he had been told not to discuss his orders with anyone. Surely, that did not include his father? But perhaps he should hold his tongue. If the women were witches he might find a way to use them to his advantage, and how sweet it would be to serve them up to his father as a surprise. His thoughts became blacker and blacker as he mounted his steed and rode towards the Cathedral to deliver the captain's message.

* * *

Aliane grinned and dropped a silver penny into the urchin's outstretched hand. He grinned back, gave her the scroll she had seen Larion tucking into his jerkin as he exited The Dancing Waters and darted away, quickly becoming lost in the crowd.

Aliane had not seen the beautiful man give Larion the parchment, but he had been holding it when he emerged from the darkened doorway of the inn. She had thought it would be wise to disappear before the men decided to leave, but some instinct had prompted her to hide herself in the crowd and watch for their departure. She was glad she had, and the urchin had been more than willing to earn an extra penny for a bit of pickpocketing. She broke the seal on the paper, experiencing a small qualm of conscience. It felt strange to read someone else's personal message, but the information she read was enough to dispel any guilt she might have felt. She smiled to herself. This was working out beautifully, better even than she had planned.

Her exultation received a check, however, as she saw the beautiful, golden-haired man leave The Dancing Waters. Seen clearly in the daylight she realized he was not as unflawed as she had originally thought. She was able to see an ugly scar that stretched from his left earlobe to the corner of his mouth, but even that imperfection failed to diminish the impact of his astounding beauty. She felt again that sharp stab of regret as she realized he fought alongside those she detested, commanded those she opposed. *Such a shame*, she thought, shaking her head. She could have sworn some communication or understanding had occurred between them in that all too-brief glance across the crowded room. But it was not to be. It was with no small regret that Aliane led Frigget away, turning from the man who had so fascinated her without ever having spoken a word.

"And as the Eye of Truth shall see, so shall she be blinded by evil and saved by the grace of Magick. So shall she save us all."
– From the Prophesies of the Eye of Truth

Chapter Eight

Gwynne awoke in that most dreary, most depressing and unnerving time of day, pre-dawn. She lay in the darkness of her room, blinking and disoriented, trying to remember the dream that had woken her from the fitful slumber into which she had finally fallen after a long and restless night. It had been one of those maddening nightmares where the terror is so real, almost tangible – she could feel it, taste it, smell it, touch it. Her heart hammered so hard in her chest it felt as if it would burst, and she could feel the blood coursing through her veins so rapidly that her body tingled with it. She could feel every nerve in her body stand to attention as she had fought to tame the panic that threatened to overwhelm her. But the cause of her fear was unknown; there was danger, she just didn't know from where or what or who. Somehow that was the most terrifying part of all.

She remembered being pursued by some unknown entity, soundless, mindless, soulless, relentless. No matter how fast she could run the thing – whatever it was – could run faster, and she knew it would not stop until it had seized her. She felt her lungs laboring and tears of terror blinding her as she ran through a nameless wood, dodging dark and forbidding trees, her feet pounding on the forest floor. Just as she had run all those years ago when her parents had died at the hands of Onnic. Just as she had run many times since from dangers she knew as intimately as she knew her true name. And in her dream, just as she felt a clawed hand reach out to grasp her, she had fought her way to the surface of wakefulness, just as a drowning woman struggles through deadly waters to reach life-giving air.

She woke as she sat bolt upright in bed, her hand at her throat, drawing long gasps of air into her tight lungs. As her heart slowed to its normal rate, her eyes adjusted to the darkness and she was able to look around. The room was still in shadow, and the embryonic rays of morning light had not yet stretched out their fingers to touch her window. The heavy furnishings of the room hunkered like squat shadows against the narrow walls, and for a moment she could not remember where she was. Then recollection came flooding back. Today was the day she and Thalan planned to leave Magir. No wonder her dreams had been troubled, she thought as she got out of bed and went to the basin to splash some icy water on her face. Goosebumps popped out all over her damaged skin as the cold air wrapped its insidious tentacles around her body. She shivered, and hurried to put on some warm clothes.

She and Thalan had spent three days at the Fox and Falcon, and had decided it would not be safe to tarry longer. Telma's oil, judiciously applied, quickly healed Gwynne's burns, so she felt confident she would tolerate the trip well. She only wished she felt as confident about the outcome of their journey as she did about its inception. But now that she had a traveling companion, she felt much more secure. With Thalan there to watch her back, Jaerak couldn't sneak up behind her and bury a knife in it. She was grateful to the young man for throwing in his lot with her, even after she had warned him of the dangers. She only hoped he realized the true gravity of their situation.

After much discussion the night before, they had decided to travel south towards Marrin. If the Eye of Truth were to be found anywhere it would most likely be in Rhyssl's kingdom, which was quickly becoming known as a safe haven for magic users. Rhyssl el'Faria was a young queen, and the unexpected death of her mother several years before had put the young, untried, unmarried Rhyssl on the throne long before she had expected the honor. These circumstances aside, she had done remarkably well. After she had ascended the throne, rumors had begun to circulate that she was a Seeker sympathizer, and people whispered that she would offer protection to any mage who came to her realm. Her reputation had incurred the love and loyalty of many people as well as the uncompromising hatred of King Morgan.

Gwynne and Thalan would therefore head for the city of Freath, which was said to be heavily enforced by Rhyssl's soldiers, and perhaps there they could meet up with other Seekers. Along the way they could listen to rumor and hear the news from the ships that traveled up and down the Freath River.

Gwynne finished her ablutions and put the remainder of her belongings in her carrysack, closing it tightly when she was finished. Thalan had taken a room at the inn the previous night so they could leave at an early hour, and his room was several doors down and across the hall from hers. She rather doubted Thalan was awake yet – he had shown himself to be sluggish and slow to waken in the early morning. Therefore, she gave the coverlet one last tweak to smooth it out and stepped into the silent, darkened corridor, noiselessly moving towards Thalan's room so she could get him up. The inn was quiet, and even the morning cooks had not roused themselves to begin baking the bread for breakfast.

The corridor was colder than her room and a fresh crop of goose bumps broke out along her arms. The early morning hush was rather eerie after the habitual noise and revelry in the evenings, and Gwynne found herself peering into the shadows as if they shrouded something that watched her, something that waited for her. She took a firm grip on her overactive imagination and hurried down the hall to knock on Thalan's door.

There was no response. She was not surprised. Thalan was truly a sound sleeper, Gwynne thought as she knocked again, louder this time. Almost like an echo of her own knocking, she heard a pounding noise from downstairs. She froze, her fist flat against Thalan's door, listening like an animal that has just caught the scent of some deadly predator. The sound came again. Someone was battering on the front door of the inn, a peremptory rapping that demanded immediate entrance. Gwynne again felt icy tendrils grip her body, but this time the cold came from within as she heard voices, now audible from the street. This was not a single traveler seeking shelter from the cold, but a group of men intent, purposeful, and commanding instant attention. Before she could formulate another coherent thought, she was through Thalan's door and shaking him awake.

"Wha...?" Thalan opened his eyes and looked at her fuzzily. "Whazzat? What's happening?" he asked, the fog of sleep clearing as he looked up at her frantic face and frightened eyes.

"Men. Outside. On the street. They're coming." As she spoke, the words coming in staccato little bursts with a voice she hardly recognized as her own, she was throwing Thalan's possessions, which had been strewn about the room in cheerful disarray, into his sack. Thalan jumped out of bed, heedless of his nudity, and began putting on his clothes, fully alert now. "I'm not sure who they are, but I think they might mean trouble," Gwynne continued, taking no notice of Thalan's bare skin. "Trouble for us."

Thalan pulled his shirt over his head and reached for the sack that Gwynne held out to him. He looked at her intently. "Do you think it might be Jaerak? Do you think he's found you?"

"I don't know. Get your boots on." Gwynne tossed his battered footwear in his general direction and went to the doorway, her ears straining as she listened. The knocking had produced the desired results. She heard a sleepy voice demanding to know what was going on, and the voices of the men had grown louder. "Whoever they are, they're inside now. We have to get out of here!"

Thalan fished a boot out from under the bed, put it on, and finished lacing them. He went to the window, moving as softly as a prowling cat. He cracked one of the shutters and peered out into the cold, dark morning. His room was situated at the front of the inn, and his window looked out upon the main street below. He paled visibly, and even in the dimness of the room Gwynne could see he was shaken. "Onnic," he said, his voice hard. "It looks like a whole party of them. It may be a routine inspection, but that would be something of a coincidence, don't you think? Why pick this particular inn, on this particular morning? It must be Jaerak. He's found you."

"Yes." Gwynne's mind raced, and she had the sinking feeling that the predator had just trapped its prey. "They'll be blocking the exits. How will we get out? If they are here for us, er... for me, I mean, then we can't let them see us."

The noise from downstairs was louder now, and they both could hear men's voices raised in official, strident tones. Another man seemed to be arguing with them, his voice raised in angry protest. Koris. Naturally he would object if the Onnic soldiers wanted to disturb his guests. "I hope Telma is down there," she muttered, thinking furiously. "Even an entire Onnic legion would have a time getting past her and her tongue. Quick, we need to figure out a way out of here."

"We have to get to the stables," Thalan said, running a hand through his hair, making his disheveled curls stick up in wild tufts. "We won't get very far without the horses, and all our provisions are there. Maybe we can escape through one of the back windows. Your room faces the back, doesn't it?"

"The windows are rather high," Gwynne said doubtfully. "I'm not sure..."

"What would you prefer, a broken bone or two, or capture? We don't have many options here." Thalan's voice was harsh, but Gwynne did not take his tone personally. He had every reason to be afraid. Thalan snatched up the rest of his belongings, grabbed Gwynne by the hand and led her out into the corridor.

Once in Gwynne's room, he went directly to the window. Gwynne closed the door behind her, dropped their packs on her bed and peered over Thalan's shoulder. The ground seemed awfully far away, but at least no Onnic stood waiting for them at the bottom.

Before either of them could move, however, Telma herself burst in through the door and the room suddenly appeared to shrink as it accommodated her bulk. She saw that both of them were up and dressed and nodded with approval. "Good. Now come with me, we have to get you out of here." Gwynne and Thalan gaped at her, and she snorted with exasperation. "Well, don't just stand there gawping at me like kunga-fish!

I'm not sure how long Koris can delay them. Follow me if you want to get out of here!" And with that, she disappeared into the corridor.

Gwynne and Thalan stared at each other for a moment, then Gwynne snatched up her carryall, Thalan grabbed his cloak, and they ran after the portly innkeeper. The inn was rousing now as servants and stewards banged on the doors of the rooms. Sleepy and disgruntled guests were milling about the corridor asking angry questions and demanding to know what was going on. Gwynne and Thalan caught up with Telma in time to see her grab one of the stewards and say, "Get as many people up as you can. Get them out of their rooms, the more people the better. Try to get some of them downstairs, and get Kane and Frist to block the upper landing. I want this place full of angry, confused people, and I don't want those Onnic to get up here. Now move!" She glanced back and motioned to Gwynne to follow her. Grabbing Thalan by the arm, Gwynne slipped among the growing throng of guests gathering aimlessly about the corridor and went after her.

Telma stopped at the end of the corridor in front of what looked like a large linen cabinet. They were at the end of the upstairs hallway, the greatest distance from the head of the stairs, but Gwynne knew they had very little time. She could now hear sounds of confusion coming from the commons room below. Some of the guests had gone downstairs and the angry voices of the soldiers shouted questions and barked orders. Soon they would be here, despite Telma and Koris's delaying tactics, and all sounds were suddenly drowned out by a voice in Gwynne's head whispering *hurry, hurry, hurry, hurry*, as if she could will Telma's hands to greater speed with mere thought. Telma pulled a large key ring from her apron pocket and quickly searched for the key she wanted. *Hurry, hurry, hurry, hurry*. Thalan pulled his dagger from its sheath and kept a lookout. *Hurry*. The loud voices were nearing the stairs, and Gwynne's breath caught in her throat. *Hurry!* Telma found the key she needed and unlocked the cabinet door.

It was not a linen closet, but a dark, narrow flight of stairs that led downwards into blackness. Telma thrust a candle and a box of matches into Gwynne's nerveless hands. "Take these. Go all the way down. It leads to the cellar. You will come across a landing with a door, but don't open it, that leads to the kitchen. The stairs continue down from the landing and you will come out in a storeroom in the cellar. In the wall on the other side of the room is a door that will lead you to the stables."

The soldiers were on the stairs now, and they were trying to get past the guests who were gathered at the top landing, curiously and fearfully looking down at the commotion. Two of the serving men that Gwynne had seen in the commons room were standing at the top of the stairs creating a barricade.

Gwynne could hear them talking to someone, and angry voices demanded they stand aside. Thalan stepped into the stairwell and began to pull Gwynne in after him. She handed the candle and matches to him, and then turned to Telma.

"I have to ask, before we go," she said breathlessly. "How did you know?"

Telma smiled at her. "I didn't, but as soon as I heard them ask Koris about an older woman with gray hair and burns on her face, I knew you were in trouble. I couldn't let them..."

"Irena!" Thalan hissed. Gwynne was impressed he could remember her assumed name under such stressful conditions. "We don't have time for this! Let's go! Hurry!"

Hurry. Gwynne gave Telma's hand one last squeeze. "Thank you," she whispered, and started down the stairs after Thalan. The darkness suddenly swallowed them as Telma banged the door closed, and Gwynne heard the click of the key as she once again locked it. Thalan scraped the match along the stone wall until it flared to life with a puff of sulfur smoke, and held the tiny flame to the wick of the candle. Soon, the stairway was illuminated, though the dancing flame of the candle created weird, uncanny shadows that moved and shifted in the feeble light. Gwynne realized she would have to be extremely careful if she didn't want to end up with some broken bones after all, despite the fact there was no longer any need to jump out of second-story windows.

The stone steps were steep and narrow, and Gwynne had to support herself on the wall to keep her balance as she and Thalan went as quickly as they could down the steps. Tiny skeletons of long-dead mice and other grisly objects Gwynne preferred not to think about scattered and crunched under their flying feet. They came to the landing that led into the kitchen, and found the next flight of stairs leading down into more blackness. Breathlessly, they made their way down the stairs until they came to a heavy wooden door. Gwynne put her hand to the handle and pushed. The door did not budge.

"It's locked," she whispered to Thalan. She could feel panic rising in her breast. "What do we do now?"

"Try pulling it," Thalan suggested, his voice muffled with amusement. Gwynne shot him a dirty look but tugged at the door handle nonetheless. It still would not move.

"Move aside," Thalan said, opening his sack. He rummaged through his belongings and pulled out a little leather case. He opened the case and extracted two curious-looking objects. They looked like long, slender silver sticks, and one of them had a hook on the end. Thalan handed her the candle.

"Hold this so I can see what I'm doing." He bent over the lock and inserted one of the silver instruments into the keyhole, and then the other. He jiggled the strange, straight metal stick carefully, closing his eyes as if his sense of touch superseded the necessity of sight. It finally dawned on Gwynne what he was doing.

"Lockpicks?" she asked incredulously. "Where by the Eye did you ever learn to do that?"

Thalan's breath came out in a silent puff of laughter. "I didn't tell you *everything* about myself, you know. Magic isn't my only talent. Hold on, I almost have it. Salt and stuff it! The bloody lock is rusted." Gwynne leaned over him to see what he was doing, and a drop of the hot candle wax fell on his hand. "Ow!" he cried, shaking it off. "Be careful with that thing. Oop! There we go." He turned the hooked lockpick and pushed the door open. He took the candle from Gwynne and preceded her into a room that was filled with cobwebs, empty barrels and wooden crates. A pile of sacking was stacked in a corner, and Gwynne could vaguely make out the indistinct shapes of discarded tables and broken chairs. Thalan crossed the room in three long strides and started searching for the door that led to the stables. Gwynne spotted it behind a pile of rubble, and they spent what seemed like an eternity clearing a space large enough for them to open the door. Obviously no one had come this way in a long, long time. The commotion upstairs seemed to be heating up, and Gwynne could hear shouts and loud banging noises, as if someone were throwing the furniture about in a fit of temper. She nudged Thalan and whispered, "Hurry."

They squeezed through the doorway and found themselves in a long, dark passageway. After about twenty paces or so, the avenue began to slope upwards, and eventually they came to another door. This door was also locked, but Thalan easily opened it with his lockpicks. They slid through the opening and the smell of horses and musty hay tickled Gwynne's nose, making her want to sneeze. They had made it to the stables.

The candlelight flickered eerily, throwing ghostly shadows and dancing lights. A horse made a whuffling sound in its sleep, and further down another stamped its foot. The quiet, normal noises of the stable made Gwynne relax, and she unclenched stiffened fingers she did not remember tightening. Thalan began saddling their horses while Gwynne crept to the stable doors and peered out through a crack in the slats. What she saw made her throat close in terror.

The doorway to the inn was still open, and the lights from inside spilled out onto the street. There were five men standing outside the inn, all of them wearing red cloaks with the Onnic insignia, two swords crossed over an eye with a teardrop-shaped iris, embroidered on the collar. There were several more Onnic still inside, and she could hear the shouts from the officers and the sounds of fear from the guests. A woman screamed, and Gwynne closed her eyes, as if by doing so she could shut out the madness altogether. When she opened them again, six men stood on the street talking amongst themselves.

The sixth man was Jaerak Thorin.

Gwynne held her breath, and her hands involuntarily clenched around the wood so hard she nearly cried out with the pain. He looked just as he had in the City of Circles. Somehow she thought his monstrous actions would have left a physical mark on him, but the only thing she saw was the pale scar on his face where her best porcelain vase had cut him when it broke. She was thankful for that small reminder; it might have been too easy to fall under the spell of his angelic face and charm once again. She had forgotten how truly beautiful he was.

Gwynne focused her thoughts and took another look outside. Jaerak appeared to be in charge – he seemed to be giving orders to the others. Then she saw, with a new clarity of vision, the Onnic insignia on the collar of his green cloak that pronounced him a Captain of the Guards in the Onnic Order. Suddenly the sight of him, that Onnic symbol, his golden hair and straight, supple body filled her with unspeakable rage. How dare he look so calm and beautiful when he was capable of such evil? Why couldn't *he* have the burn scars on his face and body, marks that would reflect the deformity of his soul and spirit? Gwynne took a deep breath and forced herself to relax her grip on the doorframe, willed her mind and body to be calm. She had known this was going to happen. She just had not expected it to happen so soon.

The Onnic soldiers accompanying Jaerak suddenly bowed their heads and touched their foreheads. They all then went inside the Fox and Falcon, leaving Jaerak standing in the street alone, watching. He must have spoken to the guard at the checkpoint, Gwynne thought, the one who had directed her to the Fox and Falcon. The guard must have told Jaerak which inn he had recommended to her. She certainly hoped he had, anyway. She did not want to think he planned to barge into every tavern and boarding house in the city, rousting all the sleeping guests searching for her. Thalan was almost finished with the horses, and he was loading their carryalls into the saddlebags. Just as Gwynne was about to turn away and join him, Jaerak turned his head and looked straight at her.

A shock of adrenaline shot through Gwynne's body. She froze, as a rabbit hopes to convince the wolf that if it does not move, it cannot be seen. The moment seemed to last an eternity. Time and motion stopped for one brief instant, etched in her mind like a woodcarving, engraved in one static, amaranthine moment in time. The rational part of her mind told her that Jaerak could not possibly see her, but his eyes seemed to bore into her own and a small, mocking smile played across his lips. *I know you are there*, he seemed to be saying. *I know you, and you are mine.*

He turned away, and walked into the inn.

Gwynne blinked salty, stinging sweat from her eyes. He could not have seen her. He could not have. He would have sounded an alarm if he had. He would have opened the stable doors, would have caught her, trapped her, and captured her, just to prove that the wolf cannot fooled by a foolish rabbit's tricks. She must have imagined that knowing expression, the almost intimate smile, the directness of his gaze. It was a trick of the light, an overactive imagination fueled by fear and strain. It must have been her imagination. It must have been.

She almost jumped out of her skin when Thalan laid a hand on her shoulder. "What is it?" he whispered. "What's going on out there?"

Gwynne swallowed, and raised a shaking hand to her throat. She opened her mouth, but no sound emerged. She swallowed again, and managed to croak, "It's clear. We have to go now. They'll be coming back any second." She made her way to Milyn and checked the saddle to make sure it was secure.

Before she could say or do another thing, she heard the creak of the stable door slowly opening. She dropped her candle and whirled around in a panic, her heart beating so fast she was sure it would leap right out of her chest. *He's come back*, she thought, despair tugging at her with insistent hands. *He did see me*. Thalan instinctively thrust her back, guarding her with his body, his dagger in his hand. The figure in the doorway took another slow step inside and then halted. Thalan and Gwynne simultaneously saw the intruder more clearly, and surprise and wonder stilled their tongues.

A young woman stood before them, peering into the shadows of the stables as if searching for something. The candle had gone out when Gwynne had dropped it in her fear and surprise, so she appeared only as a silhouette in the open door, outlined against the spreading streaks of light that slowly leached the darkness from the morning sky. Gwynne could not make out her features, but some instinct told her they had nothing to fear from her. The lines of the woman's body, her stance, her slightly rapid breath all indicated she meant them no harm. She appeared hesitant, as if unsure of her welcome, but her clasped hands and tight shoulders testified her need for haste. Her form was slim and graceful, obviously female despite the fact that her hair had been drawn away from her face and she was wearing trousers. The young woman took several more tentative steps into the stable and finally spoke.

"Hello?" Her voice was the merest whisper of sound. "Are you there? I heard voices... I thought I saw a light... don't be afraid, I'm here to help you."

It was only then Gwynne realized that the woman could not see them. They were far back in the stables, and the shadows for once worked in their favor. She put a restraining hand on Thalan's arm, silently urging him not to make a sound as she gathered a tiny thread of power from the earth, the wooden posts of the horse stalls, the hay that was strewn across the stable floor.

The woman advanced farther into the stable. Her voice was still low, but urgency saturated her words. "If you are here, please know I only wish to help. I can help you get out, and there isn't much time." Silence, and Gwynne could hear the crackle of straw as the woman nervously shifted her weight from foot to foot. Quickly, Gwynne focused the little trickle of magic she had summoned and sent out a gentle mind probe. The spell found its target, unblocked and unshielded. It was true. The woman only wanted to help, though for the life of the Eye, Gwynne could not figure out why. Perhaps even the woman herself did not know. Gwynne was quite sure, though she could not see her face, that the woman was a stranger to her. Gwynne moved forward, evading Thalan's frantic, ineffectual grab for her, and approached the woman, who looked considerably startled by her sudden emergence from the shadows.

The woman before her was small, but beautifully proportioned. She had a trim figure and glorious dark hair that was caught up and tucked under a riding cap. She was young, mid-twenties or so, and her stance had a regal bearing. A rare beauty, Gwynne thought, subtle and honest. This was no farmer's wife or merchant's daughter. As soon as she saw Gwynne, the stranger's eyes lit up, and she looked utterly charming.

"It really is you," she breathed, reaching out her hand to touch her as if she were afraid an apparition rather than flesh and blood stood before her. An expression of wonder touched her gentle face. "You're real, and you're here. You look just like they said you would."

"They said?" Gwynne asked gently, taking the small hand in her own. It was cold, and for a moment the young woman clutched her as if to a lifeline. "Who said? Who told you we would be here?"

The woman shook herself as if only just remembering her purpose. "I've come to help you. Please, we must hurry. They won't be long."

"Who are you?" Thalan asked, coming up behind Gwynne. The woman jumped and squeaked, startled by his unexpected appearance. Apparently, she had expected Gwynne to be alone. "Who won't be long?"

"There isn't time," she said breathlessly, giving Thalan a reproachful look for having startled her. "I must get you out of here." She ran to the stable door and peered out. "They are still inside, but we'd better not take any chances."

To Gwynne's utter astonishment, the woman lifted her hands and began to weave an intricately patterned spell-web between her fingers. She felt again that shivery, seductively sensual feeling in her bones that responded to magic. By squinting hard, she could discern the thin rays of amber light entwined around her hands, and Gwynne recognized the design as a protective spell of Air. The woman quickly finished weaving the spell-web and cast it upon Thalan, Gwynne, the horses and herself, binding them together with a single strand that appeared to have no beginning and no end. Those it bound together could still see each other, but they would be invisible to anyone outside the complicated matrix of light and shadow. Gwynne reached out a shaking hand to touch the gossamer tawny line crisscrossed around her, no thicker than the filament from a spider's web, though she knew her fingers would pass right through the intangible light. Magic. The girl worked magic. Gwynne's numbed brain tried to assimilate the importance of this discovery, but she was having difficulty thinking straight. She had found a woman who worked magic. Or, to be more precise, a woman who worked magic had somehow found her.

"That should do it," the woman said, nodding with satisfaction. "They won't be able to see us now. That's one of the only spells I know, and fortunately I'd practiced it often enough on myself, but it won't last long. They tend to wear off. We must leave now. Hurry, please!"

Responding automatically to the urgency in her voice, Gwynne ran towards Milyn, nudging Thalan, who was standing with his mouth open in astonishment. Thalan jerked as if shocked, and after one last stare at the young woman, clambered up onto his horse. The spell-web flexed and stretched with their movement, but did not break, and Gwynne marveled at the skill that had gone into its making. The strange woman eased the stable doors open and beckoned them to follow her.

"My own horse is hidden a few streets down from here," she whispered. "Once we are safe, I'll tell you everything. Come now, hurry!"

Hurry. The silent voice in Gwynne's head reinforced the woman's words, and she quickly mounted Milyn. Silently following the stranger, she and Thalan urged their horses into the deserted street. Harsh light drifted from the open door of the Fox and Falcon, and shying away from the glow as a thief shuns the lamplight, they stole their way down the street and became lost in the sleepy shadows of the city.

* * *

Jaerak looked over the people gathered in the commons room with satisfaction. His eyes passed disinterestedly over the overturned tables and broken chairs, not seeing the torn and splintered planks that were once the music platform, or the broken bottles that lay shattered on the floor. He did not see the fear in their faces, or the anger in their eyes. He did not notice the blood and bruises on those who had gotten in the way of his soldiers as they conducted their brutal and thorough search. He did not even look when one of the Onnic soldiers dragged away the limp body of a steward, his face a twisted mass of bone and blood and flesh, nor did he seem to hear the cries of the frightened women or the groans of the injured men. All he saw was the success of his plans, the first victory of his journey towards the ultimate power. The small, derisive smile touched his lips again, but there was no answering spark of emotion in his eyes.

Three Onnic soldiers entered the room, two of them with prisoners. They held a small man with a wispy mustache and a heavy woman whose brightly hennaed hair was in wild disarray, her dressing gown torn, revealing pallid rolls of naked flesh. There was a bruise on her cheek, but her mouth was set in a firm line, and her eyes snapped with anger rather than fear. One of the soldiers stood at attention in front of Jaerak and touched his forehead in the age-old salute.

"She was seen here, sir," the soldier said. "She had a room on the upper floor, but we found no trace of her. She must have gotten away. They," he indicated Koris and Telma, "will not tell me when she left. A guest saw her here just last night. She was talking to a man, I gather. So these two must have helped her get away. She wouldn't have left so early, otherwise."

Jaerak glanced at Telma. "You are sure they are not here?" he asked the soldier.

"They, sir?" The soldier looked confused.

"You said she had been talking with a man. Is that man still here?"

"I... I don't know, sir, but I'll find out." The soldier hurried away to question the guests once more. Soon he was back, panting for breath as if he had just run a great distance.

"He was one of the musicians, sir. He seems to have disappeared as well, but that doesn't mean anything. He might not have been staying here at all. Musicians often play more than one inn a night, and no one knows if he had a room here."

"And you are sure you searched the entire area for her?" Jaerak already knew the answer, but he asked it anyway. The men would think it strange if he did not ask the usual questions. He would at least have to act like a Captain, if only to ensure and strengthen his position and their loyalty.

"We tore the place apart looking for her, sir," the soldier said. "We found a staircase that led to the kitchens and the cellar. She must have gotten out that way. There was another door, open, that led to the stables. I can't imagine how she got past us, sir. She must have witched her way out. She certainly isn't here now."

"Thank you, Onnic, that will do." The soldier touched his forehead again and retreated. Jaerak finally moved, walking over to stand in front of Telma and Koris.

"Yes, she was here, wasn't she," Jaerak said in a mild tone, fingering a strand of his golden hair. "And you helped her escape, didn't you?" Koris wouldn't meet his eyes, but Telma regarded him steadily, and if she felt any fear for herself or her husband, she managed to disguise it. Jaerak smiled. "Do you know the punishment for harboring a magic user in Casset? Ah, I see you did not know she had magic, did you?" he said as Telma's eyes widened, and the first hint of fear crept into her face. "You thought perhaps she had avoided paying her taxes? Or that she had stolen something? You thought she was a harmless old lady, and you didn't want to see her get hurt." Telma's eyes finally dropped. Questioning her further was useless. She obviously had not known.

"Shall we take them into custody, sir?" one of the soldiers asked.

"No, I think not," said Jaerak thoughtfully. "We can put them to much better use." He glanced around the room, frowning. "Where is the High Priest, Masyl Vonnin?"

"Sir?" The Onnic soldier appeared startled by his question.

"He is not here?"

"No sir. Shall I fetch him for you?"

"Strange," Jaerak murmured. "I wrote to him... yes. Yes, fetch him here at once." The officer snapped his fingers and one of the younger soldiers went running from the room, intent on his errand.

Jaerak wondered why Masyl had ignored his message. Surely the thickheaded prince had given it to him. Shrugging, he dismissed the matter from his mind and for the first time seemed to notice all the other people in the room. He beckoned to a corporal.

"Sir?" the man said, hurrying over to his side.

"Corporal, make sure all these people get outside. Let them pick up their belongings from their rooms, and then take them all out." He went to stand in front of Telma and Koris, both of whom now trembled in fear. "You two, I'm afraid, must stay here. We have to send a strong message, you know."

Jaerak beckoned to a soldier and ordered him to bind them to a support post. Koris began babbling, begging, bribing the guards while Telma sat dumbly with tears streaming down her face. She did not struggle, and she did not say a word.

Jaerak walked to the doorway and stood on the front step, looking at the encroaching dawn. The sunrise was a vast palette of color, fiery streaks of orange and red and pink streaked across the canvas of the morning sky. Jaerak smiled, and turned to look at the Fox and Falcon. One of the soldiers came to stand beside him.

"Then she really was here, sir?" he asked. Jaerak did not look at him.

"Yes."

"And she got away?"

"Yes."

The soldier made an impatient noise. "So what do we do now?"

Jaerak pulled his cloak more tightly around his body and made his way out onto the street. He swung himself into his saddle and turned to face the young soldier, and the expression on his face made even the Onnic shudder. Jaerak looked at the inn one last time, that strange half-smile again on his lips.

"Burn it."

"Trust your instincts. They usually know something you don't."

– Common Marrindian saying.

Chapter Nine

"It's going to snow soon," Thalan said to no one in particular as he pulled his cloak closer around his shivering body.

It didn't take magic to figure that out, Aliane thought to herself, glancing at the gray, oppressive clouds that had shrouded the blue, sunny sky from their sight all afternoon. The wind tugged at her clothes like a rambunctious puppy that failed to understand that his master didn't want to play, and she irritably caught the flapping hem of her cloak and tucked it under her thigh. She glanced at her companions, wondering when they were going to stop, when they were going to ask her the questions she knew they were burning to ask, when she could find out where they were going and when would they get there. She had a thousand other questions, not the least of which was when were they going to light a fire so she could feel her frozen fingers again?

She still couldn't believe her fragile and spontaneous, though ill-wrought, plan had actually succeeded. The day after she had overheard the conversation between Larion and the fascinatingly beautiful man, she had hurried before dawn to the Fox and Falcon – that was the name of the inn written on the parchment the urchin had pinched from the Prince Larion. The message, addressed to Masyl Vonnin, had asked the High Priest to arrive early the next morning at the Fox and Falcon, where their quarry was to be flushed out into the open. It had taken her some time to remember where she had heard Masyl Vonnin's name before, and she received quite a jolt when her memory finally placed him as the second man in the treacherous conversation with King Morgan that had so incensed her all those weeks ago. That day seemed like an eternity gone after all that had happened since.

Aliane had arrived at the Fox and Falcon to find it overrun with Onnic soldiers, and for one heart-stopping moment she had thought she was too late. The beautiful man had been there, too. Jaerak. That had been the name signed to the parchment, and she had heard one of the officers address him by it. The Seeker had been right where Aliane had expected her to be – in the stables attempting to flee the siege. She had not, however, counted upon the fact that the Seeker had already found herself a protector and student.

She glanced at Thalan, hanging back a little so he would not see her gaze. He was an unexpected wrinkle in her plans, though she could not help but admire him. He had done very well, getting the Seeker out of the inn without being seen. But she was unsure, now, whether the woman would want to be saddled with another traveling partner, and the young man would probably balk at the thought of having to protect two women instead of one from the dangers of a journey. In truth, she could probably protect the party better than he could, but there was no way he could know that, and she thought it might be more diplomatic not to mention it. She wouldn't want to hurt his feelings, and in spite of his unexpected and, she had to admit, unwelcome presence she rather liked the man. At least she thought that she might, given the chance.

The man and the Seeker, whose names she did not even know yet, had spoken little since their escape from the Fox and Falcon. They had seemed to take it for granted that Aliane would accompany them, so she had followed without question. Not surprisingly, they had immediately headed towards the city gates. By the time they reached the outskirts of town, the spell she had woven had dissipated and she had wondered with a spurt of fear what would happen if the guard had been instructed to stop them. But to her surprise they had been allowed to pass, unquestioned and unmolested. Once they had cleared the city limits, she had tried to speak, eager to explain her dramatic appearance, but the Seeker had hushed her, smiling at her kindly. "Let's wait until we've put some distance between ourselves and the city, shall we?" she said, and so she had subsided, riding in silence and biting her tongue to keep from blurting out questions as they tumbled in her head.

She felt an overpowering sense of awe by being in the presence of a Seeker. Or rather two Seekers, if she had to hazard a guess – she would bet a pint of salt that Thalan also possessed a talent for magic. After Aliane's display of magic in the stables, it seemed natural that she stay with them. All her life she had wanted someone to teach her, someone to explain to her what exactly she could do, why she could do it, and how it was done. She had never understood her powers or how she used them, had never known why some people were born with the ability to manipulate the elements and others were not, and she had long hungered for more knowledge. And now it was there within her grasp.

Aliane frowned, caught between conflicting desires. Her father would be frantic, would kill himself with worry once he discovered her disappearance.

But she could not just surrender her one chance at freedom to return meekly to Morgan's palace, not after what had happened. True, she thought, she had planned only to help the woman escape, but she had been unprepared for the exhilaration that had come with her newfound freedom. If she were forced to go back to Magir, she feared she would simply fade away, sentenced to an insignificant life wasted in the hollow, beautiful, poisonous palace halls. Even the prospect of returning to her own home paled in comparison to the future that now hung before her like a bright jewel filled with infinite possibilities. Here she had purpose. Here she could make a difference.

Which left the question of what to tell the two people who rode alongside her. If they knew she was King Torrit's daughter, would they pat her on the head, thank her for her help and send her home? Would they, as everyone else seemed to, view her as a child to be cosseted and protected just because she happened to be a woman and royalty? The thought was unbearable. But was it feasible to hide her true identity? Someone, somewhere, was bound to recognize the princess of Cameon, and if they discovered she had deceived them they might not want her company any longer. Besides, the thought of lying to the kindly old woman and the rather handsome man was repugnant to her. She should probably tell them the truth. She was a grown woman and could make her own decisions. If she decided to travel with them, if they would have her, the choice was hers and hers alone. She would write to her father as soon as possible to assure him she was safe. She couldn't very well tell *him* the truth – it was possible her letter might be read by less tolerant eyes than her father's, and she would be cursed if she would do anything to put him in further danger. The situation with Morgan was complicated enough as it was; she didn't need to make it worse. And what would Morgan's reaction be, she wondered, knowing she had fled the prospect of marrying his precious son? Most likely her father would pay dearly for that as well. She sighed to herself. She just didn't know the answer, didn't know what to do.

"There's a small village several miles from here," the Seeker woman said, breaking into her thoughts. The older woman smiled at her encouragingly. "Can you hold on until then? I know you are cold, and you must be bursting with questions, but it would be much better to talk in front of a fire with some breakfast, don't you think?" Aliane smiled back, nodding her head. The young man only grunted, but the Seeker ignored him as if she were used to his moods. For the first time, Aliane wondered if she had inadvertently wounded his male pride, coming to the rescue when he had wanted to save the Seeker himself. Well, she thought bitterly, he would just have to lump it. They possibly could have escaped unseen without her help, but their chances had been slim. She had taken a great risk using magic in the proximity of so many Onnic, but she had used as little as possible, and fortunately for them all it had gone unnoticed.

Still, it seemed strange that there had been no soldiers on the street guarding the doors. Stranger still that they had not searched the stables in the first place. Thanks to Charis' teachings, she knew quite a lot about military tactics and procedures, and it appeared to her that the soldiers had been extremely lax in their duties. Well, she thought, trying to argue away her uneasiness, perhaps the Onnic did things differently. They would be livid, though, when they discovered they had let no fewer than three magic users slip through their fingers.

A short time later they reached a small village, whose name she was fated never to learn, and Aliane was very glad indeed to see the narrow buildings and unpaved streets that signified human habitation. Small though it was, the village boasted a single tavern, and they headed for it without delay. Finally, Aliane found herself warming in front of a crackling fire with hot, spiced wine to warm her chilled insides and blankets to cover her numbed feet. As she slowly sipped her drink her teeth gradually stopped chattering against the rim of her cup, and her body relaxed into the warmth of the room. Her shivering slowed, and feeling crept back into her numbed fingers with painful tingles. Winter was coming with a vengeance, early though it was. She was used to cold winters in Aryn, but she had neglected to bring a heavy cloak or warm clothes with her on her mission. Somehow, she had not envisioned herself traveling with the Seeker, only rescuing her and helping her to safety. Well, she thought, drinking more wine, that was what she would do if she had to ride all the way to Marrin to accomplish it.

The Seeker sat down next to her, and the shaggy young man took a chair on her other side, warming his hands in front of the fire. Now that he was warm, his expression was much more cheerful, and Aliane realized his ill humor had not been directed at her, but rather at the early hour and the cold. He glanced at her and smiled, his eyes flickering over her features with an appreciation she had come to be used to upon first meeting young men. She smiled back and ducked her head, suddenly a little shy.

A kitchen maid entered and brought them large bowls of thick stew, made with some kind of meat *(Aliane preferred not to guess what animal the meat came from)* and vegetables in heavy gravy. All three ate as if they had been doing hard labor for twelve solid hours, and finally, the Seeker pushed her empty bowl away with a contented sigh. Aliane chewed slowly, savoring the warmth of the stew, and Thalan shoveled a third helping into his mouth as if he were steadily stoking a fire within. The Seeker daintily patted a napkin to her lips, and turned to face Aliane.

"Well, my dear! Now we can finally talk. Don't think I was ungrateful before, but I knew we had to get out of that cold so we could talk comfortably. To be honest, I wanted to get a little distance between us and... them."

"Oh, yes," Aliane said inanely. "I understand."

"I think some introductions are in order," the woman continued. "My name is Gwynne Davanir, though you must call me Irena Savintalo when there are other people about. This," she said, gesturing to the young man, "is Thalan Dushar. He is completely trustworthy." She grinned at Thalan, and he impishly smiled back. "At least, you can trust him with your safety. I'm not so certain about your virtue."

Thalan struck his hand to his heart as if mortally wounded. "Madam! You impugn my honor? I am wounded to the quick."

Aliane smiled at their foolery, and knew that she would like them both very much indeed.

"Now perhaps you can tell us how you came to miraculously rescue us just in the conventional nick of time," Gwynne said, watching her closely. Her voice once again became serious. "I certainly did appreciate it, my dear, but really, the last thing I expected was a young woman who can work magic to help us escape. But first things first. What is your name, my dear?"

Aliane thought quickly. She had still not entirely decided what to tell them. Just then, she saw Thalan glance at her intently, and she somehow felt he was awaiting her answer with something more than casual interest. She knew then that deception was useless.

"My name is Aliane," she admitted. "Aliane el'Gregarian." She looked at Thalan. "How did you know?"

"I recognized you," he said simply, his eyes twinkling. "I'm from Aryn, originally, and I've seen you at the yearly Midsummer Festival with your father." He looked her over with candid approval, and suddenly grinned. Aliane blinked. *The smile did wonders for the man's looks!* He suddenly looked like a great, cheerful rogue with his flashing smile and brown eyes twinkling with amusement. He would be very handsome, she thought, if it weren't for that nose. But even that impressive organ leant character to his face, though perhaps a little more character than was strictly necessary. He continued, "You weren't, by any chance, going to try to foist a fake name on us, now were you?"

"I had thought about it," she admitted, "but I figured someone would recognize me eventually. I was just afraid that if you knew who I really was, you'd try to send me back." She looked at Gwynne pleadingly. "Please, my

Lady, don't make me return home. I don't want to go back." After a short pause, she added, "Not yet, anyway."

Gwynne looked thoroughly confused. "Back? Back where? And why would we send you there against your will? You are a grown woman. And why would you try to hide your true identity?" She looked at Thalan. "You recognize her? And you know her father?" Gwynne shook her head as if to clear the cobwebs away, and looked again at Aliane. "Who *are* you?"

Aliane laughed, and patted the woman's hand. "I forgot. You're not from Cameon. Thalan recognized me because I am King Torrit's daughter."

"King Torrit's daughter," Gwynne repeated stupidly. Then her voice sharpened. "King Torrit's daughter? You mean you are a princess?"

"Technically," Aliane said sourly, and Thalan muffled a laugh behind his hand. Aliane glared at him, and he smiled apologetically.

Gwynne's eyes looked glazed, like newly fired glass. "A princess... a princess who works magic... a princess of *Cameon* who works magic, rescues us from not-so-certain death in Magir..." Her voice failed, and she looked at Aliane helplessly.

"Perhaps I'd better tell you the whole story," Aliane said helpfully. So she did. She told them of her father's meeting with Morgan, told them what she had overheard in Morgan's palace. She described the ball and her meeting with Larion, and how she had found out about the renegade Seeker fleeing the Onnic from the North. She explained how she had come to know where Gwynne was staying, and how she had devised the plan to help her escape. Her audience listened in silence, amazement written plainly on their faces to be replaced with respect as Aliane finished her story.

"That took some guts," Thalan commented after a short silence. Aliane looked at him, and he smiled self-consciously. "Not everyone would have been fool... er... courageous enough to come to the rescue of a magic user."

"But of course she would," Gwynne said gently, reaching out to touch Aliane's hand. "She's a mage herself." A strange look passed through Gwynne's eyes, and her hand continued to rest on Aliane's. "Hmmm. Yes. Magic." She looked at Aliane thoughtfully. Then, her face fell. "But you are the daughter of a king, are you not?"

Aliane blinked. "Yes, my Lady. Well, mostly anyway."

Thalan was looking at Gwynne intently, as if trying to read her mind. Suddenly, he caught his breath and jumped on Aliane's hesitation. "Mostly?"

"My father... King Torrit adopted me when I was very young. He's always considered me his daughter, and I've always known him as my father."

"I see," Gwynne said, stroking her chin thoughtfully. Thalan shook his head at her, his brow furrowed.

"It can't be," he said faintly, his voice a pale echo of its usual strength. Aliane caught a note of incredulity and... hope? She couldn't be sure. "It would be too easy."

Gwynne snorted. "Easy? You call this easy? The woman took a huge risk to find us. She used great intelligence and bravery. Though my dear, you did take a great chance using magic when there were so many Onnic about."

"It seemed the only way, my Lady," Aliane explained, looking confusedly at her new companions. "What are you two talking about, anyway?"

"Perhaps nothing," Gwynne replied. "And please, just call me Gwynne, or Irena when there are people about. Now, tell me about your magic. Strong, is it?" She leaned forward, almost hopefully, Aliane thought. She wondered at her interest.

"I wouldn't say strong," she said carefully. "I haven't had much chance to use or practice it."

"Still, that was a pretty good spell you wove back there," Thalan said, mirroring Gwynne's interest. "You even hid the horses."

"Well, it would have looked pretty silly for two saddled, unmounted horses to go trotting off down the street, wouldn't it?" Aliane frowned at him. "Just what are you getting at?"

"Nothing, my dear, nothing," Gwynne said, her voice soothing. "It's just we have been looking for mages, and it seems positively providential that you just happened along when you did." She leaned back, still thoughtful. "Still... perhaps we'd better have a change of plans, Thalan."

Thalan nodded. "It couldn't hurt, could it? After all, you never know. I'd say providence owes us one, wouldn't you?"

"What plans?" Aliane asked, looking from one to the other. "If it's all the same to you, I'd like to travel with you for a while. I'd really rather not go back to Morgan's castle."

"To marry that horrid prince?" Gwynne asked scornfully. "I should think not! No, you can stay with us, and we can help you. Perhaps teach you a few things. And maybe you can teach us a thing or two as well."

Aliane was a little surprised by the intensity of her relief. She would have to send her father a message, of course, but now that she had tasted the freedom she had always coveted, had spread her wings to find she could fly, the thought of going back to Morgan's palace was unbearable. She hoped her father would not be too angry, though it was not his anger she feared most. It was his disappointment. On the tail of her less than fortuitous meeting with Larion at the ball, her desertion might be construed as cowardice.

Her companions had continued talking while she was lost in thought, but a question from Thalan caught her attention. "So we'll be heading north, then?"

"I think it would be best," Gwynne answered, nodding her head decisively.

"North?" Aliane asked, glancing at Gwynne. "What's in the north? I thought you had come *from* the north. You said you were going to change your plans." Aliane looked at them in dismay. "Am I disrupting things?"

"Oh, salt and stuff me, no, girl!" Thalan said, smiling broadly at her. Then he seemed to remember he was addressing a royal princess and a ruddy flush spread across his face and down his neck. "I mean... I'm sorry... Your Highness..."

Aliane laughed. She had a delightful laugh, clear and ringing and true. "Please... don't. Can't you just call me Aliane?"

Thalan looked dubious. "I can try."

Aliane's dimple suddenly showed itself, and now it was Thalan's turn to blink. "Here, try it. A... lye... ah... nee. You can do it, I know you can. It's not that hard."

Gwynne was helpless with laughter, and Thalan glared at her. "Well, I'm glad you're enjoying yourself! But I grew up in Aryn, and the royal family was always well respected there." Gwynne tried to answer but couldn't, her throat was filled with silvery, musical laughter, and Thalan snorted with exasperation.

"The truth be told," Aliane said while Gwynne got herself under control, "I think it would be nice to take a break from being a princess for a while. I've been cooped up long enough, and I'd like to see some of the world, and experience life!" Suddenly, a jolt of joy as potent as lightning shot through her body, and she threw her arms out wide as if to embrace them both, everyone, the whole world. "I've been dreaming of this day for years and... well, I'd really like just to be your friend." She looked at them a little shyly. "I've never really had a friend before."

Thalan looked shocked, but Gwynne nodded. Somehow, Aliane thought, the old woman understood. The thought warmed her. As much as she loved her father, Hernie, Charis and the others, she had never truly felt they understood her. For the first time in her life, she felt as if a kindred spirit sat beside her.

She brought her mind back to their discussion. "You still haven't told me why we are going north," she pointed out. She tried to visualize the map pinned on the wall of her father's library. "It seems to me there isn't much to the north of here. Just the Port of Casset and a couple lakes and some mountains to the northwest."

Gwynne smiled. "Yes, my dear, that's pretty much all there is. It's the lakes we want, though." She looked at Aliane shrewdly. "Do you know anything about the Prophecies of the Eye of Truth?"

"Not much," Aliane said slowly. "I know there *was* a prophecy, and that it had something to do with magic and a woman called the Eye of Truth. I know very little about the Seekers." She hesitated. "You two are Seekers, aren't you?"

Thalan nodded, drawing himself up proudly. "Yes, we are. I've just started my Search, but Gwynne has been Searching for many years."

"I haven't Searched for a long time, though," Gwynne said, sadly. "Circumstances have forced me to begin again."

This time, Aliane sat silently while Gwynne told her story. She listened with growing horror as Gwynne related the events that led up to their near-capture at the Fox and Falcon. She had wondered how the older woman had acquired the burn marks on her face and body, but had never dreamed that the beautiful man who had caught her eye at The Dancing Waters had caused them. Jaerak Thorin. And he had magic! What was he doing in an Onnic uniform? Surely Morgan did not know his new captain was a magic user, and obviously Larion did not. Anger and pity gripped her as she listened, touched with a tinge of sadness for what might have been but now could never happen. The death of possibilities always saddened her, and she had been so fascinated by Jaerak. She had been blind, but beauty, she knew, could be deceiving.

Gwynne had not missed her expression of regret. She smiled kindly, and said, "I, too, was taken in by his appearance. Don't chide yourself, child. The man is as charming as he is dangerous. But now that you know his true character, I trust you will stay as far away from him as you possibly can."

"Of course," Aliane murmured, blushing. She had not realized her feelings were so transparent. "After what he did to you... So you think Jaerak is after these stones? How could he possibly get them? How could *you* get them? Obviously you don't know where they are, why does he think you can lead him to them?"

"I've been thinking about that," Thalan said, looking less cheerful. "Jaerak has left Gwynne alive for a reason, but we never knew what that reason was. But now I think I have an idea."

Gwynne looked at him with interest. "Well? Do tell."

Thalan frowned. "Has it occurred to either of you that our escape from the Fox and Falcon was too easy? Jaerak practically let us go."

"But Aliane's spell..." Gwynne protested.

"You can't forget that Jaerak has magic," Thalan said, abstractedly massaging the palm of his hand. "He should have been able to sense that spell. It was a powerful spell, and anyone with the talent for magic should have been able to feel it. I did, didn't you? Isn't that why the Onnic use the Esprys?" he asked Gwynne. "Because they can sense magic in others?"

Gwynne nodded slowly.

"What are Esprys?" Aliane asked.

"Magic users who have been turned or conditioned to work for the Onnic," Gwynne said, her face bleak. "The Onnic know that all magic users can sense when magic is being performed."

"Then Jaerak should have felt the Prin... er... Aliane's spell," Thalan argued. "But he didn't come out, and he did not send any men to investigate. In fact, he herded everyone into the inn to clear the street for our escape! He let us go. He knew we were there, but his purpose was not to capture us. It was to drive us out and get us moving again."

"But why?" Aliane asked.

"Because he believes we can lead him to the one person who might actually be able to tell him how to get those stones," Thalan said quietly. "The Eye of Truth."

There was a stunned silence as the two women tried to assimilate that startling idea.

"Think about it," Thalan urged. "Jaerak now knows everything Gwynne does. He knows that the signs and warnings of the Prophecies have begun to come true. He knows the time for her to be found is drawing near. He also knows there are very few people Searching these days, but he knew about Gwynne from that book he found. Where did he find it? How did he get it?" Thalan shook his head. "I still don't know the answer to those questions, but if anyone could find the Eye, it would be you." He looked again at Gwynne, who had become very still in her chair. "He's following you because he believes you will find her. And when you do, he will take her from you and use her to get what he wants."

"But what makes Jaerak think the Eye will know what he needs to know?" Aliane asked confusedly.

Gwynne, her face looking like stone, finally spoke. "There is a passage in the Prophecies that says the Eye of Truth will remember that which she had never lived, and know that which she had never learned. Perhaps Jaerak hopes she will know the key and location of the Dark Abyss." She covered her face with her hands. "If he gets that information from her, we are all lost," she mumbled.

Thalan patted her awkwardly on the shoulder. "I think Jaerak hopes the Eye will know the information he seeks," he said soothingly, "but how would he get her to tell him? She will be so much stronger than he."

"I'm not sure about that," Gwynne said, again glancing at Aliane with that strange, darting look. "The Eye of Truth may be fairly unschooled when we find her, and Jaerak is very strong. She will probably need time to realize her full potential."

Aliane again felt as if lighting had struck her, the force of the shock that went through her body was so strong. But this time it was astonishment, not joy that prompted the jolt. She looked at Gwynne and her jaw dropped open as the impossible realization swept over her. "You think it's me," she gasped, careless of her grammar. "You think I... I... might be the Eye of Truth?"

"Well, the thought had crossed my mind," Gwynne said mildly. "After all, you appear on the scene just when we need you the most. You have, as far as I can tell, relatively strong magic. The fact that you have magic at all is incredible in this day and age, and you know some spells despite the fact that you were never taught. That means you have a good feel for the way magic works. Tell me, how did you learn that spell of protection. You used Air, didn't you?"

"I... I... yes, I did," Aliane stammered. "I didn't really learn it, I just... knew it. I've used it a couple times to sneak past people when I didn't want them to see me."

"Well, we've been Searching for a woman with magic, and we seem to have found one," Thalan, added.

"But I found you!" Aliane protested. She looked at Gwynne. "Maybe *you're* the Eye of Truth!"

Gwynne burst out laughing. "I hardly think so, my dear. My magic, as I told you, has faded to practically nothing, and I never was very strong in the first place. Besides, I can only touch the element of Earth. Can you work spell-webs in elements other than Air?"

"I... I don't know," Aliane admitted. "I've never really tried."

"Well, this is hardly the place to experiment," Gwynne said, glancing around her. "We can find out during our trip. The road to the Lake Point, where the Mirror lies, is very deserted, and there will not be many people about."

"It's impossible," Aliane said, as her heart thudded in her breast. She was suddenly very afraid. "It can't be me."

"The fact that you are adopted also points to you," Gwynne continued. "The Prophecies state that the Eye of Truth will be born of magic, but have no drop of noble or royal blood."

Relief so strong flooded Aliane that she almost gasped aloud. "But I am of royal blood," she said joyously. "My mother was my father's sister." She stopped. "Goodness, that sounds awful. I meant..."

Thalan interrupted, smiling. "We know what you meant."

"The point is I am still kin to him," Aliane finished. "We are still related by blood."

Gwynne's face fell. "Oh. Are you sure?"

"Of course I'm sure!"

"No offense meant," Gwynne said quickly. "Do you remember your mother?"

"No," Aliane said, dropping her eyes. "I only know what my father has told me."

There was a slightly uncomfortable silence. Thalan was staring down at his fingers as if they were the most engrossing objects he had ever seen, and Gwynne's face was inscrutable. A tiny, treacherous sliver of doubt pricked Aliane's heart. What if it wasn't true? What if her father had lied about her mother? *Impossible*, she told herself. Why would he lie? To protect her from censure? So no one would question her right to continue the bloodline? Ridiculous! It just wasn't possible.

"All the same," Gwynne said slowly, "I still propose we go north to the Lake Point and seek the Mirror. It couldn't hurt to make sure."

Something of Gwynne's words struck Aliane as familiar, but she could not pin down where she had heard it before. Her brain was befuddled with all she had seen and done that morning. "What is this Mirror?" she asked. "You mentioned it before."

"The Mirror of the Eye is the final test for the Eye of Truth," Gwynne explained, reaching for her wine. She took a long, steadying sip before she continued. The color was coming back to her cheeks, and the livid, puckered scars stood out in startling contrast. "It is a pool that lies far underground, and it contains the waters from the Lake of Lies and the Lake of Truth that rest on the surface above. Since the beginning of time, the waters of both lakes have slowly dripped into this pool, which is called the Lake of Chaos, otherwise known as the Mirror of the Eye. It is said when the Eye of Truth looks into the pool the waters will separate, and truth shall be distinguished from the lies." Gwynne smiled and drank more wine. "It sounds like a fairy-tale, doesn't it? There is a tale about it, but I'll tell it to you another time. It is the final sign that the Eye of Truth has come. There can be no doubt after that."

Aliane mulled the story over for a few moments. Thalan reached over and refilled her wine cup from the pitcher, and she absently nodded her thanks. She drank deeply, and felt the tightness in her chest loosen and relax, enabling her to think more clearly.

"And you want me to look into this pool?" Aliane asked finally.

"Well, I think it would be best, don't you?" Gwynne asked reasonably. "It's the only way to know for sure."

That was true, Aliane thought. If she didn't look she would always wonder, and she would probably never have another good night's rest again.

"I'll do it on one condition," she said, smiling at Gwynne.

"And what's that?" Thalan asked, looking as relieved as his friend.

"That you," she pointed to Gwynne, "look into it, too."

Gwynne burst out laughing. "It's a deal."

They shook hands on it, and suddenly, Aliane was unbearably weary. She sagged in her chair, and Gwynne clucked with concern.

"You've had a tense couple days, and a very hard morning," she said sympathetically. "We all need some sleep, I think. Perhaps we should spend the rest of the day here and begin again in the morning. We have a long way to travel, so we should start early. I think we should try to get to the Mirror before the heavy snows come."

"I'm going to need some warmer clothes," Aliane said, fingering the very fine but thin material of her cloak. "I wasn't exactly prepared for a journey to the north country."

"You can borrow some of my things," Thalan said. "I have some warmer clothes you can use."

"And we can pick up some things along the way," Gwynne added. "You can't very well wear his trousers – they'd be miles too big for you. But we haven't much time to waste. Jaerak won't let us sit still for long, and I'd prefer he not disrupt any more inns searching for us." A cloud passed over her face, and Aliane touched her hand sympathetically.

"I'm sure he didn't hurt anyone," she said hesitantly. She stopped when Gwynne looked at her with sadness and pity.

"Do you think so?" she asked quietly. "Do you really think so?" Aliane said nothing. She could not think of an answer that would satisfy both her suspicions of the truth and her loathing to think the worst of Jaerak.

"He's going to follow us, you know," Thalan said, breaking the silence. "It won't take him that long to find which way we went. What are we going to do if..." he trailed off and involuntarily looked at Aliane.

She laughed. "I don't think you need to worry about me," she said, hiding a yawn behind her hand. "I'll look in your Mirror, but I'm sure nothing will happen."

Gwynne stood up. "Let's all have a little nap then," she said, gathering up her things. "We can make an early start tomorrow morning."

"One other thing," Aliane said suddenly, stopping in the middle of rising to her feet as a thought struck her. "You never did tell me why Jaerak wants those stones. What are their properties? What use could they be to him?"

Gwynne was silent for a long time before answering. "The five stones were each enchanted with an Element of Magic. We know the Alchemist Stone lies in the Dark Abyss, and it is this one Jaerak seems to want the most."

Aliane was almost afraid to ask, but curiosity won over fear. "And what Element of Magic does it contain?"

Gwynne turned her back and began gathering her things in a bundle. She spoke in a low voice, but Aliane had no difficulty understanding her.

"It gives the Stone's user the ability to travel through time."

That night as Aliane lay in her hard, uncomfortable cot, she thought about everything she had learned that day. She still couldn't believe her luck. Against all odds, she had accomplished what she set out to do, and now she was about to embark on the adventure of a lifetime. She thought, too, about the incredible idea Gwynne had expressed. *Impossible,* she thought again. Impossible that she, Aliane el'Gregarian, daughter of King Torrit of Cameon (she was her father's daughter, no matter what blood ran through her veins!), could be the Eye of Truth. Impossible that she could possess such strength, such power. She had never felt anything even resembling such ability. Well, she would honor her promise to look into the silly pool at the Lake Point, but she was sure nothing would happen. Wasn't she? Almost regretfully, Aliane had to admit she was. Alluring and appealing as it may sound, no prophet ever foretold the coming of Aliane el'Gregarian.

Despite the warmth of the room, Aliane shivered as she recalled Gwynne's last, startling statement. She had never considered that it might be possible to travel through time. If Jaerak truly wanted that ability for himself... Aliane shuddered at the idea. The Eye only knew what damage he could do with such power. Lost in these thoughts, she did not feel the warm tendrils of sleep wrap their seductive arms around her and pull her into the comfortable release of slumber.

* * *

She could not see, and yet she could. She could not explain the phenomenon; she knew she was blind as surely as she knew her own name. Yet she could see, in a fashion, and she looked about in confusion. Then it dawned on her. She was looking through a pair of eyes that were not her own. And what she saw, or rather did not see, but did, made a chill shiver crawl down her spine.

She saw a field. It had probably once been a beautiful field, with flowers and wild prairie grasses teeming with life. There had once been trees, she was sure, for the eyes she used could still see the stumps where they had been hacked or burned away to build weapons, arrows and the hastily erected buildings that stood in the distance. Children had probably once played there, and lovers had met in secret trysts under a gentle summer sun. But these eyes saw no children, and this field displayed no trace of a lover's tenderness about it.

The field was strewn with bodies. The ones that were dead were the least horrific. They, at least, no longer suffered despite the blood that still leaked from bodies growing cold, seeping into the clumps of torn grass and dirt. Men and women littered the ground like leaves that had dropped from some hideously diseased tree. Their eyes, glazed and empty, could no longer see past the veil that had been drawn over them, and their ears were spared the agonized screams and moans of the living. Her own eyes that were not her own stared in horror at the writhing wounded and she tried to shut her ears to the terrible aftermath of a battle gone dreadfully wrong. Smoke stained the sky in strangely beautiful patterns, and here and there a fire still burned where a flaming arrow had struck an unprotected or vulnerable area. There was not one man or woman left standing. She saw nothing. And yet, she did see. She tried to close her eyes to block the terrible vision, but they were not her eyes to close, not hers to command. She looked on.

Suddenly, a woman stood. She could have sworn a moment ago that the woman had been as dead as first love after a betrayal, but still the woman stood. Aliane stared in horror at the bloody figure, unrecognizable and macabre. A few meters away, another stood. This one had a dagger in her breast and was missing most of her left arm. Then a man stood, and then another. A wounded man balanced on his one remaining leg, and to her horror a small child struggled to stand from underneath the bodies that had been piled on top of him. All across the field the dead rose and the wounded stood. They stared not at her, but at a woman who now stood atop the bloodied hill, a woman whose trailing skirts and long, dark tresses streamed behind her as the wind tried to carry them south. Suddenly, she realized that they *were* staring at her. It was her own figure that stood straight and silent on the hilltop, and it was to her body the dead and dying looked. Since the eyes from which she watched were not her own, she stared at herself with the rest. The men, women, and yes, children all faced the figure of her, not speaking, not moving, and most not even breathing. She watched herself stare blankly back at them, not knowing what to do, how to help them, how to ease their suffering. She saw herself back away, denying their silent pleas and entreaties. She finally heard herself speak, the only word that filled her mind at that moment.

"No."

A dead woman dropped back to the ground. Aliane stared at it, confused.

"No," she said again. A man dropped, once again dead and unanimated.

"NO!" It was strange, hearing the words in her mind and watching them come from her body that was standing on the hill. Apparently, the eyes she watched from had no voice to accompany her sight.

The child fell, hitting the ground like a sack of bones.

"What do you want?" she screamed. "What do you want from me?"

They made no answer, and just for a moment she thought she knew. But then, the eyes from which she watched blinked, and the scene changed. The field was empty, the smoke gone. The grass had grown over, and a few young trees struggled to reach the sun with their new, tender branches. Not a soul was to be seen. It was as if the horrific battle scene had never been. But this was worse. They were all gone, and she knew she had somehow failed them.

"NOOOOOOOOO!!!!" she cried from a heart filled with unshakable sorrow, and woke with a gasp to find Thalan shaking her gently by the shoulders. She blinked at him, relieved to be seeing him from her own eyes.

"What's wrong?" he whispered, looking worried. "You were crying out in your sleep."

Aliane passed a hand over her sweaty face and took a shuddered, steadying breath. "It was nothing," she said, though she still shook with reaction. "A nightmare, that's all."

"Will you be all right?" Thalan asked, brushing a damp strand of hair from her cheek. "You sounded... you cried so sadly."

"I'm fine," she said, relaxing back into her cot. "Go back to sleep. I'm sorry I woke you."

Thalan slipped away, and she drifted back to sleep before she could even thank him for his concern.

* * *

What seemed like moments later Aliane again felt herself being gently shaken, and she reluctantly opened her eyes. Gwynne smiled down at her, and Aliane briefly wondered if her father could possibly pass a law that forbade perky, bright moods before the seventh hour of daylight.

"Time to get up, dear. We leave soon," Gwynne said, and vanished from the room. Aliane sat up and contemplated actually standing, but decided she was better off where she was. She rubbed her eyes and blinked, trying to clear her sleep-fogged vision.

She suddenly remembered the dream that had troubled her the night before. But as soon as she tried to remember the details, the entire memory of her nightmare vanished with an abruptness that startled her. The more she tried to remember the more elusive it became, until she finally gave up. *Trying to remember a bad dream,* she thought, *is like trying to catch fingerfish with your bare hands. They will always slip away just as you think you've captured them.* Which in this case was just as well, she thought groggily, as she finally arose to dress in the frosty morning air. Whatever else the dream had been, it had been bad. She vaguely remembered someone waking her in the night, and her sleep had then been quiet and uninterrupted until Gwynne had come to rouse her before the break of dawn. A huge yawn threatened to split her cheeks, and she wondered why journeys must always begin so bloody early in the morning.

Aliane supposed it was not surprising she should have had bad dreams. The conversation the night before had been enough to throw anyone into a fit of confusion. Her head had been filled with visions of magic and the Eye of Truth, just as her heart was filled with a desperate longing to learn more about them. As she had lain in bed last night, she had questioned herself rather severely regarding her motives for joining Gwynne and Thalan on their journey. She knew it was not truly her journey to take. By all rights she should go home and face the duties and responsibilities that awaited her, but again thrust the thought from her mind as impossible. She could not go home; not when there was someone so close that could teach her what she longed to know. Aliane could not resist Gwynne's offer of knowledge, not even for her father's sake. She would send him a note today. He must be beside himself with worry.

Not that a note from her would appease him, she mused as she climbed down the stairs towards the breakfast-room. Without her actual return her father would harbor images of her untimely end, just as he tortured himself with the memories of his dead wife and sister. Well, she was not her mother. In fact, she was so unlike her mother in every other respect, why did King Torrit fear her daughter would follow her even in the manner of her death? But, Aliane knew, love was not always rational. In truth, she smiled to herself, it was often most irrational where it was most generously bestowed.

Gwynne and Thalan were already in the breakfast room when she arrived. Thalan still looked half-asleep, and his eyes drooped as he silently munched his bread. Gwynne, on the other hand, was bright-eyed and alert. *Obviously a morning person,* Aliane thought sourly. As she sat down next to her new companions, Thalan gave her a searching look.

"How are you this morning?" he asked thickly around a mouthful of bread.

Aliane looked at him in surprise. Then she remembered; it had been Thalan who had woken her from the nightmare last night. For just an instant, she almost remembered the dream, but the vague images fled once again as she tried to lock them down.

"I'm fine, thank you," she said, reaching for the pitcher of tannis. The brew was hot and fresh, and it warmed her as she sipped it. "I'm sorry if I disturbed you last night."

"What happened?" Gwynne asked with concern as she buttered a piece of bread.

"Nothing, really," Aliane said, embarrassed. "I just had a nightmare."

"Hmmm. Yes. I get those sometimes, too, still." Aliane was not surprised, considering what the woman had endured in her lifetime.

"How long do you think it will take us to reach the Lake Point?" she asked, thinking of the letter she still had to write to her father. It would help if she could give him some idea how long she planned to be away.

"It is a rather long journey," Gwynne admitted. "We will have to head north to the Port of Casset. It has the only road that leads to the Twin Lakes. With winter practically here, I don't want to be caught by the northern snows with no good road to follow. It will probably take at least two weeks, perhaps more if the weather is against us."

"Couldn't we wait to do this until spring?" Thalan asked, still tetchy. Aliane smiled, and pushed the pitcher toward him, and he poured himself another cup. She was already getting used to his moods, and she fully sympathized with the early-morning grumps.

"Somehow I don't think Jaerak would have the patience to wait that long," Gwynne said wryly. "As we have already seen, if we stay too long in one place, he will flush us out. I'd rather face the northern snows."

Aliane could not help but agree, though she still felt a strange fascination with the beautiful, ruthless man. She just wished she could get the picture of his face out of her mind's eye.

They finished their breakfasts quickly, and prepared for the long journey ahead of them. Aliane innocently asked if perhaps they could not hire a carriage to ease their journey, and Gwynne gave her a strange look. But she merely said, "No, I think not. It would slow us down, and we would not want to risk getting stuck in the snow." Aliane blushed, realizing once again how ignorant she was of the world outside her narrow, sheltered existence. Gwynne had probably never had enough money in her entire life to hire a carriage, something Aliane took for granted every day of her life. Aliane had brought quite a lot of money with her, as well as some jewels. She had thought she might give them to the Seeker when she found her, in case the woman needed coin for her escape. Perhaps she should just hold on to the money. She would not want to hurt anyone's pride by appearing to offer charity.

So, the three companions set out on a journey that most probably, in Aliane's estimation, would end in disappointment and wasted time. However, since she had no better alternatives at hand, she followed, hoping to gain at least experience and knowledge if not the everlasting fame of fulfilling an ancient prophecy.

"Those who are good of spirit and clean of soul shall welcome me. Those who are touched with evil and malignancy shall tremble before me."
– From the Prophecies of the Eye of Truth

Chapter Ten

King Torrit had managed to turn King Morgan's castle upside-down in the search for his daughter before the message that assured him of her safety arrived. Servants and attendants who had been combing the castle for her slumped with relief and went to take a well-deserved rest once it was known that the Princess Aliane was no longer in the palace. True, investigating the dark, rarely visited inner recesses of the castle had been intriguing, but all parties concerned decided they had had quite enough hunting for one day, thank you very much. They had explored sufficient musty, unused rooms containing rats and decrepit furnishings to satisfy their curiosity for a long time to come.

Torrit had been pacing up and down the length of the library for hours, unable to sit still or calm his thoughts. A huge fire roared in the wall-sized fireplace but Torrit did not notice the warmth, or the sweat that ran from his face as he paced. King Morgan, his daughter Julane and several trusted servants who stood by to oblige their needs waited for news of Aliane with him, trying unsuccessfully to soothe the poor king's tortured nerves. King Morgan had been tolerant of Torrit's frenzied orders to his servants, and he smiled benignly with the others when the message from Aliane finally arrived. Torrit pounced on the messenger and snatched the paper from his hands before the startled man could say a word. The stricken messenger stood dumbly, astonished at such indignity, until a keeper thrust a coin in his hand and gently pushed him from the room. Torrit held the precious paper as if it contained his life, as in a way it did, and he read it through quickly. He closed his eyes and sighed his relief, his entire body indicating that the need for immediate worry had passed.

"She's all right," he breathed. "Thank the heavens! She's all right."

"At last!" Julane said, assuming the air of a woman on her last thread of patience. "Now perhaps we can restore some order around here."

"Where is she?" Morgan asked, ignoring his daughter's ill humor. One of his menservants looked at him uneasily. Considering the circumstances, Torrit might be excused for being oblivious to Morgan's tone, but those who knew him best were wary when he spoke that way.

Torrit looked up, a small remnant of his worried frown returning. "I don't know. She doesn't say."

"What do you mean she doesn't say?" Morgan asked, holding out his hand for the letter. After a small moment of hesitation, Torrit handed it over.

Dearest Father (it read),

I'm sure by now you must have missed me, and I sincerely apologize for any worry I may have caused you. You know I would never intentionally hurt you. However, something has happened, something I must take care of. I cannot tell you what it is, but if I could you would want me to do it, and you would understand. I know you would. I am doing nothing of which you need be ashamed, and indeed I hope to make you proud of your wayward daughter. You mustn't worry about me, Pa-Bear. As you know, I can take care of myself – none better, as Charis will tell you! Just know that I am well, and that I will return to you as soon as I possibly can. I am not exactly sure when that will be, but I should be able to tell you in my next letter.

Please extend my apologies to King Morgan and Prince Larion and the household of the Royal Palace for my precipitous departure. I meant no offense to them, and would not have abused their hospitality in such a way if the matter had not been of such importance.

Father, you mustn't let me delay you if you are needed back in Aryn. I will find my way home. I will write again soon, and let you know where to send a letter that will reach me, and you can tell me of your plans. Until then, be happy with the knowledge that I am happy and I am safe. I am, as always, your loving daughter, Aliane.

King Morgan looked up from this extraordinary missive with less than his usual composure. He handed it back to King Torrit, who immediately began reading it again as Morgan groped for words to express his astonishment.

"This is... this is most... unusual," he finally said, feeling the enormous inadequacy of the trite phrases. Torrit smiled a little, though worry still stamped his broad face with lines that had not been there the day before.

"You would think so, Morgan," he said ruefully, "but my daughter is not conventional in any way."

"So you said before," Morgan stated, still silently suppressing the flush of anger he felt. "This, however, goes beyond the limits of what I could expect of... unconventional."

"I must say," Torrit admitted, stroking his beard, "she has never done anything like this before. I knew she wasn't happy being cooped up in the palace, but I never thought she would..." He left the thought unsaid. It was too painful to think upon.

"That she would run away?" Julane finished for him, her flat, nasal voice an insult. "Somehow, I am not as surprised as the rest of you."

Morgan took notice of his daughter for the first time. "And why is that?" he asked softly. "Did you have any reason to suspect this? If you did, and did not tell me..." He left the threat unfinished, but Julane flinched and turned white, as if intimately acquainted with the severity of punishment her father habitually dealt. Torrit hurriedly intervened.

"Of course she didn't," he said heartily, smiling down on Princess Julane's golden head. "The princess would never do that."

"Then explain what you meant," Morgan demanded, unwilling to let the subject drop.

"I... I didn't mean anything by it, Father," Julane stuttered, her usual poise shattered. "Truly I didn't. I just knew she was unhappy here, and that she didn't like doing embroidery or playing the piano or drawing or anything like that."

"And why should she?" Morgan asked bitingly. "The woman obviously has a good brain in her head, and would naturally be bored by such trivial chores." Julane flushed with resentment, but said nothing more.

"Perhaps this Charis could give you some idea of where she went," Morgan mused. "He is the captain of your guard, is he not?"

"Yes," Torrit replied, folding the letter and putting it in his shirt pocket – against his heart. "They are great friends, and he sometimes lets her... er... um..."

Morgan laughed at the king's discomfiture. "My friend, you needn't be ashamed! The entire palace knows of your daughter's practice sessions with the man!"

Torrit was surprised. "They do?"

"Of course. It's very difficult to keep secrets here. Sometimes the kitchen maids like to sneak away to watch her, and I know the lads never miss a day. I've been told it is a very fine sight."

"Hmmmm." Torrit resumed stroking his beard. "Perhaps she did tell Charis something. But if she did, why would he keep such important news from me?"

"Fetch the man," Morgan ordered, and a footman bowed obediently and vanished from the room. Morgan beckoned to another for some ouzaki, and handed the glass to Torrit. "Here, drink up my friend. You're still a bit white.

Your daughter is fine, and at least you know she is safe."

Torrit turned an even paler shade and drank down the spirits in one swift gulp. All the joy he had felt upon receiving Aliane's letter seemed to drain from his body, leaving him stooped and haggard. "Safe," he said, his voice hollow. "All my life I've tried to keep her safe. Perhaps I've been too strict. If I had trusted her, given her more freedom she might not have gone off on her own." He buried his massive head in his hands. "I was just trying to protect her, to keep her out of harm's way." And she had fought him all the way, never content to live in the jeweled cage he had tried to build for his beautiful, precious bird. He saw now that he had practically shoved her out the door himself. He had been a fool to think he could keep her penned in forever.

"Of course you were," Morgan said, oblivious to his guilt and despair. "We try to do what's best for our children." He bared his teeth at Julane. "Don't we, my dear?"

"Of course, Father," she murmured, unable to meet his sardonic eye.

Torrit, finally noticing the undercurrents of tension in the room, looked from the princess's subdued face to her father's caustic one with confusion. Obviously they were speaking of something he did not understand, and an uncomfortable silence settled over the room. Perhaps his relationship with his daughter was not perfect, but the way Morgan and Julane spoke to each other made him want to cover his ears. He and Aliane had always respected each other, and though they had had their disagreements they had never been unkind to each other. He had also thought they could trust each other, could tell each other anything. Why could she not tell him what she was doing now? Did she not trust him as he always thought she had? He again covered his face with his hands. He couldn't bear it.

Torrit bounded to his feet in relief as the footman ushered Charis into the room. As soon as the king set eyes on his captain he knew the man knew something. He had always trusted Charis beyond all others, had trusted him with his life and the life of his daughter. Charis had been a friend and an ally for more than twenty years, and Torrit had never before had reason to believe he would ever deceive him. But for the first time Torrit eyed him with suspicion, wondering how – or if – such a man might have betrayed him.

Without speaking, he handed Aliane's letter to Charis and watched the captain's face as he read it. Charis's hands trembled as he read, and his scarred, ugly face paled slightly. He handed the letter back to the king when he had finished, but still said nothing.

"Do you know anything about this?" Torrit asked. "I know you two are close, and she might turn to you for help if she needed it and felt she... she couldn't come to me." Torrit passed a hand over his eyes. "I'm not accusing you of anything, man, but if you know anything, for salt's sake, please tell me."

Charis stood silent, struggling between loyalty to his king and concern for the Princess Aliane. He knew the information he held would destroy her in the eyes of his present company, and perhaps would even put her life in danger, but he was loath to lie to the man and king he loved like his brother.

"I didn't realize she was going to leave the palace altogether," he said finally. "She told me she wanted a day out and asked me where she might go to find some... some diversion."

"Diversion," Morgan repeated, his voice dangerous. "I'm sorry there was so little here in my home to keep her occupied."

Charis stood up a little straighter. "Aliane... the Princess is a woman of strong inclination." He smiled at Torrit. "Her words, not mine, sire. I guess she just wanted to see some of the city. I thought she would only be gone a couple hours. I did not expect... this."

"You still should have told me," Torrit said reproachfully.

"Sire, with all due respect, what would you have done?"

"Why, I would have..." Torrit stopped, and then smiled ruefully. "I would have gone after her and brought her back, of course."

"She knew you would," Charis said, "which is why she begged me to keep silent. If I'd known she would actually leave I would have certainly told you, your Majesty."

"Did she tell you where she was going?" Morgan asked. Charis looked at him in surprise and glanced at Torrit, who nodded, giving him permission to answer the question. He did so, though he still looked to his own king as he spoke.

"No, sire."

"And what about this thing she 'had to do'? Did she tell you about that?"

"I know nothing about that, sire" Charis said firmly. "I just thought she might go to an inn for some music or visit the statue gardens."

"Very well, Charis, that will do," Torrit said. He did not like the way Morgan questioned his man. "We will talk more about this later."

"Yes, sire," Charis answered. He bowed, turned on his heel and left the room.

"So now what happens?" Julane asked, her customary arrogance restored. It was obvious she thought they were making a big fuss over nothing, and she never liked another woman to be the center of attention. She thought it more than likely that the Princess Aliane had gotten herself into an embarrassing situation and would surface again after about nine months, though she wisely kept that opinion to herself. "And, more importantly, what are you going to tell Larion?"

"Tell me what?" asked a voice from the doorway.

Torrit turned, startled, as Larion himself strode into the library. He was dressed in his Onnic uniform, and he looked tired and pensive as if troubled by his thoughts. Torrit by now fully realized that an alliance between the prince and his daughter was impossible. He had had great hopes for the prince, but had found him arrogant, disdainful and unkind – not a good match for his gentle if willful daughter. He nervously wondered how he was going to get out of their arrangement gracefully without provoking King Morgan's wrath.

Larion looked about the room, noting Torrit's uneasy stance, his sister's smug, expectant expression, and his father's stony countenance. "Come now," he said, beckoning a servant for a drink. "Something has obviously happened, and judging by Julane's comment you are reluctant to tell me. But tell me you must, so you might as well just come out with it." He took the glass of ouzaki and sipped it, looking expectantly at the others.

Torrit sighed. "There is no easy way to tell you, so you might as well just read this." Torrit handed him the letter. Larion read it with interest, but as he read, his interest grew into anger. The little wench! How dare she skip out on him like that! Then he remembered that he had actually seen her. Just the night before last, she had been sitting in the lounge of The Dancing Waters where he had met with Captain Thorin. She had disappeared before he had concluded his business, and he had been unable to find her afterward. He remembered, also, the piece of parchment that had mysteriously disappeared from his pocket after the young urchin had 'accidentally' bumped into him. The consequences of the so-called 'accident' had pushed the memory from his mind. His anger mounted as he passed the letter back to King Torrit.

Still he spoke mildly, unwilling to reveal what he knew – or thought he knew. "I see," he said. "Well, perhaps it is not so surprising she would be bored here without anything to do. I'm sure she will come back soon."

"It does not sound like she means to return soon," Julane sneered. "She begs her father not to wait upon her return."

"Then I'm sure the princess will write another letter to clear everything up," Larion said, shooting his sister a scathing glance. "She would not torment those she loves by withholding information about her safety. You will be able to write to her soon, your Highness" he told Torrit. "Perhaps you would be kind enough to let me know if another letter arrives? I, of course, am deeply concerned about the Princess Aliane's welfare."

"Of course," Torrit said, relieved. He had expected a much more violent reaction. "You will be notified immediately."

"And now, if you will excuse me, I have some affairs to attend to," Larion said smoothly, bowing slightly to King Torrit, but failing to show his family the same courtesy. He walked from the room without a backward glance.

"So what are your plans now?" Morgan asked Torrit as he seated himself comfortably on the chaise lounge. The bewildered king looked at him helplessly.

"I'm sure I don't know," Torrit answered. He couldn't even think straight, let alone make plans for his immediate future. His spirits plummeted to a new low. He couldn't bear the thought of returning to Aryn without his daughter, but he could not trespass on Morgan's hospitality for an indefinite period of time. Now that an alliance was out of the question, he had no more reason to stay.

"You are, of course, welcome to stay as long as you wish," Morgan told him, as if reading his thoughts. His tone of voice belied the cordiality of his words, but Torrit did not notice. "Perhaps I should send out a search party? I would be happy to spare some men..."

"No," Torrit said, his voice decisive. "I will not have her hunted down like a truant schoolgirl. She is a grown woman, though I still tend to see her as the small child she used to be. Wherever she has gone I trust she has good reason to be there. I'm sure she will come back soon." He was, in fact, *not* sure, but saying it made him feel a little better.

He turned to stare into the fire. "I thank you for your kind offer, but I will not impose upon your household much longer. There are matters I must see to in Aryn; Aliane obviously realizes that. I shall wait two or three more days for a second letter from her. If it has not arrived by then, I trust I may depend on you to deliver it to me in Aryn?"

Morgan nodded and clapped him on the back. "Of course, my friend, of course! But you will hear from her soon. Most likely she has taken a fancy to a young man somewhere, and cannot bear to leave his side yet."

"Or," Julane said maliciously, "she has taken a dislike to a young man here and cannot bear to be near him."

"Whatever the reason," Torrit said rapidly, wishing to forestall another tender father-daughter moment such as he had already witnessed, "all will be put right soon. My daughter has a good head on her shoulders, and she knows how to use it."

King Morgan and the Princess Julane soon made their excuses and left, voicing their hopes that they would see King Torrit at dinner that night. The king was then left alone with his thoughts, and he felt an inconsolable grief at the realization that there were matters his beloved daughter could not share with him. Matters of such importance that she had felt the need to leave his company entirely rather than admit him into her confidence. He did not feel the tears trickling down his face as he sat and stared into the fire, wondering if he was somehow cursed to lose all those that he loved best.

* * *

Larion seethed silently as he stalked towards the soldier's barracks. What had Aliane been doing at The Dancing Waters? Had she been following him? No, she had been there before he had arrived. Was it she who now possessed the crucial parchment that had held a message for the High Priest Masyl Vonnin? It seemed extremely strange it should disappear at the same time she herself had vanished. Larion would have given a pound of salt to know what had been in that message. He had suffered severe humiliation when he had reached the Cathedral only to find it was no longer in his pocket. Masyl had been highly displeased with his carelessness, and Larion suspected the message had been of the utmost importance. He had been forced to admit he had failed in his duty, and had been assigned scut work for two weeks, a punishment even his princely status could not prevent. If it had been Aliane who had caused the parchment to be stolen, she had quite a lot to answer for when he got his hands on her again. She had humiliated him twice now in the short time she had been in Magir.

She had written in her letter that she was attending to something she "must do." Could it have anything to do with his assignment from the arrogant Jaerak Thorin, captain of Masyl's finest guard? Perhaps it did. Perhaps he was the one the princess had been following. Larion was determined to find out.

He entered the guest barracks without knocking and Torrit's men leapt to their feet, cards, chips and coins scattering across the floor as their abrupt movements upset the table. *Not a bad looking bunch of men,* Larion thought grudgingly, looking them over. At least they were fit. *The captain of the guard must train them well.*

"Which of you is Charis?" he asked, keeping the men at attention. A large, grizzled man past his prime with a hideous scar across his face stepped forward.

"I go by that name, your Highness," the man said, bowing to the prince. Larion jerked his head, indicating he wanted a private discussion outside. Charis waved the other men back to their chairs as he went through the doorway, Larion on his heels.

Suddenly, Charis was astonished to find himself lifted from the ground and slammed up against the side of the barracks with a force that knocked the breath out of him and set the flimsy building shuddering. He stared down at the livid face of the prince with disbelief, not understanding his rage or his violence. He instinctively clawed at the hands that held him, trying to pry them from his body. Charis was a strong man despite his years, but he could not budge the prince's grip, and Larion pushed his body against Charis's legs so the infuriated captain couldn't kick him.

"What... what do you think you are doing?" Charis demanded breathlessly, his feet dangling some inches off the ground. "Let go of me you bloody bastard! King Torrit will know of this!"

"He will only know that he has a lying, conniving, treacherous, traitorous man at the head of his army," Larion snarled, shoving Charis against the wall again, hard.

Charis felt his face flame, the scar leaving a track of white across his face. "You speak dangerously, my Prince," he warned, managing to sound threatening even in his precarious position. "I'd never be false to my king."

"Perhaps not, but would you be false to mine? Where did she go?"

Charis was pretty sure he knew whom the prince meant, but refused to play the tame wolf. "Where did who go?"

Larion shook him like a dog trying to snap a small animal's neck. "Don't play games with me, man! The princess. She would have come to you, and she names you in her letter. Did she come? What did she want? What did you tell her?"

"I don't know what you're talking about," Charis said, struggling. His breath was getting short and he was having difficulty speaking. "Let me go you cursed fool!"

Larion abruptly released his grip and Charis, taken off guard, fell back to earth with a grunt. He rapidly jumped to his feet but just as quickly Larion had drawn his belt knife, which he now held at Charis's throat, right against his jugular. Charis could see the horrified faces of his men through the barracks door as they watched, and he fervently hoped they would not do anything stupid. One young soldier took a look at the tableau in the yard and went sprinting off towards the castle.

"Now," Larion continued, his face only inches from Charis's and the knife steady in his hand. "I will ask only once more. Did she come to you?"

Charis bared his teeth. "You may slit my throat, little princeling, but I'll not betray my friends. My family! Go on. Cut my throat, and start a war with Cameon. You'll find that Cameon's swords are thirsty for Casset blood!" He heard a low murmur of agreement from the doorway and knew his men stood poised, alert and ready to jump into action if the opportunity presented itself.

Larion slowly spun the knife by the hilt, the sharp tip digging just slightly into Charis's flesh. "And you think King Torrit would risk a war over you?"

"He will. I know him. He would never stand for such an insult." Charis did not wince as the sharp point slightly pierced his skin.

"His armies would be devastated, his lands seized," Larion commented, his voice conversational. "There is no way his paltry troops could overcome the Onnic army." A louder, angrier mutter came from the men in the doorway. *Easy, lads,* Charis thought. *Easy.*

"They could if Queen Rhyssl would lend her aid, which she would happily to do," he retorted. "There's no love lost between the queen and your father." He was sweating, and he could feel the prick of the knife tip against his jugular. He could not tell if the liquid he felt running down his neck was his blood or a bead of perspiration.

"Oh, but Queen Rhyssl is about to have much larger problems than your pitiful little kingdom," Larion said nastily. "Freath is ready to explode into civil war, and she's been using her troops to fortify her position there. Honestly, there are only three ways this will happen. I cut your throat, your king declares war and loses; I cut your throat, your king does not declare war and you are dead anyway; or you tell me what I want to know, and I let you live."

"You forgot the fourth alternative," Charis said, his eyes gleaming.

"And what is that?" Larion asked contemptuously. He got his answer, and paid dearly for his complacency. He did not even see the blow that laid him to the ground, clutching his groin as unspeakable pain shuddered through his body, and therefore had no way to avoid it. Charis, freed from his steely grip, stood over him, his stance all readiness and sinewy animal grace.

"The fourth alternative," he said conversationally, kicking the knife from Larion's flaccid grip, "is that I beat the bloody salt out of you, and you apologize for your insult." Charis grinned as Larion writhed and groaned. "If you underestimate an old wolf, he's likely to bite you when you're not looking."

Gasping and blinking tear-filled eyes, Larion heaved himself to his knees. "Perhaps," he snarled, hatred twisting his features into a horrible grimace, "but the younger ones are more resilient." Larion launched himself to his feet and caught Charis in the gut with his shoulder, knocking him to the ground. Larion tried to reach the dagger that had fallen only a short distance from his hand, but Charis, seeing his intent, kicked out with his leg and sent the knife flying out of the prince's reach.

A crowd was beginning to gather, and the men inside the barracks jockeyed for position at the doorway to get a better view of the fight. They jeered or hollered encouraging advice in their rough voices, but all sounds faded to the background of Charis's awareness until they became nothing more than a vague, unidentifiable buzz. The noise had attracted notice from those in the courtyard, and curious eyes turned toward the combatants, their pulses quickening with the prospect of a good brawl. They were a little taken aback to discover that their own Prince Larion was one of the fighters, but that did not in any way lessen their hungry anticipation for blood.

Charis rolled and got to his feet, and the two men faced each other, circling, waiting, and watching for their advantage. Larion moved first, turning slightly and lashing out with his leg in a vicious kick that connected with Charis's side. Charis grunted at the impact, but kept his feet. He suddenly collapsed in on himself and rolled forward, catching Larion across the knees and upsetting the prince's balance so he toppled backwards in surprise. Charis, straddling Larion, put all his strength behind his fist and smashed it into the prince's face. His entire arm went numb and he heard the crunching of broken bones as his fingers shattered under the impact. Larion howled and gave one convulsive shudder that bucked Charis off his body. Both men again found their feet, both a little less steady than before.

Charis tried to flex his fingers, but that awoke the pain that his shocked nerves had, until now, considerately numbed. He cursed himself three ways for a fool for letting his anger get the better of him. That punch had been a stupid move, and his right hand was now useless. The prince was in worse condition, however, for the blow had been a brutal one. Blood streamed from his broken nose in a crimson gush, and he would be lucky if he had escaped a fractured cheekbone. He was still unsteady on his feet from the blow to his crotch, but anger and bloodlust overrode all other considerations and Larion again charged toward the older man, blinded by blood and rage.

Charis dodged and jabbed at Larion's shoulder with his left elbow, using the prince's forward momentum to upset his balance. His own foot slipped and he frantically tried to find purchase on the wet, muddy grass that had been soaked by the late autumn rains. He fell heavily to the ground, and though he tried to shield his injured arm from the impact, the shock of the fall sent stabbing pains from shoulder to fingertips. For a moment lights danced before his eyes and he tried to breathe evenly through his nose to dispel the sickening dizziness that overcame him. His momentary weakness was all Larion needed. The prince dove toward the knife that was still lying where Charis had kicked it, and he came up with the dagger in his hand. He fell on Charis and buried half the blade into the older man's shoulder. Only the slight, instinctive movement Charis made at the last moment prevented the knife from entering his heart. Charis bit his tongue, tasting blood as he tried to choke back the howl of pain that threatened to bubble from his throat.

Larion, gasping with exertion and pain, kept his hand on the hilt. With his other hand he tried to stem the flow of blood from his nose, but because it was broken it would not stop bleeding. He was a hideous sight, bloodied and battered as he leaned his face close to Charis's.

"Now, you will tell me," he hissed, and his voice was ragged and hateful as he spit the words from his bloody mouth. Charis could feel the hot drops of the prince's blood as they sprayed onto his face, and he groaned as Larion leaned a little harder on the dagger. "Tell me what you told her. Tell me where she went."

Charis, on the very edge of consciousness, saw Larion's face only as a blurred, unfocused palette smeared with the crimson of blood and the reddish-brown hue of mud and earth. He was able to see well enough, however, to use the last of his strength to spit in his opponent's face. Larion, overcome with rage, grasped the knife more firmly and pushed down on it, hard, until he felt the point grate against bone. Charis, unable to forestall a scream of pain, lost the last shreds of consciousness and fell into a black pit that was infinitely more desirable than his immediate world of broken bones and torn flesh.

"WHAT GOES HERE?" a voice bellowed from the crowd of people that had gathered to get a closer look. The throng parted and the figures of King Morgan and King Torrit approached the two men. King Torrit looked like a huge, lumbering bear next to the trimmer, neater figure of King Morgan, but he still managed to move quickly and was the first to arrive on the scene. The young soldier who had summoned him hung back, horrified by the sight of his fallen commander. Torrit took one look at the captain of his guard lying bloodied and bruised on the ground with a belt knife embedded in his shoulder and turned a cold, hostile glare onto the prince who still straddled him, his hand still on the hilt. Torrit was by nature a gentle and kindly man, and few had ever seen him lose his temper, but it was obvious that Prince Larion was about to become the unenviable recipient of Torrit's rare but potent wrath. Morgan pushed his way to Larion's side, his face black with anger.

"What goes here?" he demanded again, pinning his son with his icy, angry gaze. "What happened?"

Heedless of polite conventions, Torrit unceremoniously shoved Larion off his officer and bent to examine Charis's wound. His face was grave as he ordered one of his men to fetch a physician from the castle. He took off his own royal coat and draped it over the body of his friend, heedless of the blood that seeped through the rich cloth. Charis lived, but his breathing was shallow and Torrit did not like the gray tinge of his complexion.

Larion stood and wobbled, his ebbing adrenaline leaving him weak and shaking. He began to feel his own hurts now that the fight was over, and he wanted nothing more than to fall again to his knees and howl with pain, but he refused to show any sign of weakness before his father. Morgan despised him enough already, he did not need further proof of his son's weakness.

"I was trying to get information from the man," Larion said unevenly, his breath still coming in whooping gasps. "He angered me and I lost my temper." He looked at King Torrit and swallowed. He looked sick, but it was loss of blood rather than the realization of what he had done that turned him slightly green. "I beg your pardon for incapacitating your man."

"Incapacitating him?" Torrit repeated, his voice a low, dangerous purr. "You bloody near killed him. You might yet still, if your knife pierced his lung."

"Begging your pardon, your Majesty," the young soldier said, stepping forward. "Charis did nothing to start the fight. The prince accused him of treason and attacked first."

"That will do for now, thank you," Torrit told him. He looked at the man – no more than a boy, really – with keen scrutiny and asked, "What's your name, son?"

The soldier looked uneasy, as if he were uncomfortable being the center of attention. "It's Nik, your Highness. Nik Ferilian."

"Thank you Nik," Torrit said, turning back to his fallen friend. "Go back to the barracks now. Everyone go back," he boomed, his voice loud enough for all to hear. Larion stood up, still trying to staunch the flow of blood from his nose.

"We'll discuss this later," Morgan told him, seeing that the physician was trying to get through the crowd to the injured man. "Larion, wait for me in my study. I'll be there shortly."

The crowd finally dispersed, allowing the physician to attend to his patient. Torrit did not like the way the man's expression deepened with concern as he inspected the knife wound.

"He will be all right, won't he?" he could not help asking.

The physician straightened. "He has sustained a terrible wound, but the shock to his system may be what kills him. We must get him to my office. I dare not try to remove the knife now, he would lose too much blood. Gently now, gently. It looks as if he's taken some damage to his hand as well." Torrit glanced at Charis's hand and winced at the sight of those swollen, blackened fingers.

Several of Torrit's soldiers gently hoisted their fallen comrade and bore him towards the castle, followed closely by the watchful surgeon. Torrit turned to Morgan, his face still shuttered with anger.

"We'll return home as soon as my man is fit to travel," he said, looking Morgan squarely in the eye. "I would not stay where such hospitality is offered me and my men."

"I hope any offense your majesty takes," Morgan said smoothly, "is against my son and not me personally. Larion is impetuous and has a quick temper, as much as I have tried to train it out of him."

"Nonetheless," Torrit said firmly, "I believe our negotiations here are finished. I could never give my daughter to a man who tried to kill her friend. I would never put her in the position where a 'quick temper' might be used against her. She would never have it, and I will not have it for her."

Morgan frowned. "Perhaps my other son, Paulis..." he began. Torrit interrupted him, suddenly very weary of the king's company.

"I think not," he said. "I appreciate the offer but I fear our houses are not to be kin. Perhaps there is another way to determine peace between our lands. After my return to Aryn I will have my counselors draw up some proposals."

"As you wish," Morgan said, realizing there was no way he could change the outraged king's mind, and in truth he could hardly blame him. Torrit nodded briefly and left, following the same path the physician had taken with the unconscious Charis. Morgan found himself alone, a rare occurrence in his busy and eventful life. He looked at the courtyard, at the grass where the two feuding bodies had torn the carefully clipped lawn and muddied the area outside the barracks. He would have to have his gardeners make repairs as soon as possible. But first, he thought, he would have to have a talk with his eldest son.

"Though you are lost, my children, you must find your way. You must see what cannot be seen, hear what cannot be heard. Only then will you find the path to the Eye of Truth."

– From the Prophecies by
Cor of Restis Haven

Chapter Eleven

The week after they left the small village outside Magir was one Aliane would never remember with pleasure. The air became biting as they slowly progressed north, and nearly constant light snow showers kept her clothes and hair damp and clammy. She bundled herself in Thalan's woolen cloak, hoping to procure better protection when they reached the Port of Casset, and her cheeks became ruddy and chapped by the ever-strengthening winds. But she did not complain. She had chosen to accompany Gwynne and Thalan and she would keep up with them if it killed her. It was, she admitted silently, infinitely better than sitting in a palace trying to embroider pillow covers.

At night when they halted their travels, while Thalan and Aliane hunted or cooked their suppers, Gwynne told them stories about the Prophecies and taught them about the properties of magic. One cold evening they made camp earlier than usual in a small copse of trees near the road. They were all tired and cold and they needed rest. Aliane built a fire, for the coming night promised to be the most frigid yet, and Thalan took her crossbow and managed to shoot a rabbit, which he roasted on a spit for supper. Gwynne somehow found wild herbs that had survived the deadly frosts, and these she crushed and liberally sprinkled over the wild, gamy meat, giving it a tolerably pleasant flavor. As they picked the stringy meat from the bones, the spattering grease burning their eager fingers and mouths, Thalan asked, "Tell us more about the Prophesies. Who were the original Prophets, anyway?"

Gwynne licked the hot fat from her fingers and swallowed before she spoke. "The Prophets were a group of mages who lived before the time of the Great Cataclysm."

Aliane looked up from the rabbit leg she was munching, confused. "What was the Great Cataclysm?" she asked, inelegantly licking her fingers. Eating wild rabbit by the side of the road was hardly comparable to the last meal she had consumed in King Morgan's castle, but the company she now kept made this meal much more enjoyable. Though she did wish she had just a little salt to season the meat.

"It is what magic users call the Onnic War," Gwynne explained, tossing a bone into the underbrush. "It is a Great Cataclysm because it marked the end of a way of life. Our way of life. The end of a people." Her eyes were sorrowful. "It has been said that the Seekers never even saw it coming. Of course they knew the church preached against magic, but they never dreamed King Retik would launch a full-scale assault against them. And no one ever imagined that the war would go on this long. Over five hundred years. Five hundred years of persecution and hatred, death and destruction." Gwynne closed her eyes. "Such a waste."

"Can you tell us about the Prophets?" Thalan asked gently, understanding her pain.

She opened her eyes. "Yes, of course. There were five Prophets altogether. Anton Calindrel, Merina Xanata, Benita Synetal, Castin Madelena and Matrix el'Lorien. All five were powerful mages, and all were given the gift of Prophecy. But such a gift has a price, and all five died. People wrote that this Prophecy was so forceful and so important that mere human frames could not withstand its power, but instead must perish from it.

"Before they died each person spoke of a woman they called the Eye of Truth, and though they were feverish and delirious they managed to give some details about her. It wasn't until much later that someone discovered that five different people had had similar Prophecies about the same woman, and that all five had perished. The Prophecies occurred at different times, and the Seekers each lived in different cities, so it took a long time to compile the entire Prophecy as we know it today." Gwynne looked thoughtful. "I've always wondered if there were any other Prophets besides the Five we know, if their words had been dismissed as the ramblings of a sick person in the grip of delirium. What more could we know today, if someone had recorded their words? But all we have are the accounts from the Five. Interestingly enough, each Prophet had a talent in a different Element. So perhaps there were only five after all – one for each Element of magic."

"Who recorded their words?" Aliane asked interestedly.

"Actually, for a long time no one recorded them," Gwynne told her, poking the fire with a stick. "No one recognized the significance of their words for years. But some time later Cor of Restis Haven was traveling through the realm and heard rumors of a story remarkably like one he had heard in a different town, many, many leagues away. He tracked down the rumor and discovered its source to be nearly identical to the other story he had heard. He wandered for many years, gathering information and writing it down in his books until he had discovered all five stories, each one similar enough to connect them, but different enough to offer new information. After that, magic users scoured the regions to learn more of the Prophecies, and many wrote their findings in books that are now lost to us."

Thalan looked utterly appalled, his face pale and drawn. "But if they were just rumors and hearsay, couldn't the Prophecies have been distorted, changed by people?"

"Yes." Gwynne looked pained. Thalan had just inadvertently struck upon one of her biggest fears. "Yes, some amount of change must have occurred. You know how rumors spread and change. Each person who told it might have added something of their own, or neglected to mention some important fact. Cor and the others did the best they could, and they talked to hundreds, perhaps thousands of people, so the words that were eventually recorded were thought to be the closest to the original foretelling."

Thalan still looked upset. "I had no idea. We could be completely... completely wrong. All these centuries we could be working from information that isn't even... isn't even right!"

Gwynne reached out and patted his arm consolingly. "Believe me, I've thought about that often, but take heart. The similarities between the five stories lend it credence, and even if the details are not perfect, they are all we have to go on. In this case we have to take what we can get."

"It's too bad the Prophets didn't survive," Aliane murmured. "Perhaps then someone could have asked them some questions."

"It's unlikely they would have remembered what they said," Gwynne told her. "People rarely remember their feverish ramblings, and I have heard that those with the gift of foretelling almost never know afterwards what they prophesied."

Thalan looked thoughtful. "Still, I don't think I'll ever have another fever again without worrying now."

Gwynne laughed. "I wouldn't worry. There hasn't been a prophecy in over five hundred years," she said. "At least, none that we know of. I think you're safe."

"I wonder why the Prophecy occurred five hundred years too early," Thalan mused. "Did the Prophets give any indication when we should expect the woman? The Eye of Truth?"

"No," Gwynne said, laughing, "and my teacher told me that we might have to wait another five hundred years before she showed up. But I don't think so." She stole another quick glance at Aliane. "Even if we haven't found her yet, I'm sure she's at least been born. All the signs point to it."

"Can you tell us some of what the Prophecies said?" Aliane asked eagerly. "What did Cor and the others find during their searches?"

Gwynne looked at her kindly. "Another night, my dear. There will be time to talk later. Why don't you and Thalan practice those new spells I showed you?" And the rest of the night passed in pleasant instruction as Aliane twined the wind around her fingers and Thalan made droplets of water dance on his hand. There was a moment of excitement when Thalan accidentally doused their campfire, soaking Gwynne in the process, but for the most part things went well.

Finally Gwynne called a halt and decreed it was time for bed. As she spread her blanket upon the cold, hard ground and lay down upon it, she propped herself up on one arm as if struck by an odd thought. She picked up a corner of her blanket and examined it as if it contained the answer to some deeply hidden secret. She looked intently at Aliane, and asked, "What color is this, dear?"

Aliane was taken aback. "Excuse me?"

"Tell me what color this blanket is, please."

Aliane looked at the blanket in confusion. "It's green."

Gwynne also looked at the blanket, and Thalan was gazing at her as if she had just sprouted wings. "Why, so it is. Now tell me it is blue."

"What?" Aliane jumped, startled. "Why?"

"Just do it."

"But it isn't blue."

"I know. Just tell me that it is."

Aliane looked at the blanket intently, trying to fathom why Gwynne was asking her to do such a strange thing. Suddenly, in her mind's eye, the blanket seemed to separate as if its very essence unraveled before her. The threads still held it together, but as she scrutinized them she saw them as individual strands rather than a piece of the whole. It was as if she could see separately every single element that went into its making. She suddenly smiled.

"You're right," she told Gwynne. "I see blue."

It was Gwynne's turn to look taken aback. She stared at the blanket and frowned. "But it's not blue. It's green."

"I know. I said that before. But you asked me to say blue, so I did." Aliane was thoroughly confused now.

"Ah, well," Gwynne said, lying back on the most decidedly green blanket. "Perhaps I was wrong."

Aliane looked again at the blanket. It was most definitely green. How had she seen blue? But she knew somehow she had. She briefly wondered if she was perhaps going slightly mad.

Thalan later sat down next to her. "She was testing you, I think," he whispered quietly so Gwynne, lying several yards away, could not hear.

"Testing me? What do you mean?" Aliane whispered back.

"Well, she told me before that the Eye of Truth could not tell a lie. I think she was trying to see if you speak a falsehood or not. By asking you to tell a deliberate untruth, she was testing you."

"Oh, I see," Aliane said, finally understanding. "She still thinks I might be the Eye of Truth, doesn't she?"

"I think she does, but she's beginning to doubt," Thalan replied, looking at her intently. His eyes were a very lovely dark brown, Aliane noticed. "You have noble blood, and you were able to say that the blanket was blue. Perhaps it isn't you."

"That's what I've been saying!" Aliane said, her voice rising with frustration. Thalan quickly shushed her, and she glanced guiltily at Gwynne's sleeping form. She went on more quietly. "I'm only a woman who wants to live her own life."

"Not just a woman. A princess. A princess with magic," Thalan reminded her. "Strong magic. That alone makes you special."

"But that doesn't necessarily mean anything!"

"No, it doesn't," Thalan agreed. "Good night." And with that, he turned over and drew his own blanket – a red one, Aliane noted – around his shoulders. She lay down, but sleep was a long time coming. When slumber finally overtook her, it was deep and dreamless, much to her relief.

They reached the Port of Casset the next afternoon, and all three were grateful for the chance sleep in soft, comfortable beds with a roof over their heads. Aliane was glad to eat something other than rabbit and hard bread, and Thalan brought out his pipe and played a cheery, gay tune in the commons room after supper. The Port of Casset was a smallish city despite the wealth of trade that went through its docks and harbors. The innkeeper of the Gilded Eagle, where they broke their journey, proudly told them that most of the goods and provisions to Magir came through their port. Magir must support them very well, Aliane thought, looking at the well-constructed buildings, the paved roads and the carefully tended landscape. Small as it was, the Port of Casset flourished richly.

Though it was still early, Aliane was exhausted. She had never ridden so far, and her legs and buttocks were still unbelievably sore from long hours in the saddle. She rather felt as if she had been pummeled repeatedly with a large mallet as she had seen cooks do with over-tough chickens. The other two were in somewhat better shape, having been conditioned to long spells on horseback already. Aliane had once thought herself quite a horsewoman, but as she hobbled up the stairs to her room, she admitted with chagrin that her equestrian talents were not as great as they might have been. Perhaps she should ask Charis to incorporate horseback riding in their daily practice sessions when she got back.

With civilization so tantalizingly close, both Thalan and Gwynne refused to waste the remainder of the day sitting in their rooms, so they decided to see some of the sights of the city while they did some shopping. Their stores and provisions were hopelessly depleted, and they all needed warmer clothing. They asked her to join them, but Aliane was content to stay at the inn and rest her aching muscles, though she gave Gwynne some money to purchase a cloak and warmer clothes for her.

"You may as well get some trousers for me, too," she said, handing over the coins. "I'm used to them now, and riding in skirts would be just too inconvenient."

"Not to mention cold. Now let's see," Gwynne said, eyeing Aliane to estimate her size. "Goodness you're small! Another jerkin, too, perhaps. A plain leather one. That one you have is a bit fine, and we don't want you wearing it out."

"Are you sure you'll be all right here alone?" Thalan asked anxiously. He was nervously fidgeting – Aliane had already noticed that the young man rarely ever stood, sat or lay completely still. She was touched by his concern for her safety, though she suspected he was probably more concerned with the welfare of the crown princess of Cameon than for the woman named Aliane who stood before him.

"Of course I will," she assured him. "It will be good to have some time to myself, and I should write my father again. He will be so worried about me, I don't even want to think about it. Besides, I have this." She patted the sword that hung from her belt in its scabbard on her hip. Thalan looked skeptical, as if he doubted her ability to use the weapon, and Aliane smiled. One day she would have to challenge him to a sparring match. That would put to rest any fears he may have about her prowess with a blade.

After they left, Aliane collected ink, pen and paper and looked for a quiet place to write. She did not want to confine herself to her room, but the only other place to sit was in the commons. The commons of the Gilded Eagle was alight with lamps, and a comforting fire in the large stone fireplace warded off the chill of the coming evening. Most of the tables were full, though the hour was still unfashionably early for dining, and the noise of the people's chatter caused Aliane's head to ache. She sat down at an empty table and ordered wine from the server, hoping the spirit would soothe her troubled thoughts and weary body. An old man in a corner plucked a tune on a small stringed instrument, but the notes were swallowed in air thick with smoke and chatter before they could reach her ears.

She sat, biting the end of her pen, trying to think what she should write to her father. How could she reassure him about her situation when her situation was not at all reassuring? How could she tell him where she was going when she wasn't even sure herself? She wished there was a way to tell him what she was doing without actually *telling* him. Not, she admitted to herself, that such knowledge would likely bring him even a scrap of comfort. It would probably just upset him more.

A loud burst of laughter from a nearby table startled her, and her elbow knocked against her cup, slopping wine all over the table. She quickly righted the cup and watched in dismay as the deep purple stain spread across the blank page before her like blood, and it was only then that she realized how tightly strung her nerves were. She had to get a grip on herself. Perhaps she was more nervous than she had expected at being left alone. Suddenly she wished she had gone shopping with the others.

Stop it, she told herself. *Stop acting the fool*. There was nothing to fear, no one to harm her. She was just being fanciful. She looked around in vain for a handkerchief or napkin with which to mop up the spilled wine on her table, and could not find one. She was about to signal one of the serving lads when a snowy white square of cloth, held by a beautifully tended, long-fingered hand, was dangled before her eyes. Her fingers automatically closed around the offering, but when she looked up to thank her kind benefactor, time and breath stopped as she stared in shock. The noise of the inn faded as if it had never existed, and the painful thudding of her heart was her only indication that she still lived and had not slipped into a dream or fantasy concocted by her wishful, if imprudent, mind.

He's even more beautiful than I remembered, she thought dazedly. Even the scar on his left cheek was sexy. She was suddenly intensely relieved that the others had gone out, ridiculously happy that she had stayed behind, and hoped fervently that they would not return too soon. Unable to articulate anything even reasonably coherent, she stared at him, gaping like a kunga-fish.

Jaerak Thorin twitched the cloth from her nerveless fingers and smiled at her.

"Allow me," he said, and proceeded to mop up the wine from her table. "I'm afraid the paper is completely spoilt. I hope it was nothing important."

He raised his eyebrows as he looked at her, and Aliane noticed they were several shades darker than his hair.

She continued to gaze at him, wondering what on earth she could possibly to say to this man. She knew what he was, knew what he had done to Gwynne. It was quite possible that he hoped to use the Eye of Truth for his own gain, as Thalan had theorized. He was undoubtedly a member of the Onnic army, though Gwynne had told her how strong his magic was. He was thoroughly unscrupulous, conniving, ruthless and depraved. And yet... somehow he continued to fascinate her. She suddenly realized she had secretly hoped she might one day see him again, had wished it so secretly that she had not even known her own desire. And here he was, standing before her as if her mind had conjured up the very object of her longing, and she blinked her eyes to make sure they were not deceiving her.

Jaerak seemed amused by her astonishment. "May I?" He asked, indicating the empty chair at her table. Dumbly, she nodded, not knowing what else to do. The beautiful man seated himself. He stopped a passing servant lad and said, "More wine for the lady, and a cup of your finest ale for myself." He pressed a coin into the lad's hand and shooed him away. Then he turned to examine his mute and gaping tablemate.

"I remember you," he said, looking at her intently. *Blue*, she thought dizzily. *No, gray. No, not gray either. Slate, cobalt, or perhaps the color of rain on a distant mountain.* Then his words penetrated, and she felt the blood drain from her face. Jaerak looked at her curiously, as if surprised by her reaction. "You were at that inn in Magir, were you not?" His eyes, whatever their color, warmed perceptibly, and Aliane felt the color flood back into her cheeks. *The tide goes out, the tide goes in*, she thought wryly as she silently cursed the openness of her features.

"Which... which inn was that?" she asked, amazed at the steadiness of her voice. There had been two inns they had been in together, and she silently prayed that he had not seen her in both.

"The Dancing Waters, I think it was called," he said. "You were sitting alone, as if waiting for someone. But you left alone." He looked at her curiously, as if he wanted to ask her a question but was uncertain whether it would be proper. Greatly relieved, Aliane managed to smile at him.

"Yes, I was," she said, gaining confidence. "I remember you, too. You were sitting in the back..." She trailed off as she remembered whom he had been waiting for, and what they had talked about.

That smile appeared again, but she steeled herself against it. "Yes, and I recall my companion expressed some interest in you," he said. "Did he ever catch you up?"

So Larion *had* recognized her. She had been so sure he had not! That could prove to be a difficulty later. She remembered suddenly the prince's orders she had overheard, that he was to wait with a legion of men at the Lake Point for Gwynne. And, she also remembered with a sinking feeling in the pit of her stomach, a woman traveling with her. Lake Point. No wonder the name had sounded familiar when Gwynne had spoken it.

Jaerak did not wait for her answer. "My name is Jaerak Thorin. May I have the honor of yours?"

"A... Ashleighn el'Faria," she said, the name coming unconsciously to her tongue. She was a little surprised that she had chosen that particular name for herself. It had been her mother's. Ashleighn el'Gregarian had married Queen Rhyssl's mother's cousin, Ronen el'Faria, Aliane's father. Aliane's full name was Aliane Ashleighn el'Faria Gracia el'Gregarian – something of a mouthful, she'd always thought.

Jaerak's elegant eyebrows zoomed up to his hairline. "el'Faria? You are then a relation to Queen Rhyssl el'Faria?"

"Only very distantly."

Jaerak took her hand and kissed it gently, and Aliane had to give herself a firm talking-to before she could speak again. "And what brings you to the Port of Casset, Lord... Thorin?" she inquired, withdrawing her hand gently, though reluctantly, from his grasp. The kiss still burned on her skin, and she hid her hand in her lap as if his lips had made a mark visible for all to see.

"I am here on business," he replied smoothly, not denying the title. *I'll bet you are,* Aliane thought bitterly. She still could not reconcile his beautiful face with his deformed soul. It just did not seem possible. But then one has a tendency to equate beauty with goodness, Aliane mused. It was a misleading assumption to say the least. Gwynne was as good a person as Aliane had ever met, but no one could conceivably call her beautiful, though she must have been a handsome woman in her youth.

"And you?"

Aliane blinked. She had lost the thread of the conversation.

"And I what?" she asked, taking a sip of wine to cover her confusion.

"What brings you to this fair city?" Jaerak expanded, smiling. "It seems you are quite the traveler. Unusual for a woman alone, so young – and so beautiful."

To her mortification, Aliane felt the tide come in again, and she was sure her face was scarlet. She really had to control her emotions. She hadn't blushed so much since she was twelve years old, when the son of a baron had tried to kiss her in her father's gardens behind the palace.

"I... the purpose of my journey is to meet up with my companions," she said. "And I wanted to see the world." Why she had added that last tidbit of information she did not know, but it seemed to interest him.

"But the world can be a dark and dangerous place," Jaerak commented, looking at her intently.

"Oh, but it holds such wonders!" Aliane exclaimed. "I've never seen mountains or rivers or grand cities." She stopped, biting her lip. She would have to guard her tongue more carefully. "Forgive me, I fear my enthusiasm sometimes runs away with me."

Jaerak smiled, and Aliane felt her toes curl in response. "Don't apologize. It's refreshing to meet someone with such passion for living. I think I understand what you mean. You must have led a sheltered life."

"Yes." She stared down at the table top, not knowing what else to say.

Jaerak leaned forward. "I'm afraid that my business demands my attention now, but I would be honored if you would dine with me tomorrow night."

Hoo boy, Aliane thought, her pulse quickening. She thought very fast. "I would like that very much," she ventured truthfully, "but I think I must be gone tomorrow."

"That is a shame." To her amazement, he seemed truly regretful. "Another time, then. Perhaps you could tell me where you will be going next, and it might be possible to meet you there."

Aliane smiled regretfully. "I'm afraid I don't honestly know. I haven't yet decided." *Why don't you just tell him you have to wash your hair?* she chided herself. *That would at least sound probable*. Though what she *had* said was true enough, now that she thought about it. *A change of plans might be in order now.*

"Well. We will just have to trust in fate then, won't we?" He stood and took her hand again. He held it for a moment, his thumb caressing her palm with the tiniest movement, and Aliane felt her entire body respond to that infinitesimal touch. "I am sure we will meet again. Perhaps if you don't meet up with your friends tonight you would like to have a drink with me. I'm staying at the Sylavan House across from the market square." He kissed her hand again, and released it. He then turned and left the room.

Aliane sat dumbly, her hand still resting on the table where he had placed it. Coherent thought was impossible, and for a moment she reveled in pure, unadulterated pleasure. Then the reality of the situation forcibly struck her and she leapt to her feet as if stung. She had to find Gwynne and Thalan and warn them. *How by the blasted sands of the Carelian Desert had he known they were there?*

She forced herself to sit down and breathe deeply. It would do no good to go flying off in all directions. Since she had no idea where her friends had gone, she must await their return. She sat at her table and wrote letters in an admirable display of outward composition until she saw her companions come through the door. As soon as they entered, she quickly gathered up her belongings and made her way through the crowded room toward them. They were loaded with packages and parcels, and they looked rather tired. Thalan took one look at Aliane's face and dropped the bundles he carried.

"What's happened?" he asked sharply, taking her hand – pen, ink and all. "You're as white as a ghost!"

"Not here," she said breathlessly, furtively glancing around her. The others stared at her as if she had lost what was left of her mind. "I'll explain in our rooms. We have to get out of here." She took Gwynne's arm and quickly led her through the maze of people to the stairs that led to the rooms above. Thalan, after picking up the dropped packages, quickly followed.

"Not my room," Aliane said, pushing them past her door. "He may decide to come by for another visit." *Wishful thinking?* she asked herself derisively. "Here." She opened Thalan's door and shoved them unceremoniously inside.

Gwynne flung her parcels on the bed and turned to face Aliane. "He's here, isn't he? Jaerak. You saw him." It was not a question, but a flat statement of fact.

"Yes." Gwynne nodded as if she had expected no other answer.

"He's here?" Thalan demanded, gazing at her incredulously. "No wonder you looked so strange!"

Aliane gave them a somewhat expurgated version of her first formal meeting with Jaerak Thorin while the others listened avidly.

"How do you suppose he got here before us?" Thalan asked. Aliane blinked. The question had not occurred to her. Jaerak Thorin really had addled her brains.

"That's right," she said slowly. "He was still in Magir when we left, and he certainly didn't pass us on the road."

"Maybe there's another road," Gwynne offered, though she knew there was not. "Or maybe he didn't come by road at all. Did you see any of his men with him?" she asked Aliane, who shook her head.

"No. He was alone, though he did say he was here to meet people on business. But he wasn't even in his uniform."

"What else did he say?" Gwynne asked, her face studiously neutral and her voice noncommittal. Aliane blushed.

"Er..." she said, thinking fast. "He told me he was staying at the Sylavan House, and that he was sure he would see me again someday."

"Strange," Gwynne murmured quietly. "That's just what he said to me." Aliane looked down at her feet, unable to meet the older woman's eyes.

"And you're sure he didn't recognize you from The Fox and Falcon?" Thalan asked, completely unaware of Aliane's discomfiture.

"I don't think he did. He said he saw me in The Dancing Waters. I knew Larion was meeting him there, so I waited in the dining lounge. I saw Jaerak there first, and that's when he saw me. That's also where I learned where to find you."

"He is anticipating our every move," Thalan said through gritted teeth. "How by the Seven Gates of Hades did he know we'd be here? And more importantly, how do we escape him?"

"He knows we would be here because he knows where we are going," Aliane said urgently. "I heard him tell Larion to station men at the Lake Point and wait for two women to arrive. I thought when you first mentioned the Lake Point that it sounded familiar, but I couldn't remember why. Now I do. They had talked about it during their meeting. Jaerak knows that's where we're going! And when we get there we shall surely be walking right into his trap."

"Perhaps we should rethink our plans," Thalan mused. "It would be foolish to walk into a trap knowingly."

"I'm not so sure," Gwynne said suddenly. "Yes, he expects us to go there, but he has to make sure we have the real Eye of Truth before he can strike at us." Gwynne looked at Aliane sadly. "And it would appear we do not."

Aliane lowered her eyes again, unable to meet that sorrowful gaze. She felt absurdly guilty. She had never wanted to disappoint the kindly old woman.

"Perhaps," Thalan said, soothingly, looking at Gwynne with concern. "We shall see."

"Besides, even when he does get the Eye of Truth, he won't want to hurt her," Aliane argued. "He'll only want information from her." Gwynne stared at her and Thalan looked at her pityingly, and she suddenly blushed. She realized she was being naïve, but she just couldn't imagine Jaerak doing anything to hurt her.

"And we are only assuming that Jaerak wants to capture the Eye of Truth," Gwynne reminded them. "As yet, it is still only a theory." She shot a quick look at Thalan. "No offense."

He gave her a watered-down version of his usual lively grin. "None taken."

"Well, it's the best one we have so far," Aliane argued, sitting on the bed and tucking her feet under her. "Why else would he be following you around all over the countryside? And since we already know we don't have the Eye of Truth, why don't we head back south? We could go to my father's castle.

He would hide you, I'm sure he would."

"Hmmm," Thalan muttered, rubbing his chin. "That's a thought. Jaerak wouldn't be expecting that."

"He would find us," Gwynne said with conviction, "and we would eventually go where he wanted us to go. He can be very... persuasive." She looked at Aliane and smiled. "I wouldn't want to involve your father in this, dear, it's too dangerous. Besides, we don't yet know if she is unfound."

Aliane sighed. "But it's pretty obvious, isn't it? I mean, I am of noble blood. I told a falsehood. I *can't* be the Eye of Truth."

Gwynne looked at her intensely. "Then say it. Say 'I am not the Eye of Truth'."

Aliane regarded her steadily. "I am not the Eye of Truth," she said. Gwynne sighed.

"Well, I guess that's that."

"But you might still be."

Thalan jerked his head up, but Gwynne merely laughed. "I told you before, child. It cannot be."

"But how do you know?" Aliane persisted. "The Eye of Truth must be found because she does not know herself, right? Well, perhaps it is you. Perhaps you don't know your own strength."

Gwynne shook her head sadly. "I have told many lies in my life, dear."

"But you said yourself it is possible not all the Prophecy is true. Remember? Rumors get changed, facts become blurred."

"If so, then you still have just as much a chance as she," Thalan pointed out. "I think it would be best to go to the Mirror and let you both look in it. That will decide the matter once and for all."

Aliane glanced at Thalan and smiled mischievously. "Perhaps the Prophecy was completely wrong. Maybe *you* should look in the pool, too, Thalan."

Thalan looked outraged and Gwynne laughed, breaking the tension in the room. "That might be going a bit far," Gwynne admitted, still chuckling. "Then it is agreed. We will continue to the Lake Point."

"And when we get there?" Thalan asked, all seriousness again. "When we meet Jaerak there?"

"We will skate across that pond when we come to it," Gwynne said firmly, "and hope the ice is not too thin. We'll be all right. We've gotten this far, and there will be three of us, and only one of him."

"Plus as many soldiers as Larion might have there," Aliane reminded her. "If neither of us is the Eye of Truth, then we shall be in greater danger than before."

"I know," Gwynne said softly. "I know. But others have faced graver danger than we, and we can do no less. We must hope that Jaerak will leave us unharmed until he is sure the Eye of Truth has been found. We are his best – his only – hope of finding her."

"Then when shall we leave?" Thalan asked.

"Tomorrow," Gwynne said, looking at Aliane. The young woman kept her face carefully devoid of emotion. "We leave tomorrow."

Aliane nodded, and Gwynne sighed with relief. The older woman suddenly gave a huge yawn that cracked her jaws, and she looked surprised. "I must be more tired than I thought," Gwynne said, laughing a little.

Thalan did not laugh, but looked at her sharply. "Then you should rest. Here, lie down." He shooed Aliane off the bed while Gwynne protested that she could not possibly take his room, but he quickly moved aside the parcels and drew back the covers.

"Well... maybe for just a little while." She gratefully lay down, and was asleep before she had drawn four breaths.

Thalan sighed in silent relief as Gwynne's breathing slowed and the lines on her face fell out of their tense, rigid grooves into more relaxed positions. She looked frail and vulnerable, and Thalan was extremely worried about her. Jaerak and his campaign of terror had affected her more than she had admitted, and the constant strain and tension were draining her. Her wounds were well healed, but Thalan suspected there were other, deeper wounds – injuries hidden from view on her mind and soul that still greatly pained her, though she never hinted at them. Thalan knew what Jaerak had done to her, but Gwynne had never spoken of it again, nor had she given him many details of her experiences. He suspected her cheerful demeanor cloaked a raw-edged pain and anger that must eventually surface and be released, otherwise it would eat away at her until it destroyed her. He motioned to Aliane to slip out as quietly as possible, and they gently closed the door after them.

"I wonder if this is all being too much for her," Thalan said quietly as they stole down the corridor to Gwynne's room. "She's not as strong as she would like us to think."

"She does look rather worn," Aliane said. "Perhaps we should stay here a few more days and let her get some rest." *And what will you do?* she asked herself silently. *Hide in your room all day so he won't see you? Or so you won't see him?*

"I don't think so," Thalan countered. "The strain of waiting is as hard as traveling for her, and it would be too dangerous with Jaerak as close as he is. No, I think we need to resolve the situation as quickly as possible." He gave Aliane a measured look. "You look as if you could do with some rest as well.

Your eyes are burnt holes in your head. Here, lie down and try to get some sleep." He gave her a long look as she made herself comfortable on the bed and a slight flush tinged his cheeks. "I'll just... um... I'll just go."

"Where are you going?" Aliane asked as Thalan took a cloak from its hook and wrapped it around his shoulders. He did not look her in the eye as he answered.

"To find Jaerak. If he's meeting with someone, I want to know who it is and what it's about."

Aliane grabbed the sleeve of his shirt. "You can't! It's too risky."

Thalan laughed. "Don't be so conventional. It's not risky, Jaerak Thorin doesn't even know I exist. He's never seen me."

"He may have seen you at the inn," she argued, still clutching his sleeve. Thalan gently disengaged her fingers and gave them a squeeze before he opened the door.

"He didn't. We've never even been in the same room together. Don't worry, I won't do anything stupid. I just want to see if I can get any information. Get some sleep. I'll be back soon." With that, he slipped through the door before she could voice another protest.

Garlands twined in
night-black hair
Crown lucent, smiling eyes so fair,
You change my prose
to purest verse,
My one star becomes
a universe.

– Old love song from Marrin, author unknown.

Chapter Twelve

Jaerak smiled as he wiped his lips with satisfaction. A good meal was always a pleasure. The Sylavan House had always spread a fine table, and he made a point to stop by every time he passed through the Port of Casset. Though the last time he had been here he'd had to forego the pleasure – he'd been forced to leave in something of a hurry. It would be awkward he if he ran into any of the militiamen who had pursued him after his assassination of a rich and prominent merchant, but that had been many years ago and he doubted he would be recognized now. If his plan worked as he hoped, he would never have to sully his hands with such work again.

As he dropped several gold pieces onto the rough-hewn tabletop, Jaerak was glad he'd had the foresight to realize he would need someone to back him if his plans were to succeed. Masyl Vonnin might be an antiquated witchhunter, but he did have his uses. As a captain in the Onnic army Jaerak was entitled to the best rooms, the best food, and the best wine. And, he mused, the best women.

The pretty one he had met tonight might be well worth cultivating. Strange, that she should appear here after he had seen her in Magir. Come to think of it, she had never told him why she had come to the Port of Casset. Or, for that matter, what she had been doing at The Dancing Waters in Magir. And, he pondered further, how could a woman who dresses in trousers, fine though they were, capture the interest of a pompous, overblown, arrogant prince? It had been quite obvious that Larion had known her. Was it the honorific 'el' before her last name, signifying her tie with a royal family? *Could she possibly be his lover? Perhaps carrying his child?* Well, Jaerak would make sure he would have a chance to ask her. She had indeed captured his interest, and the thought of seeing her again brought an unexpected surge of pleasure. It had been a long time since a woman had captivated his fancy, and this one had an air of mystery that intrigued him. For all her plain clothes and outspoken virtue, this was no ordinary woman. She had a grace and a style of manner that bespoke wealth and position, and she wore her honorific as if she had been born to it. Yes, he just might do well to become better acquainted with Ashleighn el'Faria, at that.

His thoughts turned to more prosaic matters as he spied a man coming through the door. Just the man he had been waiting for, he thought with relish. He looked quite old, though Jaerak knew him to be barely past his middle years. Years of hard labor and harder living had resulted in a bent frame, wrinkled skin and prematurely whitened hair. He had few teeth, and those that remained were stained brown and crooked out at odd angles. The teeth were bared in what was supposed to be a grin as the old man spotted Jaerak sitting alone in wait for him. He could not have looked more the ruffian had he purposely tried to cultivate the part. And, Jaerak thought, amused, he very probably did.

The man, Ratliff by name, hobbled over to the table and seated himself. Jaerak pushed the tankard of ale he had ordered toward him, and Ratliff grasped it eagerly and drank. Every man, Jaerak mused, had a weakness. *Find a man's weakness and he is yours.* Some men, like Ratliff, would commit acts for a mug of ale that they would not consider doing to feed their starving family. Others, like his old bookseller friend Thomlyn, folded immediately if they thought their loved ones were in danger. *Yes, every man has a weakness, St. Petrius bless them. Every woman, too.* He wondered what Ashleighn's weakness might be. It would be most intriguing to find out.

"Did you see where she went?" Jaerak asked once the tankard had been drained dry.

"She came to my inn this afternoon," the old man replied, with a wistful look at the empty mug before him. Jaerak caught a passing serving maid and ordered another. Ratliff grinned at him. "She looked just like you said she would, but she had someone with her. You didn't say nothing about another."

"Someone was with her?" Jaerak asked sharply. "Who?"

"How'm I supposed to know?" the old man asked querulously. "I never seen neither of 'em before. I only looked fer her, since you told me to. She was with a man... young. Long curly hair. Big nose." He gave a grotesque chuckle. "A real big nose. Can't hardly miss that one. Anyway, they went to their rooms and soon they came back out again. They went out, so I follered 'em."

"The elusive musician, no doubt," Jaerak mused to himself, remembering that the Seeker had been seen talking to a young musician at the Fox and Falcon, and both had disappeared that night. "Where did they go, Ratliff?"

"They did some shoppin'. Clothes, food, that sort of thing. They went to the farrier and had their horses checked. Strange, that. They took three horses, and 'tweren't only but the two of 'em."

"Three horses? That is strange. Could one have been a burden beast? Or pulling a carriage?"

"Nah, not those three!" Ratliff snorted, and grabbed at the fresh mug of ale that the server had placed before him. After a long draught, he gave a contented sigh. "They was too fine for that. Nice beasts, good horseflesh. One in particular. Black, it were, with a white blazon on its nose. The two I told you of were riding the others – a bay and a palomino, I think – but they was leading that black one."

"Interesting," Jaerak mused, stroking his chin. "Three. Perhaps they picked up someone else, then. You're sure you didn't see anyone with them?"

"Naw, I didn't see no one else," Ratliff said. He was shifting in his chair, clearly uncomfortable. Now that he had given his information, he wanted to be away. Jaerak was not quite finished with him, though.

"You said you saw them at your inn. The Gilded Eagle. Are they staying there?"

"Din't I just say so?" Ratliff took another pull from his ale.

"Did you see another woman there? Young, beautiful, small build, lots of dark curly hair?" He could almost still catch the lingering scent of that hair. "Big green eyes?"

"Aye, I seen that one." Ratliff licked his lips. "A tasty morsel, that one is. As fine a piece as ever put on airs in my place."

Jaerak let that one pass. Ratliff worked in the back kitchens of the Gilded Eagle and it was unlikely he would have the chance to get close enough to Ashleighn to offend her.

"Do you know what room she's in?" he persisted.

Ratliff barked out a coarse laugh. "Thinking of payin' her a visit, were you? Not that I'd blame you, with that one. Naw, I don' know what room." His eyes gleamed craftily. "But fer another mug I could sure find out for ye."

Jaerak waved the suggestion away. "Not necessary. I can find out for myself." He turned his cold gaze on Ratliff, and the little man seemed to shrink even more. "You're to leave that one alone, am I understood?"

"Yes sir," Ratliff mumbled, and shot him a murderous glance when he thought Jaerak wasn't looking. *Foolish man,* Jaerak thought. Ratliff should know by now that he missed nothing.

"Very well. Anything else to report?"

"Nah. I follered them all day, and then they just went back to the inn. Guess they got tired and wanted their beds. Not that he'll enjoy it, sharing it with that one! Twenty years his senior if she's a day, and her face all scarred like that!" A crafty look appeared on his unpleasant, weasel-like face. "But maybe he 'as another to warm his bed fer 'im now."

"Thank you, Ratliff," Jaerak said, ignoring the remark. The chink of coins sounded as they passed into the old man's gnarled, greedy hands. "Keep watch on them, and let me know if anyone comes to see them. Also, keep and eye out for their companion. See if anyone is often in their company. I'll be by tomorrow to check on our quarry."

The old man chuckled again. "Thank ye kindly, my Lord. I'll do that." He looked mournfully at the again empty cup before him. "How 'bout just one more, fer old time's sake?" he asked hopefully. But Jaerak had no more use for him. He had already spotted someone else, someone he was eager to talk with in private.

"Not tonight, my inebriated friend," Jaerak said, shoving Ratliff's chair away from the table with his booted foot. Even the drunken old man could not ignore a hint that blatant, and he stood up unsteadily and stomped away, muttering under his breath about high and mighty lords who wouldn't even share a drink with those that helped 'em.

Jaerak caught the eye of the man in the doorway and beckoned, thinking how out of place the High Priest looked in such surroundings. He stood out like a bird of paradise among sparrows. Or perhaps, more appropriately, like a vulture among chickens, Jaerak thought. Masyl Vonnin was richly dressed in crushed red velvet and trappings studded with gems, and the Onnic insignia – two swords crossed over an eye with a teardrop iris – as well as the mark of his rank were prominently displayed. Even as he crossed the room, a multitude of eyes followed him, glinting with greedy speculation. Perhaps Masyl thought his station gave him immunity from thieves and pickpockets, but Jaerak knew there were those who would not scruple to rob even an Onnic soldier where such wealth was within easy reach.

Masyl sat in the chair that Ratliff had just vacated, fastidiously passing his handkerchief over it before he settled himself down.

"I look forward to your report," Masyl said, shaking his head to the serving maid who came to take his order. He made it a rule never to drink anything in public houses. Even if the cups were clean, which they usually weren't, it was too easy for someone to slip something into his drink when he wasn't looking. He had narrowly escaped being poisoned on several occasions and now would drink only what was poured by his own hands.

Jaerak took a long draught from his mug, eyeing the High Priest over the rim. *Find a man's weakness and exploit it,* he thought smugly. Masyl's weakness was his hunger for power, for fame and glory. Even after the Eye of Truth had been found the High Priest would still have his uses, and the man's arrogance almost guaranteed he would never realize he was being used.

"First tell me what happened back in Magir," Jaerak said, wiping foam from his lips. "Why were you not at the Fox and Falcon? Surely my message was clear enough."

Masyl's expression made a thundercloud look as innocent and cheerful as a box of kittens. "The message went astray," he said shortly. "I never received it."

It was Jaerak's turn to frown. "Surely the princeling did not fail to deliver it to you? I instructed him to put it in your hands alone."

"He did come to me, but your message had already been lost," Masyl said impatiently. He did not enjoy having to explain himself to this man. "Next time perhaps you should deliver your own messages rather than trusting them to someone else."

"It was impossible. I couldn't get away. I did send for you later, Masyl."

"Yes. By the time I arrived you had already gone. Left a bloody mess behind you, too." Masyl rubbed his chin in thought. "Perhaps to forestall any further misunderstandings I should travel with you a while."

Jaerak looked at him quizzically, though the warning alarms were going off in his head with deafening shrillness. "There is no need for that, surely. It would be very uncomfortable for you."

Masyl waved the argument away. "Nonsense," he said briskly. "I must be there when we apprehend the woman. Our bargain did stipulate that I would get credit for her capture."

Jaerak groaned silently. How was he supposed to follow through his plans with the High Priest of Casset looking over his shoulder? "But are you sure it would be wise for you to travel to the North Country..." he began, but was interrupted before he could finish.

Masyl slammed his fist against the tabletop, making Jaerak's mug rock on its base. "Enough of this. Are you going to give me your report or have I just wasted a very long, very tiring trip?"

"Everything goes as planned," Jaerak said smoothly, ignoring the priest's fraying temper. "I was able to flush the Seeker out of the Fox and Falcon, and I followed her here."

"She's here?" Masyl asked, his interest quickening. "In the Port of Casset?"

"Yes. She's staying at another inn. I have eyes watching her at all times. And there is something more."

Masyl looked at him through narrowed eyes. "What?"

"She is not alone."

Masyl leaned back in his seat, digesting this news. "Just as you predicted. A woman?"

"Perhaps. She left Magir with a man, but they seem to have picked up another companion. As of yet, I don't know who it is."

"And they are moving north," Masyl mused. "You think they are going to the Lake Point?"

"I can't think of any other reason they would be heading that way. If they are, then it is most likely they have a woman with them. A woman they want to put to the test."

"And you will have troops waiting for them there?"

"They are already on their way," Jaerak stated. He looked sharply at his companion. "But remember our arrangement. No one is to harm them until I have had what was promised me."

Masyl frowned again. "I still don't like it. What could you possibly want of them except their deaths?"

"That is my business alone," Jaerak said dangerously, and Masyl thought it wise not to inquire further. There would be time enough later to divine this enigmatic man's plans. Yet another reason to join him on this stage of their journey. He had been dissatisfied with the bits and snippets of news Jaerak sent him when he bothered to write.

"When do you think they will be leaving?" Masyl asked instead.

"I'm hoping they will leave within the next few days," Jaerak replied, finishing his ale. "They'll want to get to the Lake Point before the heavy snows. They'll probably stay here a couple days to gather supplies and rest from their journey. Have no fear, as I said, I have people watching her and they will inform me the instant they move."

"And the identity of this mysterious third party?" Masyl inquired.

"I'm working on that, too. But remember – if it is a woman, and they are heading for the Lake Point, we must allow them to look into the pool before we do anything. We *must* be sure that she is the one."

"Yes," Masyl agreed thoughtfully. "And if it isn't?"

"Patience, my friend, patience," Jaerak said. "Patience is everything. If they have not yet found her, then we wait until they do."

"Eventually I will be needed back at the Cathedral," Masyl dryly pointed out. "The Triumvirate is meeting this season, and I must be there. I cannot spend all my time chasing a phantom woman that might not even exist."

"Feel free to back out of our agreement any time," Jaerak said, his voice cold. "As I told you before, I can always take my proposition elsewhere."

"Yes, well, no need to think on that just yet," Masyl said rapidly. "I'm sure we can work something out."

Yes indeed, Jaerak thought with amusement as he watched the older man backpedal. *Find their weakness, and they're yours.*

They spoke then of other things, and neither man noticed the young man with long curly hair and an astonishingly large nose at an adjoining table gather his belongings and slip through the door into the dark, cold night.

* * *

"You are sure about that?" Aliane asked anxiously. "He was a slightly overweight, gray-haired man of middle years?"

"Yes," Thalan said patiently for the third time.

"And his name was Masyl?"

"Yes, I'm sure of it."

"It was Masyl Vonnin. It has to be. We have to leave at once," Aliane said urgently, her face pale with anxiety. "Masyl might recognize me. I think he saw me at the ball."

Thalan looked at her with amusement. "You mean the ball where you popped His Royal Jackass right in the face?" Despite her worry, Aliane had to smile at the memory.

They were sitting on Thalan's bed, discussing what he had overheard that night. Gwynne, refreshed after her short nap, looked thoughtful rather than worried, but Thalan seemed to have aged ten years in one night. Lines of worry pulled his mouth down at the corners, and his shoulders drooped as if he carried a heavy weight.

"Interesting," Gwynne said, "but we didn't truly learn anything new, did we?"

"Well, some of our suspicions were validated," Thalan said. "He knows we are going to the Lake Point, and his aim is not to harm us. At least, not yet."

"He truly is looking for the Eye of Truth," Aliane murmured in wonder. "He wants to use her." *Oh, Jaerak. Why did you have to be such a bastard?*

"Yes," Gwynne agreed. "And now he thinks we may have found her." She glanced at Aliane and said no more.

Aliane, however, refused to be baited. "Then he will be disappointed," she said firmly. "At least we know that when we get to the Lake Point we will be unmolested."

"We will have to be more careful, though," Thalan said, running his hands through his hair as he always did when he was agitated. "He knows there are three of us, and now he knows what I look like."

"That doesn't change anything," Gwynne stated firmly. "The question is, how do we get out of the Port of Casset without this Ratliff character seeing us?"

"I can use the same trick I did before," Aliane offered. Gwynne frowned at her.

"It's not a trick, dear. Magic is not some sleight of hand used to fool people into thinking that what they see is real. Besides, it's too dangerous."

"But I did it before," Aliane argued.

"We don't want to attract the notice of other Onnic soldiers who might not have instructions regarding us," Thalan pointed out. "If we go about using magic, eventually we will be caught by someone who has no orders to keep us safe."

"Oh." Aliane tugged pensively on her lip. "I hadn't thought of that."

"I wonder why Jaerak has expressed such an interest in you," Gwynne suddenly mused, looking at Aliane speculatively.

Thalan snorted. "It should be obvious, don't you think? I mean, look at her." He gestured toward Aliane. "She's... well... she's very..." Thalan stumbled to a halt, suddenly confused and flaming red. Aliane hid a smile, grateful she was not the only one who could not always control her tongue – or her blushes. Thalan really was very sweet.

Gwynne smiled at his discomfiture. "Yes, she is very beautiful, and it is only natural she's caught the interest of a handsome young man, no matter how evil he may be."

Aliane ducked her head, but Gwynne reached out and put her fingers under her chin, forcing her head up to look her in the eye. "And you are just as fascinated by him, aren't you? Don't be ashamed, there's nothing wrong with that. Just be careful, my dear. Don't let his pretty face blind you to his true nature."

"I won't," Aliane muttered. She should have known Gwynne would see what she had so carefully tried to hide.

"At least he doesn't know you are the one traveling with us," Thalan said. For some reason he was scowling, and he looked more disgruntled than he usually did even in the early mornings.

"Not yet, anyway," Gwynne temporized. "But he is sure to find out somehow. If he follows us he will see her with his own eyes."

"So how do we get out of the inn without being seen if we can't use magic?" Aliane asked again. "What do we do about Ratliff? You know he'll be watching for us."

"I think I have an idea that just might work," Thalan said, his eyes twinkling with mischief. "How much money do we have?"

Gwynne gave him some silver coins, and Aliane added a gold one from her own purse. "What are you planning to do, buy his silence?" she asked as she watched him comb his hair. "You'll need more than that. But Jaerak will get the information out of him one way or another, you know."

Thalan grinned. "Not if Ratliff's too drunk to remember," he said, and with that he went downstairs.

More than two hours later he came back, a little wobbly on his feet. "If we leave now it should be safe," he stated with satisfaction as he stumbled into the room. "Ratliff is as drunk as a man the night before his wedding. Oop. Sorry. I had to have a few with him, and salt and stuff me but that man can hold his drink!"

"What did you tell him?" Gwynne asked, holding him upright so he would not fall down. She led him to a chair and gently pushed him into it.

"Just that I had just made a killing in a game of cards," Thalan said smugly. "I announsh... announced to the entire room that drinks were on me, and as soon as that lout heard free drinks were being offered in the commonsh... er... commons, he was out there fashter than... um... than – well, fast." Thalan rubbed his forehead. "Sorry, my brain's a little fuzzy."

"Brilliant," Gwynne said, rubbing her hands together with glee. "So it's safe?"

"Yup, safe. He's passed out cold. I just kept buying drinks for him until he fell off his stool. The innkeeper dragged him into the back to sleep it off. I don't know how the wretched man has managed to keep his job so long. We'd better get going soon, I think. I don't know how long he'll stay under."

"Is all this really necessary?" Aliane asked, feeling a twinge of guilt. She hated having to prey on a man's weakness for his own benefit.

"Do you really want Jaerak to know you are the woman traveling with us?" Thalan asked her as he tossed a medium sized sack to Gwynne. "Food. I got it from the kitchens before I came up."

"Ah. Right. Good point," Aliane said, snatching up her own bag. Despite what Jaerak might or might not feel for her, she knew his attitude would change once he learned she was the third traveler. "We should still be careful, then," she said as they left the room and locked the door behind them. "He may have other spies around."

"Hmmm, yes," Gwynne said. "I hadn't thought of that. Well, there isn't much more we can do, is there?"

"Isn't there?" Aliane asked her, raising her eyebrows.

"No, dear. I won't have you risking yourself."

Aliane sighed. She had been looking forward to an excuse to use magic, she so rarely ever had the chance. Gwynne noticed her downcast look and again read her thoughts with startling accuracy.

"Don't worry, dear," she said, patting Aliane on the arm. "We'll find a way to give you some practice. I promise."

And with that carrot dangling before her nose, Aliane had to be content.

Their exodus was uneventful and unseen, it appeared, by prying eyes or suspiciously interested parties. The Port of Casset boasted no city walls or gates, so they proceeded unchallenged past the city limits and found the road – if a road it could be called – that would eventually lead them to the Lake Point. It obviously was seldom traveled, for the surface had cracked with time and neglect, and a few remaining shoots of grass and weeds sprouted between the time-smoothed edges of the stones that paved their way. As they set forth, Aliane thought of the letter she had sent to her father that very day, and hoped it would reach him soon, for she guessed she would have little opportunity in the near future to write him another. She hoped he was not worrying too much, though she knew in her heart he was. Perhaps one day she would be able to explain everything to him, but until then, he must trust her to take care of herself. And she would, too. Somehow, she would.

* * *

The trip took ten days of hard riding, and often Aliane kept watch from behind but never saw anyone following them. In truth, she saw no one at all – they passed no towns or villages and met no other travelers along their way. The road was open, reaching out before them toward the seemingly unreachable horizon, and there were few trees to shield followers from view. When the weather was clear she could see for miles in all directions, but the weather was not always so agreeable. After the third day, the snows began to fall in earnest, and Aliane was grateful for her new lined cloak and warm breeches. Contact with Frigget kept her warm during the day, so she didn't truly feel the cold until they stopped to make camp each night. Even the fires they built in their camps did not dispel the icy winds that seemed to blow right through her body as if she had no more substance than a ghost. The three companions often had to huddle together for warmth when darkness fell, and once Thalan's blanket caught fire because he tried to sleep too close to the campfire, but despite these discomforts Aliane did not mind the cold nights, for it was during these stops that Gwynne taught her how to use magic.

She learned that magic was more a gift than a talent; a gift bestowed by the Elements to those who could understand and use it. Magic did not come from within one's body, but existed within the elements of the earth, the sky, the waters, the roaring flames of fire, from the very essence of time itself. Only a select few could touch these energies and manipulate them, could see the lines that binds matter and life together, and craft them into spell-webs of their own design. Magic was an integral part of nature itself, as much as both matter and energy, though more ephemeral and less substantive than either. She must, Gwynne told her, stop viewing magic as something on the fringe of the natural world just because not everyone could understand or see it.

Armed with her new knowledge, Aliane learned to listen to the air, to hear what it whispered as it flowed silkily past her ears. She learned to see the relationship between all things and to pick out the different energies that each breath of wind, each spark of flame, each grain of earth, each drop of water gave forth. When she concentrated hard enough she could see the spell-lines – fantastic patterns of yellow, ruby, emerald, and cyan light crisscrossing across the heavens and earth in intricate and endlessly complicated gyrations of movement, always changing and never at rest. She could not maintain such concentration for long, though. The effort made her dizzy and gave her a throbbing headache afterwards.

Thalan, though not as adept as Aliane, drank in the knowledge as greedily as she, and Gwynne found it gratifying to impart the wisdom she had kept to herself for so many years. Knowledge was meant to be shared, and she joyously and generously gave all she had. Aliane learned quickly and took even Gwynne by surprise with her skill.

One night, after they had fed and watered the horses, the three friends sat huddled around the campfire, trying to stave off a particularly cold and nasty wind. Suddenly, Gwynne felt that familiar, delicious tingle in her bones, a sure sign someone was using magic. The air around her began to get warm and her eyes widened with amazement. Soon she could have sworn she was sitting in the midst of a balmy, summer day had she not still been able to see the snow whirling around them and the sparse, scarce trees whipping their branches in the wind. Thalan's expression was as dumbfounded as hers, and Aliane burst out laughing when she saw their faces.

"Like it?" she asked gleefully, her eyes bright. "I don't know why I didn't think of this before."

Thalan stared at her. "*You're* doing this?" he asked incredulously, reaching out a finger as if he could touch the warmth that now so strangely encompassed him. "But how?"

"I just drew some of the warmth from the fire into the air surrounding us," Aliane explained. "Look. Like this."

She spread her fingers and spun a thin yellow spell-web of air between them, almost like she had when she was young and she and Hernie would play kitten-in-the-cradle with pieces of yarn. Then, with her other hand, she reached out and snagged another lucent strand, red this time, and tied the two together. She closed her hands briefly and then blew the puff of air she held into Thalan's face. To his astonishment, it was warm – almost hot on his skin. Aliane grinned foolishly with delight at his surprise, and he asked her to show him again.

She did, and this time Gwynne also watched intently. It was very difficult for her to see the spell-webs Aliane created, for they were made of Air and Fire. If she looked hard she could just make them out, but she could neither touch them nor manipulate them, and it was difficult for her to see how Aliane managed the spell-web. Suddenly, the importance of what she *did* see struck her, and her jaw dropped open.

"You use Fire?" Gwynne asked, her voice urgent. "You use the energy lines from the fire to make the spell?"

"Well, yes, I guess I do," Aliane said, gazing at the spell-web between her fingers. "Can't you see it? The red and yellow lines?" She looked down again at her hands. "Actually, it's sort of orange when you combine them," she amended.

"No," Gwynne sighed. "Not really. I mean, I can *see* them, but not very well. I can only easily see green ones, the ones of the earth. But I thought you said you could only use your magic with Air."

Aliane frowned. "No, I said that I had never tried anything else before. But after I had, it seemed so simple, I don't know why I didn't do it before."

"Strange, to have talent in more than one Element," Gwynne said, giving her a sidelong look. Aliane snorted in exasperation.

"I know what you're thinking, and you can just stop thinking it," she said, waggling her finger at Gwynne and losing the spell-web in the process. "Whoops. Oh, well, I can make another. I told you before, I am not the Eye of Truth."

"Perhaps," Gwynne said, smiling. "We shall soon see, anyway."

"Besides, didn't you tell us it isn't uncommon to have an affinity for another element?" Thalan asked, basking in the glorious warmth that still enveloped him. "Perhaps Aliane has an affinity for Fire and just didn't know it until now."

"Maybe." Gwynne's voice sounded noncommittal, but Aliane was undeceived.

"You still have doubts, though, don't you?" she asked, and Gwynne looked away, unable to deny the charge. "All right, here's what we'll do. I am not normally a gambling woman, but I have never lost a bet in my life. I will bet you a... a penny that when I look into the Mirror of the Eye, nothing will happen."

Thalan laughed, and Gwynne found herself smiling despite her sudden melancholy. She reached out her hand and Aliane grasped it. "It's a bet," she said, shaking the princess's dainty, but surprisingly strong hand. "A penny it is, and I just may collect from you yet."

"Well, that's what makes it interesting, isn't it?" Aliane asked, laughing as she unrolled her bedding.

"Hey," Thalan said suddenly. "Is there any way you can keep this spell going through the night while we sleep? This is a very nice change from trying to sleep with chattering teeth and shivering bodies all night."

"Ummm... I can try, but if the fire goes out during the night it won't work anymore," Aliane said. She concentrated for a moment until the spell-web that encompassed her and her friends came to her vision. It was strange, she thought as she examined the web she had made. It was almost as if she couldn't look directly at them but had to see them with her peripheral vision. If she looked straight at one of the gently hued lines it disappeared altogether, but if she looked off to the side it sprang back into her field of vision. She reached out to modify one of the delicate threads when suddenly her stomach lurched and she jerked her hand back as if she had been burned. For a moment she thought she was going to vomit, as if she smelled rotten fruit or a dead animal that had lain out too long in the sun. She let go of the spell altogether, and the nausea vanished, as did the warmth that had blanketed her. She heard the others gasp in surprise as the frigid air suddenly penetrated their clothing and skin with its sharp icicle teeth.

"W... what hap... pened?" Thalan asked, his teeth chattering wildly. Gwynne shivered violently as she snatched up the cloak she had discarded and hastily wrapped it around her shoulders.

Aliane stared at them and swallowed. "I'm not sure. I just reached out to touch one of the spell-lines and all of a sudden I felt sick, as if the air had suddenly turned to poison."

Thalan and Gwynne looked at each other, and Aliane sensed they were both thinking the same thing. "What?" she asked, suddenly frightened. "What is it? Did I do something wrong?"

"No, you did nothing wrong," Thalan hastened to reassure her. "It's just that we have all had that problem. Sometimes when I touch water or try a spell with water, I get the same feeling."

"And I with earth," Gwynne said. "It began months ago. It is a sign from the Prophecies, my dear. *'When Earth, Fire, Water and Air become one to cry out with mute voices of unspeakable danger and fear...'* I had suspected for some time the other elements felt the same." Gwynne shrugged ruefully. "Now I know. You never felt it before now?"

Aliane thought for a moment. "Never this strongly, but I guess there were times I thought it felt a little strange. But as I told you before, I haven't had many chances to practice with magic." She swallowed again. "This was definitely the worst, though."

"Don't worry, there really isn't anything wrong with you," Gwynne assured her again, patting her on the hand, "and there isn't anything wrong with your spells. It can't actually hurt you. It's just telling you that something is wrong."

Aliane looked at her uneasily. "Very wrong," she said, remembering the violence of her reaction. "That felt very, very wrong." She hesitantly focused and reached out again. This time when she twined the spell-web around her fingers, she felt nothing but a vague uneasiness that vanished after a few seconds. Quickly, for her own comfort as much as her friends', she wove another warmth spell and cast it over each of them. Then she made a few adjustments and tentatively let go of the spell to see if it would stay. It did. She still felt deliciously warm even after she had relinquished control of the spell-web.

"There. Can you still feel the heat?" Thalan and Gwynne nodded, and Aliane smiled with satisfaction. "I can't guarantee it will last all night, but at least we will be warm for a while."

"How do you feel?" Thalan asked, looking at her with concern.

"Fine." Surprisingly, Aliane felt nothing now except the delicious warmth of the spelled air about her. The foulness she had sensed before was completely gone. It had been strange, she thought. It was not something she had touched or tasted or smelled that had turned her stomach. It was as if she had made contact with a sixth sense she had until now been unaware she possessed. "It's gone now."

"Good. Now, we should all get some sleep," Gwynne said firmly. "We have a long way to go tomorrow."

Aliane lay down and snuggled under her blanket, but as soon as she closed her eyes, the image of Jaerak's face hovered against her eyelids as if she had looked at the sun too long. She wondered if he was thinking of her, and then mentally kicked herself. She should just try to forget him, try to ignore the attraction she felt for him. But she could not. She found herself thinking of his hand, as she had seen it when he offered her his handkerchief. She wondered how that hand would feel against her body, how strong it would be, how sensitive, how skillful. She thought of his lips pressed against her hand, and wanted to know how they would feel against her mouth, her throat, her breast. She imagined how his hard, lean body would feel under her seeking fingers, could almost feel the quick heat of his blood against her naked skin. She squeezed her eyes more tightly closed, and wondered why she was such a salted fool to desire the one man who sought to destroy her, even if he did not yet realize it. Finally, she fell into an uneasy sleep and though she had no nightmares that night, her dreams troubled her for entirely different reasons altogether.

I could never touch you,
But how you touched me.
I could only love you
And watch you go free.
Can't you hear me crying for you?
Can't you feel me dying for you?
– A sad love song from Cameon,
author unknown.

Chapter Thirteen

The early morning air was bright and clear, shimmering with ice and cold and infinite possibilities. Aliane felt that if she could just reach out and flick her finger against it, the air would chime and resonate like the finest, pure-blown crystal. The eternal blanket of snow, unbroken by man or beast, surrounded them like sand in some fantastic white desert, and the unending expanse of sky was the most beautiful color blue Aliane had ever seen. No trees grew here in this vast, barren tundra, and the distant mountains were only an indistinct smudge of darkness against the brilliant sky. But despite the desolation of their surroundings, she thought the landscape was beautiful in its own austere, compelling way.

They had lost the road two days ago, but Gwynne was sure they were headed in the right direction and she estimated they should reach the twin lakes within the day, or the next at the latest. As their horses picked their way through the ankle-deep snow, Aliane strained her senses, trying to detect any other signs of life. As far as she could tell, there were none. She saw no birds in the sky, nor heard their plaintive, lonely cries; she saw no animal tracks save the ones from their own horses; no winter bushes or needle-trees marred her view of the boundless horizon. It was rather exhilarating, she thought, to be the only living creatures there, but the vast expanse of nothingness made her feel very, very small.

"At least we know no one's been here before us," Thalan said, glancing around nervously. The echoingly empty atmosphere was obviously affecting him, too.

"I don't think we can count on that," Gwynne said, her voice sounding hollow in the empty air. "One or two heavy snows could have covered any tracks, and this snow looks rather fresh."

Aliane thought uneasily of Larion and his troops, who were supposedly heading for the same destination. Were they already there? Had they come by a different route? Or had the weather delayed them and she and her friends were, after all, safe? Only time would tell, though the closer they came to their objective the less she really wanted to find out.

About midday, Thalan caught a glimpse of something sparkling in the distance. Gwynne stood in her stirrups for a better look, shading her eyes from the sun that glared off the snow. Aliane's own eyes were red and sore from the constant reflections, and she wished she had something to shade them with. Perhaps that night she should put a warm compress over them, though she suspected she would be seeing sunspots for days no matter what she did.

"It's the lakes," Gwynne said. "Three hours distant, I'd guess." Aliane also strained to look, and thought she saw movement in the far distance.

"It isn't frozen?" she asked, surprised. "It looks as if the water is moving."

"These lakes are salt water," Gwynne told her, "so they never freeze."

Aliane was startled. "*Salt* water?" she said in disbelief. "I've never heard of such a thing."

"I have," Thalan said, frowning, "a long time ago. My father mentioned something about salty water somewhere... I can't remember exactly what he said, though."

"Why hasn't someone figured out a way to get the salt out of the water?" Aliane asked. "Surely it would be worth a lot!"

Gwynne smiled. "Look around you, dear," she said, gesturing at the desolate, snowy wilderness. "It's like this most of the year, even in the summer, and it would be easy to get trapped up here. People have tried, I suppose, but no one was ever able to get enough salt to make it worth the trouble."

Aliane shook her head, still unable to believe it. "*Salt* water. Incredible."

"There is an old, old story connected with these lakes," Gwynne continued. "Let me see if I can remember...

"Long, long ago before men or women walked the earth, Mother Nature and her lover, the Sun, had a child. They named her the Moon and cast her into the heavens so all could look upon her perfect beauty. Mother Nature was so proud of her beautiful daughter that she wept, and her salty tears dropped to the earth and made the Lake of Truth.

"But after a while Mother Nature became dissatisfied, for there were no men or women to worship her daughter or to admire her loveliness. So she made a man and a woman and gave them the gift of procreation so there would be many, many people to worship her daughter the Moon.

"For a time, Mother Nature was very happy. The people worshipped the Moon, and she blossomed with the pride she felt for her daughter. She made another smaller lake, this one of the purest waters, and put it next to the first lake so the Moon might see her reflection in it whenever she wished. The Sun shone down on everything he saw and he glowed with satisfaction, knowing his daughter was so well loved. The people came to the lake to worship the Moon, and the pretty daughter of the Sun and Mother Nature looked in the Mirror and admired herself constantly. This is how the pool became named the Mirror of the Eye, for the Eye of the Moon was constantly watching her reflection in the crystal clear waters.

"But after a while the people stopped worshipping the Moon. They began believing in a god Mother Nature and the Sun didn't know, and the Moon became pale and distant with no one to worship her. She looked in the Mirror one day and saw that her beauty had faded, and she missed the people who had before prayed to her and offered her gifts. Mother Nature became angry with her people, and in her wrath caused great floods to sweep the land, and huge volcanoes to erupt in the mountains. The Sun, too, became angry, and he turned his face away from the people, and darkness fell upon the lands. Their fields became covered with snow and their crops and trees died for lack of warmth and light. But the people still would not worship the Moon.

"Finally, Mother Nature grew very sad. She became too tired to keep bringing the floods and volcanoes, and she became quiet and wept. She wept and wept, and her tears fell to create a third lake, its waters as salty as the first. This became the Lake of Lies, the waters bitter with her disappointment and grief. The Sun refused to lose hope; he would look and look at the pool and wait for the people to come back, but they never did. Every night he turns his face away in grief, and darkness comes once again, but every morning, hope springs back and he looks to see if the people have returned. The Moon hid herself by day, ashamed of her pale face where she once was radiant, and only looked at herself in her Mirror by night, still hoping that someday her people would come back and renew their pledge to worship her. And still, Mother Nature wept for her daughter, and eventually she buried the Mirror in a deep cave beneath the earth so the Moon could no longer see her reflection. But a few of her tears fell into the Mirror and clouded the pure waters."

Gwynne fell silent as Thalan and Aliane digested this remarkable story and when she spoke again she sounded thoughtful.

"It has been said that when the Eye of Truth looks upon the Mirror of the

Eye the tears will be cleansed from the waters and the pool will be as pure as the day Mother Nature created it. The moon will once again grow radiant and beautiful, and look at herself in the Mirror by day, and Mother Nature will finally stop weeping."

"That's a beautiful story," Aliane said. She had always loved a good fairy tale. "What do the Prophecies say about it?"

Gwynne laughed. "Their version is hardly more believable, I'm afraid," she said. "I don't know the entire story, but they say that the Lake of Truth holds the spirit of all that is pure and good in the world, and the Lake of Lies reflects only what is bitter or evil or wrong. In a cave, far below the surface, there lies a pool into which equal drops of water from each lake have fallen for centuries. This pool – the Mirror of the Eye – is murky and clouded with the two waters, and only the true Eye can look upon them and separate them out." Gwynne shrugged her shoulders helplessly. "I have no idea what it means," she admitted. "I'm not sure anyone does, or ever did."

"It would be interesting to find out," Thalan said, shooting Aliane a sly glance. Aliane laughed, though she was getting a little tired of such thinly veiled hints.

"Yes, it would," she responded. "It's too bad we won't see it when it happens."

Gwynne laughed. "I wouldn't count on winning that penny from me just yet," she said, waggling her finger at Aliane playfully. "After all, nothing has been set in stone."

"What if there is no Eye of Truth?" Aliane asked suddenly. Her two companions looked startled at her abrupt question, and she realized that it had lain in the back of her mind for days, though she hadn't even realized it. "What if she is just a story, like the tale about the lakes? What if there never were any Prophets and we have been chasing a five-hundred-year-old folk tale? What if Cor of Restis Haven and the others just made the whole thing up? What then? You said yourself that nothing has been cast in stone."

Gwynne rode for nearly twenty heartbeats before she answered. "I have often asked myself the same question," she said, looking straight ahead of her. "It is, of course, possible that the Prophecies are false. But I think just about anything can be possible." She suddenly smiled. "I would just prefer to believe it is true, I guess."

"Just as the Onnic choose to believe that magic is evil?" Thalan asked softly. Gwynne nodded. He looked disturbed, and Aliane realized he must never have questioned the Prophecies before.

"Well, I don't know what to believe," Aliane admitted. "I don't think magic is wrong or evil or anything like that, but..." She faltered, unable to express her confusion and doubt. To her surprise, Gwynne nodded approvingly.

"That's good," she said. "It means you are not gullible, nor do you place your faith lightly. I believe in the Eye of Truth because that was what I was taught to believe. And," she continued, "because I believe the evidence I have seen or read. You haven't been exposed to that evidence, so you will not truly believe until you have seen it with your own eyes."

"That's true," Aliane said thoughtfully. "I guess I just don't take things at face value."

"Besides, if she doesn't exist," Gwynne said, her face grave, "then a lot of men and women have died for nothing. I can't accept that possibility."

"But men and women have died for what the Onnic believe as well," Thalan pointed out. "Have their deaths been for naught?"

Gwynne said nothing for a time, but after a while, Aliane heard her whisper, though she had to strain to hear – "I don't know. I just don't know."

After that they rode on in silence.

* * *

They reached the lakes late that same afternoon. They had been heading almost due west for some time, and Gwynne estimated they should arrive almost exactly where the two lakes met. The sun was just beginning to set, casting soft pinks and oranges across the glittering snow like spilled jewel-fire. The disappointed Sun was again turning his face away, Aliane thought, thinking of the story Gwynne had told them earlier. Soon the Moon would come out and gaze at her sad reflection in the waters that were tainted with the salt of her mother's tears. She shook her head, trying to dispel the sadness she felt. It was only a tale, she told herself firmly. Just as the Eye of Truth was only a tale? That was a question she could not answer. She was sure, however, with every fiber of her being that when she looked into the waters of the Moon's mirror, she would not be the one to cleanse it of Mother Nature's bitter teardrops.

But her thoughts had helped her come to a decision, she mused as Frigget plodded along through the ankle-deep snow. She would head for home after she and Gwynne had looked into the pool. Her poor father would be frantic by now, and Aliane could not in good conscience remain away much longer. *Especially,* she admitted to herself, *if it means chasing after phantoms and fairy tales.* It was odd, she reflected. When she had known almost nothing about the Prophecies and the Eye of Truth back in Aryn, she had believed in them unthinkingly. It had never occurred to her to question them. But now that she had been out in the world and had learned more about magic and had looked in the face of evil – *that beautiful, beautiful face*, a small voice within her mourned – the Prophecies and the Eye seemed an almost absurd idea. Almost as if they, too, were tales told to children to give them hope that the future held richer possibilities, offered a chance for happiness. Everyone needed hope, Aliane knew, but that did not make the stories true.

They stopped at the top of a hill – a long, steep incline that led down to the huge valley in which the lakes had rested through the ages. Looking around, Aliane could see a long expanse of water stretching out to the north and the south, but no sight of land was visible across the water itself. *Big lakes*, she thought in awe. A gust of wind carried a strange odor in its wake and she wrinkled her nose. It was not entirely unpleasant, but it was like nothing she had ever smelled before. Gwynne pulled up beside her, dismounted and took Milyn by the reins.

"We'd better lead them down," she said. "It looks a little slippery."

"What's that smell?" Aliane asked, sliding from Frigget's back.

"I think it's the water," Gwynne replied, taking a deep, appreciative breath. Thalan, dismounting his brown and white gelding Coe, sniffed more circumspectly. He caught Aliane's eye and shrugged his shoulders, and she could tell that the young musician, like herself, was having a hard time believing that lake water could smell so much like the bottom of a pickle barrel.

The three travelers navigated the steep, slick slope without incident, though by the time they got down to the valley floor Aliane was sweating despite the cold air. As she shook the snow from her cloak and boots, she examined her surroundings. She was standing on a long stretch of snow-swathed land, and the enormous lakes stretched to the horizon as far as the eye could see, the stones along their banks worn smooth and polished. Aliane goggled at the waters, marveling at their glittering depths and the beauty of the foam-tipped waves that splashed upon the rocky beach. Carefully leading Frigget to the water's edge, she reached down and dipped her fingers in the surf, and the strange scent that pervaded the frigid air enveloped her. She brought her fingertips to her lips, catching the briny drops of water on her tongue. Thalan stared at her, fascinated, as her eyes widened with surprise.

"It's salty," she said in wonder. She licked her fingers again and grimaced. "It tastes awful, though." Thalan joined her and he too tasted the water. Aliane laughed at his expression as he spat and shook the remaining droplets from his fingers.

"Yuck," was his only comment. She wholeheartedly agreed.

Gwynne, ignoring her two friends, had begun scouting the area as if she were looking for something. Thalan and Aliane looked at each other, their eyes full of questions, but Aliane just shrugged her ignorance, and Thalan turned back to watch his friend.

Finally, the suspense became too much. "What are you looking for?" Aliane called to Gwynne, who was by now some distance away. She led her horse closer, Thalan right behind her, and repeated the question.

"The Mirror of the Eye is underground," Gwynne said impatiently. "I told you that before."

"Ah..." Comprehension dawned, and Aliane realized Gwynne was looking for an entrance that might lead to an underground cave or tunnel. She and Thalan dismounted and helped search, keeping a tight hold of the reins since there were no trees to which they could tie them to secure the horses.

They searched for a long time, digging in the snow and exploring every likely crack and crevice, and they had moved several miles from their original starting point when Thalan finally gave a shout. He had found a large stone set into a small hillock that moved slightly when he pushed against it, and when the three of them together leant their weight, they managed to move it. What they saw once the rock had been rolled aside caused Aliane to shiver with trepidation. They had uncovered a hole in the ground. A narrow, nasty, stinking hole in the ground. Aliane's nose wrinkled as she peered into the filthy depths. It smelled as if many things had crawled down there and died over the years, and by the way Gwynne was shucking her bags and cloak, it looked as if they were going down too.

Sighing with resignation, knowing there was no way to dissuade Gwynne from investigating the repulsive, dank place, Aliane took off her own cloak and began to plait her hair into a long braid that hung down her back. She was going to get filthy no matter what she did, but she did not relish the idea of spiders or other creepy-crawlies getting into her hair.

"You might want to leave that here," Thalan said, pointing to the sword that was still strapped to her hip. "It might get caught on a root or something down there."

Aliane hesitated, her hand hovering over the clasp of her belt. Thalan was right, but she could not bear the thought of going unarmed into... whatever they were getting into. She shook her head and left it where it was.

"I'll leave the crossbow, but I think I'll keep the sword," she said. "I'd hate to be without it if I needed it. Larion's men might be down there, you know."

"I doubt it," Gwynne said, peering into the dark, dank hole. "It doesn't look as if anyone has disturbed this place for centuries.

"Perhaps, but the Onnic are very good at covering their tracks," Aliane responded. "I wouldn't put anything past them. I think we should stay on our toes."

"All right, if you insist," Thalan said, grinning at her. Without further ado, he raised himself onto his toes and struck an absurd, inelegant pose, teetering precariously as if he were just about to lose his balance and fall on his face. Aliane laughed and stuck her tongue out at him. He responded by crossing his eyes at her, and she giggled at how funny his face looked. Gwynne looked at them reprovingly, for all the earth like a mother chiding her errant children, and Aliane hid her smiles behind her hand.

"I'll go first," Gwynne stated, looking dubiously into the hole.

"I think not," Thalan interjected, gathering candles and matches together. "I should go first."

"You're both wrong," Aliane said firmly, taking one of the candles from him and lighting it. "I'll go first. Gwynne can come next, and Thalan, you come last to guard our... er... backs." She flushed slightly as Thalan grinned at her. "Just make sure no one comes in after us, okay?"

Before anyone could argue with her, Aliane took a deep breath, screwed up her courage, and dropped to her belly. Holding the candle awkwardly in one hand, she slithered forward like a snake, using her free hand, her elbows and legs to push herself along the foul earthen corridor.

Once she got past the first few feet, the going wasn't that bad. The tunnel widened, and she was able to crawl along on her hands and knees. The candle burned steadily, lighting her path and she could hear the others crawling behind her. The three companions spoke to each other from time to time just to assure themselves they were still all together and unhurt, and their voices sounded strangely loud in the narrow tunnel. There were no roots, since nothing grew on the surface above, but the dirt on the floor crumbled easily as Aliane touched it, and she uneasily hoped that the roof of the tunnel would stay where it was. She did not relish being buried alive under several tons of earth.

As she moved forward the darkness engulfed her, and she was grateful for the light of the little candle. She would have preferred to bring a lamp but knew it would have been too bulky. In several places, the ceiling of the tunnel came down so low that it scraped the back of her head as she passed under it. She once experienced a brief surge of fright when a small jut of rock caught her trousers at her hips and she stuck, but with a little wriggling she was able to free herself with relative ease. They continued to creep slowly forward, unable to see very far ahead in the weak candlelight and unable to move very fast in the narrow passage. After they had been crawling for what seemed like hours, the tunnel dropped off into a steep downward slope and

Aliane was nearly pitched forward as the earth beneath her hands suddenly gave way to empty air.

She called a halt so Gwynne would not run into her from behind. "What's wrong?" Thalan called to her, his voice echoing weirdly through the narrow passageway.

"The path drops off. It goes down. *Way* down, I think. I'm going to have to turn around and climb down backwards. It's too steep to go headfirst."

There was barely enough room for her to maneuver herself around, but finally she got herself turned. The others did the same, though she could hear Thalan cursing as his broad shoulders stuck between a rock and the wall of the tunnel. Gwynne, already facing him, gave him a shove and with a startled "Ouch!" he managed to squeeze his larger frame into a backward position so he was facing the way from which they had just come.

"All right, I'm going to try backing down now," Aliane called softly, and began inching her way down the steep incline. It wasn't as bad as she had feared. There were plenty of rocks against which she could brace her feet, and the angle was not as steep as she had originally feared, though it was plenty steep enough for her. Slowly, slowly, the party crept backwards down the passage.

The worst part was that Aliane could no longer see where she was going. She tried to hold the candle down low by her legs, but more often than not she needed both hands to hold herself steady. The earth underneath her had a tendency to slide beneath her hands and knees, and she did not want to start an avalanche of dirt and mud and whatever else that would carry her with it to the bottom – however far down *that* was. After an interminably long time, she felt rather than saw the passage level out, and only then did she become aware that her face was bathed in sweat and her muscles trembled with the strain of keeping herself from tumbling backwards into the darkness. Every now and then she would call out small warnings to the others. "Careful here, there's a sharp rock to the left," or "The ceiling here dips a bit – I just smacked my head against it."

Finally, after what seemed like a lifetime of crawling, she backed into a large, open area. She knew she had emerged from the narrow tunnel when the flickering bubble of light from her candle suddenly expanded, freed from the enclosed earthen walls that had imprisoned it. She tentatively stood and gazed around her, trying to assess where she was. She was so engrossed in her surroundings that she forgot to tell Gwynne that she had stopped, and soon the older woman's heels barked painfully against Aliane's ankles.

"Ow! Wait, stop a moment," Aliane said. She stepped a few paces further into the cave and said, "All right, you can stand up now."

Gwynne and Thalan stood and joined her. In the feeble light, her two friends looked frightful – they were covered in mud and cobwebs and their filthy hair was wildly askew. She knew she could not look any better. Thalan's shirt was torn at the shoulder, and she saw a small trickle of blood where the tunnel walls had scraped his skin when he had gotten stuck. She gradually became aware of painful aches in her knees and hands where small, sharp rocks had torn into her flesh, and she saw innumerable places where her own clothing had been ripped. So much for her new clothes, she thought ruefully, and hoped her old ones would hold together long enough to get her safely back to civilization.

The trio carefully made their way further into the wide room. From what she could see, they had entered what appeared to be a huge cave. Massive stalagmites rose from the floor and similar structures hung suspended from an invisible ceiling, graceful alien forms fed by an eternity of water and lime and sediment. The party carefully threaded their way through them, walking not on stone but upon some odd, soft spongy substance. Aliane wrinkled her nose in disgust.

"What is that awful smell?" she asked, holding her sleeve over her nose. It was much worse than the brackish tang of the salt-water air.

"I'm not sure," Thalan said, sounding as if he were trying not to breathe at all. "Faugh! Whatever it is, it's foul."

"I remember," Gwynne said softly, looking around her. "I used to play in caves when I was a girl, and I remember this smell. Never this strong, but still..." She fell silent as Thalan's hand suddenly grabbed the two women, forcing them to halt.

"I heard something," he whispered. They stopped and listened. Then Aliane heard it too, a strange, rustling sound that echoed strangely throughout the cavern. *The space must be huge,* Aliane thought inanely. The sounds seemed to bounce enormous distances, and it was impossible to determine where they originated. The paltry light from her candle did not touch the ceiling, nor did it illuminate the walls that enclosed the cave, so she had no way to judge how big the cavern actually was.

Suddenly the sources of the noise became immediately obvious. Indeed, they became impossible to ignore. They had apparently trespassed upon the home of thousands upon thousands of bats, for the air was suddenly thick with screaming bodies, glowing eyes and flapping, leathery wings. Bats swarmed over them, coming from every direction and obscuring even the slightest vision.

Taken by surprise, Aliane gasped and dropped the candle, which immediately went out as it hit the floor, just as the rush of wind generated by the beat of innumerable wings extinguished the flame from Thalan's. The total darkness made the situation infinitely worse – Aliane could feel wings brush against her face and entangle her hair, and a horrible shrieking sound filled her ears. She wondered briefly if the bats were shrieking or if it was her own voice she heard.

Then, as quickly as they appeared, they were gone. Silence settled again over the party, and the air stirred by countless bat wings became quiet once more. Aliane heard the scraping of a match as Thalan lit another candle, and she saw with relief that they were once again alone. She sheepishly picked up the candle she had dropped, ashamed of her fear, and held the wick to Thalan's small flame.

Gwynne laughed shakily. "I should have remembered. Bats live in caves. I used to love to watch them fly out at night when I was a girl." She lit another candle and held it high. "Phew. I had forgotten about the smell, though."

Aliane looked at her feet. "Then this stuff we're walking on...?"

Gwynne grinned. "Yep. Guano. Nasty, isn't it?"

"Hmmm, yes," Aliane said, wrinkling her nose. "My shoes will never be the same again."

"Come on, let's keep moving," Thalan urged. "I don't want to still be here when they decide to come back." Both Aliane and Gwynne wholeheartedly agreed, so they got their bearings and continued on their way. They walked about fifty paces before Aliane first caught the flickers of light reflected upon the motionless waters of a still, strange pool.

They approached it cautiously. It was almost perfectly round and rather small, only a few paces in diameter. In the darkness of the cave, illuminated only by their three candles, the water looked black, like oil slicked over a stone surface. No ripples marred its surface, and there was no way to determine the depth of its opaque waters. Two enormous stalactites hovered over its face, almost touching the water with their pointy tips. This, then, Aliane realized, was what fed the underground pool, the water traveling from the land above down to fall from these ageless, graceful upended pillars of rock. She was awed by the amount of time it must have already taken to fill the pool as full as it was.

"This is it," Gwynne whispered. "The Mirror of the Eye."

They stood in reverent silence, feeling rather like intruders in a sacred sanctuary. Finally, Thalan stirred, and looked from one woman to the other.

"So who looks first?" he asked. Aliane and Gwynne looked at each other.

"I will," Gwynne said. She moved to the edge of the pool and knelt, holding her candle over its inky smoothness. Her face was calm and her expression serene, but her pallor suggested she was not as calm as she looked and her hand, clutching her candle, was tense and white-knuckled. In the candlelight, the puckered burn scars on her face and body stood out in livid crimson contrast, like blood on newly fallen snow. She took a deep breath and peered into the waters at her reflection.

Aliane felt a tightness in her chest and realized she was holding her breath. For several moments they stood there, motionless as the giant statues of stone around them, waiting... watching... wondering. Then Gwynne looked up, and the spell was broken. Aliane heard Thalan's breath whoosh out in a gust of air and guessed that he had been as captivated as she.

Gwynne came back to stand with them. She smiled as she shook her head.

"Nothing," she said. "Not even a ripple." She turned to face Aliane. "It's your turn, dear."

Aliane took a firmer grip on her candle and nodded. She went to the lip of the pool, as Gwynne had, and knelt. The ground all around the pool was smooth stone and untouched by the bat guano that covered the rest of the floor, almost as if some unseen keeper had swept away anything that might defile the sacred waters. *Nothing will happen*, she assured herself, though her heart was racing. *You are not the Eye of Truth. You are the Princess of Cameon, you are an expert swordfighter, you are many things. But you are not the woman of the Prophecies*. Bolstered by these thoughts, she closed her eyes and leaned forward, her face suspended over the beautiful, ancient pool. She counted three rather rapid heartbeats and opened her eyes.

She saw her own face mirrored in the depths as clearly as she had seen it countless times before in any ordinary mirror. Her cheeks were smeared with mud and sweat, and a tiny rivulet of blood trickled down her forehead from a cut she didn't even remember getting. Tendrils of her curly hair had been yanked from its braid and stood in wild, disheveled masses about her face. She saw her own emerald-green eyes staring back at her, the pupils huge as they tried to absorb as much of the feeble light as they could.

But that was all she saw.

She held the candle closer to the water and blinked. Nothing happened. Nothing moved, no agitation stirred in the pool's murky depths, no magic revealed itself to her wondering eyes.

Nothing.

For a brief moment she felt absurdly disappointed. Some small part of her had actually feared Gwynne's suspicions might be correct, and she saw now that she had secretly hoped something might happen when she looked into the pool. But the rational part of her brain – a part she seemed to be using less and less as time went on, she thought wryly – had known nothing would happen, so she was able to stand and face her friends with a smile and a shrug. As she joined them, she noticed that they, too, looked disappointed, and could not meet her eye. For a moment, she couldn't think of anything to say. So, as she usually did in times of stress, she said the first fool thing that came into her head.

"You owe me a penny," she said, holding out her hand to Gwynne.

Gwynne blinked at her and stared at her hand as if it were something she had never seen before. Then she started to laugh. After a few moments, Thalan began to chuckle, and finally Aliane joined it. They all laughed helplessly for a while, and the tension drained away as if it had never been. Gwynne pulled a silver penny from her pocket and thrust it in Aliane's hand.

"Here," she said, trying to control her giggles. "You've certainly earned it, coming all this way for nothing!"

"Well, I tried to warn you," Aliane reminded her, dashing tears of laughter from her eyes and making the mud-smears on her face more gruesome than before.

"Can we please get out of here?" Thalan asked plaintively. "This place is giving me the screaming jeebies."

But for Aliane the spell was broken. She no longer saw a sacred place worthy of reverence and hushed whispers, but merely a very old cave with a puddle of water in it. A remarkable and beautiful cave, to be sure, but a simple cave nonetheless. But since she did not relish the prospect of another intimate moment with bats or other crawlies, she hastily seconded Thalan's suggestion and the party returned to the passage that would release them from the bowels of the earth back into the land of the living above.

The trip back was much less arduous and nerve-wracking, for this time they knew what awaited them at the end. The occasional breaths of fresh air that told them they were nearing the entrance spurred them on, and Aliane could not believe it when she saw the first glimmers of light ahead of them. The journey leading out of the cavern had taken much less time than the one coming in.

Aliane felt the cold air surround her as they approached the hole in the surface. She was about to ask Thalan, who was by this time halfway out of the tunnel, to toss her a cloak when suddenly something moved in front of the exit, blocking the light. Aliane stopped crawling, astonished. Before she could shout out a warning, Thalan let out a hoarse cry. Aliane could not see very well, being farther back in the passageway, but it appeared as if something had grasped him and bodily yanked him from the tunnel. She inched backward a little, unsure what she should do. Gwynne cried out Thalan's name, and then she, too, was caught and pulled from the crawlway.

Only then, finally, did Aliane understand.

Soldiers were waiting in ambush at the entrance to the tunnel. She wasn't sure who they were; Larion's men, probably, or maybe Jaerak's. She quickly extinguished her candle and thought frantically as she crouched unseen in the darkness. Should she retreat back into the cave and hide? She had no idea if there were any other paths that led to the surface, and she might become trapped in there with no means of escape. Or should she go forward and try to help her friends? She was thankful she had brought her sword along, but how would she get out of the tunnel without getting caught herself?

The decision was taken out of her hands. She heard a muffled cry – she thought it came from Gwynne – and knew she could not back away and hide in the cave like a coward. She could not abandon her friends without trying to help them. She eased her sword a few inches from its scabbard, hoping that whoever was out there would be too distracted to see it, and moved as silently as possible toward the entrance.

To her surprise, the hole was no longer guarded. She listened carefully, and heard a gruff, male voice say, "Hey! I thought she was supposed to have a woman with her! This ain't no woman!" Apparently, the men outside did not realize a third person remained in the tunnel. That would definitely work to her advantage. She took a deep breath, praying that her cramped muscles would respond as she had conditioned them to, and leapt from the relative safety of the tunnel into the open air.

Despite the fact that her dramatic entrance was somewhat marred by a clump of ice that caught her foot and tripped her as she exploded onto the scene, she took them completely by surprise. After a quick tumble, she landed on her feet and took a rapid survey of her surroundings. At a first, quick glance there appeared to be about twenty men, several of whom were holding Gwynne and Thalan at swordpoint while fastening chains around their hands. Others had emerged from their tents in various stages of undress – some were pulling on boots, others struggled into jerkins and trousers as they stumbled from their tents to investigate the commotion. Obviously the soldiers had been in the process of making camp when Thalan had popped up unexpectedly in the middle of their campsite. But at Aliane's abrupt, if graceless, appearance every last one of them froze as if they suddenly had been conjured into a still-life landscape. Most of them didn't even have their swords at hand.

The soldiers who were still fully clothed wore the red cloaks of the Onnic order and their horses had been tied to a tent stake at the edge of their camp. Aliane saw their own animals tied with the others and hope flared in her breast. If she could get to the horses... but she would have to rescue her friends first, and that would mean a fight. She drew her sword and charged toward the closest guard before her better sense could tell her she was making a grave and very stupid mistake.

She felt an uneasy qualm as she prepared to swing at the guard, for she had never in her life been exposed to anything like a real battle. Aryn was far removed and peaceful, and although she knew her father had often in the past sent troops across the river to join Queen Rhyssl's regiments against Casset, the actual fighting had never invaded their own lands. She had grieved with the others when their soldiers failed to return home and had celebrated with those who had, but she had never witnessed a battle, or tended to wounded upon a field steeped in blood. For all her practice and learning of swordplay and all the strategies and skills that Charis had taught her, she had never truly engaged in combat with another person, had never fought for her life or the lives of those she loved. She had sparred with her father's soldiers, and with Charis, but none of them had ever seriously tried to hurt her. She sincerely doubted that these men would show her the same consideration.

The startled guard had not even finished drawing his sword when she fell upon him, so she brought the hilt of her blade down upon the man's head. He dropped like a stone, and Aliane thanked the Eye he had not been wearing a helmet. They must have been rather complacent, she thought, if they hadn't even bothered with armor. But of course, they had been expecting two women and it had never occurred to them that the women might be able to defend themselves. By the time the soldier hit the ground, the others had recovered from their surprise and were scrambling for their swords. She was in for one hell of a fight.

One guard, an ugly man with a long, scraggly beard, grinned and swung his sword at her. She ducked and lashed out with her foot, taking him by surprise and knocking him off balance. He fell into one of his comrades and the two toppled to the ground together. She turned just in time to parry a blow from another. She disarmed him easily and swung her blade at his midsection. She felt the blow connect and the man gasped, clutching his stomach. Aliane caught a glimpse of bright red blood falling like rubies upon the trampled snow before another attacker distracted her. She ducked again as he thrust his sword at her, but did not see the booted foot of another soldier that kicked her in the ribs as she dodged the blade. She went down, struggling to regain the breath he had knocked from her lungs. She hoped he had not broken any of her ribs. Rolling to avoid the downward thrust of a sword, she somehow managed to regain her feet.

She wasn't going to make it. She knew she had no chance. There were too many of them, and once they got their act together they would overpower her easily. The snow didn't help, either. It was slippery under her feet and made it difficult to move quickly. *But I can take some of them with me before I go down*, she thought fiercely, and she readied her blade once again.

For what seemed like an eternity she danced among the soldiers, using every ounce of skill and strength she possessed to fend them off. Men dropped, moaning in pain as she slashed at their vulnerable spots. She went for the groin, the hamstring, and the midsection as Charis had taught her; she used her feet, her elbows and even her teeth when one man tried to grasp her around the neck from behind. He howled in pain and let her go as her teeth sunk into his hand so hard that his salty, metallic blood filled her mouth. She thrust her sword backward into his side and shuddered as she felt his body slide from her blade to the ground.

She hardly even felt it when one soldier's blade tore through her sleeve and left a deep, bloody gash along her arm, but she became alarmed when she felt herself grow weaker as her blood and strength leaked from the wound. Her own sword, bloodied to the hilt, flashed in the sunlight as it found its target in the soldier's heart. She was vaguely aware that Gwynne was screaming and Thalan was shouting something at her, but she could not hear what they said. All her concentration was focused on one thing – staying alive for as long as possible.

She had reduced the band of twenty men to twelve when it happened. A glancing blow from a fist connected with her jaw, and she was momentarily stunned. Someone kicked the sword from her nerveless hand, and she was dimly aware that she was being seized and lifted from the ground. Something pressed against her wounded arm, and the pain brought her shockingly back to full consciousness. Though she felt her strength leaching from her body, she bellowed and writhed in the soldier's arms, trying to struggle free. She flung her head back and heard the guard who held her yell as her skull connected painfully with his nose. A fresh gout of blood sprayed her, and the guard dropped her to clap his hand over his broken nose, but another instantly grabbed her and struck her across the face. Her vision, blurred by the force of the blow, told her she was overpowered and she desperately reached out with her magic to weave a suspension spell that would immobilize her attackers.

But as soon as she touched the iridescent strands of citrine energy, she was once again consumed with the wretched foulness that permeated the air, and for a moment she thought she would be sick. She let the magic go and the churning in her stomach receded, but it was too late. One of the soldiers, taking advantage of her momentary distraction, brought his sword hilt down hard upon her temple. There was no way she could avoid the blow, and

Aliane felt a brief flash of unbelievable pain crash through her head. She had time for one, brief thought before she plummeted into the depths of unconsciousness.

Father... forgive me...

...And then nothingness.

"God help the heathens who multiply and infect the lands like a plague – they must be scourged from the kingdoms, and the earth purified with the sacred fire of the one true God."

– Onnic stricture.

Chapter Fourteen

Slowly and painfully, Aliane woke from the nightmare visions that danced inside her bruised, befuddled brain to the even worse nightmare reality of her battered and beaten body. As she came to the surface of consciousness, she became aware of aches and pains, throbs and pangs that felt as if every nerve ending was afire. At first, she could not imagine why she should be in such pain. She had no recollection of what had happened.

She tried to move her head but the throbbing drumbeat that pounded behind her eyes made her groan, and she felt nausea rising from her belly. She lay quietly and tried to think. There was a nasty, burning pain in her arm, surely the kind of hurt that could only be caused by a wound – and then memory clicked and fell into place. Well, bits and pieces of it, anyway. She remembered coming up from the cave to find a legion of Onnic soldiers lying in wait for them, and remembered fighting them as Gwynne and Thalan watched, helpless in the grasp of the Church's men. *Where were they now? Were they still alive?* Aliane couldn't believe she had survived the fight. She had been a reckless fool to think she could defeat so many by herself.

She tried to open her eyes, but her eyelids, heavy as slabs of stone, refused to obey. Probably just as well, Aliane thought, and since she could not think of a good reason to stay awake, she slipped back into the more comforting realms of unconsciousness, where her pains faded into the background and she didn't have to agonize over the unknown fate of her friends.

When she again came to her senses, things had not noticeably improved. Every move she made elicited painful protests from her abused body, and she still felt a burning pit of sickness in her stomach when she tried to move her head. But at least she could open her eyes this time. Well, she assumed they were open, anyway. She saw nothing but total blackness, not even a shadow or flicker of candlelight dispelled the darkness that engulfed her. She felt a moment of pure panic, wondering if she had been presumed dead and somehow accidentally buried alive. But no, she reasoned, the air was fresh and she could feel the chill of it against her skin. She must be back in the cave, away from the dangers of cold and snow. Considerate, she thought, of whoever had dumped her there. They had made sure she could not escape, however – her hands were bound together behind her back and her feet felt as if they were tied with a thick, stout rope. They wouldn't have bothered tying her up if they had thought she was dead, she assured herself. They needn't have troubled themselves though. Even if she had been able to see her way out of the cave, she never would have been able to move with the horrible pain in her head.

She heard a rustling sound to her left and instinctively turned her head toward it. Another wave of nausea hit her, and she gagged, feeling hot bile burn at her throat. She took some deep breaths and eventually decided she wasn't going to vomit after all.

"Take it easy," a voice said softly. It came from right beside her and she jumped, startled. She hadn't known anyone else was there. "Here, take a few sips of this." She felt the edge of a spoon or dipper touch her lips and she sucked down a few drops of water. It felt wonderful in her dry mouth and parched throat, but did not feel as great once it reached her stomach. She took another deep breath and waited for things inside her to settle down.

She felt a cool compress on her forehead and was grateful, for it somewhat soothed the raging headache that pounded inside her skull. She opened her mouth and tried to ask a question, but a finger was gently placed over her lips, and she heard that gentle, whispered voice again.

"Don't try to speak. Just rest. You'll be just fine." She wished she could see the speaker. The voice sounded so familiar... She was still trying to place it when she drifted off again, this time into a gentle, healing sleep.

When she awoke the third time, it was once again to complete darkness. Why had they brought her back to the cave? she wondered. Carefully, she tried moving her arms, her legs and her head, and found it much easier this time, though she found herself still bound hand and foot. Her head dully ached, but at least the shattering immensity of pain behind her eyes had subsided. Her right arm still throbbed, and she remembered she had been wounded by one of the guard's swords. Her blood had been spilled in battle, and part of her would be forever left behind in this barren, ice-rimed northern wasteland. *Charis will be so proud,* she thought. Carefully, she flexed the arm as far as her bonds would allow, and realized it had been stitched and bandaged. She would have a scar, but at least the wound was not grave. She would still be able to use the arm. Where by the Seven Gates of Hades had those soldiers come from? She could swear they had not come from behind... they must have somehow gotten there ahead of them and hidden themselves well.

Where were Gwynne and Thalan, she wondered again. Were they, too, in the cave, trussed up like thieves caught pilfering a money chest? Try as she might, her eyes could not penetrate the absolute darkness, so she instead sharpened her ears as she had at the inn when she wanted to overhear Larion and Jaerak's conversation. She heard muted voices coming from her left, but could not make out what they were saying. Strange, she thought... there's no echo. Well, they were probably talking too quietly to cause an echo in that enormous cavern. Nor did she hear the rustling of bat wings. They must all still be out of the cave. That made sense. They would not want to come back while humans occupied their home. Suddenly two voices rang out, much closer than the others, and she winced as the noise made her head begin its throbbing anew.

"You were told to wait! I warned you not to harm them!" Aliane thought she recognized that voice through the anger that roughened and deepened it. Jaerak. She irritably wished someone would light a candle or lamp so she could see what was going on. Why were they all sitting around in the dark?

"They're not harmed," Larion's smooth voice replied. "Well, not much, anyway." Aliane's blood ran cold. She did not want to face the prince, not after what had just happened. She had killed at least four of his men, she was sure, and had wounded several others. "She'll recover, you said so yourself." So it *had* been Larion's troops, Aliane thought, and they had disobeyed their orders. And she had killed four of them. At least four. She'd never killed anyone before. *Strange,* she thought dispassionately, *how it changes everything. I must still be in shock,* she mused. *I'll probably have a nervous breakdown later.*

"You and your men are to go back to Magir immediately," she heard Jaerak say, his voice now low and very, very cold. "You are dismissed. I cannot trust a man who disobeys orders just to impress his father. Now go." Even Larion did not dare argue. She heard his footsteps as the prince walked quickly away. A second set of footsteps approached her and stopped by her side.

For a moment there was silence, and Aliane wondered what Jaerak was doing there in the dark. She was amazed he had not tripped over her – he must have eyes like a cat, she thought.

"You may as well sit down," she said after a time. "I know you're there."

There was a low chuckle and a rustle as Jaerak made himself comfortable beside her. "So we meet again, my beautiful little friend. Little did I know a few short weeks ago I was in the presence of the Princess of Cameon. How are you feeling?" he asked, and she felt his hand press against her forehead.

"My head hurts," she admitted, "as does most of the rest of me. Why don't you light a lamp or something? It's bloody dark in this cave."

The silence was almost deafening. During the painfully long pause, she heard Jaerak shift uneasily beside her. A thin trickle of fear found its way to her heart. Something was wrong. Why would he not answer a simple question? Something was very wrong. No echo, no smell of bat guano... oh, god, she thought. *Oh god.*

"Answer me," she said harshly, her voice tripping over the desert in her throat. "Answer me, salt and stuff you!"

"Hush," he said, and she again felt the dipper held to her mouth. This time she drank deeply, and the cold water tasted more wonderful than the finest wine.

"Better?" he asked quietly.

"Yes," she said, though panic twisted in her like a live, contorted thing. She took a deep breath to steady her voice and asked again, "Why is there no light?"

She heard Jaerak sigh, and knew the truth before he spoke it.

"You are not in the cave," he told her, and she felt a feather touch on her arm. "You are in my tent, and it is the middle of the afternoon. There is light, my dear, but I'm afraid you... you cannot see it."

All feeling froze in her breast, piercing her heart like a brittle shard of ice as she listened to his words with an almost detached interest.

"I cannot see," she said flatly. "I am blind." It was not a question, but a bald statement of fact. She spoke with no fear, no grief, no emotion at all. All feeling was locked and frozen in the icicle that had pricked her heart, snared in a crystalline prison where it could not escape and overwhelm her. *An interesting sensation,* she thought. She wondered how long it would last.

"Yes," Jaerak said. "You are blind."

She had been wrong. There was one emotion that had not been trapped in the glacial region that was now her heart. Anger welled up in her, anger as she had never felt before. Hot rage shot through her body like a static shock – rage at herself for being such a bloodied fool for leaving her father's protection; rage at her father for being so desperately overprotective that she had been forced to flee him; rage at Larion for disobeying his orders. And rage at the man who now sat beside her, whose beautiful face she knew so well but could not see, whose treacherous plans had wrought the unthinkable.

Her entire being was consumed with it.

"You bloody bastard," she said finally, spitting the words through gritted teeth.

She heard Jaerak chuckle. "Such language, and from royal lips, no less. Blame me if it makes you feel better," he said, patting her arm again. She twitched, trying to throw his touch from her, but she was bound too tightly and could not dislodge his hand. "We don't even know if the blindness is permanent yet. We'll have a doctor see to you once we get back to Magir."

Aliane stopped struggling. "You're taking me back?" she asked incredulously, and for the first time remembered her friends. The thought of them caused the chunk of ice burning in her breast to melt a little, and remorse flooded her for having even momentarily forgotten them. "What have you done with them?" she demanded, trying hard to control herself. "Where are my friends?" Her raised voice made her head throb, but she refused to show weakness in front of him.

"They're fine," Jaerak said, his voice gentle. With astonishment, Aliane realized he was trying to soothe her! His voice again took on the amused note that so enraged her now. "How brave you are to think of them in your time of trouble. If you're feeling better they can even come in for a little visit."

"I know what you wanted," Aliane said suddenly, tired of pretending she was interested in conversation, tired of the battle of words she had neither the strength nor desire to win. She was afraid to talk, afraid that the silent screams in her soul would escape when she opened her mouth, so she spoke in short, clipped phrases. "I'm delighted to disappoint you. I looked in the pool. I am not the Eye of Truth."

There was a pause. She must have startled him with her directness. "Yes, so they tell me," Jaerak said finally, his voice noncommittal. Aliane would have given anything at that moment to see his face. She had not realized how much communication relied on visual stimuli. A tiny voice, the voice of the very frightened woman hiding behind a tough exterior, whimpered in her head.

Oh god oh god oh god oh god oh god oh god....

Aliane clamped down hard on the voice. There would be time for that later.

"You seem to know quite a lot," Jaerak continued, and she brought her attention back to the present. "How did you know it was the woman of the prophecy I sought?"

Aliane turned her head away. If she couldn't see his face, she didn't want him to see hers either. She would be salted and stuffed before she gave this man any more information.

She heard Jaerak chuckle again, and knew he could read her thoughts. A new trickle of terror pierced her as she remembered what he had done to Gwynne, remembered that he really *could* read her thoughts if he wanted to. If he desired any information from her he could take it any time he chose.

To her surprise, she felt no mental probes or searching invasions. She heard Jaerak stand, and the panic she had until now managed to hold at bay threatened to overwhelm her.

"Wait!" she cried before she could stop herself. She bit her lip, wishing she could take back the word, but the thought of being left alone in the darkness – permanent darkness – was unbearable. Even the company of evil was better than no company at all, better than such desolate isolation.

"I have things I must see to," she heard Jaerak say. His voice came from a greater distance, so she knew he had walked away from her bed. She hadn't heard him move. "We will talk again when you feel up to it. Your friends will be here soon." Aliane listened until she could no longer hear his footsteps, and knew she was alone.

After he was gone and Aliane could no longer concentrate on how much she hated him, the icy fist that had grabbed her heart let go, and she fell into a despair deeper than she had ever known. Fear, anger, guilt and bitter grief all vied for supremacy over her spirit, and she could hold them off no longer. She bent her head and wept.

She did not hear Gwynne enter the tent, but felt herself being gathered into comforting arms, gentle hands stroking her hair and a soft, crooning voice whispering words of comfort in her ear. She knew it was Gwynne by the scent and feel of her touch, and it wasn't until her own arms had circled the older woman's neck in a desperate stranglehold that she realized her own hands had been freed. She couldn't remember when it had happened or who had freed her, but she was suddenly aware of the rush and tingle of blood in her arms as she clung to Gwynne with all her strength. Aliane tried to speak, but hoarse, wracking sobs filled her throat and she could not push the words past her inconsolable grief. She wept until her throat was raw, wept until her head throbbed and her body grew parched and thirsty for the tears she had shed. She wept until she had no more tears, and still the relentless pain filled her. She lay gasping in Gwynne's arms, clutching her as if to a lifeline, somewhat comforted by human contact and the warm, living flesh beneath her hands.

"Better?" Gwynne asked finally, smoothing Aliane's sweaty hair from her tearstained face. Aliane wanted to say, *No, everything hurts, everything's changed, I'm blind and I'm frightened and please, please, please put things back the way they were.*

Instead, she said, "Yes, thank you." She was shocked as she spoke, her voice rasped and cracked and she realized her throat was extremely sore.

She felt Gwynne squeeze her. "Liar," she said softly. She took Aliane's hand and placed it gently over her own mouth so she would know she was smiling. Aliane, surprised, traced her fingertips over the older woman's features, feeling where the burn scars gave her skin a different texture and touching the dampness where Gwynne's own tears fell in silent grief for her friend.

"What... what happened?" Aliane asked, her voice still trembling from the strain of her weeping. "How did it... did it happen?"

Gwynne sighed and drew her close again. "I really don't know, my dear, but if I had to guess, I'd say it was the knock on the head that did it."

"Knock on the head?" Aliane tried to remember but failed.

"You don't remember? Well, it's not surprising. You were lucky you didn't break your head."

"Lucky," Aliane repeated hollowly. Gwynne hurried on before she could comment further.

"By the way, Thalan has converted. He now believes you are the best fighter in all the lands."

"I wasn't good enough to save us, though, was I?" Aliane asked bitterly, and instantly regretted the words. They sounded petulant and full of self-pity. Her eyes filled again with tears.

"I don't think anyone could have gotten us out of this one," Gwynne said ruefully, tactfully ignoring her chagrin. "There were just too many of them. They snagged Thalan and me like rabbits in a trap. It was just our bad luck they made camp right where the entrance to the cave was, and we popped right out in the middle of them. We didn't even see them coming."

"No," Aliane said. "They knew we were there. That huge swarm of bats must have led them right to us. They just didn't expect us to come out again so soon. They were setting up the ambush, but we interrupted them."

Aliane's hands, loath to break contact, traveled down Gwynne's sleeve to her hands. She suddenly realized that Gwynne remained unbound and apparently free.

"Are you all right?" she asked. "And Thalan? How is it Jaerak has let you go free?"

"We're fine," Gwynne said. "We took no hurt. We're free because Jaerak knows we would not try to leave without you."

"Were you the one who freed me?" Aliane asked.

"What do you mean?" Gwynne questioned, sounding puzzled.

"I was bound before, but now my hands are free," Aliane explained. Her voice still sounded as if it were being dragged over a rough surface. She tried to move her legs and realized her feet were unbound as well. "My feet, too."

"No," Gwynne said, "I did not free you. It must have been Jaerak." Her voice was hard and cold as she spoke his name, and Aliane shivered suddenly, fully aware she was in the presence of true hatred. The hatred Princess Julane felt for her paled in comparison to Gwynne's hatred of Jaerak.

"Gwynne, what am I going to do?" she whispered. Try as she might, she could not see past the veil of darkness that had been cast before her eyes. "What if my vision never comes back?" Her hands clutched at Gwynne's again as terror again threatened to swallow her whole.

"I don't know," Gwynne answered honestly, "but let's wait until the doctor sees you before we jump to any conclusions. For all we know this might just be temporary. You could regain your sight soon. Ah, here's Thalan, come to see how you are doing."

Aliane heard his footsteps, and soon felt him take her hand in his. She had not realized how very large his hands were, and she was comforted by his touch.

"How's my girl?" he asked lightly, brushing his fingertips over her face. He wiped the few remaining tears away. "Looks like you're doing pretty well to me."

"I'll be all right," Aliane said, trying to be brave, trying not to show her weakness. "My head still hurts, though."

"You have quite a bruise," Thalan told her, gently touching a tender spot on her forehead. "We were a bit worried about you for a while there. You were unconscious for three days."

"Three days?" Aliane was appalled. She'd had no idea.

"Yup. And then you drifted in and out for a while. But you will heal soon and be back to your sword practice. I'm sorry I ever doubted your skill; I've never seen anything quite like that before."

"I'm sorry..." Aliane began, and then stopped. She groped for words, not knowing how to express herself, not knowing how to explain why she had not been strong enough to rescue them. "I'm sorry," she repeated lamely, and he pressed her hand again.

"Don't be," he said softly. "You were amazing."

"But Jaerak has us," she said, fear creeping again into her voice. "What's going to happen now?"

"I think he is planning on taking us back to Magir," Gwynne said. "He wants you to see a doctor he knows."

"But then what?" she persisted. "He can't keep us prisoner forever, and he hasn't found the Eye of Truth yet. Do you think he would just let us go?"

"It won't go that far," Thalan said firmly. "We'll find a way to escape. I think if we can make our way back into the cave, we can elude him. I'm sure there are other passages that will lead to the surface. We can use one of them to escape."

Aliane touched her eyes with her hands. "I don't think I can," she said, her voice trembling.

"Nonsense," Gwynne said briskly. "Thalan and I will help you. Besides, once we are in the cave, none of us will be able to see. It would be too dangerous to have a light, so we will all be wearing a cloak cut from the same cloth. Now, we've tired you out enough for one day, you need to get some sleep."

"Yes, but we will be close by," Thalan said reassuringly. "All you have to do is call for us."

Aliane felt herself drifting off to sleep, comforted by the presence of her friends and knowing that no matter what happened, she would not have to endure her pain alone.

* * *

Jaerak paced up and down, wondering what the bloody hell he was going to do next. Masyl watched him, a sardonic smile playing on his lips. He had never seen his captain so perturbed before, and it rather pleased him to see his usual calm and cool demeanor shattered by circumstances beyond his control.

"Don't feel too bad," Masyl said cheerfully, enjoying the scowl that marred Jaerak's too handsome features even more than the thin, white scar on his left cheek. "We've done a good day's work today. We've captured three – count them, *three* – witches, and can take them back to Magir for trial." Jaerak did not answer him, but continued to wear out the rug in Masyl's tent with his pacing. "After all, did you really believe that preposterous prophecy would come true?"

"She's still the key to the whole thing," Jaerak muttered to himself, as if he had not heard the High Priest's words. "Somehow she has to be."

Masyl snorted. "My dear man, if you mean the old woman I'm surprised she has gotten this far. She looks as if someone had already tried to burn her at the stake. Well, this time she will not get away so easily."

Jaerak halted abruptly and turned to face the priest. "And the princess?" he asked. "What of her?"

Masyl raised his eyebrows in affected surprise. "She's traveling in the company of magic users, my friend. She has looked in the pool. I'm sure it will not be a difficult task to prove she is one of them." He rubbed his hands together with relish. "Unfortunate that she is of the royal house of Cameon, but it cannot be helped. The law is clear. There can be no exceptions." Masyl grinned. "A shame, really. She's quite a beauty. Morgan had such plans for her, but what good will she be to anyone now that she's blind?"

Jaerak irritably waved that objection away. "That's probably a temporary condition caused by the blow to her head. She'll most likely recover at least some of her sight. But what will Torrit do if you execute his precious daughter? I believe the princess has ties with Rhyssl el'Faria's family as well. Torrit is already allied with the queen, and if he attacks Magir with their combined strength Morgan might be hard pressed to fend them off."

Masyl shrugged. "That's not my concern. My job is to find witches and prosecute them. It is for the greater good."

Jaerak turned away, suddenly disgusted with the man. Masyl had no idea how to look past the present circumstances to the future, juicier prize beyond. He was willing to give up the ultimate glory for a speedy trial and a meaningless execution. "You may leave," he said shortly, forgetting they were in Masyl's tent. "I must think."

Masyl stood, but only because it suited his own purpose. "Don't be too long about it," he warned as he lifted the tent flaps back. "We leave for Magir in the morning." He left, leaving Jaerak to his unpleasant thoughts.

Things had not turned out quite as he had planned. That fool Larion had disobeyed his direct orders by attacking the three magic users as they emerged from the hole in the ground. Salt and stuff it, he had been so sure the old woman would find the Eye of Truth. Aliane had admitted that she had looked in the pool, but nothing had happened, and now she was blind. Despite his words to Masyl, he was uncertain whether the beautiful woman would ever see again.

He had been somewhat surprised to find her here with Gwynne and the large-nosed musician whose name he couldn't remember, if he had even bothered to learn it at all. Jaerak had once entertained the thought that the woman calling herself Ashleighn el'Faria might be the third companion Ratliff had told him about, but had dismissed the idea as unlikely. When he had first seen her lying on the cot, pale and bloodied and unconscious, a very strange sensation had come over him. At first he could not put his finger on what it was, but eventually he managed to pin it down. Part of him had been ridiculously happy to see her, and the other part was enraged by the sight of the large, ugly bruise on her temple. Strange, he thought. He couldn't remember the last time he had truly cared about someone. True, she had been in his thoughts from the first day he had seen her sitting alone at the Fox and Falcon, and he had hoped he might see her again someday, but he had not expected the strength of emotion he felt when he saw her lovely, unconscious form. Little had he known, back in Magir, that he held company with the daughter of King Torrit, ruler and monarch of the western region! He shook his head, trying to compose his thoughts. He had no time to moon over women, no matter how beautiful or captivating. He had to concentrate. He had to make some new plans.

Obviously, he had to let Gwynne and the others escape. It would be more difficult this time with Masyl breathing down his neck, but he thought he could manage it. He had to get them back on the trail of the Eye of Truth, otherwise everything would be ruined. But how? He knew the old woman would not leave without her friend, and he wanted to take Aliane to Magir to see a physician. Perhaps he should let her go... her father was a king, she would be cared for when she got home. But for some reason he was reluctant to release her.

He looked up irritably as the flap of the tent rustled, and a meek voice announced the presence of a messenger. "Come in," Jaerak ordered, schooling his features back to their regular stony countenance.

The flap opened and a young Initiate stepped inside. The boy held a sealed parchment in his hand, and he looked confused. "My Lord," he began, "this message was just found by the perimeter of the camp. It is addressed to you." He held out the paper, and Jaerak automatically took it from him.

"What do you mean it was found?" he asked, frowning at the message he held. "Who delivered it?"

"I don't know, my Lord," the Initiate said. "There was no one about."

"Thank you, you may go," Jaerak said, and the young Onnic soldier left him in peace. He examined the parchment and broke the seal, which had no identifying marks imprinted in it. He opened it and received a jolt as he again recognized the handwriting as his own. Interesting, Jaerak thought, remembering the old book he still carried with him. First Restis Haven and now here. Very strange. He read the message eagerly, and then read it again more slowly because he did not believe his eyes the first time.

Interesting, he thought again as he held the parchment over the flame of a candle and watched it smoke and burn. *Very interesting indeed.* He would have to think on this, but suddenly the question of what to do with his captives had been very neatly answered. He did not realize that he was smiling, and his expression would have frozen even the salt water in the Twin Lakes had he gazed upon it with those eyes.

"If at first you don't succeed, you obviously didn't try hard enough."
– From the writings of Cith Carrigan, famous Cameonian philosopher.

Chapter Fifteen

Over the next few days Aliane's body healed well, but her spirits remained damaged. Though her head ceased its infernal throbbing and the bruise on her temple faded, her sight remained elusive and not even the smallest spark of light penetrated the total blackness of her vision. The only times she could see were in her dreams, and she would wake every morning full of hope, only to confront the reality of her sightless existence. Gwynne and Thalan spent a great deal of time with her trying to keep her spirits up, but Aliane knew with every passing day that nothing would ever be the same again. She was blind, and she would have to learn how to live without ever seeing another sunset, never again looking upon her father's face, never able to read another page of her favorite books. These realizations broke her heart and the pain of it made her mood as black as her vision.

She had to relearn almost everything, and her slow progress frustrated her almost more than she could bear. She hated getting dressed only to be told she had put her shirt on inside out, and she still could not bring a fork to her mouth without stabbing herself in the face. She was determined to get it right, though, because as much as she hated her mistakes, she hated more the thought of continually depending on others to perform such simple tasks for her.

Jaerak paid her a visit every day. At first she had refused to speak with him, refused even to acknowledge his presence, but after a while she no longer had the energy to go on hating him. Hatred was exhausting to sustain, and she just didn't care enough to expend that kind of strength on him. So now she answered his questions and wondered when he would decide she was well enough to endure the journey back to Magir. She knew Thalan and Gwynne were still planning an escape, but Aliane feared they were running out of time.

Jaerak did not bind her hands and feet again, and when she walked he,

Gwynne or Thalan led her steps. She didn't think she would ever get used to walking in the dark, but if she were to escape with her friends she would have to learn to walk on her own, so one day after she had been awake about a week she decided to get up and try it.

She was alone in Jaerak's tent, alone for the first time in a week. She got to her feet and stretched out her arms, but her fingertips touched only empty air. She shuffled sideways until she felt the coarse material of the tent wall under her hand, and took a few tentative steps forward.

It was utterly terrifying. Every step felt as if she were about to plunge down an endless abyss, and she carefully tested the ground in front of her just to make sure it was still there before she placed her foot on it. Any obstacle, any irregularity in the ground would cause her to fall, and sweat beaded on her upper lip as she fought back panic. She kept her feet low to the ground and inched her way around the tent.

Suddenly she barked her shin against some hard object and cried out with pain. Losing her balance, she toppled over, falling heavily to the ground. She gritted her teeth in frustration, determined not to cry. She was afraid if she began she would never be able to stop, and her tears would make yet a third salt-water lake filled with bitterness and sorrow. She heard the tent flap open as someone came in to investigate the cause of the noise she had made.

"Well, I see you're up and around," Jaerak's voice said. "You must be feeling better."

Aliane, already brimming with anger, hurt and outrage, turned her head towards the sound of his voice and spat. Jaerak only laughed and she felt him grasp her under her shoulders to lift her to her feet.

"You *are* feeling better," he said. "That's the biggest response I've gotten from you yet."

"I wouldn't expect much more," Aliane snarled, shaking off his hands.

"Oh, but I do," he replied, leading her to the chair she had banged her shin against. "Much, much more."

"Think again," Aliane replied rudely, settling herself down and surreptitiously rubbing her leg. She'd have a bruise there. "I wouldn't bring you water if you were expiring from the plague at my feet."

"But you already have helped me, my dear," he said. She couldn't tell from his voice if he were teasing her or not. "You see, I know you have. And you will again."

"I have no idea what you're talking about," Aliane grumbled, suddenly tired. "Please go away, I'd like to rest now."

"There will be time to rest later," he said smoothly. "Now it is time for you to fulfill your destiny."

Aliane laughed scornfully. "My destiny? I know my destiny, thank you very much." Her voice rose in bitterness as she fought to keep her temper under control. "I will somehow get away from you, I will somehow return to my father in Aryn, and *will* somehow learn to live the rest of my life as a blind woman. *That* is my destiny."

"No," Jaerak said. "No, that is not your fate. You have magic, remember?"

Aliane winced, shying away from thoughts too painful to bear. "I can't use magic anymore," she said nastily. Concentrating on her hatred kept her from concentrating on her fear. "I can't see, remember? How can I use the spell-lines or make spell-webs if I can't see them?"

Jaerak made a rude noise. "The same way you eat jumpernuts without seeing them, or the way you breathe without consciously making your lungs move. You have not lost your magic, it is an integral part of you."

"Well, magic can't help me out of this, can it?" Aliane abruptly stopped. It had never even occurred to her to ask that question. "Can it?" she breathed. For the first time in days, a tiny ray of hope rose in her heart.

"I don't know," Jaerak replied. "Perhaps it can. You tell me."

Aliane frowned with confusion. "How can I? I don't know the answer."

"Perhaps you do and you don't even know it."

Aliane shook her head. "No, it's not possible. I know hardly anything about magic, and I've learned that from Gwynne." She sneered nastily. "You know more than I do, I'm sure. You're magic is quite strong, I've heard."

Jaerak laughed. "Don't think you can blackmail me with that knowledge, my pretty princess. No one would believe you. But you are stronger than you know, my dear. Stronger than any of us. You just have to trust yourself."

"I don't know what you're talking about," Aliane grumbled again, growing tired of his enigmatic remarks. "Say what you mean."

"This is not the time. But, since you are determined to be up on your feet, you will come with me now and then perhaps you will understand a little better."

"Go where?" Aliane asked warily. It helped, she found, not being able to see him. When his beautiful face did not distract her she could more easily recognize the evil in him, and she did not trust him as far as she could throw him. Even less, really, since she suspected she could throw him quite a distance, given the chance.

"Back to the cave."

A profound silence settled over them, broken finally by Aliane's humorless bark of laughter. "Are you deaf or just stupid?" she asked harshly. "I told you before, I already looked in the bloody pool. Nothing happened."

"I know. You must look again."

Aliane bit her tongue to forestall all the rude things she wanted to say. "How can I look in the pool if I can't even see it?" she demanded instead, speaking as if to a child lacking wit.

"I don't have to explain my reasons to you," Jaerak said, his voice cold.

"Why should I do anything for you?" she demanded. "You haven't exactly helped me a great deal. If it weren't for you I wouldn't... wouldn't have these problems."

"You have little choice in the matter."

"What you ask is not possible!" she said, anguish coloring her voice. "You know I cannot see the pool. Why are you doing this? Why are you doing this to me?" Her voice caught on the tears that suddenly spilled down her cheeks, and she hastily wiped them away.

"You think you know me," Jaerak said unexpectedly. There was a note in his voice she had never heard before. "You think you know what I want, what I've done, what I desire."

"I know you seek power for yourself, power you have not earned," Aliane retorted. "And I know why you so desperately want to find the Eye of Truth."

The sound of Jaerak's pacing stopped. "And why is that?" he asked with interest.

Aliane cursed her imprudent tongue, but answered honestly. "You want her to find the Alchemist Stone for you."

"Very good," Jaerak said approvingly. "I knew there was a brain under that beautiful face."

"Oh stop it," Aliane said irritably. "Your flattery tires me."

She heard his footsteps as he resumed his pacing back and forth before her. "No flattery. I just speak the truth."

Aliane snorted. "I'll bet that's a first." She paused, and then asked, "Why do you want it, anyhow? What would you do with it? Change things in time to suit yourself? Get rich, manipulate history, and become supreme ruler of the world?"

"Enough of this." The sound of Jaerak's pacing stopped again. Apparently he did not appreciate being questioned, and it amused her how accurately she could gauge his degree of perturbation by his pacing habits. "You will do what I ask because I ask it. If you will not, you will do it because I force you. Which would you prefer?"

"You haven't given me much choice, have you?" Aliane asked bitterly. There was nothing she could do. She and her friends were in his power. It was so frustrating, because had she been able to see she might have been able to escape him, but as it was... She stood and felt him grasp her arm. Despite herself, she clutched at him, afraid of losing her balance.

"Don't worry, I won't let you fall," he murmured. Aliane shook her head in amazement. When he spoke in that gentle voice, it almost seemed as if he actually cared for her. Which was completely ridiculous. Anyone who cared for her would not keep her captive in a tent, or force her into caves when she couldn't see, or stalk and terrify her friends for his own gain. Someone who cared for her would not have blinded her in the first place. He may not have struck the actual blow, but he was as responsible as anyone for what had happened.

Jaerak carefully led her to the mouth of the cave, holding her arm the entire way and warning her of rocks and rough spots on the ground. Somehow, Aliane managed to crawl through the narrow tunnel again, though later she couldn't have told anyone how she had done it. She would just as soon not remember that nightmare journey. Doing it by the light of a single candle had been bad enough – doing it in complete darkness was nerve shattering. She had once fantasized about being alone in the dark with Jaerak, but this was not even remotely what she had envisioned.

Soon she found herself back at the pool. She recognized the echoes in the vast expanse of space in the cavern, the smell of water under the pervasive odor of bat guano, the stillness of the air that had no breezes or winds to sweep the staleness from it. She could tell they were near the water – she could almost taste it on the air. Jaerak held her arm to guide her around stalagmites and cautioned her when to duck her head under the huge, inverted towers of lime that cascaded from the ceiling. Suddenly he jerked her to a halt, and she yelped in protest at his roughness.

"Sorry," Jaerak said, though he didn't sound sorry. "We're here."

There was a long silence. Aliane could not think of anything to say. She could not understand why he had brought her here. She had already looked in the pool, and nothing had happened. What could he possibly expect to happen now? She couldn't even see the waters.

Jaerak was the first to break the silence, but what he said was not at all what Aliane was expecting. She heard him draw breath, and slowly let it out.

"I had not expected it to be so beautiful," he said.

Aliane raised her eyebrows. "So you are a lover of beauty?" she asked sardonically. "Then why do you try to destroy it?"

Jaerak gave her arm an irritable little shake. "Enough. Come to the edge, but be careful. I've got you." Slowly, Aliane inched forward until Jaerak told her to stop, and then she once again knelt. He let go of her then, and if she had not been able to hear him breathing she would have thought she was completely alone.

"Now," Jaerak said, his voice echoing weirdly throughout the cave. "Look."

Aliane bent her head obediently but saw only blackness. "I can't," she said, tears pricking in her eyes. She tried to blink them away. "I can't see anything."

"Look with your heart, not your eyes," he urged. Again, Aliane wished she could see his face. It was probably more expressive than his voice. She could not tell him that her heart had frozen, had closed off so completely that she dared not look into it for fear of confronting a vast, empty, barren wasteland where her emotions and trust had once dwelt. She could not explain why she had detached herself from her emotions, could not tell him why she was afraid to face the pain they caused while refusing to accept the warmth they brought. Jaerak continued, unaware of her thoughts. "Use your magic, feel your powers. They can help you."

Aliane shut her eyes, though she couldn't have said why – it made no difference. She tried to calm down, tried to relax. She felt Jaerak's hands on her shoulders, and she instinctively stiffened.

"Relax," he whispered, and she could tell he was bending over her. His hands moved in gentle rhythm, easing her tension and smoothing away the knots in her tired, aching muscles. All the while, he murmured a soothing litany in a soft tone, too loud to ignore but too soft to irritate.

"Remember," he whispered to her, "remember how it felt, the last time you used your magic. Remember how sweet, how powerful you felt. Remember the warmth it gave you, the protection you felt from it." Aliane felt herself ease back into his hands and thought how strange it was he had said that. It was almost as if he had known about her spell that had warmed the air around her and her friends. His voice continued. "Try to get back to that place, try to feel again the power flowing through your fingers, your hands, your body, your mind. Remember."

Head drooping, she succumbed to his voice. She felt the tension drain from her body, leaving only delicious, sleepy warmth in its place. She wondered briefly what Jaerak was doing to her, but whatever it was she didn't want him to stop. She had not felt like this since... well, for a long time, anyway. In a semi-daze, she began to remember.

She remembered the spell she had used to shield herself and her friends from sight as they escaped from the inn in Magir. She remembered the little bits of magic she had practiced on the road, the spells Gwynne and Thalan had taught her, the designs she had made up on her own. As she concentrated, she felt the air around her buzzing, as if alive with the tiny vibrations of infinitesimal movement – living, breathing, watching, waiting.

Beckoning. She reached out, unconsciously, trying to touch it and felt the spell-lines brush against her hand. For the first time since she had gone blind, Aliane smiled.

Completely forgetting about Jaerak, she twined a spell-line between her fingers. It felt wonderfully familiar and responded to her touch as easily as if she could see it. Since she could no longer concentrate on what they looked like, she realized in wonder that the spell-lines had a texture and a feel of their own that was quite unlike anything else she had ever felt. They had no substance, and yet they felt dense, almost waxy on her fingers. For a moment she forgot all else as she fingered the strands in pleasure, grateful that they had not forsaken her as all else seemed to have done.

"Look at it," a voice whispered to her. For a moment she wondered where the voice was coming from, until she remembered Jaerak. He still held her between his hands, and his grip had tightened as if in response to a strong emotion. "Don't be afraid. Just lean forward and look into the pool with your magical eyes."

Wonderingly, Aliane opened her eyes, and found she was staring down at the back of her own head.

She yelled and scrabbled backwards, her feet slipping on the smooth stone surface by the pool, almost falling headfirst into the motionless waters. The spell-lines fled from her fingers as her concentration was suddenly severed, and darkness again descended upon her vision like a slammed door that blocks out the light. She gasped and wheezed in shock, trying to get control of herself.

"What the bloody hell was that?" she demanded, badly shaken. She received no reply. She began to feel uneasy. "Jaerak?" she softly called.

"I'm here," he said, his voice muffled. "You knocked me off balance and I fell into a rock."

"Well, I can't say I'm very sorry about that," Aliane muttered to herself. She just wished she could have seen it. "What did you do to me?"

"What?" Jaerak sounded genuinely confused. "I didn't do anything to you. I just was trying to help you relax."

"No," Aliane said adamantly. Her heart slowed back to its normal rhythm. "No, you did something. I saw something. What was it? What did you do?"

"You saw something?" Jaerak's voice sharpened intently. "Tell me. What did you see?"

"I..." Aliane hesitated. "I don't think you'll believe me," she finished lamely. She wasn't sure she believed it herself.

"Try me."

"Well..." Aliane groped for words, but they all seemed inadequate to describe what had just happened. "I saw myself."

"In the pool?" he queried.

"No," she replied, frowning. "I can't explain it. I had just touched the spell-lines, had just felt the magic when you told me to open my eyes. So I did. And I saw..." She faltered to a halt.

"Go on."

"I saw myself kneeling down, as if I was looking at the back of my own head," she finished in a rush.

There was a strange pause as he took in her extraordinary words. "Almost as if you were standing over yourself looking down?" he finally asked.

Aliane did not answer, but that was exactly what it had been like. Jaerak interpreted her silence correctly, and she heard him approach.

"Amazing," he whispered, the sound of his voice carrying far in the enclosed air. "Then it's true."

"What?" Aliane demanded. "What's true?" She received no reply. "Look, if I don't start getting some answers here, you're going to have a lot more trouble with me than you'd like." She was beginning to get frightened again. Things were happening that she didn't understand, and she didn't think she could take much more. Normally it took a lot to frighten her, but she had been through a lot and was on her last thread of self-control.

"You actually saw yourself?" Jaerak asked finally. His voice was strangely muffled, as if he had his hand or some object in front of his lips.

"I... I must have imagined it," she said slowly. "I guess I wanted to see so badly that I tricked myself into thinking I could."

"I don't think so," Jaerak replied. "I want you to try again."

"Try *what* again?" she asked with asperity. "I didn't *do* anything!"

"Of course you did," Jaerak said reasonably. His voice still sounded a little breathless, as if he had not gotten his emotions completely under control yet. "You worked magic, didn't you?"

"You think it was magic that made me see?"

"I don't know. It could have been. Try again. This time, if it happens again, look at your reflection in the pool instead of your real self."

But Aliane was too keyed up to concentrate, and this time the spell-lines remained elusive. "I can't," she finally gasped. "I can't get them back."

"You're trying too hard. Here." Jaerak sat down next to her. She was suddenly very conscious of his body next to hers, touching her arm, her shoulder, her thigh. *Even now!* she jeered at herself. *Even now you want him.* She was disgusted with herself for her weakness, but did not object when she felt his arms circle her body and pull her close to him.

"You just need to relax," Jaerak said softly. She felt the hairs on her arms stand on end as his breath tickled her ear. *Kick him,* she thought fiercely. *Jab him with your elbow, punch him in the nose, anything! Just don't sit there enjoying this!*

Moments later, blissfully ignoring her own good advice, she relaxed back into his arms, the back of her head resting against his shoulder, and tuned out the voice of reason that was still trying to bring her to her senses. It had been so long since anyone had held her, so long since she had responded to a man's touch. She just couldn't bring herself to pull away. And she would guess from the rapidity of his heartbeats that he was not entirely unmoved, either. She heard him extinguish the candle and felt his cheek resting on the top of her head as he drew her closer to him.

For a beautiful, timeless moment they sat like that, both in darkness, both content. Forgotten were evil deeds, heartbreak and fears; suspended were accusations, blame and grief. Aliane lay back against Jaerak, their arms and legs intertwined like lovers. Her heart beat an emphatic, rapid cadence as his lips touched the sensitive skin behind her ear and his hand brushed gently against her breast. She lifted her arm and twined it back behind Jaerak's head, feeling between her fingers the silky softness of his hair over the hard, smooth muscles of his neck. She felt his fingers on her chin, gently tilting her head back, and shivered as his mouth closed warmly over hers. His lips were so soft, his touch so sensuous, and Aliane responded to his kiss with a passion that surprised her. For just one moment there was no such thing as good or evil. They just were.

Finally, Aliane sighed and reluctantly detached herself from Jaerak's embrace. *With all that's going on,* she thought wryly, pushing her face slightly into his upper arm, *after all this man has done to me and my friends, I sit here canoodling with him in a ruddy cave. There is definitely something wrong with me.* She sat up, forcing herself away from the warmth of his body, away from the seductive strength of his hands, and once again reached out for the magic. She felt the slightly viscous texture of the spell-lines of Air as they once again revealed themselves to her. She felt Jaerak move behind her and felt a soft brush against her hair as if he had gently touched or kissed her. She sensed a pulse of magic in her bones as he conjured a small flame to re-light the candle, and the spell-lines that twined about her hands flexed in response to his magic. Much the same way she responded to him, she thought, leaning forward once again over the pool.

Then she opened her eyes.

"When she looks upon the waters of the Eye, they will reveal her to be the Eye of Truth, the savior of magic users, and the earth shall tremble with the signs of her coming."

– From the Prophecy of the Eye of Truth, recorded by Cor of Restis Haven

Chapter Sixteen

As she stared at herself kneeling next to the pool, Aliane finally remembered the nightmare that had fled her memory the night she had rescued Gwynne and Thalan from Magir. In the dream she had seen herself on the bloody battlefield, just as she now saw herself kneeling beside the waters of the Mirror of the Eye. But this was no dream. At least she didn't think it was. Her dream-self had not looked nearly as surprised by such circumstances as her living-self did at this moment.

She had no control over the eyes from which she saw, but she didn't care a whit. She could see! It was wonderful to see the colors of the cave that appeared bleached and faded in the glowing magic light of the single candle Jaerak had lit. She hungrily gazed at everything in her line of sight and wished Jaerak would turn his head so she could see more.

Jaerak. It struck her then. She was seeing through his eyes. He had been watching her, and now she was watching herself with his vision. Just as he had been looking down on her when she had seen the back of her head through his eyes the first time. She wondered vaguely if he could still see her, or if she was using all his sight herself. It was bizarre to see her own expressions change as revelations and thoughts came to her. She could feel them happen, but watched them as well. *So this is what I look like*, Aliane thought wonderingly. It was completely different from looking in a mirror. She saw herself at and angle she would never have otherwise seen, and she gazed at herself in astonishment. *Goodness*, she thought, a little embarrassed. *I am rather pretty*. She briefly wondered if she was seeing herself as she truly was, or if she saw herself as Jaerak did. Was she using only his eyes, or did his perception carry over, too? She was well aware that the eyes of affection

– or in this case attraction – could magnify the slightest beauty. Was this how only Jaerak saw her, or did others see the same woman with their eyes as well?

Just then, Jaerak turned his head and her body moved from her... his... line of sight. It was a very odd sensation. She felt as if she were floating as he moved forward towards the Mirror of the Eye. She gasped as he sank to his knees, feeling a lurch in her stomach as if she were falling. She clutched a nearby stalagmite, feeling as if she were about to lose her balance, and saw herself out of the corner of her... his... eye mirror the action. All other senses – touch, smell, hearing, taste – were still firmly locked in her own body, but her sight seemed to have found housing in the body of another. *This is too weird*, she thought, holding her breath as Jaerak leaned forward out over the surface of the water.

She saw Jaerak's image reflected in the pool. It was like looking in a mirror, only the face she saw was not her own. She gazed at him, hungrily drinking in every detail of him. She saw the thin line of the scar that marred his left cheek and wondered how he had gotten it. His hair was longer than she had remembered, and he was wearing different clothes. He did not wear the Onnic uniform now, but wore instead a regular shirt and cloak. He wore leather bracers on his arms and she could see his breath coming in small, white puffs in the cold air. His limestone eyes gazed back at her from the surface of the water, and she again caught her breath at the beauty of his features, but Jaerak did not let his gaze linger on his own reflection for long. He turned his head... and looked at hers.

For an instant nothing happened, and Aliane saw her reflection frown as she herself frowned, sadly watching her now-vacant, sightless green eyes in the water. But as she watched, a faint ripple passed over the surface of the pool, distorting her reflection into something that might be seen in a warped glass or mirror. At the same time, a breath of wind extinguished the flame of the candle Jaerak still held, and for an instant she was afraid she was once again as blind as she had been before.

She felt another small puff of fresh air glide gently over her cheek. Wind? Where had the wind come from? They were in the bowels of a cave where no breeze or breath of air could penetrate. But she could still feel it on her face, and it was growing stronger. Through Jaerak's eyes she could see small flashes of yellow as the air blew by, and she looked in astonishment at the little spell-lines. *She could* see *the wind!* It swirled and tumbled about her, moving in liquid luminescence through the cave towards the pool. The spell-lines came together in a circular motion around the Mirror of the Eye, creating a small, glowing eddy of air a few feet above the surface.

Suddenly Aliane grew very afraid. She reached out a hand, blindly groping in the darkness to feel it clasped in Jaerak's, who had also instinctively reached for her. The air was charged with magic; Aliane could feel it crackling around her as the stones, the water, their very bodies hummed with vibrations of power.

Another faint light, different from the amber Air-light, caught her... or rather, Jaerak's... eye, and he turned to look at it, allowing her to see it as well. It was red this time, a deep crimson stirring deep within the pool itself, spreading its reaching tendrils of light as it rapidly fought its way toward the surface. Suddenly, it burst from the waters and the entire cavern was awash in it, every rock, every limestone column, every surface was bathed in glowing, brilliant carmine light. Jaerak instinctively turned away from it, shielding his eyes and Aliane cried out in protest.

"No! Don't look away! Let me see it, I have to see it!"

His eyes again opened, and Aliane saw an incredible sight. Hundreds of thousands of bats, disturbed by the light and noise, were fleeing the cave in huge hordes of tangled wings and reddened eyes. They rushed through the air in a frantic effort to get out of the cavern as quickly as possible. In only a few seconds they were gone. Aliane briefly wondered if they knew something she didn't and resisted the urge to follow them. The ruby-red spell-lines, now thicker and stronger than before, were suddenly pulled into the whirling vortex of air above the pool. The vermilion light mingled with the saffron to make a beautiful gleaming orange.

Jaerak looked back at the water, which now bubbled and frothed as if heated over a huge furnace to boiling point. Flashes of blue spell-light were now jumping around the pool like indigo sparks, twisting and turning as if goading the water to foam higher, and higher yet. The cerulean incandescence merged with the gentle glowing orange whirlwind of light and air hovering above the pool and a very pale, very gentle purple light emerged from the union. As each element joined its lucent strand to the mix, the whirlpool of air spun faster and faster until Aliane's curls whipped about her face in angry, snapping locks and Jaerak's cloak flapped sharply around his body.

Still grasping Aliane's hand, Jaerak lifted her to her feet and pulled her back from the water's edge. It felt bizarre to watch her body move while still seeing through Jaerak's eyes, but she did not resist. She and Jaerak both backed away as the foaming waters inched towards their feet.

Aliane heard vague noises behind her and automatically turned to see what had caused them, but could not see what was happening for Jaerak was still staring at the heaving, churning waters. Suddenly the earth started to shake beneath her feet and she stumbled, falling heavily against Jaerak who was also thrown off-balance. Lightning bolts of green spell-light shot from the ground, the rocks, the ceiling, everywhere, until the two astounded magic users were surrounded by flashing emerald lights. The verdant spell-lines streaked toward the Mirror of the Eye to join the ever-growing cyclone poised over the heaving waters, and as the colors touched they changed, forming the clearest, sharpest, most beautiful white light Aliane had ever seen. The wind was so strong now that she and Jaerak clutched each other to keep their feet. The miniature tornado of bleached, opaline light and wind suddenly condensed, shrinking into a pulsing orb that illuminated the entire cavern. Aliane had no time to marvel at how huge the cave was, or appreciate the surreal beauties within it, for an ominous cracking noise alerted her to a new danger. Aliane and Jaerak fell to their knees as the cave shattered to pieces around them in a deafening symphony of falling rock and splintered stone.

Aliane did not see what happened next because Jaerak flung her to the floor and landed heavily on top of her, his face buried in her hair and his body shielding hers. As she wheezed and gasped for air, trying to regain her breath, she heard a horrendous thundering cacophony as if the world had split asunder beneath their feet. She felt Jaerak flinch and jerk against her as if he had been struck by a piece of falling rock, and realized they were about to be buried alive. She desperately reached out with her senses and felt dozens of spell-lines in the dust-choked air, jumbled and crossing and impossible to distinguish from each other. Rapidly and without thought, she grasped and wove them into a complicated web of protection and flung it over herself and Jaerak. The rocks stopped falling on them and she heard strange, thunking noises as they bounced off the shield rather than their bodies. She wanted to see what was happening so she shrugged Jaerak off her. Coughing on the dust now trapped within their little bubble of protection, Jaerak, realizing he no longer felt rock and stone raining down on him, opened his eyes and both of them looked in wonder at the sight before them.

The ceiling of the cavern must have been quite close to the surface above, because where there used to be only rock and stone there now was a gaping hole through which they could see blue sky and clouds. The cave floor was littered with large chunks of broken earth and rock that had fallen through the great height of the cave, as well as the body of at least one Onnic soldier who had had the misfortune of standing where the ground had split apart. Aliane shuddered at the sight of the torn and bloodied red cloak protruding from beneath the pile of rubble, hoping no other bodies lay crushed beneath the tons of rock and stone.

The unnaturally brilliant orb of white light pulsed and throbbed as if it were a living thing. The light had to be hurting Jaerak's eyes, but he somehow managed to keep them open. Aliane felt no pain, but of course she wouldn't for the eyes she used were not attached to her body. It was obvious his arm also pained him, for it hung from his shoulder at an odd angle as if broken or dislocated, but he paid it no heed.

A gurgling noise brought Jaerak's attention back to the pool of water. It was roiling in earnest now, splashes of frothy water spilling over the sides of the pool and creeping like sea-foam across the stone-littered floor. The earth gave one last mighty heave, sending a huge geyser of water gushing up from the Mirror of the Eye. The water soared into the air through the newly opened hole in the ceiling. The strange fusion of rainbow-colored spell-lights fell on the jet of water, outlining every droplet in clear, shimmering brightness. For a moment it seemed as if time stopped altogether and a billion tiny diamonds hung suspended from silver chains in a celestial necklace spanning the sky. It was so beautiful that Aliane felt a lump form in her throat as she gazed in star-struck wonder through Jaerak's eyes.

The waters of the pool hit the sky and split, forming two shining, dawn-tinted arcs that hung pendent in the air for several heartbeats before they plummeted back to the earth, one towards the Lake of Truth, the other headed for the Lake of Lies. The two jets of water hit the lakes simultaneously, causing huge sprays of salt water to plume skyward. Campfires were extinguished, people doused and horses soaked as large amounts of water fell onto the camp. Aliane could not see the pandemonium that ensued, but she could certainly hear it. Yells, curses and high-pitched shrieks told the story of what was happening well enough.

Then it all stopped as abruptly as it had begun. The earth fell quiet, the bright white light suddenly winked out, and the water stayed on the ground above where it belonged. A few stray stones and rocks clattered down onto the pile of rubble and the dust began to settle once the wind died away. Aliane almost laughed at the sight of cautious faces peering down from the large rift in the cavern ceiling, dripping with water and eyes wide. She was still looking through Jaerak's eyes, but she saw the looks the men were giving her nonetheless, and she shivered as if she were cold. Come to think of it, she was cold. The opening had let in the frigid air and she was soaked to the skin. She wished she could see Jaerak's face, but there was no longer any water in the pool to reflect his features.

"We need to get out of here," Jaerak muttered to her. He sounded strangely subdued. "It looks as if the whole cavern is about to collapse on us." But when they turned to make their way back through the tunnel they found several tons of rock and dirt blocking their way. That must have been the noise she had heard earlier, Aliane realized. Jaerak swore under his breath and called up to one of the startled men to toss down a rope.

After anchoring their longest rope to a tree, the soldiers above threw it down to the captives. Aliane watched as the end of the rope fell toward them and bounced off the protective shield she had created around them. Jaerak glared at her, though she didn't see it, and she watched herself give a slightly hysterical giggle.

"Whoops," she said inanely, and let go of the magic.

Instantly the darkness came crashing down on her again, and she clutched her eyes in shock. It was incredible how easily she had become accustomed to seeing again, even in such an unconventional way. The return of her blindness was almost as painful as its onset, and she gave a small moan of regret, trying very hard not to scream her frustration and anger. She heard Jaerak grunt as he looped the rope around her shoulders and under her arms. She wondered if he knew she no longer saw through his eyes. She grabbed at the rope as she felt herself being lifted from the ground.

It seemed as if she spent a long time dangling from the end of that rope, but eventually she felt hands grasp her and pull her to the safety of solid ground. The harness was removed and lowered again to retrieve Jaerak, and Aliane lay on the ground, heedless of the wet blanket of snow beneath her, panting and spent as if she had been the one hauling someone up the length of the cavern.

The ground beneath her vibrated as she felt rather than heard footsteps pounding toward her – the snow muffled much of the noise. She found herself caught up in someone's arms, held tightly against a broad, hard chest and squeezed as if she were about to fly away and never come back. She heard the beating of a frantic pulse as her face was squashed into the approximate region of someone's manly heart. From the smell and feel of him, she would guess it was Thalan who held her, and she laughed softly through the tears streaming down her face. This must be her day for canoodling.

"Are you all right?" he asked breathlessly, squeezing her even harder.

"Erk," she squeaked, unable to speak with Thalan's arms wrapped like steel bands around her ribs. She pushed him away and sat up.

"I'm fine," she said, though she wasn't sure it was entirely true. The enormity of what had just happened was beginning to dawn on her. *She* was *the Eye of Truth!* At least maybe she was – the Mirror had certainly put on a spectacular display for her. She wasn't entirely sure, though. She had looked in the pool with eyes that were not her own. Did that make a difference? Did it matter that it had not been she who had physically looked – that it had been Jaerak? But it had been her vision. Or had it? Aliane's head began to throb, so she gave up trying to think at all.

She heard someone else approaching, panting and puffing with exertion. Gwynne. The older woman dropped down beside Aliane and flung her arms around her in an affectionate and slightly hysterical embrace. Returning the hug, Aliane wondered what she could possibly say to the older woman after what had just happened, but as usual Gwynne had the perfect thing to say for any situation, and when she spoke, Aliane could tell she was smiling.

"I want my penny back."

* * *

"I don't know what you want me to say," Aliane said for the third time that hour. Gwynne feared for the girl's patience if Jaerak continued to question her, as he had been doing for the last three days. "I don't feel any different. As far as I'm concerned, nothing has changed."

Gwynne sat silently, staring at the beautiful princess in wonder. It was finished. The Search was over, the Eye of Truth found. A lifetime of learning, searching, hoping, yearning had come to an end. The culmination of history, the fulfillment of the Prophecies. The Epoch of the Eye was upon them. She just couldn't take it in.

"But things *have* changed," Jaerak insisted. "It's been proven you are the Eye of Truth."

"But that doesn't mean anything to me," Aliane said, exasperation giving a rough edge to her voice. "I'm still the same woman I was when I went down there. I don't have any extraordinary, secret knowledge, I don't suddenly feel enormous surges of powerful magic – I'm just... me." She paused briefly before adding, "But I'm not really even that anymore, either, I guess. I still think of myself as someone who can see."

All of which was probably true, Gwynne mused. Recent events had put the entirety of the Prophecies into question – at least Gwynne now questioned them. Aliane was of royal blood. She had been able to speak an untruth. Gwynne could see no signs of the Old Blood in her features and, though her magic might be powerful, she had seen no signs of the cataclysmic, irresistible pull of power she had expected. How was this woman, a princess, blinded by a cruel blow, armed with unschooled magic and a wicked swordfighting technique, supposed to save the world?

And yet, there were explanations for each discontinuity. Aliane had said she was not the Eye of Truth, and indeed, at the time she had not been. She had not become the Eye of Truth until she had looked in the pool, a process Gwynne still didn't fully understand. But Aliane had said her blanket was blue. No, Gwynne amended, trying to remember the woman's exact words. She had said she *saw* blue. She should have realized sooner that in order to dye something green you needed to mix blue and yellow dyes together. Or perhaps half the threads in the close weave had been blue and the other half yellow to create a blanket that *looked* green. So if Aliane had said she saw blue, she probably had. As for having royal blood... Gwynne was still skeptical about the girl's parentage, though she would never voice her suspicions. She was obviously very attached to King Torrit as her father and close kin.

It was clear, however, that it would be foolish to rely on Aliane's strength to get them out of their present predicament. The poor woman was still blind and her magic, though adequate to deflect falling rocks, was not strong enough to fend off an entire army. Thalan's idea about using the cave for escape was no longer an option since the rockfall had blocked any alternative escape routes they might have taken. So Thalan had spent the last three days devising another plan, and Gwynne decided it would be best to implement it as soon as possible. Jaerak's patience would not hold out forever, and neither, she suspected, would Aliane's.

Jaerak paused in his pacing, halting right in front of Aliane. He directed a ferocious glare at her, a futile gesture, Gwynne thought with amusement, since the girl couldn't even see it. It probably relieved his feelings, though.

"Enough of this," Jaerak snarled. Aliane recoiled, as if she had never heard him use that tone of voice with her. She probably hadn't, now that Gwynne thought on it. Jaerak had been uncommonly gentle with her until now. Glancing at Jaerak, she caught him flashing an almost apologetic glance at Aliane, which the girl was, again, unable to see. Interesting. Was it possible...? No. Gwynne shook the idea from her mind, though the seed of suspicion had already taken root. Evil villains may have some uses for beautiful women, but they did not fall in love with them.

"I don't know what else you want from me," Aliane was saying. "You tell me I have information you want, but I don't know what you're asking me! I'd never heard of the Dark Abyss until Gwynne told me what it was, and I know nothing more about those stones than you do. I don't know where they are, I don't know how to find them, and I don't know how to use them!"

Jaerak dropped into a chair and ran his fingers through his flaxen hair, and when he spoke his voice was once again mild and controlled.

"Yes, you do know. I know you know, you just have to try to remember."

Aliane gave a snort of contempt. "It's that stupid prophecy, isn't it?" she asked. "Something in the prophecy makes you think I know something. Well, it hasn't exactly been right on the mark up until now, has it? So I wouldn't bet my last grain of salt on it being right about anything else. So something happened when I looked in the bloody pool. That doesn't mean I know how to save the bloody world!" The woman stopped and took a deep breath, obviously trying to calm down. Gwynne was impressed. She didn't think she could do half as well if she were in the princess's dainty slippers. "I still say there is no way I could remember something I never knew in the first place," Aliane finished, apparently biting her tongue on the other, less agreeable things she wanted to say.

The Eye of Truth shall know that which she had never learned and remember that which she had never lived. Gwynne wondered if it was true. Jaerak obviously thought it was.

Jaerak clenched his hands into fists, evidently trying to control his temper. Then, as suddenly as a summer storm blows over, the anger seemed to drain from him and he smiled. It was probably just as well that at that moment Aliane was blind, Gwynne mused to herself. That one would have knocked her off her feet.

"There will be time for this later," Jaerak said, standing. "You mustn't expect me to give up, though. You see, I have proof you will help me find the stone. It will come to you. And then," he murmured, as if to himself, "you will come to me." With that, he left the tent.

Gwynne stared after him in utter confusion, and even Aliane's brow wrinkled as she tried to figure that one out.

"What did he mean, proof?" Aliane asked finally. Gwynne moved to stand behind the girl, her hands resting on the princess's shoulders.

"I have no idea," Gwynne sighed and closed her eyes. She was so tired, she just wanted to sleep for days and days and days. The events of the past few days had taken a lot out of her, and the coming weeks promised only further hardship.

"Where is Thalan?" Aliane asked suddenly. "I haven't seen him... I mean... he hasn't been here all morning." Aliane's hands twitched, and Gwynne squeezed her shoulders in silent sympathy. She knew how it hurt the girl when she made slips like that.

Instead of answering her question, Gwynne absently replied, "Come, my dear, let's get you something to eat."

"I'm not hungry," Aliane protested as Gwynne pulled her to her feet. She lost her balance slightly and reached out to steady herself against the table that stood next to her. Her fingers touched a soft, smooth surface... leather, she decided. A book. She barely had time to pick it up before Gwynne pulled her from the tent. "Gwynne... slow down. I can't go so fast!"

"I've got you, don't worry," Gwynne said softly. "Just don't try to fight me... trust me. I won't let you fall."

Aliane was silent for several more minutes, but Gwynne could tell she was beginning to suspect something was wrong. The woman was smart, and she should have known she couldn't fool the canny princess for long.

"Gwynne, where are we going?" Aliane asked finally, tucking the book she had taken into her pocket. She would examine it later. "I may be blind, but I know this is not the direction to the mess tent. It's not nearly this far."

"Hush. I'll explain when we get there. Just trust me," she said again, and Aliane fell silent. Gwynne felt a rush of affection for the girl. If she could have chosen a daughter for herself, Aliane would have perfectly fit the mold. Both Gwynne and Thalan had felt it would be better to keep their plans from Aliane, at least for a little while. Gwynne was not sure how to categorize the relationship between the princess and Jaerak Thorin, but she didn't want to take the chance that Aliane might inadvertently give something away.

Making plans had been difficult, for even though they were not bound or locked up there was always someone watching them, following them, and checking on them. They never had a moment alone, and even late at night there was a guard watching their tents. They could not use magic, since Jaerak would have known immediately what they were doing, and they could not speak privately for fear someone might overhear their intent. So they had devised a method of passing short notes to each other and destroying them once they were read. Gwynne grimaced as she remembered several times when no fire had been available and she had had to stuff the note in her mouth and swallow it as she heard the approach of a guard's footstep.

But it had all been to the good and their chance for escape had just arrived. Jaerak was sulking in his tent, trying to figure out a way to get the information he needed from Aliane. The soldiers were either eating or sleeping or polishing their weapons, trying to keep warm as the icy breeze sliced through the camp. Masyl Vonnin could be heard in his tent muttering prayers and would probably not wish to be disturbed for some time. Gwynne had seen the High Priest's shocked, white face after he had witnessed the fulfillment of a prophecy he had never believed in and he had not been seen since.

That left two lone guards who followed the two women at a distance, and Gwynne was reasonably confident that she and Thalan could take care of them.

Thalan was waiting by the horse pens, just as they had planned. Aliane lifted her head and sniffed the air as Gwynne propelled her towards the young man.

"We are near the horses," Aliane said, a hint of confusion creeping into her voice. "What are we doing here?"

"Shush," Gwynne whispered. "We are going to get you out of here."

"Escape?" Aliane asked, lowering her voice. To Gwynne's relief she sounded hopeful rather than disappointed. "Is it possible?"

"It had better be, unless you want Jaerak to take you back to Magir with him." Gwynne purposefully hardened her tone. "You are what he wants, you know. Not because you are beautiful or funny or kind or good, but because he thinks you can give him what he needs and wants – power. He wants to use you, exploit your knowledge for his own gain."

Aliane was silent for a moment, and then sighed. "I know," she whispered back. "I know."

"This may be our only chance for escape," Gwynne told her, still leading her towards the horse pens. "Are you willing to try?"

"Yes," Aliane whispered. "I guess I haven't much left to lose."

Gwynne privately disagreed with her but this was not the time to argue the point. "Then just follow my lead," she whispered as they approached Thalan, who was leaning against the fencing that penned the animals in.

"How are they?" Gwynne called to him, loud enough for guards behind them to overhear.

"Milyn and Frigget are fine," Thalan replied, "but my horse, Coe, seems to have thrown his shoe. He's favoring his left leg."

"Hmmm..." Gwynne said, leaning over the rail to take a better look. "You're right, he is. We'd better get someone to re-shoe him."

"I can't find the one he threw," Thalan told her. He was now standing next to the two women, and he slid his hand under Aliane's arm and squeezed it reassuringly. "We'll have to get their smith to make a new one."

"Hmmm, yes," Gwynne replied, examining Coe's hoof. "There's no way you could ride all the way to Magir with three shoes. He'd be lame in less than a day."

Thalan looked around as if unaware of his surroundings and caught sight of the two guards who stood at a discreet distance, as if noticing them for the first time.

"Hey, you there!" he yelled, gaining the attention of the guards. "A little help over here!"

"What is he doing?" Aliane hissed to Gwynne under her breath. Gwynne could feel the tension snap through the girl like miniature tidal waves. "He's going to get us killed!"

"Hush," Gwynne whispered back. "It will be all right."

"Is there a problem?" one of the guards asked, coming a little closer.

Thalan walked out to meet him. "We need the smith," he said, pointing to the horse corral. "My horse threw a shoe, and Captain Jaerak is preparing for the journey to Magir. Could you run over to the smithy and give the message?"

The guard, a big burly man who usually took a long time to think things through, scratched his head and looked at his companion. The other guard shrugged, obviously unwilling to commit himself.

"Well... I guess it would be all right," the first guard said, reluctantly making a decision. "Don't you try nothing, now," he warned. "Julian will be keeping an eye on you."

"Hey, wouldn't think of it," Thalan assured him, holding his hands in the air in a conciliatory gesture. "Appreciate the help, friend." He watched as the large, burly man lumbered off towards the campsite.

Once he was out of sight, Thalan turned to Gwynne and whispered, "All right, now!" Instantly Gwynne let out a heartrending groan, as if her heart had broken and her belly ruptured all at the same moment. Aliane gasped and clutched her. Gwynne fell to her knees, clasping her arms around her middle and cried out pitifully. Aliane put her arms around her shoulders and shouted, "Help! Someone help! Please!" Gwynne hoped the girl realized it was a ruse and would not really think she was in imminent danger of expiring at her feet. Thalan dropped to his knees beside the groaning woman, and Julian, the remaining guard, came to see what was wrong.

Two quick hits – one to the belly and one to the head – dispatched Julian easily. Thalan dragged his unconscious body behind a snowdrift so he would not be visible from the camp. Gwynne straightened up and grabbed Aliane's hand.

"Miraculous recovery," the young woman said, her voice nearly lost in a puff of laughter. It was nice to hear her laughing again – it had been a long time.

"Thank you, my dear," she replied. "Thalan?"

Thalan brushed off his hands and gave a last look at the unconscious guard. "Right. Let's move before anyone comes looking for us."

Gwynne told Aliane much, much later that she and Thalan had already saddled and tied their horses to the railing so it would be easier to catch and mount them. Once they had abandoned their plans to escape through the cave, they knew they would not get very far without their mounts. Therefore, Thalan was able to save a great deal of time by grabbing the pull-ropes and leading their horses from the corral with ease. They had talked about setting the other horses loose as well, but thought it might attract too much attention;

they wanted time to escape, not an angry mob of Onnic on their heels.

Unfortunately, that was exactly what they got – they were mounting when they heard the shouts. Someone, perhaps the first guard suspecting something odd, had come to investigate and was now sounding the alarm. Gwynne cursed and Thalan quickly threw Aliane on Frigget's back. By some miracle she managed to stay on, and Frigget, a big, powerful black with a white blazon across his nose, danced uneasily as she settled herself in the saddle.

"We'll have to run for it!" Thalan shouted as he sprang onto his own mount. Gwynne looked behind her and saw what looked like a small army of men running towards them. With a shout she wheeled Milyn around and dug her heels in. The gentle bay, startled by this unusually rough behavior, took off like a shot.

Out of the corner of her eye she saw Thalan on Coe, heading in a direction perpendicular to hers. The men had entered the corral and were hastily mounting their horses to chase them, and Gwynne's hope for escape died. There was no way they could outrun so many, and Milyn was an old lady now. It would kill the gentle mare to push her so hard.

Just then Gwynne remembered Aliane and gasped. She pulled the reins so hard that Milyn squealed and reared up on her hind legs. Gwynne wheeled her around and searched frantically across the field for the princess. *For the Eye of Truth*, Gwynne growled to herself, *who couldn't see and therefore wouldn't know which way to ride*! She had forgotten all about the girl's affliction and had left her to fend for herself while she ran away like a coward.

She saw Aliane on her beautiful, powerful black horse. The girl was still frantically trying to fit her feet into the stirrups. Gwynne couldn't hear her, but it looked as if she were calling their names, desperately trying to hear their voices in the chaos that erupted around her. It was clear the princess could hear the pounding of horse hooves, but it seemed as if she could not tell where they were coming from. She didn't know which direction to run.

"This way!" Gwynne screamed, trying to attract the princess's attention. "Come this way!" She nudged Milyn forward again, more gently this time, but still urgently. She had to help the girl. Aliane's head cocked as if she heard the voice, but she wavered, unable to tell where *it* was coming from, either. The Onnic were close now, and Aliane obviously could sense them. She leaned over Frigget's neck and dug her heels in, urging the horse forward. Unfortunately, she rode him right into the thick of the oncoming Onnic siege.

Gwynne screamed something incoherent and saw a flash of white and brown as Thalan streaked by on Coe, riding like a centaur. Gwynne knew he was going to be too late. One of the Onnic guards already had his hand on Frigget's bridle, and they were reaching out to pull the frightened woman from her saddle. Gwynne heard more noise and turned to see Jaerak riding towards the princess, his fair hair and green cloak flapping in the wind. Jaerak gave a shout and the Onnic froze, their hands still clutching Aliane's clothing.

Gwynne was never entirely clear about what happened next. She sometimes thought her eyes must have deceived her – she had never seen anything like it before. One moment Aliane was on the back of her horse, trying desperately to unfasten her crossbow from where it was still strapped to her saddle and the next moment she was gone, vanished. Gwynne, standing in her stirrups, saw the whole thing.

Aliane had been leaning low over Frigget's neck, trying to urge him forward while fumbling with the leather straps that held her crossbow to the saddle. Frigget was hampered by the men who grabbed his reins and bridle, and could not break their hold. Aliane, in a final desperate attempt to break free, reached out in a flash of magic – Gwynne could actually see the spell-lines, the magic was so strong – and began to weave a complicated spell-web. The next moment Aliane seemed to disappear, or disintegrate, or break apart into a billion pieces; Gwynne could not decide which description fit the process best. She did know, however, that one second the woman was there, and the next she was gone. Frigget's saddle stood empty and the princess was nowhere to be seen.

She could have used a protection or invisibility spell, but somehow Gwynne did not think she had. That spell-web was like nothing she had ever seen before, and the magic stronger than any she had encountered. Aliane's body had seemed to break into dust-sized particles that were instantly swept away on the wind. But whatever had happened, it was clear the girl was gone.

Thalan brought Coe up short and looked wildly around. When Aliane did not immediately reappear, he galloped to join Gwynne.

"Wha... what happened?" he panted, still looking around in bewilderment. "Where did she go?"

Suddenly something clicked in Gwynne's mind as a piece of memory fell into place. *Amazing*, she thought. *Then it really is true.*

"I don't know where she is," Gwynne said slowly. "I think she could be anywhere. Literally. She could be anywhere in the world, and we would not be able to find her."

Thalan stared at her. "What do you mean?" he whispered. "What did she do?"

Gwynne closed her eyes, remembering that bright flash of magic just before the princess had disappeared. “She seems to have rediscovered an ancient method of traveling,” she explained. “It was called ‘riding the wind’ and it hasn’t been used in centuries. The knowledge of how to ride the wind died out a long time ago.”

Thalan looked disbelieving. “You’re kidding. How did she do it?”

Gwynne shook her head ruefully. “I have no idea. She’s the Eye of Truth.” That was the only explanation she had, but Thalan seemed to understand. He took her hand and pressed it.

“Don’t worry so much,” he whispered to her. “She’s probably safer wherever she is than she would be here. We’ll find her again.” Despite his confident words, his usual jolly smile was absent and his forehead was lined with worry.

“Or more likely,” Gwynne murmured, “she’ll find us.” She hoped with all her heart that wherever Aliane had ended up, she was safe and unhurt and unafraid. She watched as Jaerak, his arm in a sling, realized his prisoner had escaped him. He went white with anger, clenched his gloved fists, turned his horse and started back to camp without saying a word to anyone.

Gwynne felt despair hanging over her like a thundercloud as guards surrounded the two friends and dragged them from their horses. She had found the Eye of Truth, and then, in keeping with the rest of her luck, had promptly lost her again.

"Magic is the key to all things... the key to magic is magic itself."
– From Melanrys an'Tereal's Book on Magic

Chapter Seventeen

Aliane fell to the earth with an emphatic "thud." Bruised but not broken, she wonderingly fingered the firm, solid rock beneath her hands and body. She was whole again. For a while there she had wondered if she was doomed to travel the earth as a wraithlike cloud of magic dust and atoms, without form or figure, for all eternity.

It had been the oddest sensation. She still wasn't exactly sure what had happened, or how she had managed it. She remembered being thrown on a horse – presumably her own – and then hearing the beats of hooves as her companions ran off in all directions. She could tell they had taken different paths but she had hesitated, not knowing which one to follow. Then, suddenly the sound of two hoofbeats had become twenty and she knew she was in trouble. She had become confused, she couldn't remember which direction her friends had gone, and she didn't want to move for fear of running headlong into her pursuers. Which, of course, was exactly what she had ended up doing. *Quite a nasty situation,* she thought, rubbing a particularly painful spot on her bottom.

She vaguely remembered a piercing scream that sounded as if it might have come from Gwynne, and then she had been surrounded by stamping hooves and snorting horses, the smell of sweaty men and leather filling her nostrils. She had felt the reins jerk under her hands as rough men seized them, and Frigget tried to toss his head to dislodge the grips on his bridle. Aliane knew she was overcome, but she would be salted and stuffed before she would give up without a fight. It was difficult to undo the straps of her crossbow with Frigget prancing around, but she had almost managed it.

But then she had heard a voice that drove everything else from her mind – Jaerak's voice. Panic had overwhelmed her, and she knew she could not let herself be taken again. She was afraid that if she spent much more time with Jaerak she would succumb to him – in more ways than one. Her response to him in the cave had proven she was not to be trusted in his company, and even now the memory of his kiss burned on her lips. This was her last chance to escape and she couldn't afford to lose it. She had reached out blindly – her mouth twisted in a mirthless smile at the appropriateness of the word – and grasped a handful of spell-lines. Even now she could not remember what she had done with them – she had felt an incredible surge of power and the next thing she knew she had lost all form and substance. She had no arms, she had no legs and it didn't matter that she was blind because she had no eyes. She had suddenly felt every part of herself separate from every other part of herself as time, feeling, hearing, touch – in essence the reality of the world had dissolved around her.

Her only thought was to escape, so she had found herself moving, though how she did so without any muscles she not know, at incredible speeds on the breath of the wind. It had been incredible, exhilarating, exciting, and terrifying all at once. She had only to think about a safe place, a place where Jaerak could not find her, and she would find herself moving. Then, after what seemed like only moments, she had once again become whole. Unfortunately, she had re-materialized some distance from the ground and had fallen painfully to earth. *Thud indeed,* she thought wryly, again rubbing her sore posterior. She'd have an impressive bruise on that spot the next day.

Of course, now she had no idea where she was. She still could not see. She had no idea how far she had traveled, or in which direction, or even *how* she had done it. The ground under her hands was stone; polished stone, it felt like, so most likely she was in some kind of building. She stood warily, wincing as her bruised muscles pulled and protested. She reached out her hand, but felt nothing but empty air.

The first thing she had to do was find out where she was. She remembered wishing herself somewhere safe, some place where Jaerak would never be able to find her, where he could not reach her, could not hurt her. Could not touch her as he had in that all-too brief moment in the cave. That, Aliane thought, was the real danger. He was so salted charming, her willpower and common sense dissolved when she was with him.

So, apparently she had woven some magic spell that had transported her to such a place. But where? Her father's castle? No, she thought. Too obvious. That would be one of the first places he'd look. It would be no trouble for him to use Onnic posted in Cameon to search for her. But where else could she go? She didn't know anywhere else well enough to feel safe there. She hadn't been out of Aryn until just recently, and she couldn't imagine she'd consider Morgan's palace a safe haven from anything, especially Jaerak. So where had she gone? Where was she now?

She shuffled a small way to her right, her arms outstretched, but felt nothing. She bit her lip. She had never been afraid of the dark, but this was altogether different. She was in unfamiliar territory, and if something dangerous happened to be out there she would not be able to see it, and it would be able to see her. The thought made sweat bead on her upper lip, and she clamped down hard on her rising fear. The bombardment of terror over the past several hours was taking its toll – she felt enervated and listless, but forced herself to concentrate.

She stood perfectly still and listened. She heard no sound whatsoever. That was strange, she thought, frowning. She should be able to hear something. A breath, a creak, a whisper, a rustle – *something.* But there was nothing. The only sounds were the rapid beating of her heart and the sound of her own breath, coming somewhat faster than usual.

Every nerve in her body pricked to attention, and she fancied she could feel danger, smell it, taste it, though she could not see or hear it. It was a tangible feeling and it wrapped its insidious arms around her, willing her to lose control, urging her to surrender to her fear. She took a deep breath and dug deeper into her reservoir of strength. She silently thanked Charis, who had taught her more than how to wield a sword and control her muscles, but also how to calm her mind and quiet her soul under extreme duress. She could almost hear his voice: *A finely tuned body is not enough – you must have equal control of your mind and emotions. You cannot go into a fight if you are flying in all directions. Focus, and you will prevail.* And now, of all times, she needed to keep her wits about her.

She moved again, sliding her feet along the smooth, stone floor, reaching out with seeking hands, testing each step before shifting her weight. Before long, her foot bumped against a hard object, and she reached down to touch it. It felt like a wooden crate, several feet long and a little narrower in width. Her fingers explored the area around the lid, and she felt the slight indentation where the top met the sides. Digging her fingers in tightly, she tried to pry the lid off the crate. It would not budge.

She pulled on the lid with her considerable strength, but to no avail. She finally had to give up, and she sat down on the crate to catch her breath. As she sat, her foot bumped another object, this one much smaller. She could tell it was small, because it skittered across the floor as her foot pushed against it, and she heard a quiet *thunk* as some object in its way stopped it. She got down on her hands and knees to feel the floor with her hands. She bumped into three more crates, each one smaller than the first, before she found the object she had accidentally kicked. It was another box, this one small enough to hold in the palm of her hand. She picked it up and tried to open it.

It must be a puzzle box, she finally decided. She could feel no seams, no latches, no locks and no hinges. Yet, when she gently shook the box she could hear the rattle of an object or objects moving inside. There must be a way to open it. Whatever was in the box and the crates might give her a clue where she was.

Further exploration revealed a total of four smaller crates scattered around the larger one, none a very great distance away. She could not open any of those either – the lids stuck fast and she could not figure out how they were being held down. She could feel no nails or pegs in the wood, and the smooth sides and edges held no locks or chains.

Since she could not do anything more with the crates, she decided to explore. Putting the small puzzle box carefully in her cloak, she began to move forward. Hesitantly at first, but then with growing confidence, she walked and walked and walked, never straying from her direction, never faltering in her step. Therefore, when she ran into the crate again she barked her shins rather severely against it, drawing blood and a painful hiss through her gritted teeth.

She could have sworn it was the same crate. It felt the same, had the same dimensions, everything. She felt the area around the box and sure enough, four smaller crates flanked the main one. She must have been walking in a large circle without realizing it. *Strange,* she thought. She had been so sure she'd been going in a straight line. She faced a different direction and set off again.

Less than twenty minutes later she ran into the crate again. Something was definitely wrong here, she mused, sitting on it and trying to make sense of things. It was very unlikely she would have made the same mistake twice, and it was even less likely there were three identical sets of crates and she had managed to bruise her shins against all of them.

Aliane felt the hem of her cloak and felt for the warm, thick woven lining inside. She tore some stitching and picked at a thread with her fingernail until it came loose. Pulling her sword from its scabbard, she used the tip to chip at the lid of the crate until the wood splintered. She pulled on the loose thread and wound it around a small splinter of wood. Then, holding the thread between her fingers she walked away from the crate again, the lining of her cloak unraveling as she moved forward. She walked in a studiously straight line, but in what seemed like only minutes she was once again bumping her sore knees against the wooden crate. She felt around the edges of the box, felt the splinter around which was twined the thick, coarse thread, taut and reaching out in the opposite direction. Aliane fingered the thread in bewilderment. She gently pulled on it, and felt the thread in her hand vibrate slightly. It was impossible, she thought. The thread was stretching out away from her, heading off into the distance. She tugged sharply on her end of the strand and it abruptly broke. She felt the crate again to find the now limp thread, still attached to the splinter, drift down to rest on the floor, all its tension gone. Aliane sat down on the large crate again, since it seemed pointless to try to move anywhere. It appeared as if she would just end up back in the same place, and she was tired of whacking her legs against crates.

Well. This certainly wasn't her father's castle. The crates and threads in Aryn did not behave in such a bewildering and inexplicable manner. One could expect a wooden box to stay put and a thread to remain in a straight line there. Obviously things were different here.

But that brought up an even more troubling question. Where exactly was she? And how could she have transported herself to a place she didn't even know existed? The answer was obvious. She could not have. It just wasn't possible.

She must be some place she knew, then, somewhere she had at least heard about. And there was only one place she *knew*, without question, Jaerak could not find. She must be in the Dark Abyss.

It made perfect sense. Made of magic, accessible only by magic, the Dark Abyss was Jaerak's goal, the reason he needed her in the first place. If he had known how to enter it, he would not have needed her. Jaerak believed, then, that he could not enter it without her help. If she were already *in* the Dark Abyss, there would be no way she could possibly help him find it, so she had instinctively brought herself to the one place she knew Jaerak could never, ever find her.

Now the question remained: how was she to get out again? She could not exactly remember how she had managed her unexpected disappearing spell, and she was hesitant to try it again. What if something went wrong? What if she dematerialized and never came back together again? Or what if she reappeared all wrong, with no arms or three legs or two heads or something? Could that happen? With magic, Aliane mused to herself, anything was possible. How was she supposed to recreate magic she had woven in an instinctive moment of panic?

Experimentally, she reached out with her fingers and senses and felt the spell lines surrounding her. She was getting better at identifying them by their feel rather than their color now. It was actually a lot easier than trying to look at them, which took an enormous amount of concentration. The amber Air felt slightly drier and sharper than the warmer, waxier lines of Fire. Aliane had wondered how spell-lines of fire could exist where there was no fire, and Gwynne had told her that if the *potential* for fire existed then the spell-lines would be ever present. The emerald green lines of Earth had a cooler, moister quality, and the deep blue lines of Water felt thicker and denser than the others. Then there were the very, very thin, brittle lines that intersected and crossed all things, held them together, inextricably bound them. These, she knew, were the spell-lines that dealt with Time, but she knew no spells that affected them, nor did she understand how to manipulate them to create spell-webs. She could touch them, but if she tried to craft something from them they broke apart like burnt sugar on her fingers. She knew so little about magic – perhaps Gwynne would know why they did that. Or, Aliane thought very privately to herself, maybe Jaerak would know. Would she ever have the chance to ask him? She shied away from the painful question and concentrated again on the spell-lines.

Aliane thought carefully. When she had dematerialized herself, she had grabbed the first spell-lines that came to her hand. She reached out and met with flexible, arid ones. *Air, then,* she thought. *That makes sense, I have more experience with Air than with anything else.* She laughed silently at herself. It seemed ludicrous in the extreme that someone who was supposed to be the Eye of Truth was stuck in some magic dimension and didn't know how to get herself out.

The Eye of Truth. Aliane still couldn't take it in. She kept thinking that there must be some mistake, there had to be another explanation for what had happened at the Mirror of the Eye. Jaerak had been the one who had looked in the pool, not her. Maybe Jaerak was the Eye of Truth. Or maybe she was only the Eye of Truth when she could look out of his eyes, or when he mingled his magic with hers. *Or maybe when he mingles other things with you, you dolt,* she thought scathingly. *You just want an excuse to be with him!* She did not deny the accusation, but she cut off that train of thought before it could go any further. Even though she had always tried to be honest with herself, there were some things she just wasn't ready to face yet. Her feelings for Jaerak bloody Thorin were one of them, and if she kept arguing with herself she really would go mad.

But how was she supposed to save the world if she couldn't even get herself and her friends out of even a minor pickle? If the world was depending on her to rescue it, then a lot of people were in for a big disappointment. She frowned as her horrible dream came back to her once again. She remembered the army of dead standing before her as she stood on the hill, and she remembered how they had fallen as she had denied them, denied her responsibility, refused their piteous appeal. She banished such unproductive thoughts and brought her mind back to her present predicament.

First, she had to decide where she wanted to go when she escaped her enchanted prison. If she were indeed in the Dark Abyss, she would have to use magic to get out. Hadn't Gwynne told her that the key to entering the Abyss was magic? Well, then it stood to reason that the only way to get out was to use the same key. But where should she go? She could go to Aryn, but she didn't even know if her father was back from Magir yet. She could go to Magir, but she'd be willing to bet a pound of salt that Larion had already told his father that she had been traveling in the company of witches and was most likely one herself. The prince had seen her after the fateful fight that had blinded her, and she remembered with a chill the conversation she had overheard the day she had regained consciousness. Maybe Larion even knew she had fulfilled part of the Prophecies. The prince had been ordered to leave, but she would not have been surprised if he had been skulking around the camp looking for something that would make him look good to his father. Maybe by now everyone knew. Maybe even her father had heard, but the Eye only knew what he would think when he found out. Suddenly Aliane giggled. *If the Eye only knew,* she thought, giggling some more. *I have to stop saying that. I don't know anything at all.*

After a bout of semi-hysterical laughter, which probably did her more good than harm, Aliane composed herself and seriously considered how she was going to get out of... wherever she was. She only suspected she was in the Dark Abyss – she could be on the surface of the Moon, for all she knew. Well, if wishes were wings she could fly to town, as her father often said, and nothing would happen if she didn't try something.

Screwing up her courage, she reached out, unthinkingly grasped some spell-lines and quickly twisted them around her body as she had done before. Then she envisioned her rooms in her father's palace in Aryn, outlining every detail, remembering every particular as clearly as she could. She reached out to draw the magic spell-web into her body as she had done before – or thought she had, anyway – but just as she felt the silky cords of light touch her fingers an overpowering wave of nausea came over her like a giant tidal wave.

She did not so much drop the spell-web as fling it away, gagging and retching as her stomach churned. As soon as the magic left her fingers, the burning pit of sickness within her disappeared. Unfortunately, the crate she had been sitting on also vanished from *its* place and she tumbled ignominiously to the polished stone floor.

She sat up, dazed and confused. What had happened to the crate? She felt around on the floor, but could feel nothing. Crawling on her hands and knees, she frantically searched the area with trembling fingers. All the crates were gone! The four smaller wooden boxes flanking the larger one – the box she had been sitting on – had vanished into thin air.

Sitting on the cold, hard floor, Aliane clutched her head in despair. Her spell. She had thrown away her spell-web as she was casting it and it must have caught and transported everything away *except her*!

If she truly was in the Dark Abyss, then the crates and boxes she had found most likely contained the remnants of the magic items – the Pyaerea – from the Onnic War. All the objects in the inventory, the book Jaerak somehow found, had been housed here. It made sense – the crates must have been sealed with spell-webs she couldn't see, which was why she could not open them. One of the items was the Alchemist Stone, the very item Jaerak had expressed great interest in, the item he had wanted her to find for him. And she had just transported it out of the Dark Abyss, where it had remained safely for over five hundred years, into the world where it could be found and misused by any number of people, including Jaerak himself.

She groaned and lay down on the floor, feeling like a cursed fool. As she rolled onto her back, she heard a 'clunk' as the side of her cloak, weighed down with a heavy object, came into contact with the floor. Puzzled, she felt in her cloak pocket and brought out an oblong wooden container and a soft, leather object. She shook the box and heard the faint rattle of something inside the box. *Oh yes,* she thought. It was the small puzzle box she had found and could not open. *Perhaps she would be lucky,* she thought hopefully. Perhaps the thing that rattled in the box was the Alchemist Stone and Jaerak wouldn't get it after all. She shook the box again, more carefully this time. Disappointed, she had to admit it probably wasn't the stone. Whatever was in there sounded as if it were made of metal.

Abandoning the box for the moment, she turned to the other object she had found in her pocket. It was the book she had taken from Jaerak's tent just before her escape. She ran her fingers over it gently, feeling little flakes of leather come apart at her touch. She recognized it now. It was Gwynne's book, the one Jaerak had found, the one that listed the magic items in the Dark Abyss. The magic items she had just lost.

Maybe I can get them back, she thought, idly fingering the little book. *If I can send them somewhere, surely I can bring them back.* Aliane reached out again to touch the magic spell-lines that permeated every thing, twisting and twining them around her fingers, but soon the nausea again engulfed her and she turned her head and vomited. Again, the sickness vanished and she felt perfectly sound as soon as she released the magic. She lay there, gasping and swearing, facing the realization that if she couldn't use her magic she would not be able to get herself out of this unbreakable prison. She was trapped. And she *had* to get out. She had to retrieve those Pyaerea before Jaerak found them. Aliane groaned again – she couldn't believe she had done such a stupid, unthinking thing.

She lay there for a while, trying not to think, trying not to feel, trying not to cry. A wave of homesickness, almost as strong as the nausea, came over her, and she found herself wishing she were safe in her father's embrace where nothing bad could touch her. But even her father could not keep her safe now, she thought despondently. If it became known she was a magic user, let alone the Eye of Truth, her father would be in as much danger as she was. *I've really bollixed things up now*, she thought, pressing her face into her arms. *Somehow when I pictured the Eye of Truth I never saw a blind woman, trapped with no hope of rescue, alone and ignorant and in desperate need of a hug.*

But that wasn't the worst of it. She didn't even want to consider the truly horrific aspect of what she had done, but it kept intruding on her thoughts, as inescapable as the Abyss itself. When she tried to transport herself she had been thinking of her father and the safety of his castle in Aryn, hoping to direct herself there by her will. She figured she'd be as safe there as anywhere, and at least she could consult her father and ask his advice. But as the nausea had gripped her and as she had flung her spell away, transporting the crates rather than her person, she had not been thinking about her father or Aryn at all.

She had been thinking about Jaerak Thorin.

* * *

King Torrit had delayed his departure from Magir three times already, not wanting to leave Charis to the tender mercies of King Morgan and his son Larion. Charis's wound had been graver than even the doctor had feared, and his Captain of the Guard had lain in a feverish delirium for four days. Finally his fever had broken, but it was a long, long time before Charis was strong enough to endure a journey back to Aryn. But as soon as the doctor pronounced him fit to travel, Torrit had begun preparations to depart.

He was sitting in his salon, gazing idly out the window and watching his carriages being brought round and loaded with luggage and supplies. He had ordered his daughter's things packed, but he didn't know exactly what to do with them. He had hoped she would return before he left, hoped she would come back to him safe and sound. He had wished she would confide in him, tell him what she was doing and where she had gone. But he had received two letters, and then nothing. She had warned him in her last letter that she might not have the opportunity to write for some time, and Torrit missed her abominably.

She had told him almost nothing of where she was or what she was doing. She said only that she was safe and happy and involved in something of the utmost importance. She had apparently made some friends – he had seriously mixed feelings about that piece of knowledge – but more than anything he wanted her back in his life, back in his arms, back in his confidence. He did not even know where to write to tell her he was returning to Aryn. He only hoped she would eventually find her way back to him there.

He sighed and looked down at the crumpled and stained piece of parchment in his hands. It had been read and lovingly fingered many times since he had received it more than twelve days ago. He knew it by heart, but still he opened it, careful not to tear it along its fragile creases, and read the final lines yet again.

Do not be cross with me, Father, it read. *I wish I could tell you where I am, but I'm sure I will be with you again soon. My adventure is almost at an end, and then I will come home. I miss you so much. Say hello to Charis and Hernie for me. Love, Aliane.*

He sighed again and refolded the letter. Mandras, his manservant, entered the salon and gently cleared his throat.

"We shall be ready to depart by midday, your Highness," he said deferentially. "There is still the matter of the Princess's trunks to be decided."

Torrit stood with his back to his servant, still looking out the window. "Put them in the carriages," he said shortly. He had not realized how painful the decision would be. Mandras bowed and left the room, leaving him alone with only his unpleasant and painful thoughts for company.

She had taken only a few clothes and jewels with her, she had no books, no trinkets, and her treasured possessions had all been left behind. How was she living? What was she eating? What was she wearing? Was she warm enough? Did she have any money? She had taken some of her jewels, including her mother's ring, but Torrit knew she would never sell it. Aliane had money of her own, but Torrit had no idea how much or where she had kept it. He hoped she had taken it with her, hoped she was able to travel in some comfort. He'd had to decide whether to leave her trunks with Morgan in case she came back or to take them to Aryn in case she stayed away longer and needed them once she got back home. The time had come to face the facts. She wasn't coming back, not soon anyway. Ordering the trunks back to Aryn basically constituted his acknowledgment of that fact – something he had refused to do until now.

He was also worried about the company she was apparently keeping. He knew nothing of these people she was with, for she had told him almost nothing.

Irena is a dear woman, open and loving though she has seen some hard times. I could not just abandon her when she needs my help. You understand, Father. Thalan is a nice young man who helps her, and he has been very friendly with me.

His daughter could have no idea how terrifying that last statement would be to a fond father. An icy fist clenched around his heart as he thought of the unthinkable possibilities. She was so innocent, so naïve... at least, he thought she was. Torrit was learning quickly that there was more to his daughter than he had realized. She truly had grown up, and he just hadn't noticed. Or, he amended silently, he had simply looked the other way and refused to admit it. But the fact remained there was nothing he could do right now but get Charis and his men safely back home. If Aliane needed his help she would ask for it.

The sound of hooves ringing on stone brought him back to the window. His lips, hidden by a luxuriant growth of beard, twisted in unconscious disgust as he saw a group of approximately fifteen men clad in the red uniforms of the Onnic order come through the gate. Prince Larion was leading them, he realized, and he silently groaned. He had wished to leave without having to face Larion again. It amazed him that he had once hoped for an understanding between the haughty prince and his beloved daughter. He understood now that he wasn't nearly good enough for Aliane. She deserved much, much better.

The prince seemed to be in something of a hurry. Torrit watched as he brought his steed to a rearing halt, dismounted and threw the reins in the general direction of a servant. He took the steps to the palace at a dead run and vanished from Torrit's sight. His fellow officers or soldiers or whatever they were followed more slowly. They all had the look of hard riding and little sleep about them – their shoulders were slumped and they surreptitiously rubbed sore muscles. One man, an older man with graying hair and a loose, almost flabby figure, looked vaguely familiar. Someone important, he thought. He had seen the man talking with King Morgan on several occasions. One of his High Priests, then. The man followed Prince Larion into the castle, managing to look dignified while at the same time moving at a fair clip.

Losing interest, Torrit went back to his couch. Though he had lost a little weight in the past month he still found it difficult to sustain his bulk for any length of time without frequent rests, and he sank gratefully into the soft cushions of the elegant divan. Ever since the prince had tried to kill his Chief of Arms, Torrit had had no use for the boy. Such a temper. Torrit frowned. Come to think of it, he never had discovered what that fight had been about. He had been too worried about Charis to ask. *Not that it matters much now,* he thought. They would all be leaving within a matter of hours.

Suddenly the door burst open and several men in red streamed in. Mandras scampered breathlessly behind with less than his usual dignity, demanding in high-pitched, ringing tones that they cease and desist and he would check to see if his Royal Highness was available. Torrit leapt to his feet, angered and offended at the rude and unusual intrusion. The man he had noticed below, the older one with graying hair, strode into the room closely followed by King Morgan and Prince Larion. Now that Torrit could see him up close, he finally recognized the priest. He was Masyl Vonnin, one of the most brutal and ruthless of the Onnic witchhunters.

Torrit opened his mouth to demand an explanation, but before he could do more than draw breath, Masyl Vonnin spoke.

"You, King Torrit el'Gregarian, ruler of Cameon, the Western region, father of Aliane el'Gregarian, witch and magic user, are under arrest. You are hereby remanded into the custody of the Onnic army where you shall await your trial in the Cathedral prison."

Torrit choked on the breath he had taken. "What?" he sputtered, looking astonished and bewildered as two young men in Onnic uniforms came to stand by him, one on either side. One reached out to pull his hands together, and then Torrit saw the rope in his hands, the rope they meant to bind him with. His face turned ruddy with anger as he snatched his hands away.

"What is the meaning of this outrage?" he demanded, glaring first at Masyl Vonnin, then at King Morgan. "How dare you? How dare you accuse me? How *dare* you speak so about my daughter, who isn't even here to defend herself?"

Masyl Vonnin gestured to the two Onnic to continue binding the affronted king. "My only obligation to you is to inform you of the charges upon which I arrest you. You are hereby charged with harboring a magic user in your home and protecting her. You are charged with treason, conspiracy to defraud the Crown of Casset and unlawful consortium with a witch. You are charged with criminal neglect for failing to report a magic user in your lands and with entrapment for trying to marry the Heir to the throne of Casset to a filthy witch." He looked coldly at the Onnic soldiers and said, "Take him away."

"STOP!" bellowed King Torrit, and the Onnic hesitated. One did not treat King Torrit lightly when he spoke that way. He was a huge bear of a man, and his fists, which were tightly clenched with rage, were as big as Solstice hams. He turned his glare onto Morgan. "You allow this?" he demanded, trying to control himself. "You allow such treatment of your guests? Your *royal* guests? And you..." he turned to Masyl. "My daughter is no witch. How can you say such a thing? I would have known. There must be some mistake."

"There is no mistake," said Masyl. "I was there. I saw what happened."

"You saw what happened," Torrit repeated stupidly. "You were there. You were where? You mean you saw her? Where is she? Is she all right?"

"We are not obligated to tell you anything," Masyl said crisply. "I suggest you cease all resistance. I would hate to have to... punish... you."

Torrit looked at the stony faces surrounding him and felt cold desperation rising within him. "But my family," he said, "my kingdom..."

"Until the time of your trial your lands will fall under my jurisdiction," Morgan informed him frostily. "As for your family, we are all very eager to speak to your daughter. Perhaps while you are in prison you could give us some idea of where she can be found."

Torrit felt the blood rush from his face. He knew how Onnic Catechists elicited information from their prisoners. He also knew that whether the accusations against Aliane were true or not, his daughter was as good as dead if the Onnic got their hands on her. It would be better to go along with them for now. If he made a scene it might be his daughter who paid for it later.

Before he could do or say anything, however, a messenger stumbled into the room through the already open door. He was dripping with sweat despite the frosty air, and he looked as if he had not rested in at least three days. Morgan frowned in annoyance, but Masyl Vonnin held up his hand as if to stop his angry words.

"Be still, Morgan," he said. "Obviously he has important news. Someone must have told him you were here."

The messenger nodded, still panting and wheezing. "Aye, Sire," he gasped, holding out a large scroll. "I come to you with a message from Freath." At the name of that troubled city, nearly everyone in the room stopped breathing. Morgan tore the seal from the scroll and read quickly. He went slightly pale.

"It's war," he said. Torrit felt his throat go dry. "Rhyssl's armies have marched against the Onnic garrison in Freath and there has been fighting there." He glanced up at Masyl. "Have you units you can send?"

"Of course, your Majesty," Masyl said smoothly. He looked inordinately pleased with this turn of events. "I will get them ready at once." With that, he turned and marched from the room.

Torrit looked at Morgan with fire in his eyes. "You can't imprison me now, Morgan," he said. His jaw hurt from clamping his teeth together in an effort not to curse and swear. "Not with war! My people will need me!"

Morgan looked at the frantic king coldly. "Until the time of your trial, and unless you are acquitted of your crimes, they are not your people. Cameon falls to me until such time as you are considered fit to return. Besides," he said with a contemptuous look, "I would hate to think you might send your troops to help Rhyssl against me, for I have a suspicion you might favor her as ruler for Freath." Morgan gestured to the Onnic guards flanking King Torrit. "Take him."

Under his quelling gaze the Onnic who stood ready to bind his hands with the rope stepped back uncertainly, and King Torrit took a deep breath and stood tall, his chin up and eyes forward. He spared only a glance for Mandras and made a very slight signal with his fingers as he passed. Mandras gave the barest inclination of his head to show he had understood and would obey. Feeling slightly easier, but still sick with anger and fear, King Torrit walked before his accusers toward the dungeon into which he was about to be thrown.

Epilogue

The streets of Restis Haven were empty and still, devoid of midnight activity. The market square was barren, the vendors' stalls stripped down and vacant for the coming night. Beggars slept in dingy bricked doorways, softened by the shadows of night and masked by the cloak of darkness that hid their disfigurements and illnesses from incurious and indifferent eyes. The smell of raw sewage, ripe garbage and inclement rain mingled in the air, causing Jaerak to cough as he made his way through the empty streets toward the bookshop.

Jaerak Thorin looked around at the familiar surroundings and smiled, remembering the last time he had walked these streets only a few short months ago. But it wasn't a few months ago, he reminded himself. It was in the future – tomorrow, to be exact. On this day he had not yet ventured to the bookshop to find his destiny waiting for him on the shelf in the guise of a spelled book with his handwriting in it.

He looked down at the book he carried and smiled again. The one he had taken from Thomlyn's bookshop had disappeared the same day Aliane had, but that did not trouble him much. Stealing it back had been no problem, once he had learned how to use the Stone. The Alchemist Stone. Jaerak felt his cloak pocket with his good hand and relaxed as he felt the hard, oval shape still resting in its place. It had been something of a shock when he had returned to his tent at the Lake Point to find five wooden crates – one quite large and the others smaller – stacked neatly on the ground next to his clothes-chest. No one could tell him where they had come from, and no one admitted delivering them. He had tried for hours to open them before he had realized they must be spelled shut. Once he had found the spell-web pattern it had been an easy job to neutralize the spell and remove the lids.

Once opened, he found a staggering array of unbelievable objects inside, many of which he recognized by their descriptions in the Seeker book he had found at this very shop. The Pyaerea. He finally had them in his possession. How they had come to be there was another question altogether, one he was sure would be answered in due course. Little by little the answers were coming, the pieces of the puzzle were fitting together. With a little patience, he felt sure this piece would fall into its place eventually. *It had all started here,* he thought, looking at the awning of the bookshop. There had been so many questions then, and now he had answers. Soon he would know everything. Soon.

Two of the Pyaerea Stones had been in the large crate. About the size and shape of a duck's egg, one was a deep, lustrous crimson, blood red and glowing with inner fire. This was the Aurora Stone, the ruby that had been infused with the power of Fire. When Jaerak had picked it up and held it in his hand he had felt the pulse of the stone, the radiation of power that emanated from its scarlet depths. Fire was his strongest element, and he had stood in wonder for some minutes, fingering the stone and marveling at the energy it broadcast. He could feel an answering stir of power within himself and had closed his eyes with the pleasure of it.

But it was the second stone that made him tremble with anticipation as he lifted it from its protective nest in the wooden crate. The clear, white brilliance of the stone threw rainbow lights when the sun glanced off its intricately faceted surface, and he marveled as he held the large diamond in his hand. The Alchemist Stone. The object of his desire since he had first learned of its existence from the book he had stolen from Gwynne's shelves in the City of Circles. The book he had left to find himself. The book he was on his way to leave at the bookshop now.

Yes, stealing the book had been easy. Once he had learned how to use the Stone, it had been no problem to go back in time to before he had ever met the aging Seeker. He had found Gwynne's house as whole and unburned as it had been the day he had first met her there, and after forcing the lock had entered. Everything was as he remembered it. The shelves were still lined with dusty books, the chairs and tables were piled with papers and used dishes. He spotted a vase perched on a pillar-like table and fingered the scar that ran across his cheek. That vase, when it had broken, had given him that scar. But here, in this time, it was as whole and unbroken as the day it was fired. Incredible.

He'd had no idea where on the shelves the book lay, so he had randomly started looking through them, pulling them off the shelves and putting them back where he'd found them. It was awkward with one arm in a sling, but he had managed. He opened several books that looked interesting just to look at them, and in one he saw the name *Gwynne Davanir* imperfectly crossed out and *Silvya Brenn* scrawled underneath it. *Ah yes*, he thought. *I had almost forgotten.* He finally found the book he wanted and left, touching nothing else.

So now he was back in Restis Haven, and he had come full circle. With the book safely under his cloak, Jaerak picked the lock of the bookshop, making sure there was no one around to see him as he did. He had no problem picking it one-handed. He was, after all, an experienced thief and assassin. The lock opened easily and he stepped into the familiar shop, breathing again the familiar scent of dust and mold. Under Thomlyn's counter he found pen and ink, and inside the front cover of the old and fraying book he wrote the names 'GWYNNE DAVANIR, AKA *SILVYA BRENN*, CITY OF CIRCLES' in his boldly spiked handwriting.

Next, he seared the page with a bright flash of ruby-colored magic and his enchanted mark – a dodecahedron inside a seven-pointed star – melded into the ancient parchment. Perfect. Jaerak nodded to himself in satisfaction and headed for the stacks.

He found the correct shelf and slid the book into it so that it was lying crossways between two others. Then, quickly and efficiently, he wove a protective spell of air around the book, the spell-web encasing it and causing the casual eye to pass over it as if it was not even there.

That should do it, Jaerak thought. *That should be everything*. His eye fell on the pen and bottle of ink once more, and he remembered something else. *Might as well get it over with all at once*, he mused as he rummaged through Thomlyn's desk for a piece of parchment. Jaerak smiled. No wonder Thomlyn had thought the Onnic had sent a night-search to his shop, he thought, finding a relatively clean piece of parchment. He made no effort to hide his tracks and knew the shopkeeper would be able to tell someone had disturbed his things.

On the parchment he wrote, in careful letters, *Aliane is the Eye of Truth. Take her to the cave again and all will be revealed. Just get her to relax, and she will see*. He thought carefully. Yes, that was the exact wording of the message that had been found outside his camp at the Lake Point. He had burned the parchment, but he would never forget the words that had been written upon it. They had been the clue that had shown him the next direction to take. Now all he had to do was take himself back – or forwards, rather – to that day and leave the message to find for himself. Nothing easier.

Jaerak folded the parchment and glanced around the bookshop one last time. His eye fell on a strange shadow moving in the corner and he went very still, listening and feeling for the presence of another man. He let out his breath again as the shadow came forward and he saw it was only the white cat he had met in the shop once before. The cat looked at him with unblinking copper eyes and sat on its scrawny rump to wash its face. Shaking off a strange foreboding, Jaerak removed the Alchemist Stone from his pocket and gazed into its glittering diamond depths. As before, the milky spell-lines jumped into view as he looked at them through the stone, and he gathered them around his fingers, encircling the stone with their light. The cat watched disinterestedly as Jaerak burst into billions of atoms, disappearing, scattering himself through time and space and, once he was gone, calmly went back to washing its face.

* * *

Printed in the United States
18918LVS00004B/316